Where the Lotus Flowers Grow

MK Schiller

LYRICAL PRESS
Kensington Publishing Corp.
www.kensingtonbooks.com

To Papa with love. You will always be in my heart.

Acknowledgements

Thank you to Corinne DeMaagd, my fearless editor, and all the great folks at Kensington for believing in this story. Thank you to the readers who make this crazy business of writing worth it!

Even in darkness, love can bloom...

Heir to a multinational hotel empire, Liam Montgomery thinks business is everything—until he goes undercover to check out their locations throughout Asia. As cosmopolitan as Liam is, from the bright lights of Mumbai to the tranquil beaches of Goa to the bustling streets of New York, he's never met anyone like lovely Mary Costa. He can't understand why this delicate, educated woman works as a maid. Or how she is reigniting his long-buried desire to be an artist. They are apart in so many ways—especially in the things Mary won't tell him. But more and more, Liam can't imagine his life without her...

Mary knows this unexpected desire for Liam must end. It's true that his gentleness and sense of fun inspires her and makes her hopeful for the first time in her life. But she has a grim promise she feels compelled to keep—and painful experiences she fears he could never understand. And with secrets soon reaching out to separate them for good, can they dare risk a future together if it means confronting the scars of the past?

Books by MK Schiller

Unwanted Girl
Where the Lotus Flowers Grow

Published by Kensington Publishing Corporation

Chapter 1

Liam

I was too exhausted to sleep. Despite the twenty-two-hour plane ride, the ten-hour time difference, and the three bloody bourbons consumed on the flight, sleep refused to come. That's how I found myself wide awake at the ungodly hour of three a.m., studying the pale glow of a Rajasthani moon. At precisely 5:36 in the morning, I finally decided to make my insomnia useful and call my secretary, Monica Penny.

"Hello Miss Moneypenny," I said, imitating the Sean Connery brogue. It made her giggle every time.

"And who would this be?"

I could imagine the blush that crept around her face whenever we played this game. At sixty years young, she'd always been formal and efficient, but when I burst into Bond, she acted like a giddy schoolgirl.

"Montgomery. Liam Montgomery."

"It's gotta be five in the morning there."

"Five thirty-six, actually." Can we go over the schedule and your notes from the meeting yesterday?"

"I love the way you say 'schedule.' But seriously, Liam, you have to be exhausted."

"I am, but I can't sleep. May as well be useful."

"Fine. Well, I booked the rest of your flights. You'll leave for Mumbai on Saturday and Goa the following Saturday. Then back to New York on Sunday." She went about the specific details, meetings, and agendas that would take place over the coming weeks. I had most of it memorized, but I needed her to remind me of all the upper management at each hotel.

By the time we'd finished, the sun had crept slowly over the horizon. I opened the window to let in some air.

"Make sure you wear plenty of sunscreen, drink lots of bottled water, and buy a Pashmina scarf."

"What kind of protection will a Pashmina scarf offer me?"

"Nothing, but it's a really nice gift for your secretary."

"Noted."

"Liam, what's that sound?"

I blinked, taking in the huge hulking creatures that flew across the sky, their shrieking calls growing exponentially with the rise of the golden sun. Their cackles drowned out all other noise.

"Birds."

"You're kidding?"

"Afraid not, Moneypenny. The wingspan on these birds would give Hitchcock a heart attack." I ducked outside the window to get a closer look. Another flew by, nearly grazing me. Holy shit…was that a falcon? I banged my head against the sill as I backed away.

"Fuck."

"What happened?"

"Just banged my brain a bit."

"Are you all right?"

"I'll live."

"I'm sure you will, seeing as you have a very hard head. Which reminds me, Natalie called." Moneypenny's typically soft voice hardened over Natalie's name. "She asked about your schedule, too. She's trying for an Indian visa since she's filming a shoot in Hong Kong." Her heavy sigh gave the birds a run for their money. "I thought you broke up."

As if my bloody head wasn't already aching.

"We didn't break up. We were never going out. She rings when she's in or around the same general vicinity as me. We get together. That's all."

"Liam Montgomery, I maybe older than you, but I know what a booty call is."

"Booty call?" I almost dropped the phone. "I believe the kids are calling it a hook-up these days. Yes, that's the correct terminology."

"I don't like her. She's very rude."

"Well, it's good you're not sleeping with her then. But in any case, please send two dozen roses to her hotel in Hong Kong with a note relaying my sincere apologies. I'll be far too busy these next three weeks to entertain her."

"I'll send it right away," she said, sounding incredibly happy at being assigned the task.

"And Moneypenny?"

"Yes."

"Make the note sincere, yeah?"

She huffed over the phone. "What do you want me to do? Quote Shakespeare?"

"That's a nice touch."

"Fine. I'm sure I can find a line from *The Taming of the Shrew*."

"You're a funny girl. I have to go."

"Be careful, Liam. I'll tell Stephen you arrived safely."

I wanted to tell her not to bother. My half-brother could care less. In fact, he'd probably be happy if I hadn't arrived safely, but I simply thanked her instead. Keeping up appearances had become second nature. If anyone looked below the surface, they could easily identify the large fissures in my family, but we'd done an outstanding job at plugging the leaks.

What looked like a hawk came to the window next. He perched on the ledge, fanning his large wings. It appeared more curious than anything, staring me down as if to say I was on his territory, not the other way around. I could almost hear his taunting thoughts: *You wish you had my freedom.*

I did.

He flapped his wings before swooping down toward the grounds. I followed his descent across the infinity pool, the manicured gardens, and finally the water fountain. Prabhat, the manager here, had given me a brief tour yesterday. I told him to get rid of the eyesore. It wasn't in a spot guests would go to, but the crumpling stones blemished the otherwise spotless façade. Not to mention it was a haven for mosquitoes and the water looked dirty. He went on about how he agreed with me, insisting it would be no problem. So why it hadn't been done in all the years he'd been general manager?

I focused on the shining figure standing next to the fountain. It looked like every ray in the sun was pointing at her and reflecting off her at the same time. That was until I realized that her long white skirt and scarf had tiny mirrors patched into the embroidery. She moved with grace despite the large pot balanced on her hip. She placed the pot on the ground. From within, she took many small silver bowls. Ten, to be exact. I counted as she placed them around the fountain, occasionally swiping the tiny broken stones gathered on its ridge. The strike of a match against the box cut through the air as if even the birds had decided to be silent out of respect for her. She lit each bowl. Who lit candles in the daylight? Was it some type of religious ceremony?

When she was done, she fell to her knees in front of the fountain and removed her scarf. Her hair cascaded in dark waves. A soft echoing music filled the air, the melody haunting. She looked toward the sky.

Whatever she prayed for, I wanted her to have it.

My fingers twitched. I wished for a piece of charcoal, a paint brush, or even a fucking pencil. The once-familiar longing had been absent from my life for many years.

Her gaze drew back to the fountain.

"What's so interesting?" I asked, as if she could answer me. I didn't know what was so interesting for me either. I blamed it on a combination of sleep deprivation, curiosity, and bad bourbon. Whatever it was, I couldn't look away.

A single flower in the middle of the pool opened up. The bud stood out in ethereal white above the still, dark waters. What the hell kind of flower grew in water? A lily? No…no, this wasn't a lily. I knew this. I racked my brain until the memory finally came.

Mum sitting at the rickety kitchen table, her elbows bent in concentration as she tried to fashion some kind of pin. She based her design on the tropical flower book she'd checked from the library. She swore under her breath as she tried to shake off the arthritis before it settled into her fingers.

I tapped the book with my pencil. "What is it?"

"A lotus flower. I want the pin to look like this. Isn't it lovely?" She prattled on about some stone she'd found at the thrift store.

"No, Mum, it's very ugly" was my flippant reply. I hated her doing this kind of work. It only made her hands hurt. It was the reason all my weekends were spent at street fairs instead of hanging with my mates. Hell, it wouldn't have been so bad if we made money from it. In the end, I felt so guilty for my outburst, I finished the pin for her, bending the stiff silver wires with small pliers, following the lines in the book, until they resembled petals. I pasted the cheap stone in the center.

Mum said the lotus flower was special. I didn't see anything special about it then, and I certainly didn't now.

I couldn't see Lotus Girl's face…not from this angle, ten stories up, but I imagined it anyway. She was as enamored with the flower as I was with her.

I wasn't the only one watching. He came from the shadows and stood in front of her. My hand clutched the sill. She straightened, but there was no fear in her posture. I recognized his uniform and shape as the driver who'd fetched me from the airport.

Their voices didn't carry, but even if they did, I doubt I'd understand what they said. It didn't matter, though. Their body language slashed through any language barriers. He was taller than she was, but she looked him in the eyes when she spoke. She patted his arm, a docile gesture meant to comfort. She kept an ample amount of space between them, each of her movements careful, perhaps even guarded. His words were accompanied with shakes of his head, his hands barreling though his hair, and finally a defeated slump in his shoulders.

I chuckled to myself. *Sorry, mate, but at least she's letting you down easy.*

He took her hand and pulled it toward his mouth. She yanked it back so fast, his lips met nothing but air.

Don't go embarrassing yourself, bro. No bird is worth that. As if to contradict me, a fucking Pterodactyl soared past, squawking loudly. I stumbled back.

Bloody birds.

Once I regained my balance and confirmed my heart was still tucked inside my chest, I shifted my attention back to them. He kept talking, closing the gap between them, his fingers curling around her arm. In reaction, I tightened mine into a fist.

You're starting to piss me off. Keep your fucking hands to yourself before I come down there and break them.

Her stance stiffened. She slapped his hand away. Whatever she said, she spoke it with force, pushing his chest so hard he staggered back.

"Good for you," I said. "Let the wanker have it."

She uttered some final words that must have been harsher than any slap. He shrunk against her voice, shoving his hands in his pockets. She grabbed the large pot and walked away…well, more like sashayed. The girl glanced back once more, but not at him. At the flower in the fountain. I swear, even from this distance, I could see her regret at being disturbed, her solitude ruined.

I felt it, too.

Chapter 2

Mary

My knocks went unanswered. *What type of person requested additional towels and didn't bother to answer the door?* And of all the guests, this one should know better. Although there was no invitation to enter, there wasn't a Do Not Disturb sign either. Prabhat had warned us of this guest—a man who came from our corporate office to look over our burdened shoulders.

Prabhat had even called a mandatory meeting with the whole staff, including maids like me, who were normally left alone. He reiterated that we not only had to be exemplary, but extraordinary. With each passing week, the warnings grew and shuffled downward until each supervisor rendered a perfect imitation of our general manager, right down to his stern glances, wagging fingers, and the nervous tick of his lips. Ironically, all the frenzied energy surrounding this visit had the opposite effect. Rather than putting our best foot forward as the guest-centered hotel we were, we fluttered about, tipping around nervously like meek mice in the presence of a hungry cat.

Prabhat would have my head if the man complained about not getting his towels. Then again, if the guest, especially this particular guest, complained I'd intruded on his privacy, it would have the same result. I stared at the soft, fluffy, brand-new towels in my arms. I had no idea what Prabhat thought this deceit would accomplish, except all the fanfare on the man's behalf was an annoyance. He would have to settle. He was a man, after all, not a god.

It took three swipes of the electronic all-access keycard until I managed to unlock the stupid door. I breathed a sigh of relief at the empty room, glad I didn't find anyone sleeping on the four-poster king-size bed. He wasn't here. I wondered why he hadn't chosen a suite or, at the very least, a room with a nice view. I placed the towels on the corner of the bed, making sure their edges were neatly tucked. I pivoted toward the door.

That would have been it. Should have been it. Except my gaze lingered on the bureau. It didn't just linger, it full-out paused. My heart beat several decibels louder than usual. It was love at first sight.

A book.

Not just any ordinary book, but leather-bound with gold lettering etched on the spine. The kind of book my father had kept in his library, and by library, I meant bookshelf. But it was reserved for only the most revered novels. If my father had shown any signs of religion, the shelf would have been his altar, an organized place free of the dust and clutter of his carefree, sometimes careless life.

Although my head kept blasting warnings to leave, my rebellious feet carried me in the wrong direction. I stroked the stiff ridge of the spine and traced the embossed letters. But touching it wasn't enough. To leave would be like seeing an old friend without saying hello. How rude would that be? So despite all my best efforts and misguided intentions, I found myself picking up Charles Dickens's *Nicholas Nickleby*.

It felt solid in my hands as I turned it over, completely at contrast to the dog-eared paperbacks I currently read, but substantial like the books of my childhood. The pages, thick and uneven, would give a satisfying turn. With so many people at the hotel using e-readers, I had begun to wonder if real books were becoming as archaic as rotary phones.

I flipped through the novel. The sound of rifling paper was louder than I remembered. I missed that sound. There was something comforting about it, a lost melody of my youth.

A card fell out. I bent and retrieved it. The stiff cardboard had yellowed over time, washing out the flowers on the stationery. But the handwritten words remained sharp, written in neat ink: *To Liam on his fifteenth birthday. Always remember what Dickens said...Happiness is a gift and the trick is not to expect it, but to delight in it when it comes. May you always be delighted in your life, Love mum.*

I remembered the quote. Remembered that it was early in the book. In this book. This book that belonged to Liam...not me. The right thing to do was to leave Liam's possessions alone. I tucked the paper back between the pages, but more cards fell out, scattering all over the floor.

Oh, no. No. No.

Clearly, they marked pages. They also had the same writing. I stuck them back in, praying I wasn't messing up the order too much.

I stood to place it back where I'd found it, but I couldn't help myself. One sentence, I promised. I turned to a random page and read it quickly. It wasn't enough. One paragraph. I could read a paragraph quickly. My eyes lowered, my lips moving as I devoured the words. One whole page. I deserved it, right? One stolen page of Dickens would sustain me for a long time.

My eyes scanned the well-written sheets, careful to avoid the private note cards wedged into the spine.

My thumb leafed across the pages once more, searching for another random passage to read. Air wafted across my face, blowing a strand of loose hair. Ink, glue, cardboard, and paper were not so distinctive on their own, but when combined, they created the headiest scent. I sniffed, inhaling the memory.

"Read this one, Mary," Papa said. "You'll enjoy it."

"My teacher says Indians should only read Indian authors."

"Then your teacher is a fool, beta. *What a shame since your tuitions are so high."*

I stared at the huge book. Surely, he didn't expect me to read the whole thing? I was twelve years old.

"Priya's mother says reading will make your eyes go bad. Men don't want to marry girls who wear glasses and squint."

I chuckled, remembering the way Papa had tilted his pipe, jabbing the mouthpiece into the air with each point he made. *"Then Priya's mother is also a fool. Pity you're surrounded by so many ridiculous people. Why are you even thinking of marriage at your age?"*

I shrugged, unsure myself, except that movies, clothes, and weddings were the only subjects of conversation among my friends. Unlike my father, I had no desire to be an outcast, so I followed suit.

He bent to my level, as he always did when he wanted to capture all my attention. "Don't clutter your mind with nonsense. There are many people who will try to educate you, including me, but you are and will always be your own best teacher. There are many wonderful Indian authors, and you should read them. But don't limit yourself. Never be afraid to read about other times, other places, other cultures. On the contrary, it won't cause your eyes to blur, but rather open them wider. The choice is yours, lovely. But I fear you listen to others too readily. That your horizons will be so narrow, you'll have to squint the rest of your life."

"I'll read it," I said, more to please him than any real desire on my part. My sister, Hannah, always soaked up everything he said with a reverence I found annoying.

Hannah. I thought about her every day, but the memories were always tangled with grief. This one was different. She had sat next to me on our worn red couch, a tattered, threadbare blanket wrapped around her, begging me to read Dickens to her. The couch had been my papa's doing because he invested all his money in us. In our education. But the blanket, I had hated with a passion. My mother had left it, and Hannah clung to it as if it would shelter her from any storm.

"You won't understand it," I said to her with an air of authority I didn't deserve. My father looked angry then, his eyebrows knitting so tightly they almost joined. He said I was never to speak so disrespectfully to Hannah. His anger subsided as quickly as it came. He led me to the other room. He said in hushed tones we should both try to be more like Hannah. He'd always said Hannah had something special in her spirit that the two of us sorely lacked.

At the time, I thought he was speaking literally about her extra chromosome. But of course he wasn't. It was her inner strength—a rare combination of joy, loyalty, and faith. There was nothing cynical or bitter about Hannah. She was the tiniest jewel, but she could bring light to the darkest corners.

Holding these same words in my hands again made my heart heavy and full at the same time, a bittersweet wave of emotion. My eyes darted across the sentences on a random page, my lips moving to a cadence that was too fast for rhythm. Was I an avid admirer or an addict?

A clearing throat intruded on my inner monologue, snapping it shut the way I did with the book. My spine straightened with such speed needles shot through my lower back.

"Is it common for the staff to pilfer through the guest's belongings?" The deep voice was British.

British? He was British? I stared into the mirror, watching my body tremble before focusing on the image of him behind me.

Holy Mother of God.

I changed my mind.

He *was* a god.

Steam from the bathroom swathed him as he stepped out, a towel looped low around his hips. His naked chest, revealed muscles chiseled to perfection. I'd seen him when he arrived, but I wasn't paying attention. And now my attention would not go anywhere else. His damp hair, the color a mix of sun with flecks of sand, lay unruly against his head. His expression conveyed annoyance. I pivoted, my bum backing into the bureau. He narrowed his eyes. Green eyes? Brown? They were both. They were neither.

"I'm waiting for an answer."

My fingers clutched the book, digging into the hardback cover, holding it against my chest as if it could shield me from his voice, deep and husky. I shrank back farther, praying the floor would quake open and swallow me up.

His eyes shifted to my hands. He blinked, staring at the book. As much as my eyes were absorbing, my mouth refused to work. What could I possibly say to him? There were no excuses. I'd trespassed and, as a result, I'd be sacked.

"I've frightened you," he said, his voice a shade softer. He held up his hand. "Wait."

He picked up a few articles of clothing from the open suitcase on the bed, then looked back at me. "Stay." He closed the bathroom door behind him, disappearing into the diminishing poufs of steam.

I should run. But my feet were stuck to the floor, even though my legs were shaking. For once, I was grateful the sari would hide that.

When he came out a few minutes later, he wore soft, faded jeans and a green rugby shirt. He stood a few feet away, but I could smell fresh soap and sweet mint radiating from his body.

He slapped his chest three times. "My name is Liam Montgomery."

I continued to stare, dumbfounded. Was he introducing himself to me as if we lived on the same plane? I had found comfort in being a maid because the attention paid to me was on par with my paycheck. That was my preference. My choice. Perhaps a penance in a way. But now...I had all his attention and no idea what to do with it.

He sighed, shaking his head with disappointment. "Lotus Girl, why would you pick up a book you can't read?"

Lotus girl? Was he talking to me?

"Let's try this again. *Mera Nam*, Liam Montgomery," he said in poorly pronounced Hindi.

"You don't speak Hindi either?" When I didn't respond, he picked up his phone and pressed a few buttons. "So many languages in this country. Rest assured, I'll find yours."

As if rest were a possibility.

"Ah, here we are." He repeated the introduction in Punjabi, Gujarthi, Marthati, Tamil, Bangali, and even Sanskrit. Each time, he looked at me with a hopeful expression. With my continued silence, he grew more disappointed. Somehow, his desperation to talk with me made the tension dissipate just as the steam had. Finally, he threw his phone on the bed.

He shook his head in resignation, offering me a self-deprecating smile. "That's all I got. I suppose we shall never speak." He stared at the book again. I held it out to him with both hands. He stepped closer, his bare feet oddly beautiful. Later, I would wonder why I didn't just lay the book back on the bureau. His hands, large with long fingers, gripped the other edge and stilled the wobbling tome. I tilted my chin, forcing myself to look at his face. I knew I'd regret the moment if I chose to…squint.

He nodded toward the book, but kept us at a distance. "It's a shame, really. This is my favorite Dickens's novel. It's almost an autobiography." He tugged on it. I wouldn't let go.

He chuckled, rubbing the back of his neck. "Why the hell I'm still talking to you when you can't bloody-well respond, I have no idea." He gestured to the door. "Either it's heatstroke, or I'm going mad."

"You're wrong."

He swallowed, his eyes widening. "I'm not going mad?"

"It's not an autobiography. Dickens said his most autobiographical book was *David Copperfield*. Not *Nicholas Nickleby*." I thought I'd said it in my head, but the way his jaw dropped made it clear I'd articulated the statement.

Liam smiled again, his expression a mixture of curiosity and suspicion. "She speaks. And what interesting things she has to say."

I closed my eyes tightly. Now that I'd spoken, and in English, an avalanche of words tumbled out of my mouth. "I'm sorry. I wasn't trying to steal it, sir. I was only looking at it. I'll resign, sir. You don't have to bother yourself with sacking me."

His voice was cool but strong, a rush of water quenching an out-of-control flame. "Calm down. No one is getting sacked."

My eyes popped open. "No?"

"I believe you."

Why did he believe me? I wondered if I muttered that aloud as well because he answered the question.

"Of all the things on the bureau, the book is the least valuable. You skipped over a Cartier watch, gold cufflinks, and several hundred dollars in favor of a novel."

"You're wrong again. It is the most valuable."

"Perhaps."

He held out his hand for a handshake, but I couldn't bring myself to do it. Most people in a prestigious hotel as this believed I was contaminated. They avoided touching me.

"Now then, my name is Liam Montgomery."

I backed away.

"I know."

He smirked, taking a step forward, but stopped, his foot hovering in midair before he stepped down. "Ah yes, I introduced myself already." He dropped his hand.

I swallowed, realizing I'd rebuked him on some level, but instead of being angry, he seemed concerned, unsure, and cautious.

"In seven languages no less. Impressive," I said, hoping my pathetic stab at humor had made a mark.

His grin returned, and I let out a breath so long, my diaphragm sighed with relief.

"And what is your name?"

"Mary. Mary Costa."

"That's not a very fitting name, is it?'

I straightened, exposing my stubborn, sardonic side I'd done so well in hiding from the world. "It's a Catholic name. There are many Christians in India, sir."

He arched a brow. "Of course." His eyes wandered to the skin below my neck.

I covered it with my hand, feeling the cool glint of the cross that hung there, trying and failing to ignore the way my toes curled under his intense gaze.

"You misunderstand me, Mrs. Costa. I only meant that it's a very simple name for an exceedingly complicated girl."

A nervous giggle escaped me. The sound was so foreign I was sure it had come from someone else. "I'm not complicated, sir."

"Liam. Call me Liam."

"That's not proper, Mr. Montgomery...sir." With that, I relinquished the book.

He clasped it in his large hands, appearing slightly amused before his expression sobered. "As you wish, Mrs. Costa."

"Miss. It's Miss." Had he called me by my surname? Did he not know I was a maid? I'd gotten used to being referred to as "maid," or my first name, and sometimes just "girl," but no one...no one ever called me by my last name.

"Miss Costa, would you care to borrow the novel?" He held it out to me.

I shook my head, backing into the dresser once more. The very thing that had rooted me in this room now acted as a deterrent. I held out a hand in protest. "I couldn't."

"Please, it would be my honor to lend it to you. I'm here for a week. You can return it anytime before then."

I wondered if this might be a test on his part. "No, Mr. Montgomery, sir. Thank you for the generous offer, but hotel staff cannot accept gifts from guests."

His smile tightened. "I'm very aware of the rules. We both work for the same company, after all. But this is not a gift. It's a loan."

"No, please." No please? Did that even make sense?

He frowned. "Understood."

"Have a good day, sir." I said, doing some ridiculous curtsy as if he was a king. He did look regal, and at least the gesture caused the amused smile to come back. A deep line imbedded into his right cheek when he smiled just wide enough. I would call it a dimple, but it didn't indent in a pucker, but creased the defined angle of his face in a solid line. For a moment, I wondered what it might be like to touch it, trace it with my finger, my lips.

As the thought appeared, I brandished it, mentally whipping my own dirty mind. I backed out through the door, stumbling once as my foot caught on the hem of the sari.

"Have a good day yourself, Miss Costa."

Chapter 3

Liam

Mary Costa. Her name repeated in my head, a blasted record that skipped with irritating regularity. She was pretty…not breathtaking. Okay, perhaps a little breathtaking. Her skin, the color of coffee with one shot of cream, radiated with a soft rosy blush when I caught her. Those chocolate eyes had gone wide. Her pouty mouth spun words so beautifully they rolled off her tongue in a lyrical way. Her long black hair twisted in a tight and complicated braid, except for a few loose rebellious strands that framed her face. The innocence of her stare did nothing to detract from her strong backbone. Not many people corrected me. It was the last thing I expected from her. I wanted to sketch her so much. I imagined mixing the colors and outlining her form, capturing each feature, freezing them on a canvas.

I shook my head, snapping out of it. My mum had wanted to be a writer, and she told me once what it was like. When an idea hacked into her head or she caught a snippet of interesting conversation, she didn't walk, she ran to her typewriter to get it all down so it could exist in the world instead of just her head. It was a deep need, almost an addiction, she'd said.

That wasn't what this was. I had found inspiration where I least expected it, but I didn't want it. I sure as hell didn't need it.

Still, the girl intrigued me. Besides her looks, the most interesting thing about Mary Costa was the way she aroused….my curiosity. Okay, she aroused other things, too. There were so many questions I had. Why was she a maid? She spoke perfect English. Surely, she could get a job at one of the new IT companies sprouting up all over India, or better yet, work the front desk here. Why sell herself short?

I contemplated this while watching her from the restaurant window, half-listening to Prabhat go over the financial analysis I'd already reviewed on the plane. She scrubbed tables by the pool, picked up discarded items, and refilled the towel rack. For some reason, I wanted to carry her away from this place. This life even. Ridiculous thought, that. Although I was careful in my leering, I had no right to look at her, or regard her at all for that matter. She was an employee. Any deviation from a professional relationship would ruin my reputation…and hers. She had her life. And I had mine. My very good life. Still, why was she here?

"Mr. Montgomery, you can see we have good prospects for an auspicious year ahead."

"That may be, but the hotel is still losing money at an alarming rate."

"But sir, this is a short-term issue. The downward pattern will change."

Short-term, my arse. "Three years, Prabhat. That's not a downward pattern. It's a spiral. That's not entirely your fault, but unless we see some growth possibilities, we cannot continue this way. I'm sorry, but difficult decisions will need to be taken."

I hated this part of my job. Looking at this man, who no doubt had a family to support, and telling him the job he'd had for the past ten years was an uncertainty.

"I understand, Mr. Montgomery."

I sighed, gathering up the sheets of paper. "Before we do anything, I'll take another look at the books and run some comparisons."

He straightened in his seat, his smile too wide for my small concession. "Thank you, sir. I think you'll see if you just—"

"We'll talk about it later. Now, have you set up the interviews for me?"

He sipped his tea. "Yes, all of our high-level staff is ready. I beg your pardon, sir, but I still don't understand the purpose of the interviews."

"Often times, the people who work for us have the greatest insight. They can see problems we cannot. Problems we need to provide solutions for."

"Very smart, sir…brilliant."

I didn't care for or need the ego stroke. But I wouldn't waste my breath telling him as much. Beneath the cloak of praise, it was clear the man didn't like me. Under the circumstances, who could blame him? I was fine with the dislike. Hell, I would even respect it if he didn't hide his hostility behind kissing my arse.

"Shall I start sending them in now?"

"I don't want to speak with the high-level staff only. I told you I wanted conversations with all areas of the hotel."

"Sir, most of our lower-level staff do not speak proper English."

"Then get a translator."

The teacup shook in his hand. "Of course, sir. I would be happy to translate."

The last thing I wanted was him acting as translator. Everyone here feared me as it was. Except for Prabhat and senior staff, they didn't even know I owned the hotel. But it didn't matter. I was an outsider from the corporate office. That was enough to cause suspicion and distrust. They wouldn't be honest in the first place. And even if they were, he'd make each response work in favor of the hotel.

"You're far too busy, Prabhat." I hated playing these games. I would rather tell him I didn't trust him, but that wouldn't be good for his productivity or mine.

"I'll find someone to translate." He looked pleased, following my gaze out to the courtyard. "It's a nice day. Would you care to sit outside while doing the interviews?"

"Maybe." He thought I was staring at the elliptical pool, not Mary Costa.

"What about her?" I asked.

"Her who, sir?"

"I think her name is...Mary." As if her name didn't roll around in my head at all odd hours.

"The maid?" he asked, as if the idea disturbed him. Not because he could detect my salacious thoughts, but perhaps the suggestion itself. "Is there another Mary?"

"Ah...no, sir. It's only she isn't capable."

"She speaks excellent English."

Prabhat looked more nervous than I'd seen him since I arrived last night. "I'm afraid you are mistaken, Mr. Montgomery. Mary only speaks Hindi. Maybe she knows a few broken words of English, but nothing that would suit the skill set of a translator. Did she bother you, sir?"

Now it was my turn to be surprised.

Prabhat called for the woman in charge of housekeeping, giving her orders in Hindi. A few moments later, my beautiful Lotus Girl stood before us, visibly shaking under Prabhat's glare. I cursed myself because I knew better. This was such a small thing. In the States, in England, in France, in any other fucking place we had a hotel, this would not be an issue, but here...here my stupid fascination would cause her distress.

"Do you speak English?" Prabhat asked, ironically in Hindi. It was one of the few phrases I'd memorized in preparation for this trip. She stared between us, a doe caught in a trap. One I'd mistakenly set. Why didn't anyone else know she spoke English? Why had she only revealed that part of herself to me?

Mary parted her lovely mouth, but nothing came out. She shook her head furiously. She looked lost, a girl in need of rescuing. And although I wanted answers to all the questions rattling in my head, I wanted to rescue her even more.

"Sorry, Prabhat. My mistake. This isn't the girl I meant. I mixed up her name with someone else's."

"Are you sure, sir?"

"Positive. I've met so many people since arriving. It's difficult to recall names."

He looked smug for a moment. "I can understand such mistakes. They are very common to foreigners who come here." The accusation was clear. He thought I was some kind of racist who thought all Indians looked the same. He dismissed her. I caught her look of gratitude before she turned away.

I'm sorry. You're welcome. You're beautiful. What I might have said in a different circumstance. Instead, I cursed to myself and bid her good-bye, wondering when I'd gone completely mental.

Chapter 4

Mary

I found myself drawn to Liam, even spying on him as he prepared for an early morning swim. The pool area was surrounded by vegetation, which normally annoyed me when I tried to move about, but today it served me well. I'd wager he was part-fish the way he swam, his arms flexing with each rotation, his muscles glinting as he rose to the surface, shaking his head. He'd rubbed sunscreen over his body first. I didn't recognize the brand. He might as well have put baby lotion on for all the protection the pretty white bottle would give him despite the promises on its western-style label.

I clutched the list in my hand that the woman in room 313 had given me. Getting a shopping list wasn't unusual. I normally didn't mind shopping for guests. It often resulted in a nice tip. But I didn't want to run this errand. Not just because I'd have to miss the personal erotic theater of Liam Montgomery swimming, but also because I didn't care for the contents of the list, especially one very unnecessary item. I also hated the way the woman had spoken to her daughter, belittling her, pinching her belly as she barked commands at me.

The girl was a few years younger than me, maybe eighteen or nineteen, but it felt like decades stretched between us. I offered her a reassuring smile, and she replied in kind but her chin quivered. Her uncertainty veiled her natural beauty as her mother hurdled insults at her. "You're too fat. You're too dark. You're too spoiled. You're too…" Always too something. Women were always *too*. Men were always *just*. "You're just fine. You're just perfect. You're just right."

I wondered if Liam had ever been a *too* or was he always a *just*? He carried himself with a confidence I admired. But it was his compassion I found most attractive. He smiled…not just at guests, but at everyone—the cook, the driver, the other maids. I might have been jealous which was ridiculous in itself, except it was a more composed, good-natured-but-stiffer version of the easy smile he had offered me. He said "please" and "thank you." He left generous tips and had a kind grace about him. I exhaled, reminding myself he'd be gone in a few days. I wouldn't have to think about him. I honestly did my best not to, except it was near impossible with all the whispered murmurs about his looks, the gossipy guesses about his personal life, the deep dreamy sighs of affection women had whenever he walked by.

Pooja said he looked like an actor, not a businessman. Although he filled out a suit well, his hair was too long, cut in harsh chops befitting a musician, not someone in his position. His body was long and lean muscles, unusual on someone who sits at a desk for long hours. His lips were full, and when they smiled just right, the knee-weakening creases would appear on the chiseled planes of his face. But most of all, it was his age. He was young. They said people in the west aged slower, the sun less harsh, the water less polluted, the air cleaner, not to mention the wide assortment of vitamins and skin remedies. Still, I doubted he was older than mid twenties.

A hand clasped around my arm, ripping me back to reality.

"What are you doing?" Kishore barked. The large mirrored sunglasses he used when driving covered his eyes. It irritated me when he wore them for show. He was very proud of having been promoted from a grounds person to a driver, but it boarded on a hubris I found unappealing. Ironically, I'd been the one to teach him English. He'd discovered my secret when he spotted me in the city reading a weathered paperback novel. He begged for my help. We'd worked each night on his pronunciations until he'd felt confident enough to apply for the open position. Somewhere in those late-night sessions, the flow of words stopped as we gave into the needs of flesh. I'd been paying for my lack of judgment ever since.

I stared at his fingers pressed into my skin. "What are you doing? You're not supposed to back here." My voice was a harsh whisper, followed by a harsher stare.

"And you are supposed to be cleaning, not acting as a peeping tom." He looked disgusted as he turned toward the pool. "What is wrong with you girls? Has everyone gone gaga for *gora*?" *Gora*…white man. I considered that for a moment because I'd never been attracted to a white person. In fact, I'd say the opposite was true. But what else could explain the wild magnetic draw of Liam Montgomery? I had a stupid, stupid crush.

"I don't start for an hour. I was on my way to the market."

"I'll drive you."

"You know I cannot ride with you unless Prabhat allows it."

"That lazy motherfucker has his lips so far up *gora*'s ass he wouldn't even notice."

"Don't be disgusting."

"We need to talk."

"We did talk."

"No, we didn't. You walked away from me."

"I said what I had to. You chose not to listen. For the last time, I cannot marry you."

"Why the fuck not? Do you know how difficult it was to convince Mummy to allow me to propose? And you...you have the nerve to reject me? Someone like me won't come along again. I am willing to marry a girl far beneath me because I love her, and that should mean something to you."

"Just how far beneath you do you think I am?"

He smirked. "In this world, you're the floor and I'm the sky. You will not find anyone better. I may not be Christian, but I am capable of taking care of you."

"This has nothing to do with religion. I don't need taking care of. I thought I made it clear to you that we were—"

"Were what, Mary? Having sex? Fucking on your terms?" He fingered my cross. I smacked his hand away.

He'd never treated me this way, not until that day last month when he made a spectacle by getting down on his knees. "What the hell has gotten into you?"

"I don't know the Bible very well, but aren't there two Marys? One is wholesome and strong. The other is a whore. This is your time to choose the right path. The one I'm giving to you. Which Mary do you want to be?"

He curled his fingers against my skin. I stood on my tiptoes, staring into his eyes, my nose almost touching his. "I am a whore? I wasn't alone those nights, Kishore. I wasn't pleasuring myself. Then again, you weren't pleasing me very much either."

His eyes widened with fury. The sting wasn't called for, but his verbal assault put us on the same level. "Don't talk your filthy rubbish to me."

"I don't want to talk to you at all. Take your hand off me."

His eyes softened, his fingers slackened. "Mary..."

"If you don't get your hand off me, I'll yell bloody murder."

"Then we'll both lose our jobs."

"But as you've pointed out, I'm already close to the ground without much of a fall. It's you who has the long drop…one that's likely to crack your neck." I pulled back once more. "Now, let me go before I break your arm."

"*Wah Wah*, keep talking your nonsense."

My knee jabbed into his groin. "You're right, I can't break your arm. I'll settle for another part of your anatomy you're not using."

His swallowed a scream, his arm dropping. I marched away before he caused any unwanted attention.

I turned back once. This time I wanted to scream. Liam was standing at the edge of the pool, drops of water rolling down his finely sculpted chest. I forced myself not to watch their descent. Our eyes locked for a brief moment until he turned toward the shrubbery. The planes of his jaw clenched. God, had he heard us? I pivoted and rushed toward the gate. I had walked away from Kishore, anger welling in my chest. But with Liam, I felt a need to run, to escape the intensity of his gaze before it rooted me in place as it had that first meeting.

Once the gate was closed behind me, I breathed slowly until I could reason again. I would have told Prabhat about the harassment, but I knew how it would play out. Kishore was more valuable than I was. Ironically, the position I'd helped him obtain had changed the scenario. There were tens of me for every one of him. It was that skill that would save him and sack me. But now, Liam Montgomery most likely had heard everything. What would he do?

Stupid, stupid girl.

Why would he even care about me?

If anything, he'd sack us both. The idea wasn't frightening. I would survive.

As I made my way down the choppy pavements of the city, I thought about severing the roots that had held me in place for the past four years. By the time I reached the shop, a sharp surge of rebellion coursed through me.

When I returned, the mother from room 313 was waiting in the lobby. She tapped her foot and crossed her arms, clearly annoyed I'd taken so long. I held out the brown paper bag to her. She snatched it from my hands, nearly ripping the paper.

"This isn't the right cream," she wailed in Hindi, then turned to the other woman with her and switched to English. "They hire these stupid illiterate girls at these places. Where is the class?"

There was a benefit to secretly understanding a language. You got to hear what people really thought, not that she wasn't saying the same thing with her sighs and tsks.

Eyeing me with a sharpness that pierced my defenses, she returned to Hindi. "My daughter needs this cream. Her marriage ceremony is in two days."

She didn't need it. She didn't need anything more than what she was.

"How could you get the wrong item? You only had to ask the clerk to help you if you can't read."

"I'm sorry, Auntie," I said. "I thought it was what you wanted. It's cheaper."

"*Arey*, cheaper?"

I shrunk back, cursing my choice of words. She'd counted out the money so carefully, telling me several times she knew the exact change due back. I will know if you steal from me, she'd said. I'd hoped the words would make her soften, but they did the exact opposite.

"Do you think I cannot afford it?" Her eyes narrowed into tiny slits. "Stupid *kutiya*." At least she was insulting me in our native tongue. "Do you not see we're staying at a first-class hotel?" Her hands gestured around the opulent lobby as if I didn't realize where we stood.

No good deed....

What had I been thinking when I purchased this product? It was too personal. The past had slithered its way through the open cracks to the present. This woman berating me could have been my own mummy.

I couldn't run from the dark. Not when it was a part of my flesh, my bone, my very soul. No matter how far or fast I ran, I was always there.

"Is there a problem?" A deep British accent interjected. His tall frame stepped between us. I took a step back from him—his imposing body, his spicy cologne, his throaty voice...all delicious and all equally as dangerous.

"Problem? Yes, a very big one," she said, pointing to me. Her face scrunched up, make-up caking into all the lines she'd worked so hard to mask. She looked at me as if I were something she'd scraped from the underside of her fingernail.

When Liam cleared his throat, the woman's focus shifted to him. She grew quiet, eyeing his suit with a slow up-and-down movement. She broke into a wide smile. Liam Montgomery obviously had the power to sweeten the bitter.

He lowered his voice so that I had to step closer to hear. "How may I help you? Obviously something is quite wrong since you are yelling at my employee. Our guests are very important to us."

"Yes, that's why I chose this place for such an auspicious occasion," she said.

"We appreciate it. We do," he said. "But you are mistaken if you believe that allows you to abuse our personnel. Although I don't know what you said, your tone was quite clear on the matter. I assure you I— Wilshire Hotels—has no tolerance for this sort of behavior."

"You're taking her side? She's incompetent and stupid."

His jaw flexed. He took a deep breath and adjusted his tie. They were stall tactics designed to dam the turbulent waves threatening to overflow. "I want to resolve your problem, but if you say one more unproductive or negative word against any person who works here, I will personally escort you from the building."

The woman looked as if he'd thrown a bucket of water on her. I doubted anyone had ever spoken to her that way. Liam smiled at her, further throwing her off. That smile remained frozen on his face, as though they were having a friendly conversation, but the green in his eyes had brightened with a simmering rage.

The women nervously knotted her colorful *dupatta*. Liam had no idea how much work went into planning a Hindu wedding or how ridiculous she'd look if she had to tell her guests to go to another hotel. Or judging from the smile on his face, maybe he did.

"You cannot. I have paid for the room for two nights. We have booked the banquet hall." She crossed her arms, an expression of righteousness, but her shoulders shook slightly. I almost felt sorry for her.

"I will be happy to refund your money and find alternative lodgings for your party."

"That...that won't be necessary."

"Good. Now then, what is the problem?"

She pointed toward me. "I gave her a list with a specific item. She returned with the wrong type."

"That can easily be fixed. I'll send someone else to get exactly what you need. Why don't you return to your room? I'll have some vouchers for our restaurant brought to you as well."

She nodded her head, clearly too stunned to speak.

"What item did you want, madam?"

"The girl...the girl has it."

"Her name is Mary. We'll get it to you."

Liam stuffed his hands in his pockets, watching the woman and her friend walk away. His jaw unclenched as soon as they were out of sight. He turned to me, lifting an eyebrow. I held up the list, pointed to the door, and then back to myself in some kind of ridiculous pantomime I hoped he'd understand. *I'll get it. I'll make this right.* When he didn't respond, for reasons I couldn't understand myself, I let out a barrage of Hindi stating the same. It was the automatic response I had with foreign guests.

Still, he was silent. He shifted, his face focused straight ahead as if there were something interesting in the long corridor ahead of us. I decided not to wait for his dismissal. I walked away, but his footsteps clicked behind me, his shadow reflecting on the white marble floors casting over me. I headed the back way through the employee entrance. The steady click of his shoes gave way to hard thuds as the floor switched from the marble to the soft rug, each sound pumping more blood to my heart.

He cleared his throat. I paused. Pivoting toward him, I tried to ignore the tension in every one of my muscles. He opened a door to a vacant banquet room and jerked his head, indicating I should enter. Taking a much-needed steadying breath, I walked inside. "Sir?" I asked, embarrassed by how timid and weak my voice sounded.

He closed the door behind him and leaned against it. The air suddenly felt thicker and warmer against my skin. I closed my eyes, preparing myself for the inevitable.

"How many languages do you speak, Miss Costa? I believe you fully grasped each of my botched attempts at an introduction."

I was struck silent by his question.

"How many?" he asked again. I was wrong. It wasn't a question, but a demand.

"Four fluently. Two not as fluently."

"Do you know how many I speak?"

I shook my head slowly.

"One. Just one. Luckily, it's one you know. I'm not playing charades with you. You can communicate with me just fine, Lotus Girl. In fact, you speak the Queen's English a damn sight better than most Englishmen." He leaned in closer to me, the safety of our gap disappearing. His voice dropped to a husky whisper, sending a silent shiver through my whole body. "So when you speak to me, Mary Costa, bloody well use words I can understand."

I swallowed, every cell in my body urging me to run. I could handle Kishore's unwelcomed advances. I could ignore a mean guest berating me. And I could take a lot worse, too. But Liam Montgomery's challenging stare was not something to be handled or ignored. "As you wish, Mr. Montgomery."

"Good." He held his hand out, and I wondered if he was trying for another handshake. "Now then, give me the list. I'll have someone else fetch it. I don't want you having any more contact with this particular guest."

I clutched the paper, crumpling it in my hand. "Let me fix this. I won't aggravate her any further."

"It's not you aggravating her I'm worried about."

"Then what, sir?"

He dragged his hand through his hair. It fell back into place, two strands splaying against his forehead. "I believe you already know the answer to that question." I did. He had defended me. But maybe, he'd feel differently if he knew the truth.

"I'm sorry, sir."

"Don't apologize. She was out of line."

"Let me correct my mistake. I've put us in a bad situation."

"Us?"

"The hotel."

"Ah, of course," he said, as if that statement could have another connotation. "You made an error, Miss Costa. Everyone is allowed the occasional error. But no one. No one is allowed to speak to *you* in that manner."

I forced myself to remember he was talking to me as my employer and nothing else. Staring at the intricate design of the rose carpet we stood on, I decided to come clean. I lifted my head, taking in the cut of his dark designer suit, the navy pinstriped tie, the stretched fabric of his crisp white shirt. I forced my head up to meet his fiery eyes. As my father had said, "If you need to confess, don't do it behind masked doors." Liam's eyes were more green today, shining as brilliantly as the foliage of the Banyan tree. "Sir, I purchased the wrong face cream intentionally."

He blinked at me. I expected some anger, but his expression held only curiosity, maybe even a hint of amusement. "You botched it on purpose? Why?"

"I didn't feel it was right. What she was asking for. But I know better. It was none of my business."

"You're right. It wasn't. Unless the substance she sent you to buy was illegal. Was it illegal?"

An hysterical laugh echoed through the room. Although it was mine, the sound startled me just the same. "No, just face cream."

His expression didn't waver. The weight of his intense stare was suffocating.

"What is so controversial about face cream that caused you to stage a silent protest?"

"She wanted whitening cream."

"You'll have to educate me as I don't know the first thing about women's beauty products. What exactly is whitening cream?"

"Exactly what it sounds like. It lightens skin color. The kind she wanted contains bleach. It can burn your skin if it's not applied correctly or left on too long."

He regarded me with a look of concern. "Do you speak from experience?"

Don't ask me anymore, Liam. He had managed to learn more about me in two days than anyone else had in years.

"I'll go fetch it now," I said, hoping he would drop the subject. I felt foolish for bringing it up in the first place. For allowing him to defend me when my actions didn't warrant it. Now, I only felt stupid for my admission. He didn't budge from the doorway.

"May I be bold and improper?"

"Better than meek and weak," I said, a little too loudly.

"Right you are." He took a step back from me, shoving his hands in his pockets, rocking on his feet. "You're lovely as you stand. You have beautiful skin, Mary."

A warm flush spread across my body as my mouth went completely dry. I tried to swallow, unsure if a body could die from spontaneous dehydration.

He exhaled. "Anyway, it's an awful thing, but there is nothing we can do about it. We are not the morality police. We have a business to run."

I nodded. "I shall go now, sir."

He backed away from the door. I went to turn the knob, but his voice halted me. "Mary." There was a silent command in that voice. Something in me wanted to heed it…needed to. I'd never felt that way. It had nothing to do with our business dynamic. My stomach flipped, and my knees knocked against the stifling sari. "You are not to deliver it. Have someone else take it to her room. Also, have one of the drivers take you this time. Do you understand?"

"Yes, sir."

"And what is that you understand…specifically?"

"I understand you won't risk the guest's satisfaction. Any more contact with me will only upset her further."

"Not her satisfaction. Despite what our mission statement says, guest satisfaction currently ranks number three on my list of concerns right now."

His statement was like a cracked doorway, too tempting not to open further. "May I ask what the first two are, sir?"

He stepped closer, not touching me, but only a thin span of space separated us. "Someone speaking to you disrespectfully is the first. Me not losing my temper when it happens is the second. Any further questions?"

"No, sir."

"Good. You are dismissed, Miss Costa."

Dismissed? I grasped the doorknob, fumbling nervously, as if I didn't know the mechanics of the object. "Yes, sir."

His hand clasped over mine, turning the knob.

"Liam. My name is Liam."

I pressed my forehead against the door. "Thank you, Mr. Montgomery, sir."

"Formal it is. Good day, Miss Costa."

I hurried toward the driver's area of the lot. He didn't follow me, but I felt his eyes on me with each step. I prayed Kishore wouldn't be there, because this day was already weird enough without another encounter. He wasn't there. After two seconds, the other drivers filled me in. I needn't have to worry about Kishore again.

He'd been sacked.

When I returned from my second trip, I asked Pooja to deliver the correct face cream and also another item I'd purchased from my own funds for Mr. Montgomery, telling her he'd asked me to get it. I sent a note with the product, explaining how to apply properly. He wouldn't be able to read the Hindi lettering on the bottle. I lied and told Pooja he'd written the note for me to give the clerk, knowing she wouldn't be able to read it.

She looked at it curiously. "He asked you for sunscreen?"

"Yes, the other kind made him burn."

I didn't understand my own motivations at the time, except that the sunscreen had stared me in the face at the shop. I thought he had beautiful skin, too. I would hate to see any damage come to it.

Chapter 5

Liam

Her personnel file stated she had been with us since she was eighteen. She was twenty-two now. There was little information, except that she did her job with proficiency. She cleaned rooms and worked in the kitchen making room-service deliveries. I almost choked on my coffee when I saw how little we paid her. Maybe enough to indulge in a Starbucks latte in the States...after a week's salary. Of course, the wages were aligned with our competitors in this region. That didn't make it right, though. She didn't even have an emergency contact listed. That made me sad. Who cared for her?

I had every right to this information, but my purpose was personal, not professional. I stared at the bottle of sunscreen she'd sent me, unfolding her note once again.

Sir, please use this as your sunscreen while you are in India. The other kind is worthless. You might as well hang a mirror around your neck. You have nice skin, too. This will protect you.

She'd written some additional instructions about its use, but didn't sign the note. I smiled at the last line. She wanted to protect me? Guess what, love? That went likewise and double for me. I'd almost lost it when that hostile woman was yelling at her. Knowing that Mary earned so little and had used that money to buy something for me made me feel like a complete sod. Mary didn't belong here. She definitely had an education. The cross on her neck, although old, appeared to be gold. The bangle she wore on her right wrist was more fitting though...a large, tarnished, fake silver band. She was always adjusting it. When I'd first seen her, I hadn't thought much of it, but she wore it every day, and it wasn't part of the uniform. But it was definitely part of *her* uniform.

God, she was a strange girl. Strange and intriguing and the last person I should be thinking of. Yet, she held the distinction of occupying all my random thoughts.

I picked up the bottle of sunscreen. Worried about an allergic reaction, I had placed only a small amount on my right shoulder, using the other brand on the rest of my body. As it turned out, it was only my right shoulder that didn't sting from burn.

I chuckled, remembering this morning when she was picking up the discarded glasses at the pool. I wanted to talk to her, but she had given me her silent look of warning. So instead, I held up the bottle and mouthed the words, "Thank you."

She'd nodded in response.

I wasn't an idiot. Even behind the cloak of her nervousness, her gaze lingered on my body. Yet she was able to go on as if the conversation didn't hold the same weight for her as it did for me. Each day since, I found myself searching for the girl who didn't want to be found. Why had I gone against my own promise when I pulled her aside like that? It showed a lack of self-control on my part, but even worse, a blatant disregard for her. I understood the ramifications of rumors better than anyone. She didn't need that. I'd told her that she was beautiful. I had needed to tell her. The words had been a fire in my belly, refusing to ease up until I said them.

Fucking idiot, Liam.

I checked through my emails, trying to appease the board and fend off my half brother, Stephen's, ridiculous suggestions. *Sod off, Stephen.* I wondered if my father was having a good laugh over the torturous situation we'd inherited. I disliked my brother because…well, because he was a tosser who'd had everything handed to him. By the same token, he hated me intensely, showing off his feelings with brilliant displays of disloyalty. The most recent of which was suggesting to the board someone in our position should come on this trip. He'd meant me.

It was a private company, at least for the next few months. I could have declined, but truthfully, I wanted to get the hell out of Manhattan, and our Asian hotels did need a closer look than the quick figures we went over each month. I opened the email he'd sent with the subject line *sold*. I read through it three times, my anger rising with each sentence of the long contract.

I rang the obnoxiously long number, my fingers gripping the phone. It went to voicemail so I rang again.

"What the fuck, Liam. Do you know what time it is here?" Except he didn't sound tired. He was wound up and awake.

"Yeah, Stephen, I know exactly what time it is. I just read your email. What the bloody hell? You know I'm trying to work through the problems here, and now you go and try to sell it."

"You can't fix it. I'm sure you'll spin your wheels trying, but it's time to admit failure and move on. The buyers came to us. The land is worth more than the building. It's a solid contract. We need to clean up our bottom line before we take the company public."

All good reasons, yet I argued. "You can't sell without my permission."

"Thanks for the reminder, bastard Brit brother from another mother."

"Oh, that term of affection never gets old." He did almost as good a job of getting under my skin as the scorching Rajasthani sun.

"Just look over the fucking contract. We are not in the hotel business. We are in the making-money business. And this place isn't making any."

"At least be original, bro. Stop copying lines from our father."

A girl laughed in the background. Stephen sniffed. He fucking sniffed.

"Are you coked up?"

The line went quiet. "That's no concern of yours."

"It damn well is since we run a business together."

"And if it were just you, it would be run into the ground by now."

This was pointless. Conversations with Stephen were impossible under normal circumstances, let alone when he was under the influence. Despite his lifestyle, he did have a good mind for business. I would admit—never to him--that it was better than mine.

"Jesus Christ, Stephen. Get yourself sobered up and call me back."

"Read over the contract, Liam."

"Okay, brother. In the meantime, you should go over the proposal I'm presenting to the board at the next meeting."

"What proposal?"

"All our employees will be randomly drug tested at least once a year, maybe twice. That includes us too, mate."

He laughed, a mixture of irritation and fear. "Fuck you. They'll never go for that. It's too expensive."

"I've done a lot of research and figured out ways to cut the expense. Besides, you don't want drug addicts working for us...or do you?"

"What is your problem with me?"

"With you? Nothing. I don't think about you. I don't care about you at all. I do care about this company left in our charge. I am doing you a favor, though. It'll give you an opportunity to get clean and stay clean." If there was one thing Stephen cared about, it was his position.

"I fucking snort coke once in a while. It's recreational. Do all British people have sticks up their arses or is it just you, bro?" He did his very weak, much too high-pitched, imitation of my accent.

"Don't justify yourself to me. I'm not your therapist or your mother."

"Read the fucking contract," he yelled as I hung up.

I almost punched a hole in the plastered walls, but that would be counterproductive. I went to the hotel gym instead and lifted weights. Then I went swimming. I wanted to go for a jog, but the grounds weren't set up for that, and I wasn't in the mood to run about the city. It was early afternoon by the time I'd showered and gotten through the rest of the emails. The contract could wait.

I had planned to tabulate results of my interviews. That was my idea, and what a fucking useless idea it was. No one had been honest. Everyone loved working here and, accordingly, there was not one damn thing we could do to improve ourselves. I'd even made sure that Prabhat hid the fact that I owned this company. But it did nothing to lessen people's inhibitions when answering my questions. Even the reassurance that their responses would be private did no good. I wondered what kind of scare tactics Prabhat had used on the employees. Did he not realize if I couldn't come up with solutions to increase our bottom line, that the entire ship he was so desperately protecting would be sunk?

Including her.

Mary Costa... I bet she'd be honest with me, but how could I talk to her without mucking up her life? I picked up the phone, dialing down to the kitchen.

"Hello, Liam Montgomery here. Can you please get me the staff schedule for today? Yes, I want all shifts and breaks. Thank you."

Chapter 6

Mary

The whole kitchen staff grumbled about how much our Western taskmaster ate. I chuckled as the fourth round of room service was placed on the cart. The things he ordered didn't even make sense. Dessert first, then tea, then lunch, then breakfast items.

I stood in front of his door with this cart—the fourth cart. I took a deep breath before knocking.

Today he wore long khaki-colored shorts with many pockets—cargo shorts, they were called. His white button-down shirt was open at the collar.

His soft lips broke into a welcoming smile. One I couldn't help but return. "Hello, Miss Costa."

"Sir."

He opened the door wider, gesturing me in.

"Everyone is wondering how much you can eat."

He laughed, patting his stomach. "I am a growing boy."

I stopped short, staring at all the food that took up every meter of space on the small table against the window. "You haven't touched anything."

"I had other reasons for ordering it."

"What reasons?"

"I'm sure you're aware I've been conducting interviews with the staff?"

"Yes."

"I'd like to interview you if you're game."

"Me? Why?"

"I value your opinion."

There was something in that simple statement that made me deliriously happy. I didn't think I had anything of value, especially not my opinion. "When?"

He rubbed the back of his neck, a gesture that put me at ease because it spoke volumes about his own nerves. "Now. That is, if you're free. Your answers would be completely anonymous. Or, if it would make you more comfortable, we can do it downstairs and have the translator between us, but I think that might be odd and a waste of resources. Another kind of charades, and I suck at games."

"Here is fine. I'm done for the night."

He started clearing away the dishes, placing them on the cart I'd brought in. I couldn't believe he'd done this to spend time with me. I told myself to relax and get over it. It didn't mean anything personal. He wanted my opinions to make the hotel better. Not for any other reason.

"May I offer you something?" he asked, gesturing to the cart. "As it happens, I have an abundance of food."

"I'm fine, thank you."

He pulled out a chair. I stared at it in confusion, waiting for him to take it, but I soon realized it was for me.

"Please eat something, Miss Costa."

I smiled, trying to downplay the giddiness that threatened to well up in me. I had to act professional…but maybe on this occasion, I could be friendly as well.

"Call me Mary, please."

"Will you call me Liam?"

"No, sir. That's improper."

He sighed, taking a yellow legal pad and pencil from his briefcase. "As you wish, Mary."

Perhaps I should not have asked him to call me by my first name. He said it slowly, emphasizing the syllables.

Maarry.

I'd never thought much of my name, but I enjoyed it a great deal when it came out of his sexy mouth.

"What would you like? I'll fix you a plate." He wanted to fix me a plate? If Prabhat knew I was cavorting with a guest socially, let alone dining with one—especially him—he'd kick me into the streets without a second thought. Still, it didn't mean I couldn't enjoy it. Only that Prabhat couldn't find out. Liam seemed to understand that. It gave me a measure of safety in this daring dance between us.

"I'll only eat if you join me," I said.

"With pleasure. What shall we try first?"

I removed the domes. "How about this?"

"What is it?"

"It's called a *dosa*."

"Dosa," he said slowly.

"Yes, traditionally from south India, but it's eaten everywhere. It's a rice crepe flavored with masala. We stuff ours with potatoes and onions."

He cut the long folded pancake in half, placing a portion on each plate. "Sounds good."

I spooned a thick dollop of chutney on the side of his plate. He regarded it with suspicion.

"You should try it with chutney."

"I don't know. It looks spicy. It's the same color as Wasabi."

"I've never had Was—was—"

"Wasabi...used for sushi."

"Raw fish? Do you enjoy that?" I asked, trying not to make a face.

"Yeah, I love it. But I can only handle a little bit of the Wasabi. You should try it sometime." His statement had codified our differences. I couldn't just go out to a restaurant on my budget.

"This particular chutney isn't spicy. It's made from coconut and mint."

He cut into it gingerly.

"Use your hands, sir." I demonstrated with my own plate. "If you are willing to eat with the natives, then you should eat as we do in all ways."

"Very well." He poured himself a glass of wine. "Do you drink?"

"Only during communion."

"So you don't drink?"

"I don't have an aversion to it, but I don't want any wine right now." The last thing I needed was to lose the tiny shred of sense I had left.

"Would you like a soda? Water?"

"Water is good."

He retrieved a bottle from the honor fridge for me.

He followed my lead, chewing the food slowly. I tried not to stare at the way his mouth moved. His lips were full and sensual, especially against his strong-set jaw.

"It's tasty."

We chatted about food. He told me about different kinds of sushi and other things I'd never heard of, like calamari and tilapia. I had no idea why anyone would find squid appetizing, but apparently it was one of Liam's favorite things. He asked questions, too. I told him about the diverse cuisines of India. He finished the dosa, scraping his plate clean.

"Now what should we nosh on?" he asked, arching a brow.

My skin flushed as his gaze raked over me. We made our way through all the different dishes. I offered him suggestions on what to try next. Some things he appreciated more than others, but to his credit, he tasted them all.

"I'm full," he declared after several plates. He patted his stomach again. The sound was as solid as the wooden base of *nagara* drums.

I started clearing the table, placing our dishes back on the trolley. He stood to help me.

"Please sir, I can clean up. It's what I do."

"It's not your mess. It's our mess, and you're not working. You're my guest. Let me take care of it."

"I need to do it." He regarded me for a second as I cleared the plates. The work kept my mind occupied. I stacked our dishes and wiped down the table. I hoped he'd understand. It wasn't a servant mentality, but my need to always have order in my life.

Once it was done, I stared at the cart.

Before I could say anything, he pushed it to the other side of the room. He glanced at me and then opened the door. "I'll be right back."

It took a while for him to return.

"Where did you go?"

"I took the cart back to the kitchen. I gave the chef my compliments and apologized for keeping him busy all day."

"That was nice of you."

He shrugged, as if people brought their carts back to the kitchen all the time. "You would have kept looking at it, wouldn't you?"

"Probably."

"I figured. I wanted you to be here with me, not thinking about dirty dishes. Are you able to do that, or would you prefer to leave? You understand the choice belongs to you and you alone."

"I want to be here, sir." I twisted a strand of hair. The sun filtered through the windows, casting a golden glow. I swiped a napkin across the table, gathering a few stray crumbs. "Are you going to ask me questions now?"

"Sure," he said, picking up the legal pad. He tapped the pencil against it. "Why are you here?"

"You ordered food."

"I mean, at the hotel."

I shrugged, not expecting such a personal question. Then again, it really wasn't that personal. "What does that have to do with anything?"

"Just wondering what motivates people."

"I moved to Rajasthan from Mumbai when I was eighteen. In my search for work, I inquired if they had open positions, and they did. There is not much else to tell."

"I doubt the story is that simple."

How did he see right through me? "I am not as complicated as you seem to think."

He leaned in. "And I'm much simpler than *you* think."

I had no idea how to respond to that. He leaned back, not expecting an answer. "Why settle in Jaipur of all places?"

"I wanted a place bigger than a village, smaller than a metropolis. Here it was. A city with massive hilltops, overlooking clusters of castles occupied by Raj's that are surrounded by a lake so pure it gleams brighter than any jewel."

He listened to me with a quiet intensity. "You should be in charge of tourism. You make me want to explore it…every beautiful meter."

My fingers gripped the armrests of the chair. Were we still talking about the city? A crisp breeze circulated, but it only fanned the sparks between us. This flirtation was dangerous and delicious. I licked my bottom lip.

"I'm going to Mumbai after this," he said.

"You are?"

"We opened a hotel there a few years ago. I'm going to visit, and then my final destination will be Goa. That is actually one of our most profitable hotels."

"Goa is lovely." People from all over the world traveled to its lush beaches.

"You've been there?"

"No, but I've heard it is."

"May I ask you something without sounding completely ignorant?"

"I doubt you ever sound ignorant, sir." I braced myself for a difficult question.

"Why do you have a Spanish last name?"

All my bunched muscles relaxed. "As you probably know, the Brits ruled India before independence."

He smirked. "Yes, I'm aware of that."

"But before that, we belonged to Portugal. When the Portuguese came ashore on Goa, they brought missionaries along with the sailors and traders. The missionaries converted many families. Along with those conversions, they adopted Spanish names. Mine was one of them."

"Interesting. I didn't know that. So you come from Goa?"

"Originally, but this was centuries ago. We migrated to Bombay eventually…or Mumbai, depending if you use the new name."

"Does your family still live in Mumbai?"

My quota for easy questions was up. "My parents are gone."

"I'm sorry for your loss," he said, his striking green-brown eyes shining with a compassion I wasn't prepared for.

I swallowed down a silent sob before taking an unladylike gulp of water from the bottle. "Thank you. But only my father passed away. My mother ran off years before. No one has heard from her since, not that we were looking."

"Where did you live after your father passed?"

"In an orphanage until I turned eighteen."

"Do you have any family?"

I opened my mouth, but was struck silent. The lump in my throat threatened to crack open. Shit.

Liam's concerned expression only made it worse. *Do not pity me,* I wanted to scream. But I might have dissolved into a pool of tears if I opened my mouth.

"I'm sorry. Obviously I'm trespassing on your privacy. I noticed you didn't have an emergency contact." My mouth gaped, but before I could respond, he continued, "I checked the other employees, too. You're the only one who doesn't have one. I'd like to fill that line in for you. Who shall I put down?"

The silence between us stretched. I twisted the cheap silver band on my arm, reminding myself it was time to buy a new bracelet. "Leave it blank."

He placed his hand flat on the table, close to mine, as if to offer an invitation to reach out. I refused the offer.

"I lost my mum in a car accident when I was sixteen."

Guilt pricked at me. "Were you close?"

"Yes."

"She bought you the book. I…I read the card. I'm sorry. The other ones fell out. I probably put them back in the wrong place."

"I can figure out where they all go. I've read them enough times to know."

"What do they mean? The note cards."

He considered my question for a moment. We'd been tiptoeing around each other's boundaries since I'd arrived. His reaction made me wonder if I'd unknowingly crossed into hostile territory. He smiled softly, putting me at ease. "Mum fancied herself a writer. She always bought me a book for my birthday. She put note cards inside with parables or lessons or thoughts she'd written for me. Sometimes, they had to do with the book. Most of the time, they were just generalizations to guide me."

"What did she write?"

"Poems, short stories, and a novel that never saw an end. It was her dream, but dreams don't pay rent. She worked as a supermarket cashier and crafted junk jewelry, too."

The realization struck me our differences were not as vast as the oceans between our homes. Liam Montgomery had been poor once. "Her gifts were very thoughtful."

He laughed, a sad, cynical laugh. "When I was a kid, I hated them. What the hell was I going to do with a book? I wanted a new bike or a skateboard or even a fucking shirt without a hole in it. I never read the books then…nope. Too busy playing rugby and chasing birds." He looked disgusted with his admission, as if he'd eaten something spoiled.

"Birds? You're a bird chaser?"

"Birds…girls."

"Oh, I see."

"Anyway." He tapped on the notepad. But I didn't want him to steer us again, so I took the reins from him.

"It doesn't matter."

"What doesn't matter?"

"That you may not have shown gratitude at the time. We're not always ready to appreciate every present in the…present."

"Very true."

"Obviously, you knew deep down how great they were because you saved them."

"They were all destroyed except for *Nicolas Nickleby*." His eyes darkened, the green overtaking the brown, a quiet hurricane of anger. I winced when he cracked the pencil in two. "I don't want to talk about it."

I was torn, searching for the right response to the swirling fog of emotion. He was inside some toxic mixture of anguish and anger. My heart broke, realizing he offered to lend me the only book he had left.

"Sir."

He lifted his face to meet my gaze.

"You still have the words, right?" I pointed to my heart. "You have them here, don't you? It doesn't matter if they're not on the same paper in her writing. Words never die."

He blinked several times, focusing on me. His jaw tightened. "Are you a maid or a philosopher?"

"I am a maid."

His hand reached for mine, but I pulled away before contact.

"I'm sorry. I am." He shook his head. "God, I can't believe I said that."

"Why? It's the truth."

"It's me being a complete dick is what it is."

I understood why he'd snapped. It wasn't to lash out at me, but to protect himself. I employed the same exact methods. I shouldn't have pressed. Each of his movements had been a clear warning, a plea even, to step lightly.

He offered me an apologetic smile. "It's the funny thing about childhood. You think it's the worst of times when you're living it."

"And the best of times when it's over." I finished his thought. "Very Dickensian, sir."

"Please don't call me 'sir,' especially when I'm referring to you by your first name."

"I can't."

"Why not?"

"Will you tell me something she wrote?"

"I'm supposed to ask you questions, remember?"

"Questions about the hotel, but we're not doing that, are we?"

"No, I suppose we're not."

"Motherly advice is something I've never had." Unless it involved whitening creams or the proper way to apply kohl. "If you share the words with me, I'll pass them on. They'll go into the universe and then maybe, one day, you'll hear them again. You'll see what I mean about words not dying."

"Your persistence surprises me, Miss Costa."

It surprised me, too…my persistence and my lack of resistance. "Sorry, sir. We can move on." I folded my hands in my lap and waited for him to ask me something.

"Here's one I rather like. It's the story of two roads. There are only two roads in life. The high road and the easy road. The high road is difficult, full of jagged rocks and pits and steep curves, but the journey is worth it. The easy road is smooth and straight, but it's also paved with regret. Always travel the high road, Liam. Always the high road. That's what she wrote."

"Good advice. Do you follow it?"

"I wish I could tell you I did, but I don't always."

"Maybe there's a place where both roads intersect."

I hoped a place like that existed because being with Liam Montgomery was both easy and difficult. Which path did I want more? Or was there even an open path for me to choose? The way he looked at me said yes. But all the ways of the world said no.

I jumped as Liam's phone buzzed, the harsh sound sawing through the thick tension in the room.

He glared at the screen. "Excuse me, please. I have to take this." He answered the phone and told the other person to hang on the line. I wondered if it was a bird calling him.

"I'm going to go now." I stood and walked toward the door. As I turned the handle, his husky voice coiled around me, almost pulling me back into the room.

"Next time I order room service, don't make me do it four times, Miss Costa."

Thankfully, I wasn't facing him, because I smiled so wide, my jaw protested. "Yes, sir."

Chapter 7

Liam

Stephen argued we needed to execute the contract soon. The lawyers had signed off, and the buyers were anxious. I stared at the vacant chair across from me the whole time he spoke. At least he was sober.

"I'll call you tomorrow, Stephen."

"What? No, we need to talk about this. We have—"

"Fuck. Off."

I slammed the phone on the bed. It bounced three times before landing on the pillow.

Why the hell did I tell her all that stuff? Details I had never told anyone. The girl was calm and chaos rolled into one. Every time she called me 'sir,' it was a reminder our relationship was imbalanced and improper. Still, the fucking term turned me on. I had slapped it back in her face, hadn't I? I'd stung her with my words...and guess what?

Words. Don't. Die.

The girl, both subservient and rebellious, was becoming more of a mystery to me. How brave was she? She'd lost her entire family and moved to a new city on her own. Although my stepmother, father, and Stephen weren't exactly loving people, at least I'd had a home. I had a fucking emergency contact, and I didn't have to worry about supporting myself.

She had no one. Yet, somehow that made her stronger. The questions I had asked Mary harpooned straight into inappropriateness. They discredited my reputation as an honest businessman. But she'd turned the tables on me.

Get your shit together.

Maybe I needed to take Mum's advice. Take the high road and not order room service tomorrow night. I'd forget about her. Forget the way her body moved as she walked across a room. Forget her long limbs and soft curves. I'd forget about her pouty lips and silky hair. Or the way she parted her mouth or the crimson blush that settled over her face when I flirted. I'd forget how hard I was, too. Well…some things couldn't be ignored.

* * * *

I spent the next day convincing myself I'd forgotten all about her. Even as I dialed room service, I blamed it on hunger. Yeah, I was hungry all right.

I didn't know what to expect this time, but I sure as shit didn't expect Mary's anger. I got a full dose as she rolled the cart past me so fast I had to get out of the way.

"How are you?"

"Pissed off, sir." She turned back to me, hands on her hips. "Is that the right term?"

"Oh yeah, you nailed it."

She dropped the cloche on the table, its silver platter clanging as it landed. "May I get you anything else, sir?"

"An explanation perhaps. What has you so upset?"

"Are you planning to demolish the fountain?"

It was the last possible thing I expected her to bring up. "Yes. It's an eyesore."

"The stones are crumbling, but the inside structure is still intact. If you take it down, the flower will die."

"Why is the flower so important to you?"

"It's a lotus flower."

I had no idea how that answered my question. "Yes, I'm aware. If you care to make a valid argument, please do. I'm willing to listen."

"It was a present to me."

"From who?" I hope to God it wasn't from the bastard driver I sacked.

"When I left the orphanage, the sisters gave me a packet of seeds and told me to plant them wherever I was. Like you, I didn't appreciate the gift. When I arrived here, I threw the seeds in that stupid fountain and never thought of it again."

"But it blossomed."

"Yes, a single flower took root. It should not have. I never took care of it. But it grew anyway. It's not much, but it's a tiny miracle. At least it is to me. They are the most special flowers in the entire universe. Did you know that?"

I raised my hands. "I did not. Tell me, Mary, why do they hold such a prestigious place?"

"The Buddhists believe they are a symbol of purity. I do, too."

"Purity?"

"They grow in darkness and muck, in the dirtiest places possible, but when they emerge from the water, they are clean and pure. They symbolize resurrection, because even in darkness, there is light."

"That's a sweet sentiment, but you aren't convincing me."

She crossed her arms. "You're such a bully."

I held back my laughter, but I couldn't suppress my smile. How did she manage to look so damn beautiful when she was angry? "We're progressing from 'sir,' but I don't really care for the term 'bully.' Can we negotiate something in between?"

She swiped a wisp of hair from her forehead. "Everyone who works here loves that flower. Not just me. It brings them some small joy to walk past every day. Even Prabhat likes it, and he never likes anything."

"Mary, I don't want to take anything away from anybody, but you can't call me a bully because I want to remove a dilapidated old fountain that is a haven for mosquitoes."

She sighed, staring out the window. At the very spot where I first saw her at the same damn fountain we were arguing about. "Every morning, I lay out candles around the perimeter. I make sure they stay lit throughout the day. It keeps the mosquitoes away."

"I see."

"I remove any litter. I can't do anything about the stones, though."

"I'll have the flower relocated."

"You'll kill it."

"If it survived once, I'm sure—"

"It's strong, but delicate. You can't change the habitat without destroying it."

"Then we'll plant a new one. Okay?"

"Don't you think it's special how one seed hung on? How it beat all the odds?"

I think you're special, Mary. That's what I think.

"I'll take it under advisement. Can we move on now?"

Her shoulders slumped with defeat. "Yes, sir."

Fuck it. If fixing a stupid fountain made her happy, then I'd do it. I moved to her. Her spine straightened. I placed a hand on each of her shoulders. Her breathing changed. The pale moon cast her face in a soft glow. I inhaled her scent...spiced vanilla and citrus. God, I wanted to run my nose against her Audrey Hepburnesque neck. "Okay, Mary. We won't get rid of it."

"Don't do it just because I want you to. Do it for the right reasons."

"What other bloody reason do I have? You think I believe in resurrection and purity? Trust me, neither of those concepts are high on my list. But it means something to you, so in turn, it means something to me. That…that is the right reason as far as I'm concerned."

"Why am I the right reason?"

I didn't have an answer. Hell, I couldn't even make sense of it myself. "You just are."

She fingered her cross. I almost wondered if she'd hold it out toward me to repel my sinful thoughts. I pulled my hands back. As quick as an autumn wind, she changed directions.

"It's your birthday tomorrow, isn't it?"

"How did you know?"

"Prabhat is throwing you a party." She clamped her hand over her. "Shit. It's a surprise party."

Although I hated the idea, I chuckled at hearing her swear.

"Don't laugh. It's not funny. I just ruined it."

I pulled out a chair for her. She eyed it warily.

"Please sit. Our supper will get cold."

"You're treating this romantically."

"Romantic? You have no idea what romance is. It's certainly not your coming to my room, all cloak and dagger, with a room service cart. This is just a business dinner."

My words must have done more harm than good because she looked hurt.

"Do you often have business dinners with maids?"

"Stop."

"Stop what?"

"Stop making this about what we do. We're two people having a conversation. If you don't want to be here, then you're free to go."

"I want to be here."

I exhaled in relief. "Good, but you have to promise me you'll check all those doubts and fears at the door. Can you do it?"

"I'll try, sir."

"Works for me." I fetched a bottle of water for her

"Thank you."

I slumped into the other seat. "You know what's not good, though?"

"What?"

"Surprise parties. I'll tell Prabhat to cancel. Don't worry, I won't tell him how I found out."

"He'll be upset."

I wanted to tell her I didn't give a fuck about Prabhat being upset, but my stomach grumbled. "Let's eat."

She took two plates from the tray. I opened the dome and ladled out lamb stew. We tore pieces of buttered naan and scooped it. "Are you afraid of Prabhat, Mary?"

"Yes."

"Has he treated you unfairly?"

"No. He is my boss. Everyone is afraid of him to some degree."

"You shouldn't be afraid of him."

"Please don't cancel it. They are allowing us to work extra time. It may not mean much to you, but there are a lot of people counting on those wages."

"Who says that doesn't mean anything to me?" I sighed, wanting to get off this stupid topic. Our time was limited, and the last thing I wanted was a debate. "Okay, Mary. I'll attend and act surprised."

She relaxed a bit. "Thank you."

I downed a bottle of Kingfisher. I preferred Guinness, but it wasn't bad. She explained how the lamb was seasoned with fresh spices and cooked over a low flame, simmering for hours. She moaned after her first bite, closing her eyes, her mouth chewing slowly. It was fucking delicious…and the lamb was good, too.

My hand twitched as the light caught her hair. I wanted to touch it, but I also wished to draw those strands. I imagined what it might look like loose, flowing against her back, tangled between my fingers.

"Why doesn't anyone here know you speak English?"

She stared out the window. I tapped the pencil against the blank paper. Blank paper and a fine lead point…so many possibilities. I never took notes with a pencil. In fact, I hadn't even realized there were a few in my briefcase until I pulled out the legal pad. It was a subconscious choice on my part, but what my brain couldn't comprehend, my hands did.

"It didn't seem important. No one ever asked me."

I wanted to bring up the fact that Prabhat had asked her point blank the other day, but I thought it better to muzzle my curiosity on that issue. This was my time with her, and I really didn't want to spend it talking about Prabhat.

"Are you taking notes about this?"

"Just jotting down a few things I need to remember. You could do better with your life."

"Better how?"

"Make more money. Work an office job. Something less…manual."

"That's important to you, isn't it? Money."

"It's important to everyone."

"Not true. I'm happy with this work. It's hard work at times, but I need it. It helps me focus."

"Focus on what?"

She sighed, fidgeting impatiently. *Stay still, Mary,* I silently commanded.

"Do you have any real questions?"

"Was he your boyfriend?"

"Who?"

"The man I saw with you at the fountain the first morning I arrived, and then later at the pool."

"Did you hear us?"

"Answer my question first."

"We were a fling. He wanted more." A realization flickered over her features. "Wait…you saw me at the fountain? That's why you called me Lotus Girl? And you sacked him because of me?"

"Yes. Yes. And hell yes. He was harassing you. Everyone should feel safe where they work."

"Don't do me any more favors. I can take care of myself. If I need help, Mr. Montgomery, I am fully aware of the proper channels as outlined in the Wilshire Hotel Corporate Handbook."

"I would have done it if I'd witnessed any employee being mistreated by another. I'm sure you are capable, but I don't want you to handle anything outside of your job description."

We looked at each other, the irony of my words hanging in the air. The tension grew thicker than the humidity. She surprised me with a laugh. I found myself laughing as well. What I'd just said was ridiculous considering we were having a quiet dinner for two in my hotel room. Definitely not part of her job description.

"Do you always need to control everything?"

"Not at all. I'm very flexible, actually. For example, just recently I was talked into saving a fountain and convinced to attend a surprise birthday party. So you see, I'm pretty easy going."

She tilted her head. "Touché."

"Ah, do you speak French as well? What else don't I know about you, Lotus Girl? You have a black belt? Maybe you're a spy engaging in a form of corporate espionage."

"No, no, and certainly not."

"Do you really think I'm a bully?"

"Sir, I completely understand your need to rule. It is in your blood, isn't it?"

"Ouch, is that a barb on the British imperialism of India?"

"Possibly." Her grin turned sly, fucking sexy.

"Your country has been free since before you were born...way before. Still holding a grudge, then?"

She placed her fingers together to indicate a pinch. "Maybe a small one."

"And you're placing all that on my shoulders, yeah?"

Mary shrugged. "You have very broad shoulders. I think they can sustain it."

"I assure you none of my ancestors made any decisions regarding Her Majesty's pleasure when it came to this country or any other."

"How can you be sure?"

"I come from a long line of surly bastards. None were proper enough for Parliament or Her Majesty. As a matter of fact, my grandmother was Scottish, so you could venture to say both our cultures have sustained suffering under the same flag."

Her mouth crinkled with amusement. "Scottish? Have you ever worn a kilt?"

"No...never."

Her mouth turned downward.

"Does that disappoint you?"

"Slightly. I think it would suit you."

I turned on the Sean Connery brogue. "You have a thing for lads in kilts, do you?"

She chewed on her bottom lip, a pretty shade of crimson reddening her cheeks. "There is something...appealing about it. At least based on books I've read."

"Historical novels?"

She nodded, playing with the label on her water bottle. "Highlanders and the lasses they love."

"And where do you procure such books here?"

"There is a store some distance away. I take the bus there on my days off. Not much selection, but I can usually find something to rent."

"Rent? Like a library?"

"Sort of. You pay for the book and return it for partial refund. I buy a book in the morning, drink my tea, devour the whole thing in one sitting, and return it at night. You can also purchase books outright, but I never have." She pulled her legs up, wrapping her arms around them.

I almost asked her to shift so I could capture her profile better. "I see. You know, your pronunciation is perfect. You actually sound British sometimes."

She graced me with a lovely smile, the kind of expression that made men want to freeze the image of beautiful women on canvas, stone, or clay.

"My family lived in England for a few years when I was younger. I was only two, and we moved back when I was eight, but it was where I learned English. I suppose I retained the inflection. My papa studied at Cambridge."

The pencil fell from my hand. She picked it up.

"I lived in Luton. That's about an hour from Cambridge."

She dropped the pencil. We both went to pick it up. Our foreheads bumped on the way back up, like some silly Monty Python bit.

"Sorry," I said, stroking her hair. God, it did feel like silk. Her body tensed against my touch. I dropped my hand immediately, unsure which I regretted more, starting or stopping the action.

"It's okay. We were close."

"And here we are again. In the summers, my mum sold jewelry at different booths and craft fares around Cambridge. Sometimes, I'd go with her. What if we crossed paths before?"

She played with the hem of her sari. "I doubt our circles ever overlapped, sir."

Yeah, Mary. Not then and not even now. That was what she was telling me.

"Still kind of amazing, don't you think?"

"Yes." She wrapped her arms around herself. "When I think about my time in England, all I remember are long trains, Dusty Springfield, Cadbury bars, and the cold, wet chill in the air."

"Dusty Springfield?"

She laughed, the kind of laugh only faraway memories brought. "Papa was a fan of rock'n'roll. He amassed a huge collection of records when we lived in Cambridge, but my mother hated them and insisted we couldn't fit them in our luggage. They got left behind. I used to dance to them as a kid."

I could almost picture her doing that. It was easy to read between the subtle lines of her dialogue. Dad was "Papa" and Mum was "Mother."

She shivered, rubbing her arms, although the room was warm. "You came at the right time. It has to be freezing in Luton."

"I'm sure it is, but I haven't lived there in ten years. Manhattan is my home now."

"Of course, you moved there for work. That's the corporate headquarters, no?"

"I shifted to America at sixteen after Mum died. It's where my father lived."

"Lived?"

"He passed a few years ago. I suppose another thing we have in common."

She twisted a loose strand of her hair. The same strand I'd touched. "I'm sorry."

"Thank you. So, your father went to Cambridge?" I wondered how she got here for the thousandth time.

She nodded. "He moved us back before my sister was born. He loved England, but he missed home, and he wanted to teach here." Her eyes misted over talking about her dad, pride in her voice.

"Did you ever think of going to university yourself? I can make inquiries on your behalf."

She shook her head rapidly. "No."

"Mary…"

"I'm not interested, sir." The sharpness in her tone surprised me. God, she was stubborn. She didn't have pockets of sorrow—she had landmines. I could feel the blast coming, but I didn't care to stop it either.

"You're brilliant. You can do so much with your life. I would like to help you in that regard."

"I didn't ask for it, and I don't need your help." She stood and headed for the door.

"Stay."

"Why?"

"Because you want to be here as much as I want you to be here." I took her hand and held it, staring at her.

Her gaze lowered to our joined hands. She let go. Relief came when she finally sat again. Holding the legal pad higher, I focused back on my work, although the pencil felt shakier in my hand. If she hadn't let go, I would have pulled her onto my lap and tangled my fingers through strands of ebony silk while my mouth crushed against hers.

Get a grip.

"Do you enjoy your job, Mr. Montgomery?"

"No," I replied without pause. I had no idea why I was able to answer so quickly. I could barely admit that to myself, let alone tell it to someone else. In fact, I'd never told anyone else.

"Why not?"

I shrugged. "Take me up on my offer and become a therapist, Miss Costa. Look at how many confessions you're getting out of me."

"Will I get a straight answer?"

"I don't care for the bureaucracy of business or making decisions that impact the livelihood of others. Because, at the end of every bottom line, there is a person, a family, a life that is affected. Satisfied?"

"Why do you do it then?"

"Lotus Girl, I swear it's not complicated. I do it for the money. Money can make up for many things. I understand you don't share that ideology, but horses for courses as they say." I didn't know if I'd ever been this honest with someone. Why stop now? Why not just go completely starkers? "Does that make you think less of me?"

"No, sir, but here is the thing. I do like my job. As you said, I'm fine where I stand."

"That's not exactly what I said. And your statement doesn't offer me any greater insights into your position. You're wasting your life."

Her mouth tightened. I thought she'd leave then, or slap me, or some other gesture I deserved. Instead, she cut me with the harsh tone of her words. "That's an opinion, not a fact. And it's not exactly a very solid opinion when coming from someone who isn't passionate about his own life."

"At least warn me when you're about to gut me."

"I should go. It's late. Unless you actually have any questions involving my job or this hotel?"

Fine, we'd play it her way. I had a whole fucking list of questions. I skipped right to the most important one.

"I'm sure you're aware this hotel is losing money."

"I am. Everyone is."

"Do you have any suggestions or opinions on the matter?"

She looked around the room. "May I be bold and improper, sir?"

"Better than meek and weak."

Her smiled widened. "The hotel is a fraud."

"A fraud?"

She stood and knocked on the decorative molding that framed the window. "This is plastic. The floor," she said, tapping her foot against it, "is not real stone, but a cheap factory-made porcelain imitation. The rug is a mass-produced, made in China, reproduction of a Persian rug."

"What is your point?"

"We should not try to be something we are not. This is Jaipur. You can cross the lake and stay at a real Raj's palace. Why would you want to stay at a fake one?"

I paused, my grip tightening on the pencil. She'd successfully expressed the very issue that eluded me. "You make a strong point."

"Thank you, sir. Are you writing this down?"

"Yes."

"You're not. You haven't been taking notes this whole time. What are you doing?"

She held out her hand, gesturing to the pad. I gripped it tighter. "It's chicken scratch you won't be able to read."

"Then why won't you let me look at it?"

What use was it? We—no, not we—I had crossed so many lines tonight that I might as well have walked a marathon.

I set down the pad. It was a rough sketch at best, but she looked at it as if was a fine work of art. Her finger hovered above the lines, following them in the air. I drew her with her hair down as I imagined it would look, her pouty lips in that carefree sexual smile that rarely surfaced. But whenever it did, my heart jumped, as did another part of my body.

"It's me?"

"I was paying attention to what you said, but I really wanted to draw you, which is weird considering I haven't drawn anything in a long time."

"You're very good."

"Hardly, it's a hobby." Not even a hobby anymore.

"Have you had any formal training?"

"No."

"Then you are naturally talented."

In my head, I snorted at the compliment. "I have professional opinions to the contrary."

"What do you mean?"

"When I was eighteen, I wanted nothing more than to be an artist…a painter. My father had other ideas."

"So you didn't do it because of him?"

"Oh no, I wasn't a docile boy. I rebelled. He threatened to disown me. I'll have you know I didn't balk at that idea. I accepted it. Things are always easier when you're young."

"What changed?"

"He made a deal with me. It was a fair deal, and I accepted the terms."

"What deal?"

"He said I couldn't make a living with the bohemian lifestyle I chose for myself. I disagreed, of course, but he wanted to prove that to me. He offered to pay all my living expenses for six months. After that time, I would have an exhibition. If I made enough to cover what he'd spent, then he'd send me to the art school of my choice. Or to Europe to study with a master. I really wanted that, Mary. I wanted to improve and hone my skills. So I accepted."

"And?" she asked as if I was withholding a captivating plotline from her.

"And I worked hard those six months. I lived as frugally as I could, intending to prove him wrong. My girlfriend and I moved into this tiny loft and split the rent. I think it was half the size of this room."

"You didn't sell enough then?" Her disappointment was almost adorable, except that shortcoming in my life still hurt.

"One. One fucking painting, and to my father no less. A pinch of salt for my wounds. The critics blasted me, and these are New York critics, so they were especially harsh."

"That made you stop? Because you didn't make any money?"

"People cannot live on their dreams. I went onto college and business school, the path he'd planned for me."

"But there were other options. You could have gotten a temporary job and continued to paint. Just because you didn't make money doesn't mean you're not good."

"It most certainly does mean that. It's basic commerce. Besides, after I put everything into it and failed so epically, I didn't have the heart for it. I parted ways with my paintbrush."

"And the girlfriend?" she asked, a little sharply.

"We parted ways, too."

She stared down at the picture again. "I look beautiful in this picture."

"You look beautiful every day."

"May I purchase this from you, Mr. Montgomery?"

I replayed her request in my head, unsure if I heard correctly. "You can have it. After all, you're the reason I wanted to sketch in the first place."

She stood and reached into her blouse. My cock stirred at the sight. But when she pulled out a bill, I almost fell from my chair.

"I have to purchase it."

"I'm not taking money from you, Mary. Have you gone mad?"

"This isn't much. It might get you some hard candy at the market, but it's important I pay for it."

"Why is it important to you?"

"It's not important to me, Liam. It's important to you." Fuck, she picked now to say my name? As if I could refuse her anything. God, she was clever. "I don't mean to offend you. But you've made it clear you don't think you're talented unless there is a monetary value associated with your work. It's my way, a symbolic way, of showing you that you are." She held out the note. "Please take it. I really want your sketch, but I won't accept it unless you let me pay for it."

Reluctantly, I took the note from her. The gesture, even though it was strange, touched me. She brought something out in me I didn't know existed. "You're emasculating me. You know that, right?"

"I'm empowering you." She bowed her head for emphasis. "Sir."

And that gesture…well, that made me want to spank her, to kiss her, to send her away, to hug her, and to fuck her at the same time. Where Mary Costa was concerned, I checked the box that read *all of the above.*

She carefully ripped the paper from the ledger and folded it into a neat square. "I have to go. It's very late."

"I'll walk you."

"That wouldn't be wise."

"Wise people are boring. We're going to be foolish." I mentally forced my dick into submission before I stood.

She opened her mouth to argue.

"Don't speak—not a single word. You will walk ahead of me, and I will follow a few paces behind until I see you safely behind your quarters. Is that understood?"

She took a step back, her breaths coming out quicker than before, her breasts heaving. I hadn't even touched her…yet. At least not the way I wanted. *Oh God, Mary, you love this, don't you?* She was stubbornly independent, but she also had a desire to be dominated…at least on some level. Or was it just me who brought this out in her?

The former suited me just fine, but the idea of the later caused my erection to become painful. The same could be said for me. I enjoyed dominating, but I wasn't a dom, for God's sake. I didn't know the first thing about that particular lifestyle except for a passage of *Fifty Shades* a girl read to me one night. But with Mary, I found myself with all kinds of kinky thoughts about tying her up and having her kneel before me. *Get it out of your head, Montgomery.* Mary Costa and I made absolutely zero sense in every way.

"Yes, sir."

"Say. My. Name."

She bowed her head slightly. "Yes, Liam."

Fuck…we were in trouble.

Chapter 8

Mary

I double-checked my wrapping. I hadn't bought a present in years, not since my family was alive. Here I was buying two in one week. Well, technically the sunscreen didn't count.

I'd traded shifts with Pooja so I could make the two-hour journey to the bookstore. Instead of renting a book, I bought one for the first time. The clerk almost fainted when I handed her the money.

The whole day I wrote little messages and stuck them inside the stiff pages of the hardback novel. I had no idea if he'd appreciate it or be offended. I wished I could talk to Pooja about it, but one sentence, and she'd figure out the whole sordid thing. The rumors would spread quicker than malaria and attract just as many flies. Instead of trying to avoid the gossip surrounding me, I'd actually be the gossip. I didn't want that. I kept everything in my heart hidden. No time to start sharing now.

The same banquet room where we'd had the strange discussion about face creams was also the location of Liam's party. He did a good job of acting surprised. He even appeared grateful to Prabhat. I gathered dirty plates and empty glasses during the party, stealing glances at Liam the whole time. A few times his gaze was already on me. Prabhat had invited the high-level staff as well as guests, splurging on the higher-end suites.

I wasn't sure of the right word for him...dashing, handsome, striking? His sandy hair swept across his face, and his intense green-brown eyes captured more light than the twinkling chandelier in the center of the room. The dark suit and emerald striped tie contrasted nicely with his skin, which had taken on a golden hue since he'd arrived.

My heart skipped entire beats whenever I looked at him. But I wasn't the only one. The women all made excuses to be near him. I did my best not to notice…or at least pretended not to.

"Oh, my God," one lady with considerable breasts mused to another when I cleared their table, "he's like the British Channing Tatum."

I made a mental note to ask Pooja later who that was. She had worked for a western family before coming to the hotel and knew lots of things I didn't.

When I cleared his table of the cake plates, he leaned in close to me. "Thank you," he said, pressing a tip into my hand.

I quickly walked away, afraid all of my hidden feelings would spill out in one lusty look.   Liam's deep voice boomed across the room. "Prabhat, the party wore me out. I'm going to retire for the night."

"But it's so early, sir. We have entertainment."

"I'm really tired."

A selfish part of me wished I hadn't talked him out of cancelling the party. It meant no room service for him tonight. I craved our nightly chats. After every dish was cleaned and all the guests had left, I unfurled the bill he'd given me. A note with a tiny drawing of a lotus flower fell out.

Meet me outside at the rear of the building next to the garden. Unchain the rope.

What rope? Did he really want to risk us being seen? Did I?

I did.

* * * *

I had to use every ounce of control not to run there. The rope stopped me short with the large wooden sign that stated the garden was closed for the night. Ah, this rope. I removed the chain and hooked it back up after me. None of the lights were on to illuminate the path, but it still didn't stop me from running. I searched all the dark shadows for him.

An arm hooked around my waist, pulling me to the side of the building. His breath warmed my skin.

"About time. I've been waiting for over an hour."

"I just saw the note. You waited for me?"

"I would have waited a lot longer. You're worth the wait."

My knees buckled at his words. He rubbed my arms, his hands curling around them. Dear God, how would those large hands feel on the rest of my body? But he let go all too soon, before wicked thoughts could turn into wicked actions. I lowered my head. I wanted him in a way that scared me. I wanted him to kiss me with his soft mouth. I wanted to run my fingers through his thick hair, making it even more unruly. I wanted to watch the muscles in his arms flex as he lay on top of me. He tilted my chin so I was looking at his intense eyes.

"How was your day, Mary?"

Getting much better, thank you. "It was a good day for me. Did you enjoy your party?"

"The company was lacking. I missed you."

Butterflies hatched in my stomach, their wings fluttering like crazy. The air between us crisped and sparked. His hands settled on my hips. He wanted to kiss me. I wanted it, too. But he took a deep breath instead and let me go. A crooked smile lit up his face as he jerked his head toward the garden. "Come, I have something to show you."

He took my hand and led me down the dark path of the garden.

"Why is the garden closed?"

"Patience, Miss Costa."

He placed me in front of the fountain. "Stand here." He went to the other side. Under the dim light of the full moon, he picked up two extension cords. "I hope I don't get electrocuted," he said as he joined them.

There were no words. The trees canopying the fountain sparkled with tiny white lights. Polished stones lined the fountain, the smell of fresh mortar slightly masked by the rose petals floating around my proud surviving lotus flower.

"They fixed it without disturbing the flower. I made sure of it."

"It's beautiful. You've given me the best gift. And on your birthday, too. Thank you."

"I told Prabhat I'd like an outdoor going-away party tomorrow night."

My stomach burned, a caustic acid dripping on delicate, fluttering butterfly wings. He was leaving. Why did I keep forgetting that? "You hate parties."

He tucked a strand of hair behind my ear. "I do, but how could I explain I wanted it done in one day without making him suspicious?"

"You did all of this for me?"

"Yes, but I had my own selfish reasons, too. I wanted a dance with you."

"There's no music."

"But there is."

He took out his phone and set it on the fountain. Two seconds later Dusty Springfield was singing "Don't Forget About Me."

Staring at Liam, I completely understood Dusty's lyrics. "You remembered."

"Of course, I did. I told you I was listening." He bowed slightly. "Will you do me the honor, Miss Costa?"

"Yes, Liam, I will."

The green took over his eyes, his hands grasped my hips, and he bent toward me until our foreheads touched. "I love the way you say my name."

He pulled me against him and spun me around. I giggled like a teenage girl. I had never danced with anyone. But there were silent commands in the firm grip of his hands, the penetrating stare of his eyes, and the fierce pull of his body. I surrendered to all of it. It was easy to follow him…so, so easy.

I was out of breath by the time the song finished. God, if he could exhaust me with just one dance, what would he be like during other intimate pursuits? I pushed the thought out of my mind because, for once, I was not going to run away or think too hard. I was only going to enjoy the perfect night he'd given me.

He pulled me toward a bench. I rested my head on his shoulder. Dusty started crooning "Spooky."

"Dinner is served," he said, pulling out a brown paper bag from under the bench. I peered inside. There were mangos and bananas. At the bottom was a plastic container with a piece of his birthday cake. "I'm sorry. It's not much. I had to pack it myself, but I know this is usually the time you eat. I've had my dinner already, but I didn't want you to go hungry."

"It's perfect."

I took a mango and sniffed. "It smells delicious." I held it toward him.

"Mmmm," he agreed, except he didn't smell the mango. He buried his nose in my hair.

Then he shifted away, perhaps thinking the trespass was too much.

It wasn't enough.

I found a knife at the bottom of the bag and used it to cut through the amber flesh of the mango, holding it steady in my hand.

"Do you want a plate? I can get one."

"I do this all the time." My bracelet slipped. I stopped and pushed it back up. I had linked the chain too loose this morning. I started cutting through the mango again. The bracelet inched down once more. I stopped to fix it, sighing in frustration.

He took my wrist. "Let me take it off."

"No!" I pulled my hand away.

He flinched. "You okay?"

"Yes, I'm sorry. I just don't want to take it off."

God, Liam, don't ruin this perfect moment…please.

"Then let me finish this," he said, taking the mango and knife. I calmed myself by watching him and listening to Dusty. Liam rolled up his sleeves, the fabric of his shirt stretched across his frame. His hands were large, but far from clumsy—they could handle a small knife with mastery, yet cover a great expanse. I'd never noticed how long his fingers were, only the electric tingle my body had whenever they touched me. He had the hands of an artist.

He worked swiftly, making two halves. He started to chop them into smaller pieces.

"That's enough." I took a slice. "This is the way a mango should be eaten."

I demonstrated, cupping the smooth red-yellow skin as I bit into the juicy sweet flesh of the fruit. The sharp tang of the nectar slid across my tongue and coated my lips. Liam's eyes locked on my mouth. He sucked in a deep audible breath when I licked my lips.

"I do believe you're seducing me, Miss Costa."

"I do believe it's working, Mr. Montgomery."

"Indeed." He held up his end of the fruit, his mouth twisting into a wicked smile. "Are you going to watch me while I eat it out?"

My skin prickled as he bit into it. A drop of juice ran down his chin. I cupped his face and wiped it away with my thumb. He grabbed hold of my wrist and sucked my thumb.

Was this seduction or torture?

He put my hand on my knee. "Breathe."

"I am breathing."

"I was talking to myself."

I cupped my mouth to cover my laugh, but it exploded anyway, quieting the chirping crickets.

"Cake," he said, a word that sounded even more decadent than the actual dessert.

I looked at the fountain, surrounded by glorious lights. "It's really beautiful, Liam."

"Yes, I see why it's special to you. But I have to warn you, Mary, it's temporary."

"What do you mean?"

"It's what I wanted to talk to you about. About the hotel."

He handed me a fork.

I didn't want to talk about the hotel. Right now, it felt as if we were the only two people in the world. Bubbles of happiness welled inside of me. I refused to let anything burst them. "You have to make a wish before we have cake."

"I already made one earlier when I blew out the candles."

"What did you wish for, Liam?"

He placed a hand on each side of my face. "This." He moved his sensuous lips close to mine, creating the tiniest sliver of space between us. I realized what he wanted. For me to make the choice, to finish the kiss.

I did, brushing his mouth gingerly. But as soon as the contact was made, he took over, crushing his mouth against mine.

He tasted of mint and mango and liquor. His long, talented fingers twisted in my hair, swiftly undoing the knot at the nape of my neck. Liam's tongue found mine. I heard a clinking as the fork hit the ground, not even aware I'd dropped it. His muscular arms wrapped around me. He claimed me with his mouth.

I wanted to get lost in that kiss and never find my way out.

When we came for air, we were both breathing heavily.

"Best fucking birthday, ever," he said.

Then I remembered I had something for him. I desperately wanted more kisses, caresses, and just more him, but I didn't want to miss the opportunity. "I have a gift for you."

"You just gave me the best gift. But so we're clear, I'm happy to sit on this bench and talk to you. We don't have to go any further, Mary. I only ask that you refrain from eating anymore mangos tonight. I can't handle another one."

I traced the ridge of his mouth with my thumb. "Let's go to your room."

His smile, full of lust and need, made me go limp for a moment. "Sounds like a plan."

"But let me fetch your gift first. I want you to open it now."

Before he could answer, I ran back to the employee lodgings. The bubbles inside me grew with each step, making me feel as if I could float away. The package almost slipped out of my hands despite my tight grip. When I returned, I was sweaty and out of breath, hair plastered to my forehead and a smile too wide to hide any of my dirty thoughts. I slowed my steps to regain what little composure I could.

He stood next to the fountain.

Except he wasn't alone.

I had seen a doll once, the kind with a small waist, perky smile, perkier breasts, and hair the color of sun. That's what this girl resembled.

Dusty sang, "Take Another piece of My Heart." How appropriate.

"Why are you here, Natalie?" he asked, his voice sharper than I'd ever heard it.

"I came to see you, silly. Is there any other reason to travel to this shithole?"

"My secretary told you I was busy, didn't she?"

"Liam, sweetie, it's your birthday. I wasn't about to let you spend it alone. Now, let's go to your room where I can properly give you your present." Her hands settled on his waist, a position of familiarity and possession. All the sparking flutters coursing through me suddenly burned red hot, scorching me from the inside out.

The thud made both of them look in my direction.

Oh, dear Lord, I'd dropped the book.

"Mary," he said, approaching me. I stepped back.

Her heels clicked in perfect rhythm right behind him. "Oh, good, a maid. I need water."

I stood, frozen as a statue.

Liam and I stared at each other. The bubbles of anticipation inside of me popped...every single one. She snapped her fingers in front of my face. "Waaatttter."

"Shut up, Natalie." There was anger in his voice. Was it because I had ruined their moment?

She turned, her silky hair swinging in sync. "What? Isn't that her job?"

"She's not working right now."

"Well, then, she can tell someone who is working." She turned back to me. "Bottled. You understand me." She mimicked an unscrewing cap motion. "And cold but no ice. God knows what bacteria lurks in the ice."

I nodded and turned away.

"And make sure it's American or Swedish. None of this foreign shit," she screamed after me. I wanted to tell her that in India, American and Swedish waters *were* foreign.

"What the hell is wrong with you?" I heard him say.

This time I ran faster. I had to get *memsahib* her damn water.

Just as I rounded to the servant's entrance, I heard his footsteps behind me.

The kitchen, cleaned and shut down for the night, was eerily quiet. *Don't cry...be strong.*

"Mary..."

"Leave me alone."

"You got me a book," he said, revealing the ripped paper. "I've never read Elizabeth Gaskell. I'm sure I'll love it. You wrote note cards, too. I can't wait to read those."

Why did he keep talking?

"Shut up." I thought I'd said it under my breath, but his reaction made it clear he'd heard me.

"Shut up?"

"Yes."

"It's not what it looks like."

I opened the fridge, grateful the door provided a barrier between us, except he was so tall, his head peered over the top.

"Really? Maybe I'm just an ignorant maid…"

"There is nothing ignorant about you. Don't insult yourself that way again."

I let the cool fridge air wash over me. "All right then, it looks to me as if some girl is visiting you on your birthday to help you celebrate in a way you're accustomed to. Am I right, sir?"

"She isn't my girlfriend. She isn't anything to me." His deep voice echoed through the room.

"Shhh, someone will hear."

"Then talk to me," he said, his voice much lower.

"Unless you'd care for more towels, there is nothing for us to discuss, sir."

He dragged his hand through his hair. "You call me 'sir' with that inflection, and it's not pleasing at all."

I pulled out a bottle and shoved it at him. "Is this American? Swedish? I don't know."

He slammed it on the counter. "Forget the damn water. Please just listen to me. I asked her not to come. We're not together like that. There is no commitment between us."

"It's none of my concern."

He looked surprised, his shoulders slumping. "I can live with your anger, but not your indifference. Indifference implies you don't care. I know you do."

Defeat crept into me. I hated myself for it, for allowing myself feelings I had no right to. "What do you want from me?"

He swallowed. "I care about you, too. I never wanted to hurt you in any way."

"Save your pity for someone who needs it."

"Pity? This isn't pity."

"I'm very grateful to her. She stopped me from making a horrible mistake." My statements were low whispers, but he flinched as if I yelled. I refused to read into his reactions. It was good for me to see this. To realize my place in the world, and more importantly, my place in his world. If he wanted a woman like that, I would never be right for him. If he wanted a woman like that, I didn't want to be right for him either.

How silly I'd been to think we could have one night together without any repercussions.

"You really think we're a mistake? That's your opinion, Miss Costa, but I need you to listen to me." He put his hand on my arm to still me. "I have to tell you something."

"What?"

"The hotel. We're selling it. It's like you said. It's not the right fit for this area. It'll happen quickly. You need to look for another job. I can help you if you'll allow it."

I moved out of his grip. "I don't want a damn thing from you."

He backed away from me. "Fair enough. I ask you keep this between us. People tend to jump a sinking ship."

"Why are you telling me then?"

"Because I want you to have a life raft."

I tasted the bitter seeds of reality. He felt sorry for me. If seeing the woman hadn't been enough, he'd salted the wounds.

"Try to understand—"

"No sir, you try to understand." I jabbed my finger into his chest. He moved back with every poke. "I can take care of myself. I always have. I don't need anyone looking out for me. Especially you."

"Everyone needs someone to look out for them. You're an exceptional girl, but you're not an exception."

"Let me make it clear. My life, my choices, are none of your business. You are management. I am a maid. There are no other distinctions. This is some type of power trip for you, and I'm done with it. I'm done hiding behind closed doors so I'm not seen with you. Stop harassing me, Mr. Montgomery." I knew each sentence was a sharp slap, but my anger had formed into dark storm clouds bursting with chaotic lightning. "Do you pick a maid at all your hotels to fuck, or am I just special?"

A vein pulsed in his neck. The knuckles on his hands turned white as he gripped the edge of the countertop. His eyes turned the darkest shade I'd ever seen.

"You really think that's the kind of man I am? Harassment?" He put his hands up in surrender. "First of all, fuck you, Mary Costa. Secondly, you're making yourself out to be some naïve, gullible girl. We both know that's the furthest thing from the truth. You had a choice in everything. Thirdly, I told you things I've never told anyone. I had no idea what I wanted from you except, when I'm around you, I feel more like myself than I ever have. I'm sorry about our goddamn circumstances, but I am not embarrassed to be with you. Closed doors? I wanted you sitting beside me tonight, not in a fucking garden, not sneaking around like teenagers, and definitely not serving me. You cloak yourself to everyone. I felt honored you let me in. But you know what, Lotus Girl? You're right about one thing—our relationship is a power struggle, but it's you that has all the power over me. Or at least you did." He took the water bottle from the counter. "I'll see she gets this. Good night, Miss Costa."

He walked out, leaving me reeling, the emotion swelling inside of me until I gripped the counters. If you measured our relationship in typical standards of time, we hardly knew each other. Yet, he knew me better than anyone else.

The tears came then, fat, hot drops running down my cheeks.

I ran back to my room. I hid my sobs when the last of the crew came to bed. Six of us shared a room, sleeping on thin mattresses on the floor. I lifted the cover over my head and took out Liam's sketch of me. I'd stared at it so much, I could trace the lines and curves with my fingers. I struggled not to rip it into shreds.

At least tonight, I didn't have to dart the questions of where I'd gone. Everyone was jabbering away about the *gora's* girlfriend. Their conversations echoed against the dark night, drowning out the cricket's chirps.

"Last-minute checkout. The woman barely checked in when Mr. Montgomery said she was leaving. My God, the lady was crazy."

"Crazy…did you see her luggage? You'd think she was moving here."

"The way she talked about India? I doubt it. I've never seen a white person so angry. Her face turned red as a chili pepper."

"She was so beautiful. Why would he turn her away? She looked like a princess."

"But she acted like a frog."

Liam had sent her away? When all the chatter had finally died, I thought about everything he'd said without the storming clouds of fear, insecurity, and jealousy.

She was a girl he shared a bed with in his life in New York…no commitments, no ties. Hadn't I done the very same thing with Kishore? Why had I imposed a double standard between us?

I had made my own choices when it came to Liam Montgomery. There was no force on his part. I saw him for the man he was—kind, generous, passionate. He saw me, too, even through the veils of deceit I'd sewn together. I wasn't foolish enough to believe we could survive anything outside our Rajasthani bubble, but why couldn't we share in a little bit of happiness?

A final tear rolled down my face before I shut my eyes to the world.

Chapter 9

Liam

She had painted me with vicious strokes, like some fucking villain twirling his mustache, waiting to take her chastity. God, didn't she know? I wanted to be her hero. But she didn't want one. She thought I pitied her? She couldn't be more wrong. I admired her, respected her, fucking revered her.

Now, I would forget her. Maybe we shared some intimate things, but the reality was we'd only known each other for a few days. We came from opposite sides of the globe. We were forcing odd-shaped puzzle pieces to snap together where they didn't belong. I was leaving, and she was rooted like that goddamn lotus flower of hers. So why did I even care?

The realization came to me when I finally slammed the book shut at five in the morning.

In the cards, she'd written all kinds of messages about the first time she'd read the book, what her favorite parts were, and a few random sentences. Those were my favorite.

My favorite season is right after the Monsoons. You can hear the sound of earth giving way to new growth. I close my eyes and inhale it all.

Guess who Elizabeth Gaskell's editor was for this book???? Guess Guess!!! Okay, I'll tell you. It was none other than our friend, Charles Dickens. PS—they did not get along.

Although I'm partial to Highlanders, this is one of my favorite romances. It's all about embracing differences and finding similarities where you least suspect. Sound familiar?

Yeah, Mary, it sure as hell did.

I had not slept. I had battled an epic fight with Natalie, which set the steady turns of the gossip cogs into high speed. And worst of all, I'd really fucked up on so many levels.

My room had become suffocating. I needed air to get away from all the things that reminded me of her. So I decided to spend my last day sightseeing around Jaipur. Besides, I needed to avoid her.

I wondered if I was seeing a mirage when a girl in blue jeans and a yellow embroidered shirt stood right outside the hotel gates. I'd never seen her in western clothes, but it suited her. I honestly never cared for the sari. Wait, that wasn't true. I thought it was sexy as hell, but she wasn't comfortable in it. I walked past her.

She followed me, her flip flops clopping against the narrow cobblestone path.

Finally, I turned. "What do you want?"

"You shouldn't be traveling alone. Why didn't you bring someone with you?"

"You think you're the only one who can take care of yourself?"

"I can go with you. You're shopping, right? I can translate for you. They'll take advantage of you otherwise."

"I don't want you. Is that clear enough?"

Her lips trembled, and I wanted to kick myself. I'd really fucked this up. She was right. We were wrong. I'd just proven it once again.

She turned and walked the opposite way.

I took a deep breath and moved on. Street children surrounded me. Some of them were missing limbs. But I had this under control. I could keep walking and not give them money. I'd been warned not to since this was a cottage industry here, and it would only support their current situation. Sure, I could do that. It didn't matter that they were starving and some spoke English while others just pointed to their mouths with their outstretched hands. The universal sign for "I'm starving, you prick." Didn't matter that they were following me like the fucking Pied Piper.

I stopped at a chai shop and did the quick math, depositing a sum large enough to feed an army. I pointed to the bread and the tea. Then I gestured to the crowd of kids. I knew the guy would keep a good chunk, but I told him in my own broken way I'd be back to check.

I moved on. Mary was right about Jaipur. The city was a cocoon of pink under the bluest sky, with fiery reds and oranges and every other color I ever imagined. I found the park Prabhat had told me about. He, too, had thought I needed a chaperone. I probably did, but this was just a quick visit. Hell, if Siddhartha could journey six years in the forest living like a caveman, then surely, I could make the few-mile stretch down the market street. I stopped to purchase two bottles of water, placing one in my backpack. Settling on the park bench, I took out the yellow legal pad and pencil. I gulped down the water and tried to capture the architecture of the building across from me. But I couldn't get it right. My thoughts kept returning to Mary.

Finally, I stashed the blank pad in my pack and made my way back. The cobbled pavement cracked and fissured in several places. I wondered how people didn't fall. I watched each step, while the old and young passed by me with curious glances.

A young girl stood before me, no more than six, her bare feet dirty. She smiled at me. I reached into my pocket, ready to give her something, anything, when a man swooped in and snatched her from the road, her cries echoing down the path.

"Stop," I said. He was small but fast. I ran down one alley and up the next, my feet hitting the steps hard until I had no more places to run. The street was a dead end. Where had they gone to?

He came out of the alley.

"Where is she?"

He didn't understand, but two more fellows joined him. No more language barriers existed. The rusty knives they held took care of any confusion. They yelled something at me.

"Take it easy." I reached into my back pocket for my wallet. "Where's the girl?"

But they were still screaming. One held a knife against my chest.

I couldn't fucking understand. I said a little prayer to a God I hadn't talked to in years. Maybe one I'd be seeing soon.

But not without a fight.

The first one was small. I kneed him in the groin and then pushed him so hard he slammed into the opposite wall. The second, who had looked unsure to begin with, just ran away. But the third was tall and sure and large.

We sized each other up with desperate circling steps. "Where the fuck is she!"

He didn't answer. He only showed me the edge of his knife.

She came from nowhere, standing between us, bringing with her the faintest scent of spiced vanilla.

"Mary?"

There was something so strong and fearless about her, it scared the shit out of me. She said some fast-paced words at him. Pretty sure it included some swearing.

The man looked just as surprised as I was, holding back his knife.

"What are you saying?"

"He wants to kidnap you. I'm telling him that if he does, even his grandchildren's children won't be able to repay the debt on his head."

The man swooped in and repeated some harsh language of his own.

"That didn't work, I take it?"

"Afraid not."

He made fast strides toward us. Toward her.

No!

I reacted on pure instinct and adrenaline. I pushed her out of the way. Somewhere in my peripheral, I saw her hit the ground.

He lunged for me, but his movements were sluggish. He wasn't as large as he was stout. I pushed him against the wall. We tussled for a minute. Something nicked my side before I finally caught hold of his wrist. I hammered his hand against the stone building until the knife fell with a clink.

Then I bashed his head back a few times.

"Where is she?" I repeated over and over.

He screamed something before running off. I turned to Mary, ready to help her up. I'd thrown her with enough force to cause pain. I took a few shaky steps. A little girl's cry sounded somewhere in the distance. Then everything went dark.

* * * *

"Liam."

I blinked my eyes open.

"Can you walk?"

"Of course I can."

But when I tried to stand, my gut screamed like it was being torn in two.

"You've been stabbed," she said.

I looked down to see the thin tear in my shirt, soaked through with blood. "Just a graze, I think." As I said it, an overwhelming sickness entered my body. She helped me up and put my arm around her shoulder.

"There was a little girl, Mary. Did you see her?"

"The girl is safe. See, look."

I looked down the alley where a frantic woman clutched the little girl.

"You'll be all right. I promise you."

I didn't know how we got there, but I found myself in a cab.

"We're going to the hospital. You'll be fine." I looked down at my waist where her hand was holding a ripped piece of her shirt against my side.

"Where did you come from?"

"I followed you. I wish I had something to clean your wound."

A mixture of gratitude for what she'd done and anger at how she'd done it washed over me. But mostly it was pain. I couldn't breathe. "I have water in my backpack."

I gestured to it on the floor. Had she picked it up?

She reached inside and took out the bottle. Suddenly, a strong thirst seized me. I reached for it, but she moved it.

"Where did you get this?" she asked.

What the hell was she doing? My mouth was like the fucking Sierra right now, and she wanted to know where I shopped?

"A vendor." I reached my hand out again, but she still didn't relinquish it.

"Look." She pointed to the cap. "It's been tampered."

"What?"

"It's very rare, but some corrupt merchants search for empty bottles in the street and refill them so they can pass them off as new."

"Why?"

"Money."

I tried to sit up, but a million battles were being fought inside my gut, and I wasn't winning a damn one. "What do they fill them with?"

"Nothing good."

"Fuck me."

She smiled, a sad worried smile. "It was a new bottle, right?"

"Yes."

She exhaled a breath. "Good, you didn't drink any."

I swallowed, which was a bad idea because bile was rising in my throat, ready to erupt. "I bought two bottles, Mary."

"Where is the other one?"

I patted my gut.

She banged on the back of the driver's seat. "*Jeldi, jeldi, jeldi!*" she screamed at the cabbie.

One of the few Hindi words I recognized.

Faster, faster, faster.

Chapter 10

Liam

I woke up to the sound of her voice, a damp rag pressed against my forehead.

"Liam, there isn't much time. I need you to wake up for a minute so I can tell you what's happened."

It was dark out. My body was drenched. I was sweating through something silky. She adjusted the fan on the bedside table so the cool air would blow on me.

"What happened? Are we at the hospital?"

"We were, but now we're back at the hotel. They pumped your stomach and sutured you up. Do you remember that?"

"How could I forget? Why am I at the hotel?"

"Prabhat was worried you'd get sicker at the hospital. He had you brought here."

"Sicker than this?"

"He is a bit neurotic, in case you haven't noticed. But even I have never seen him so frazzled. He didn't even ask me why we were together."

I tried to swallow, but my tongue stuck to the roof of my mouth.

"Are you thirsty?" she asked.

I arched my brow, a small movement that took way too much strength. "Depends. Where's the water from?"

She laughed, holding a bottle out to me. "I'm glad you still have your sense of humor. Don't worry, I checked it personally. It's safe."

I took a few eager sips. Then I gagged. She held a bowl under my mouth. I pushed it away. "Did I hurt you when I pushed you down?"

She seemed surprised by my question. I blinked, looking for any signs of harm on her body.

"No, Liam. I'm fine."

Only when I was satisfied with her answer did I fall back into bed. A bed that felt more like a tub of boiling water. Well...I was kind of dressed like a lobster. I stared down at the red silk pajamas I wore. Where the fuck did these come from?

"Who changed me?"

"One of the men here. They looked through your bags but didn't see any sleeping clothes. Prabhat figured you forgot to pack them."

"So you dressed me like Hugh Hefner?"

"Who?"

"Never mind."

"Prabhat procured these from the hotel store for you. He figured this is what a western man sleeps in."

"Yes, it is...if he were sixty years old."

"What do you normally sleep in?"

"Nothing."

"Tell me. I can get it for you. You should be comfortable."

"I did tell you. I don't wear anything."

Her eyes widened. "Oh, I see. Well, that might be a problem."

"It's fine."

"Prabhat is worried to death. He thinks you're going to hold him personally responsible. He's gone to fetch a nurse for you."

Right now, I didn't give a fuck about Prabhat or what he thought.

"Why did you do it?"

"Do what?"

"Step in front of a fucking knife?"

"I was stepping in front of you."

"Same. Fucking. Difference."

"I looked for a police officer or someone to help, but when I saw him come toward you, I just reacted."

I took her hand. "You have no idea how grateful I am to you." I squeezed her fingers to emphasize my words. "Don't ever put yourself in that situation again."

She nodded.

"Swear it to me. Say that you won't ever put yourself in harm's way."

"I swear."

"Whole thing. And put your hand over my heart while you say it."

"Why do I need to do that?"

"Because I need to feel your sincerity."

She put her hand over my heart. "I swear I will never put myself in harm's way again. You need to rest now."

"You killed me today. Were you trying to kill me, woman?"

"I was trying to save you."

"Maybe you did a little bit of both, but mostly you killed me."

She ran the cool cloth down my neck. God help me, it felt so good I almost forgot why I was angry with her.

"I told the police what happened. I'm sure they'll apprehend the men."

"How's the girl?"

Mary smiled. "She's fine, Liam. You did a heroic thing. Her mother said she'd do special prayers for you at her temple."

I exhaled, making my ribs hurt even more. "How long have I been out?"

"Just a day. You won't have a scar, but you do have a fever." She leaned closer to me. "I'll have to leave once Prabhat comes back. He's gone to make arrangements for a private nurse and doctor."

No.

I heard Prabhat barking orders. Mary straightened so fast, the air pulled with her movement.

Prabhat stood over me, his expression frantic. "Sir, sir, I am so so sorry. I have brought Manny. He is a nurse and will take care of all your needs. Dr. Singh will be here soon as well. He is one of the best doctors in the region. You must rest comfortably. This never happens here. I swear, very safe."

I sat up, which zapped what little strength I had. A burly fellow stood next to Prabhat. I shook my head. "I don't want him."

"But sir, you need someone to watch over you."

I fought my eyelids as they became heavier. He went in and out of focus. "Mary can watch over me." The words came out slurred. I wasn't sure if Prabhat understood, because he looked more confused than ever.

"She's not qualified."

"There is no one I trust more."

"She cannot even speak English. How will she communicate with you? Be reasonable Mr. Montgomery. You need a nurse, not a maid."

"I'll take care of him," she said in perfect English.

I would have laughed at the way Prabhat's jaw dropped, but I was in too much pain.

She walked over to him. "I can read medicine bottles, and I have the hospital instructions. Let Manny stay in another room close by in case I need help."

There was something so succinct and matter-of-fact about the way she said it that Prabhat stumbled over himself. "You've been lying to me." He scowled at her and looked over to me. I had no doubts what he was thinking. What everyone would think.

She'd revealed her secret because I wanted her here.

He began some long diatribe in Hindi. She winced at his words, which I didn't have to understand to know they were foul.

I took a deep breath and swung my legs over the side of the bed. I needed to take control in this situation. To let Prabhat know not to mistake my illness for weakness. My legs almost gave way, but I leaned against the bed. The stitches on my side smarted.

"Not another word, Prabhat. Not one more," I said, doing my best to convey authority. "This woman saved my life, and you will not speak to her with disrespect ever again. You need to leave."

I wasn't sure who was in more danger of going into shock—Prabhat or Mary. Or maybe it was me.

He stood there, his mouth opening. "But sir…"

"Get out."

He threw his arms up in frustration and stormed out the door. Manny stood there, confused and silent, until Mary told him to follow Prabhat.

She turned to me. "What are you doing? Get in bed. You're very sick."

"I just made some trouble for you."

"I'm no stranger to trouble. Trouble I can handle. Your faith in me is worth that. But now, if you really want my help, you have to listen to everything I say. You have six stitches on your left side and a serious infection. You have a fever. It needs to work its way out of your system. It will with rest, medicine, and care. But not if you insist on being stubborn. Is that clear?"

I let out a weak smile before collapsing onto the bed. "Yes, sir."

Her laughter was the last thing I heard before sleep took a powerful hold on me.

Chapter 11

Mary

There were many girls in a dark room made darker by our lack of hope. I would have given up entirely if not for Hannah. Someone had to watch out for Hannah. She was so tiny and precious and frightened. I held her on my lap, stroking her fine hair.

"Papaji will come for us," she said with quiet conviction. "I am praying for it."

"He will, little one. He will." I had nothing more to give her other than hollow reassurances.

I followed her gaze to the darkest part of the room, where a girl wearing a head covering ripped a piece of long dress into even strips. I wondered what she was making. Possibly a noose? If so, maybe I could ask her to borrow it after she was done.

I laughed cynically. There would be no need for the ask, would there? I could just take.

Hannah turned to me with questioning eyes. "What is she doing?"

"I don't know."

The girl moved toward the center of the room, where the beam of light gathered from the lone window. Squinting, she knotted a small section of the fabric. She repeated it until she had made several tiny beads. When she got frustrated, she'd undo them and start again. There was nothing to do except watch each other, feel sorry for ourselves, and pray. I doubted if any temple, church, or mosque had as much prayer going on as this tiny room did.

Finally, Hannah's curiosity would hold no more. "What are you doing?" she asked the girl.

I shushed her, but the question was already spoken. I didn't trust anyone here, not even our fellow prisoners.

It didn't matter, though. Hannah had never learned Hindi, since my father insisted we speak English. So she asked the question in her soft, slow manner. I doubted the scarf-beading girl would understand.

Except she did.

She looked in our direction, sizing us up. Distrust ran both ways.

"A subha,*" the girl said.*

Hannah looked at me. I gave her a reassuring smile, grateful that my sister had avoided becoming a miserable creature like me. As Papa always said, Hannah was special. God gave her to us so we could remember what it was to be innocent and joyful.

Oh, Papa, I failed. I didn't protect her. But even as I thought it, I could still see the gleam in her eye, the curve of her mouth, the way she embraced me. Some things cannot be stolen, not even by monsters.

"What is a suber?"

"Subha," I said. "Muslim prayer beads. Like our rosary."

"We have that, too," a girl with long hair interjected. "The Hindus call it a mala.*"*

"Are you Muslim? I've never met a Muslim before. What is your name? I'm Hannah. This is my sister, Mary." Hannah's welcoming smile was infectious, even in this dismal place.

The girl returned it. "I'm Amira." She knitted her brows together, clicking her tongue. "I've messed it up once again. I can't get them small enough."

Hannah stood. I almost pulled her back to me, but she needed to stand. We'd been here for five days. Hannah was not the type of flower you locked away behind a glass dome. She was the kind who thrived in large gardens with people around her.

I steadied her, a physical reminder not to run. I followed close behind.

"Let me help," I said. Amira handed me the fabric. I ripped it into a thinner strand and formed tighter beads, showing her each step.

"I thought if I made something that reminded me of home, then it wouldn't be so lonely."

"Can I help, too?" the Hindu girl asked. She wore a faded pink dress that had seen better days.

We didn't answer, but Amira waved her over. The girl introduced herself as Divya from Walkeshwar.

Hannah's fingers were too stubby for the intricate work. Her beads were the largest, but the three of us said they were the best ones. The work was tedious, but it kept our minds occupied. We talked about our lives outside, what we would do when rescue finally came. For Divya, it was wearing a fine pink sari every day of her life and giving thanks to Ganesha for removing the horrible obstacle. For Amira, it was finishing school and taking care of her ill mother. For Hannah, it was listening to Papa read a story. I never told them what I wanted. My thoughts ran much deeper...much darker than theirs.

We'd each donated shreds of fabric for the cause, ripping them from the few garments we owned. In the end, we had not a noose, but a long thin rope of a necklace adorned with multicolored beads. Although it wasn't blessed by a priest or guru or imam, it was holy to us. We ran our fingers over it constantly, staining the cloth with our grubby hands.

I didn't know how or why we had found each other and had become friends in this place where friendship shouldn't exist. What I did know was that heaven had no religious divides.

How could it, when hell did not?

I almost fell off the chair when I woke, the old dream haunting me. My legs cramped, the cloth rosary in my hand. I had been circling it, praying for him. Although I put on a good show for him, the niggling worry would not cease. The doctors said he would be fine once the antibiotics took hold, but I had my doubts. Hannah had died from an infection despite all the medications.

None of my prayers had worked then.

I closed my eyes again, touching each of the small beads. I hadn't run my fingers across this necklace since Hannah died, but it gave me some strength nonetheless. It wasn't blessed by any holy person, yet it was the holiest thing I owned.

Liam stirred. I wiped the sweat from his brow and adjusted the covers. He was in pain, but he never complained.

God, he was a good man. He'd put his life in jeopardy to save a child. *Please don't take him. Keep him safe.* The world needed good men.

As the low light of sunrise filtered through the window, I repeated my prayer, my mantra, holding back the tears. The shrill sound of the phone broke my concentration. I snatched it up, expecting Prabhat with his hourly check-in.

"Hello?"

"I'm Liam's brother."

I almost dropped the receiver. Liam had a brother? And why did he sound American?

"Hello? Hello?" he yelled into the phone. No doubt he thought the call dropped.

"I'm sorry. I'm here."

"I've been trying his cell for the past few hours."

I looked over at the backpack. Liam's cell was probably in there, and I was sure it needed a long charging.

"I just got my messages and found out what happened. They tell me you're taking care of him. Mary Costa, right?"

"Yes."

"You're a nurse?"

"A maid, but there is a nurse here, too. Also, a doctor. They both check on him regularly and are staying in rooms close by."

If the man was shocked, he didn't express it. All I could hear was concern and worry in his voice.

"Can you tell me what happened? I think Prabhat might be exaggerating."

I told him everything that happened, and what the doctors had said.

He took a deep breath when I finished. "Wow...I guess he wasn't exaggerating. That's Liam, always the hero. Thank you for the update."

"I'll tell him you called."

"Thank you...and Mary?"

"Yes."

"Please take care of him."

He disconnected before I could answer.

Chapter 12

Liam

Ever wonder what it felt like to have your insides retreat and rebel at the same time? Try drinking tainted water and being stabbed with a blunt, rusty knife in the same day. You'll wonder no more. I swallowed the sun, ate it whole, and it scorched my flesh from the inside out. When the sun went down, winter flowed through me as if my veins had turned into icy, arctic roads.

I got sicker and weaker before I got better. I hated for her to see me this way, at my very worse, but she never faltered. I was only conscious for brief moments, but I always felt her presence. She read to me. She spoon-fed me soup. She sponged me off with a damp towel. She gave me my medicine. She massaged my arms and legs. Although I could barely keep my eyes open, another part of my anatomy had no trouble staying awake for that session. Figured.

In the low light, I could hear her reading Dickens.

"You're at the end of the book. Did you read the whole thing?" My voice sounded distant, weak, and pathetic, as if it belonged to someone else.

"Yes."

"Read from the other one."

"Which one?"

"The one you gave me."

She turned on a side light. I shut my eyes from the harsh glare. She looked around the room.

"It's on the sideboard," I said, lifting my arm to point, a small gesture which took a grand effort.

Mary seemed surprised I would have it. I wanted to say how much it meant to me. How much she meant to me. But right now, I could barely control my own bowels, so I kept quiet.

I forced myself to stay up, though. I felt like shite, but I could keep my eyes open, and the sheen of sweat on my body started to evaporate. I focused on her lyrical voice.

Groaning, I rolled toward her. Every muscle screamed. I shook my head as she rushed to help. "I can do it."

She nodded, her face turning back toward the book. She read for a while.

I waited until I had the strength to voice the thoughts in my aching head. "I'll talk to Prabhat. I'll make this right."

"No need."

"Of course there is."

She twirled a lock of hair. "I've been thinking of what you said. I gave my notice. I told Prabhat I would leave as soon as you were healthy."

"Why?"

"It's time." Such a simple statement, but clearly, there were more complex thoughts behind it.

"Where will you go?" Would she take my help? But I already knew the answer to that question. Mary was stubborn and independent. As much as I admired those qualities, I also cursed them.

"I'm not sure yet."

"Do you have funds?"

"I've saved some money, and my father left me some. You don't have to worry for me." She flipped the page in the book. "Now, where was I?"

She continued reading.

I wanted to fall asleep again, but I forced myself to stay awake, to prolong this time together.

The tarnished silver bracelet she usually wore sat on the nightstand. The skin on the underside of her wrist caught the light as she flipped a page. It was as if the knife sliced my gut once more.

Oh, God, Mary…why?

I clasped her wrist.

I figured she'd snatch her hand away, but she didn't. I rubbed my thumb across the jagged scar, my eyes never leaving hers. Her pulse quickened, but she never moved her hand. I swallowed my questions. I wasn't sure if she would answer, or if I even had the strength to hear her explanation.

So we just sat in silence.

Chapter 13

Liam

The next time I awoke, I was more alert. Although my muscles were stiff, it didn't hurt as much to stretch. She smiled at me.

"The fever broke this morning," she whispered. She looked so damn happy and relieved, I grinned.

Then a whiff of something sour hit me. "What the bloody hell stinks?"

She laughed, adjusting the blanket. "It's you, sir."

"Oh man, I reek."

"I had Manny give you a few sponge baths, but they aren't as effective."

A few? "How long?"

"Since when?"

"Since I've been…incapacitated."

"Four days."

My head spun. I thought maybe a day or two. Time had passed without me. The only constant was the feeling that Mary was near. "I need to call my office."

"Prabhat did that. Also, your brother rang. You should call him. He sounded worried."

"He's only worried about the meetings I missed."

"I don't think so, Liam." She opened her mouth to argue some more, but the last thing I needed was to talk about Stephen.

I interrupted her, "I'll call him later, Mary, but right now, I have to call my secretary and get caught up."

"Don't spend your time worrying about what cannot be undone. It'll set back your recovery."

Those were wise words. I caught a whiff of myself again, the silk garments aggravating me as I shifted. I wore royal blue pajamas now. When had that happened? How had I slept through it all? "I need a shower."

"I'll get Manny," she said.

I shook my head in protest. "I can do it on my own."

She looked unsure, but stood aside while I sat up on the bed. My legs had turned into rubber. I wasn't sure if they could sustain my weight. She sidled up next to me. "Put your arm around me."

She was remarkably strong for someone so petite.

"I think you should take a bath," she said as we entered the bathroom.

As if I hadn't been emasculated enough, now she wanted me to take a bath like a child. To prove I was capable, I walked the rest of the way on my own. "I'm fine."

"I'll get you a change of clothes."

I glanced at the mirror. Several days of stubble covered my jaw line. My hair had always been longer than suitable for a businessman, but it hung fine and limp over my forehead. The tan I had sported was gone. In fact, I was three shades paler than I'd ever been. The ridiculous silk-pajama shirt plastered against my chest. I ripped it trying to peal it off.

I saw her in the mirror. She was staring at me, relief on her face.

She left the room, closing the door behind her. I shed the rest of the clothing and walked into the shower. Leaning my palms against the tile, I stood under the hot spray of water for a long time. Long enough for the feeling to return to each limb. I soaped my entire body, scrubbing away the last of the stench and illness.

I wasn't alone, though.

Pulling back the curtain, I found her standing near the sink.

"Why are you in here?"

"I brought you a change of clothes, and…"

"And what?"

Steam clouded the entire room, making her appear like an apparition. "In case you fall. You're so stubborn."

There was something about how she looked at me or, rather, turned away. It wasn't due to shyness or embarrassment. Her chest heaved as she bit her lower lip.

She was turned on.

And so was I.

I swallowed, doing my best not to focus on my damn erection. I hoped to God she couldn't tell through the curtain that separated us. How could she be turned on right now? I looked awful.

"Go into the other room and wait for me."

"Don't fall. I won't be able to lift you."

I chuckled, bending my head toward the spray. "Promise."

I'd taken hot showers for granted all my life. This one I thoroughly enjoyed. When I stepped out, I headed straight for my toothbrush and did all the motions in triplicate. I wiped down the foggy mirror. I almost felt like me...except for the beard. I found my razor.

"I don't think you should shave right now." I caught a glimpse of her standing behind me before the mirror fogged up again.

Yeah, probably best if I refrained from placing sharp objects against my jugular.

I scratched at the beard. "I hate this."

"Do you trust me?"

"Implicitly."

She moved a chair into the bathroom. "Sit."

I did.

"Tilt your head, please." I closed my eyes and leaned back. "I'm not sure how to use this," she said, holding up the razor. "Shall I go get a normal razor?"

I laughed. "This *is* normal, Mary. It's the way men have been shaving for centuries." I placed her thumb on the side of the blade and showed her how to grip it. I brushed the fingers of her other hand on my cheek. "Shave in the direction of the growth." I sucked in a ragged breath as her fingers caressed my face.

"Are you sure?"

"Yes, I'm sure."

In slow, circular motions, she lathered my face with shaving cream. I tried not to breathe too hard when she ran the straight-edged razor against my throat. Her strokes were sure and swift. Her plump breasts were very close to my mouth. The scent of spiced vanilla drifted toward me. I did my level best not to think about how erotic this was.

"I may have missed a few spots, but you can wash your face now."

By the time I emerged from the bathroom, freshly shaven and myself again, she had arranged fresh linens on the bed and aired out the room. Her lips parted in surprise as she gave me the once-over.

"Was I a cranky patient?"

"Never."

"I am very grateful to you. You have healing hands."

She waived away my compliment. "It was the least I could do."
She gestured to the table, set up with several dishes. My stomach
grumbled at the sight.

"I ordered food for you. I'm sure you're hungry."

"Starved." But food wasn't going to quench all my cravings.
That much I knew.

"I should go now."

"Stay. Eat." When had I turned into Monosyllabic Man?

I pulled out a chair for her. She took her place across from me. The
meal was simple fare of shredded chicken, bland potatoes, *naan*, and
fruit. Mary said I should start slow, since I'd only had broth for the past
few days. We shared a plate since she'd ordered only for me.

She told me about everything I'd missed. The doctor's visits. Prabhat's
constant checking. Manny helping me to the toilet because I was too
stubborn for a bedpan, thank God. I had no recollection of any of it. I
only remembered her voice, the massages, and the cloth beads she ran
her fingers over. And that night when I took her wrist and rubbed the scar
etched over her veins.

Although her smile was bright, full of relief, she looked so tired. The
tight braid she usually wore hung loose, many strands escaping the band.
Darkness circled her eyes.

"Were you here the whole time?"

She swallowed a chunk of mango. "Practically. I left to bathe and get
something to eat."

I looked around the room. No cot had been brought in. "Where
did you sleep?"

"Sometimes on the chair next to the bed or on the floor. You'd get up at
all different times, so I wanted to be close in case you needed me."

What kind of bastard let a woman sleep on the floor? The hard wood
of the chair had to be even worse.

"You look exhausted."

"I'll sleep tonight."

"Sleep now."

She shook her head, cupping her mouth as the yawn escaped. "There is
too much noise and traffic in the employee quarters at this time."

"Sleep here on the bed."

She arched a brow as if the suggestion was crazy. "I couldn't."

I rubbed her arms. "Let me watch over you for a while."

She looked unsure. I took her hand and led her to the bed. I turned down the covers for her. "Mary. You're exhausted. That's my fault. Please let me do this little thing for you."

To my relief, she slid into the bed. "Okay. Just a nap."

"Shall I fetch you some water?"

She shook her head. "What will you do?"

"I have a million emails to occupy me. Just sleep now. As long as you need."

She flipped over on her stomach, her face turned toward me. I ran my hand down her spine, settling on the dip in her lower back. She had a very nice dip. Emails could wait, right? "I'm not as versed on the fine art of massage as you. But if you'd like, I'll do my best."

"I'd like."

I rubbed her back and shoulders, feeling the tension in them. She moaned softly as my hands kneaded her. God, that fucking beautiful moan.

"You gave me many rubdowns over the last few days, didn't you?"

"You remember?"

"Yes."

"They help with circulation. I didn't want your muscles to atrophy."

The fan above us blew a strand of hair against her face. She pushed it out of the way impatiently, but it refused to yield. I tucked it behind her ear.

"It's better, thank you," she said.

Crossing the room, I fetched my laptop. I took her place on the chair, which was more decorative than comfortable. I couldn't imagine her sleeping in it. Yet, hadn't I woken up several times to see her in this very spot? Guilt and regret plagued me. The illness had robbed me of all consideration.

I rested my feet against the bed frame and opened up my laptop. Emails filled the screen. I focused on the most important ones of the lot. I shot off replies to Stephen and Moneypenny with an update on my status. Stephen sent another back immediately, asking if I was coming home. That would make sense, wouldn't it? I should cancel the rest of the trip and leave. Yet, I still wanted to finish what I'd started. I peered over the top of the screen. She had closed her eyes, her breaths soft and steady.

I snapped the laptop closed. I found my pack and took out the yellow legal pad. With a dull pencil, I sketched her. Definitely not my medium of choice, but when I was in the presence of my greatest inspiration, I'd take anything I could. Hell, I'd use a bloody chisel and rock right now.

I'd just drawn her outline when her eyes fluttered open.

"Why aren't you sleeping, love?"

Love? Where had that come from? I didn't know, but I also didn't regret it.

Her eyes widened for a second before she graced me with a smile. "What are you drawing?"

Just the most beautiful creature I'd ever seen. "You. You seem to have woken something I thought was long dead."

She crooked her arm and leaned her head against it. "I will buy this one, too."

"Will you?"

"I want all of them. Then I will have an exhibition featuring your work. I'll become very wealthy when all the pieces sell."

"Your ambitions are misguided."

"Not ambition...faith. Faith in you, Liam. You'll see how rich I am, and then you'll know exactly how talented you are. I'll prove it to you."

I lost my focus with her words. I was a successful businessman who made multi-million- dollar deals every day. I had every luxury at my disposal. This girl...this girl who had so little had given me so much.

I glanced at the bracelet encircling her wrist. *Why did you hurt yourself, Mary?* I wanted to fix it, to make that hurt go away. Hell, to turn back time and make her world whole. "Are you still leaving?" I asked.

She adjusted the bracelet on her wrist, a flicker of emotion crossed her face. "You remember our conversation?"

I wondered how many I'd forgotten. "You said you'd given your notice. That's my fault."

"It's the best thing for me. I was rooted to this place, afraid of leaving and loathing my life at the same time."

"When are you leaving?"

"Now that you're well, I'll go in a few days' time."

"Where?"

She shrugged. "I don't know."

"How can you be cavalier? Are you just going to hop on a train to somewhere? To nowhere?"

She laughed as if I was being ridiculous. "That's the beauty of having no one. You never have to leave a forwarding address. I speak perfect English. I'll take your suggestion and get a job at one of the outsourcing companies."

"I don't suppose you'd be open to staying in touch? I have connections. I can help you find suitable work."

"I think it's better for both of us if we part ways completely." She stared at me. "Don't look so sad, Liam. I'm sure we'll talk again someday."

"How can you know that?"

"When you have a problem with your software or you need to order a new something digital." She cleared her throat. "I'm going to be Lola from Seattle." Her voice inflected a very bad southern accent.

My laughter echoed through the room. "You sure you're not from Alabama, Lola?"

"I suppose I'll have to work on my geography. Surely, they'll train me in such things."

I focused back on my drawing, trying to capture the way the light illuminated her hair. She stretched and yawned.

"Go to sleep, Mary."

"Will you keep drawing when you're back in the States?"

"Paint is my preferred medium."

"Painting then."

"Maybe."

A sleepy smile brightened her face. I wasn't sure which I wanted more, to capture it on paper or just enjoy it. Did she know she sliced me deeper than a knife? Pierced through my very heart.

"There is a scandal circulating the hotel about us."

I looked up from the sketch. "Yeah? What are people saying?"

"That you weren't ill at all. We were having a sexual liaison."

"For four days? That's impressive stamina, even for me."

"The rumor is you have a very large appetite." She laughed, but I could not join her.

"I was very stupid to ask you to stay. You divulged your secret because of me and destroyed your reputation."

"Are you joking? I don't care what they think. There was nowhere else I'd rather be."

Me either, Mary. I stifled a yawn.

"You're tired, too," she said.

"I'll be fine." The shower had done me in. My muscles ached from the little physical activity.

"The medicines make you tired. You need to rest, too, Liam."

"I've slept enough."

She shifted to the far side of the bed. "There's enough room for both of us." She patted the area next to her. "Come."

If I got in that bed, I just might...come.

But never had an invitation been so inviting.

I couldn't refuse an opportunity to be close to her. I was good, though. I laid on my back, keeping a gap between us. I looked up at the ceiling, all the while feeling the heat of her gaze on me. It didn't matter. I wasn't in the best shape. I doubted I could give her the pleasure she deserved. In fact, I doubted she even wanted me to. It was concern, not lust, that had elicited the invitation. I sucked a harsh breath through my teeth. "Go to sleep, Mary."

"Okay."

But she didn't. She shifted around restlessly. She hit the pillow with her fist. She rolled all over the damn bed.

"What the hell is wrong?"

"This bed is too soft. I think you misunderstood me. I'm used to sleeping on the ground. I should probably go."

"Please stay with me. Just a little while longer." I hated the desperation in my own voice. But I could see in her pained expression, she was fighting something, too.

She sat up, running a hand through her messy hair. "Will you do something for me, Liam?"

I cupped her chin. "Anything, love."

"It's a strange request."

"Fitting, since you're a strange girl. What is it? Don't keep me in suspense."

"Will you hold me? Just hold me for a bit?"

"It would be my honor." I patted my chest. "Come here."

She leaned her head against my chest. "Yes, this will do very well." Her breath softened.

Her body curled around me. I stroked her hair. My erection stretched against the fabric of my shorts. *Down boy, you already got your fix in the shower.* But it would not be silenced. "Since we're already the subject of a scandal, perhaps we should rid the good people of idle gossip and give them something real. You're no longer my subordinate." I would have said we were equals, but that would be a lie. Clearly, she was my better.

She tilted her head up. "I want to."

"I am sensing a contraction in that sentence."

"Liam, how can I explain this to you?"

"I don't know, but I really wish you'd fucking take a stab at it." Poor choice of words.

"You're like...*Sidr*, honey to me."

"It all makes sense now."

"It does?"

"No, it sounds fucking ridiculous. What is cedar honey?"

"Sidr. Sid—har." She rolled her tongue on the syllables. "It's this rare and expensive honey harvested in Yemen. Do you know who Constance Dakata is?"

"The celebrity chief? Yes, I know her. Why the hell bring her into this conversation? I'm really not into three ways."

"Stop being naughty. I'm trying to explain this really difficult thing to you. Listen."

"Yes, sir."

Her mouth twitched, fighting the smile. "She did this around-the-world special about a year ago. When she visited Jaipur, she stayed at our hotel. She filmed her show from our kitchen."

I was aware of that. Stephen had set it all up. It turned out to be great publicity for us.

"India was her last stop. She made some traditional Indian dishes. But she did a very special dish...a dessert. The cake combined flavors from each country she visited. I was lucky enough to watch the production. Then she poured this honey over the cake. It was slow-poured sunshine. I never tasted it, yet I was already addicted to it. Silly, right?"

"Not silly at all." Hell, she'd just described the way I felt about her.

"Chef Dakata said it was the most sinful and decadent ingredient she had ever come across. Afterwards, I was tasked with cleaning the kitchen. There was still some honey left in the cup she'd used."

"And you tried it?"

The crimson blush swept over her skin. "I licked the cup, Liam. Licked it clean."

"I take it you were disappointed after all the hype?" The analogy cut harder than a rusty knife.

"The very opposite. I've never tasted anything so delicious in my entire life."

"I'm not following what this has to do with..."

She put her finger against my mouth. "In the months that followed, I found myself craving it again. I've never been a huge fan of sweets, but I purchased many just to recreate the feeling of honey melting on my tongue. Nothing compared, nothing even came close to it."

Was she trying to kill me? All her story was doing was turning me on. It took every fucking ounce of strength not to lick her...cup.

"I really need you to get to the point. Get there now."

"Don't you see, Liam? It would have been wiser to have never tasted it. I couldn't crave what I didn't know. Even now, I have a crazy hunger for it. Not hunger, thirst. Like it's the only thing that can quench me. Yet, if I were able to obtain a jar, it wouldn't be enough. Do you understand?"

It did make perfect sense. But unlike her, I could not rationalize it. I wanted the honey too much to think how bitter my life would be once the taste dissolved. "Yes."

She rested her head against my chest. We lay together in silence for a few moments.

"I'm disappointed, Mary."

"You don't think it's a good reason?"

"It's a brilliant reason."

"Then why?"

"I always thought if I were compared to a food, it would be something more masculine. A bouillon cube, perhaps."

Chapter 14

Mary

I'd used three buckets of hot water for my bath, lathering myself with sandalwood soap, a forgotten luxury purchased eons ago. But I needed luxury tonight. It smelled like him. I loved his scent, so I'd been very liberal.

Desperate to scour my mind of him, I'd touched myself to the point of perversion. But my dangerous thoughts refused to yield. The usual tactics provided no relief…only more remorse. Now, I sat by the fountain he'd fixed for me, surrounded by a million tiny lights under a heavy moon—a completely aroused, sandalwood-scented mess.

I hadn't seen him for the past two days, but I felt his presence everywhere. I ignored the lecherous remarks of my former colleagues and Prabhat's admonishing eyes. Tomorrow, I'd go to the train station and randomly pick a destination. I was leaning toward Hyderabad, a place with many call centers and opportunities. Distance and time healed all wounds, or so I kept telling myself.

Thoughts of Liam swirled around my head no matter how many times I tried to swat them away, squash them, or slam the door. How safe and secure I'd felt in his arms as we'd slept. I had awoken in the middle of the night. Staring down at his beautiful body, I debated between kissing him awake and pushing him away. In the end, I'd slipped from the bed quietly, stealing a few last glances like a thief in the night.

He'd made me laugh in a way I never thought I'd do again. He'd seduced me with his sensuous British accent and his muscular form. He'd mesmerized me with his intense eyes and deep dimples. But never…never did I think I would actually care for him. I had stopped really caring for people a long time ago. I'd already experienced the gut-wrenching pain of a full heart being emptied. I wouldn't survive it again.

I stared at the blossom, sitting proudly in the middle of the fountain, hoping it could give me some much-needed guidance. It remained stoic and silent. The flower gave me a sense of balance, but even its beauty couldn't control my chaotic thoughts.

"There you are," Pooja said, taking the seat next to me.

"Here I am."

"Are you packed?"

"Yes."

Pooja handed me a parchment-wrapped parcel. "Prabhat gave me this. He said I was supposed to give it to you right before you left, but I'm very forgetful."

She wasn't as forgetful as she was curious. Before she could ask, I took the package from her. "It's the cream I ordered."

Her gaze turned suspicious since we didn't buy creams fancy enough to mail-order. Before she could ask, I walked away. I went to the same alcove where Liam and I had danced to Dusty. Under the dim overhead light, I tore through the paper.

The jar of honey gleamed against the night. Beneath it was a note card, folded into a neat square, with a rendering of a hand-drawn lotus blossom. Squinting against the low light, I read his words.

Hello Lotus Girl, you don't belong here, but I am too selfish not to be happy to have found you. Besides all the obvious things you did, there is something else you gave me that I cannot name, but I sense it all the same. Something I lost long ago without ever realizing it. So I thank you for that. I know you said we shouldn't keep in touch, but I've listed my contact information in case you ever need anything. Although I doubt you will. There is a rare strength in you that I admire.

The honey is an extremely small gesture of my gratitude. How could you ever satisfy your hunger if you never give into your cravings? It's beyond me, but as I said, I am a selfish man.

Humbly yours, Liam.

He admired me, the girl who buried herself in routine to keep all the cracks from fissuring. He credited me with restoring something in him?

I licked my lips and curled my fingers around the honey jar. But it wasn't the honey I craved.

Chapter 15

Liam

I sat in the chair, my feet on the window ledge, drowning my sorrows with King Fischer. I closed my eyes, drumming my fingers to La Traviata-Brindisi. Some days called for Nine Inch Nails, but today I wanted Pavarotti.

If I had turned it up another notch, I might have missed the knock.

She stood in my doorway, wearing a loose-fitting yellow shirt and long flowing skirt. Her hair hung in cascading waves, framing her face. She held a small satchel so tightly her knuckles strained. She scanned me from my unbuttoned shirt, down to my jeans, and ending at my bare feet.

See something you like?

Me, too.

"May I come in, sir?" she whispered with a slow seductive grace.

I kicked the door open and waved her inside. "You may."

I shut the door, latched it, and leaned against it. "You should not call me 'sir.' I am not your boss."

"That's right. You don't like it, anyway."

"I like it too much, but then you already know that, don't you, love?"

"I suspected." She turned toward me, biting her lower lip. "You look fit."

"I've been eating like an ox the past two days. I'm surprised the kitchen hasn't run out of food."

"You have all your strength back."

"Yes." Although, staring at her, a different type of hunger made me weak once more.

She looked at my luggage, lying open on the bed. "You're leaving."

"In the morning."

"I'm sure you'll be happy to get home."

"I'm finishing my work here first."

This seemed to surprise her. "I thought you'd want to leave India after your horrible experience."

"It wasn't all horrible. In fact, some of it was exceptionally good."

She walked over to window, looking out at the stars. *God, Mary, I don't have the strength for this.* I'd been battling a civil war. My brain insisted she'd made a choice, and I needed to stay away. All the while, my dick was still debating the topic.

She turned, her damp hair swinging. "Is this opera?"

"Verdi."

"It's lovely."

You're lovely.

The sensuality of the music surrounded us. "It is."

Her breasts heaved with each of my steps. I hoped to God this last dance between us would end in a merciful crescendo. She reached into her satchel and brought out the jar of honey. I paused, the gap between us feeling as large as an ocean.

"I wanted to thank you for this and your letter."

"You weren't supposed to get it until I left." I wanted to smash the jar. Had she really just come to thank me? *Keep killing me, Mary.* "It wasn't meant to solicit an invitation."

"Then you don't want me here." The jar shook in her hand.

I stilled it, drawing closer. I bent until my mouth hovered over her ear. "I didn't say that."

"Did you try it yourself?"

"I was only able to procure one jar. From my understanding, it's the only jar within a hundred miles."

"How many kilometers is that?"

"About a hundred and sixty, give or take."

"Wow."

"I have to admit, your description aroused my…curiosity."

"You're lucky then."

"How so?"

She tilted her head back, her lips parted. "I am willing to share."

She held out the jar to me.

"You first, love."

This was slow-poured hot seduction. The sound of the metal as it scraped free of the glass catch. The way she swiped her finger around the inside rim and brought it to her lips. Her mouth curved around her finger and she sucked, closing her eyes in bliss.

I loved that look, but I wanted to be responsible for it. I wanted to make it happen again and again.

She held up the jar. "You try."

I mimicked her movements, but instead of my own lips, I placed my finger against hers, gliding the honey across them. She opened her mouth, ready to lick what I'd given her. I clasped her chin. Her breaths quickened.

"You think that belongs to you? You're wrong. That's mine. All mine." I crushed our mouths together greedily. The rough, needy kiss was a few shades past passionate. She moaned. The honey was delicious and pure, but it was nothing compared to how she tasted. That fucking moan would get me every time.

I took the jar and slammed it on the table. "I'm going to eat the rest of that off your body, but right now, I just want to taste you." I walked us to the back wall, my mouth never leaving hers. Her fingers tugged my hair. I pulled off my shirt fast and carelessly. Then I lifted hers over her head. She wore a plain white bra, no lace, no fringe…just beautiful breasts. My fingers trailed down her waist. My erection, swollen and painful, begged for release.

Then panic set in. Did I have a rubber? Fuck, how could I not?

"Liam…" she murmured.

"I'm having a little crisis." Little? No…this qualified as a huge crisis. "I don't have protection for us." I buried my head against her shoulder. "Fuck."

"I do."

I backed away from her. "Don't tease me."

"I'm not. They're in my satchel. An American brand."

Sweet relief spread through me. I took her face in my hands and sought out her mouth. "Smart, beautiful girl."

"Shall I fetch one?"

"Not yet."

"No?" She chewed her bottom lip as if worried.

"My body's been waiting to meet yours for a while now. I think they deserve a proper introduction."

I unclasped her bra. As I pulled it away from her, I had to steady my breaths. I kissed her nipples. Then I sucked and flicked and nipped them. Her fingers twisted through my hair. I was glad I'd left it long.

"You're teasing me now," she said, each word coming out harsher than the last.

"We're just getting started. Take off the rest of your clothes."

She hooked her thumbs into the waist of her skirt and lowered it until it puddled around her feet. The knickers were next. There she was…my beautiful lotus blossom, completely unfurled for me.

Her beauty was both obvious and subtle. The shape of her collarbone. The feel of her hips as my hands clasped her. The softness of her wet hair brushing against my skin.

Give me fifty lashes with that hair, Mary.

I traveled a slow path south, tasting and touching her along the way. Her knees shook as I finally had my first taste of honey. Holding onto her waist, I took her to the edge of the precipice, but pulled back just as her moans heightened with intensity.

She hooked a leg over my shoulder. Encouraged, I fucked her with my tongue. Her hands fisted my hair. Verdi didn't hold a candle to the aria Mary sang to me.

I stood and kissed her, tenderly this time, exploring her mouth with desperation, cupping the back of her head. She nipped my lip with her teeth, releasing the savage inside me once more.

"Naughty girl."

I twisted her hair around my hand. She gasped as I pulled her hair back, my body pressed against hers. Her hands tugged at the button on my jeans. Her fingers inched around my belt. I moved her trembling hand toward the clasp. She undid it quickly. My belt fell with a thud, followed by my jeans.

I pushed myself off her before I forgot all about the condom. I was too wound up to fish through her bag, so I shook it until the gold foil packets fell out. She leaned against the wall, her arms covering her breasts.

"Don't cover yourself, love. I want to see all of you." My steady voice was at odds with my shaky fingers. Her hands dropped to her side.

I pulled down my boxer briefs. My dick sprang, painfully erect and screaming at me for making it wait so long.

She looked so fucking beautiful, wanton and lusty. Part of me wanted to paint her this way, but the thought was laughable. I could barely hold it together. All the blood had rushed straight to my sheathed and fully erect groin.

I pressed her against the wall. She threw her hands over my shoulders. I picked her up. Her legs wrapped around my hips. I should have been more gentle, but my need overtook me. I plunged inside of her.

She let out a startled gasp. I pulled back, a feat of heroic proportions considering how fucking wet and tight she was. "You okay, lover?" She nodded, tightening her legs, pulling me deeper inside her. That non-verbal message spoke volumes. I pressed my palm against the wall, leveraging myself. I growled with my first thrust. Her nails raked my back.

Was I really about to fuck her against a wall? *Take her to the fucking bed, man. Do it properly.* It was better to see her face that way. I'd been imaging that expression of pleasure since I'd first laid eyes on her. I turned us around, carrying her. I was so busy kissing her I almost missed the bed. We landed with a bounce. She titled her head back, her ecstatic groan encouraging my advance.

I inched her up the bed. Her shoulder hit the open suitcase. We both pushed it with aggravated annoyance until it crashed to the floor. I paused inside of her, wanting to make it last longer than I was capable. I traced her lips with my tongue. She opened her mouth and sucked my finger. I plunged again, my hand resting on her neck. She panted louder, crying in rhythm to my thrusts.

I fucking knew you'd like it rough, Mary. I knew it.

Fuck, I enjoyed it, too. More than I ever thought possible.

I nudged her face so she met my eyes. The rich cinnamon color was both calming and mesmerizing. I had to see her face in climax. I focused on her mouth as my thrusts deepened.

She closed her eyes, her body shaking. As desperately as I wanted to prolong this, I lost control, too. I pulled her leg over my hip, buried my face in the crook of her neck, and fucked her to crescendo. She shuddered all around me. We laid there, a mess of ragged breaths and tangled limbs and pounding hearts.

We held onto each other. Maybe to make it last longer. Maybe because neither of us wanted to let go.

"I'll be right back," I whispered as I broke our connection.

When I came out of the bathroom, she was sitting on the edge of the bed, getting dressed.

No.

She had on her bra and knickers.

I crawled on the bed until I reached her. "You're staying the night with me."

"Liam, it was…amazing. But I should go."

We had fucked hard, but I wanted to take my time and make love to her. There was so much more to explore.

I kissed her cheek and worked down to her shoulder. "Stay. Spend the night with me. Let me love you again."

She leaned against my chest, the struggle inside her evident. I was selfish for her, so I did some more convincing. I cupped her breast and nibbled on her earlobe. I brushed her hair aside and worked my way across her back.

Then I stopped.

She straightened immediately.

The scar right below her neck froze me. It was in a place normally concealed by her hair.

She inhaled sharply. "I have to go." She pulled away from me.

I tightened my arm around her waist to keep her steady.

"Who did this to you?" My voice was calm, completely at odds with the boiling rage threatening to erupt.

"I burned myself."

I traced the perfectly symmetrical diamond seared into her flesh. Although it was healed, it shined a dark red welt against her smooth brown skin. "This is not an accident. It looks...." God, I couldn't even say it. "Someone branded you. Who did this, Mary? Tell me."

She shook her head. "I don't know." Her voice choked with emotion.

She squirmed for a minute. I didn't want her to run from me. My fear of losing her too soon was stronger than my need to punish the person responsible. I wouldn't let her go. She went limp in my arms.

"Mary?"

She pulled her legs against her chest and rocked back and forth. She was somewhere else. I had put her there with my demands.

She cried.

I held her tightly. "It's okay, love. I'm sorry. You don't have to tell me. You're safe. You're with me. I won't let anything happen to you." I made these promises without any reasoning. I only wanted to pull her away from that place of darkness. I kept whispering reassurances, holding her and wiping her tears. She leaned against me once more. I laid her down on the bed. She turned away from me, her body shaking.

"May I hold you?"

She nodded. I shifted so we were both on our sides. I spooned her, whispering hollow words and promises I couldn't keep until she fell asleep.

Chapter 16

Mary

I scrubbed my face in the bathroom, trying desperately to wash away my shame. Not shame that I'd slept with Liam. That was glorious, and I wouldn't regret a single second of it. Not shame for the mark on my back. I'd accepted it long ago. No, this was shame for the way I'd reacted. I'd taken all the beautiful and delicious things we shared and transformed them into a horrible, tragic mess.

I had fallen apart in front of him. This…this would be the memory of us. In the moment when he'd seen my scar, I'd disintegrated from a strong, independent woman to a whimpering child. He saw all the weaknesses I'd kept buried for so long. Then again, emotion begets emotion. Liam was a hurricane, flinging all my tightly locked doors wide open.

This wasn't what I wanted him to remember about me…about us. It wasn't how I wanted to look back on our time, either.

I walked back to the bed completely naked. He'd shifted to his back. The orange glow of the rising sun captured the chiseled planes of his face. I pulled back the covers and kissed his muscular chest. He had the warmest, hardest body. It made me weak with a lust I could not resist, let alone deny myself. I was no saint, but with him I wanted to become a sinner.

Liam moaned as I took him in my mouth. I pursed my lips tightly around him. My fingers circled his shaft. He sat up and stroked my hair away from my face.

"Oh God, Mary."

I felt powerful pleasing him this way. His erection grew with every lick of my tongue and every stroke of my hand, making it impossible to take all of him anymore. His moans turned into primal grunts as I moved faster.

"Come here," he whispered.

I replied by cupping his balls.

"Come here," he pleaded.

I surged deeper, tasting the hard column sheathed within the soft velvet of his skin.

"Come. Here," he demanded, pulling me up.

"Why did you stop me?"

He held a golden packet in his hand. "I was going to come."

I pouted. "That was the idea."

"We do it together. But no worries, Miss Costa, I'll yield to your charge and let you fuck me this time." He put the packet in my palm, closing my fingers over it. "Put it on me."

He understood my need for the power. I rolled the condom down his length. He guided me, my body settling over all of his inches. I'd never been in this position. At first, it was uncomfortable, until his large hands glided down my sides and settled on my hips. I could have been clay... putty in those hands. Sunlight filtered the room, casting our shadows on the wall. He gripped me, lifting and releasing until I figured out the rhythm. I placed my hands on his broad shoulders for leverage. His eyes darkened with a wicked sparkle.

"Mary...so good, lover. You fuck me so good."

I relished the compliment and increased the tempo. He kissed me with those crazy, desperate, toe-curling Liam kisses. A trickle of sweat ran down my back as I reached the summit. Shivering, I collapsed on top of him. He put his arms around me and thrust a few more times before he shuddered. I laid against his chest, taking in the sound of his heart as he rubbed my back.

"I'm going to wash up." He pressed his lips against my temple. "Be here when I get back. That is not a suggestion."

I watched him stand. He pulled up his boxers. How could a man's backside be so beautiful? He looked at me, a clear warning in his eyes before heading into the bathroom.

I'd wait for him, but the sun signaled our time was over. At least, I'd ended it the way I wanted, the way we deserved.

I dressed quickly. I made the bed because...well, because it was part of my nature to clean up. I sat at the edge. The bed dipped when he took the seat next to me.

"I have to go, Liam."

He twisted a strand of my hair over my ear. "Come with me, Mary."

I blinked in confusion. "Where?"

"To Mumbai and then Goa. It'll give us a fortnight." I shook my head, but he silenced my protests with his kiss. "Listen to me. You're leaving, anyway. Think of this as a holiday, and if anyone deserves one, it's you. I'll be working, but I'll have time for us. I'll make time for us."

"I can't." Even as I protested, my conviction waned. Because two weeks with Liam sounded almost greedy, but God help me, I was greedy when it came to him. How could he still want me after last night? Clearly, my outburst had done nothing to dissuade him.

He caressed my cheek, his thumb running across my bottom lip.

"Don't answer yet. My flight leaves in two hours. That gives you one hour to make the decision. Let's be bold for a bit longer, love."

Chapter 17

Liam

She wasn't coming. I had shaken everyone's hand twice and exchanged enough pleasantries to fill an entire Regency novel. But there was no sign of Mary.

"You should go, sir," Prabhat said, pointing to the car.

It was her choice. I had to let her go, but damn it, not without a fight.

"I'll stop at the employee lodgings. I wanted to say good-bye to them as well."

Prabhat's expression was ripe with disapproval. He, like everyone else here, thought I was using her. Maybe I was. All I knew was I couldn't get enough of her.

"She left half an hour ago, Mr. Montgomery."

"Left?"

"She had her bags and said good-bye. It happens a lot in our business. These village girls come and go all the time."

"I see."

Now I wanted nothing more than to leave, but he kept talking. "I'm sure she'll be fine. These girls are more beguiling than they appear. A man has to be careful."

"I don't appreciate your tone. I would suggest we end this conversation."

How could she leave? Was it because of the mark on her back? Was it because I'd taken her to the darkest place? Or did she just not want to stretch our journey a bit longer?

I got into the car. I didn't look back as it left the gates, only forward. Thank God I did, because I probably would have missed her standing on the side of the road beside a worn-out suitcase.

"Stop the car."

"Sir?" the driver questioned.

"Stop."

The poor man didn't know what was happening. I opened the door and had my foot on the ground before it reached a stop. Cars honked behind us.

"Do a circle," I told the driver.

"Sir, you might miss your flight."

"Circle," I repeated, not taking my eyes off her.

"You just keep killing me, Miss Costa."

"It was better this way. To leave with you outside the gates." She nodded toward the hotel. "Instead of in there. The driver will tell everyone, anyway. Like I told you, I don't care. But I wanted us to leave without all the stares and gossip following us out."

I nodded, trying and failing to wipe the idiotic grin off my face.

"You ready to spend a fortnight with me?" I asked.

"Yes, I want it. I have a few conditions, though."

"Are you going to impose rules on us?"

"Just two. Two small rules."

I gave her my full attention. Even took a step back so I wouldn't take her in my arms or throw her over my shoulder. The early afternoon streets of Jaipur jostled around us, but we were the only two people in the world as far as I was concerned.

"What is it, love?"

"Don't ask about my scars again. None of my scars, okay?"

I tucked a loose strand of hair behind her ear. "Only one question, then. I need you to answer honestly. Has the danger passed?"

"I don't understand."

"Is there danger?"

She shook her head. "No, I would never ask you to put yourself in harm's way."

She misunderstood my intent. I had come to the conclusion she was hiding at the hotel from something...someone. And the thought drove me mad. "I wasn't asking because I'm worried about me. I want to know if there is someone in this world who wants to hurt you. And if there is, I need a name."

"No. No one."

I wanted to ask if she had included herself, but I didn't. Whatever she harbored, I would not make her go to the dark places again.

"And the second rule?"

"When this is over, we end clean. No keeping in touch or anything."

I wanted to argue this stipulation, but I wouldn't risk what she was offering. "As you wish, Mary.

Although I made the vow, I doubted I could keep it.

Chapter 18

Mary

He'd asked me if I was safe, not because he was worried about the ramifications for himself. His question was as simple and as complicated as that. I replayed it in my head, his expression of concern and his look of relief with my answer.

Liam held my hand through the flight. I hadn't been on a plane since I was a kid, and never first class. He ordered champagne and told jokes. I had to admit, after two glasses, I wasn't nervous anymore. It was all new to me, but Liam was a seasoned traveler. When we arrived at Chhatrapati Shivaji Airport, though, it was Liam who had the culture shock.

We stared out the window on my side of the car as we passed through the crowded city. Me, sentimental and nervous, searching for pieces of my past in the tall skyscrapers and cramped streets. Liam, wide-eyed and stunned silent, his hand gripping my hip, as he took in the blaring car horns and near-miss collisions.

"You've gotta be kidding me," he said as a family of four pulled up next to us.

"They're just heading off for the day."

"On a motorbike? Four people on a motorbike and two of them children." The father had the helm, two small children behind him, and the mother took up the rear.

"I'm sure you don't see things like this in New York."

"Or anywhere. Also, I've never seen cars share the road with horses and cows. And why the hell is everyone bloody honking?"

"Welcome to Bombay, Liam."

Bombay had stayed the same in many ways, but there

were even more people than I remembered. The buildings looked grander, more westernized. But other things hadn't changed. There were churches, temples, and mosques on every corner. Women wore every color and style of clothing, from patterned traditional saris to plain black burkas. There were plenty of jeans and T-shirts in the mix, too.

Children ran up to our car at every intersection with outstretched hands.

"They're going to get hurt darting through traffic," he said, his face holding a grim expression.

I didn't want to tell him that this was probably the safest thing they did all day. "They'll be fine."

"How does it feel to come home again?" he asked.

"Strange. I never thought I would return."

"Are you happy you're here?"

I snuggled close to him. "I'm happy to be with you."

"Where did you live?"

"In Bandra. It's some distance from here. The orphanage was in Navi Bombay."

"I have an appointment there in a few days. I'm going to check out a piece of property for a new hotel. Would you like to come with me?"

"I don't know."

He placed his hand over mine. "I'll leave a car for you in case you want to visit friends or anything."

I nodded, unsure if I had any friends to visit.

* * * *

The Mumbai hotel didn't look like it belonged to the same family as the Rajasthani one. It was a modern, imposing building with a glass and steel façade. It took a while for the car to make its way through the gate.

"Sir, I'm very sorry," the security guard said. "This will only take a moment."

"Let it take as long as it needs to. There are no exceptions."

The man nodded. I watched from the window as he placed the mirror beneath our vehicle, while another man walked a leashed dog around the car.

"What are they doing?"

His mouth stretched into a grim line. "Checking our car."

"For what?"

"Bombs."

This was the real change, wasn't it? When had differences, once respected, turned into obstacles to be conquered?

He rubbed my shoulder. "The terrorist attacks have made this necessary. Don't worry. It's just a precaution."

The extravagant suite he'd booked had a lovely view of the city. We were on the top floor, and I could see the terraces and roofs of all the tall buildings. Hear the noise of a million people and smell the chaos of it all. A warm breeze came through the open veranda. Most of the time the city didn't smell very good. But there were other times when it was scented with the aroma of spices and flowers and sea. We had arrived at such a time. I took it as an auspicious sign. Liam's arms wrapped around me as we stared at the Bombay skyline.

"It's a beautiful room."

"I always opt for a regular room and reserve the nicer ones for guests, but I made an exception."

I held in a laugh since we *were* an exception, a complete contradiction to normal.

"I have to tour the facilities and meet with the management here. I'll be a few hours. Will you be alright, love?"

"Yes. I think I'll go out for a while."

"Why don't you wait for me?" There was a worry in his voice. When I tilted my head back, he was staring at the traffic, his brows drawn. "We can go sightseeing together."

I was in Bombay, and there was only one sight I had to see. I had to do it alone. "Liam, this is where I was born. It's my home. I'll be fine."

"Have the driver take you. If you need anything, charge it to the room." He put a key card in my hand.

"May I borrow your book? *Nicholas Nickelby*? I'll be very careful with it. I know what it means to you."

A flicker of surprise crossed the chiseled planes of his face. "Of course, Mary. If you want something different, though, there is a bookstore downstairs. I'm sure they have some Highlander novels." He arched a brow, his smile turning wicked. "It might serve as fodder for other activities."

My face flushed. "I'm really in the mood for Dickens. Thank you."

The valet cleared his throat. We both startled, unaware he was still in the room. "Sir, the front desk wanted me to give you this message from Mr. Stephen Wilshire. He asks you call him immediately."

Liam's smiled tightened into a thin line. "Thank you," he said, tipping the man and closing the door behind him.

I realized that he'd been worried about my job, but I'd never given a single thought to his.

"Liam, will you...will you get in trouble because of us?"

"No worries on that account."

"Why is Stephen Wilshire calling you then?" I chided myself for the question. Liam was in upper management. It would make sense he would talk to the owner of Wilshire Corporation once in a while.

"Probably to annoy me."

I gestured to the spacious room. We were in a country where you paid steep premiums for space. "This room? My airline ticket?"

"What about it?"

"I know you're in a high position, but can you afford all this?"

He chuckled as if I'd made a joke.

"Something funny?"

He adjusted his tie in the mirror. "I forgot you don't know."

"Know what?"

"I own the Wilshire group...or at least half of it. Stephen owns the other half."

His statement echoed in my head. Surely, he was joking. It made no sense. I turned the bracelet on my wrist. "You're teasing me."

"I'm not."

"It's a family-owned hotel."

"Right, Stephen and I are half brothers. Although I wouldn't call him family."

I recalled the phone conversation from his brother. Why hadn't I made the connection? But I realized now the man never told me his name. Stupid, stupid girl.

"But it's an American company. You're British. You have a different surname." I blurted out, as if he didn't know all those things.

"You're correct on all counts. I told you I come from a long line of surly bastards. I'm no different. I didn't find out who my father was until my mum passed away. Despite all his pressure, I insisted on keeping the name I was born with."

Liam took a step toward. I took a step back. My knees hit the back of a chair. I collapsed onto it, feeling a crushing weight on top of me.

He knelt beside me. His hand stilled my shaking knee. "Hey, you okay, Mary?"

"Why didn't you tell me?"

I felt betrayed. I thought we weren't on the same plane before, but now I questioned if we even existed in the same universe. What was I even doing here with him?

"The upper management all know who I am, but I find it works in my favor to keep a low profile and not flaunt it."

"You deceived me. I knew you had wealth…but you're a billionaire."

"You say that like it's a bad thing. I've never had that reaction before. You're a very peculiar girl."

A very stupid, stupid girl.

I remained silent, trying to control the million different threads pulling all at once, ready to rip me apart. There was a dark sorrow in his eyes.

"I have no idea who you are, and here I am running off with you."

"You know me better than most…maybe all. If you want all the sordid details, I can give them to you. The car accident with my mother? I was driving. The roads were slick, and I was going too fast. I ran a light. A truck slammed into her side. I woke up in the hospital with a broken leg and no mother."

I wasn't sure if he was speaking to fill up the empty air between us. When the emotion cracked his voice, it split something inside of me, too. "You blame yourself." It wasn't a question. I could see years of guilt and anguish reflecting in his eyes. The same emotions I saw whenever I looked in the mirror.

"Of course I do. It was my fault. The rain made her arthritis worse. She had a hard time driving. There were other options, though. We could have called a cab, but then we would have had to dip into the money for my rugby cleats. I couldn't have that now, could I? We could have taken the bloody bus, but I didn't want to stand outside in the rain. She argued with me, especially since I didn't have a license. But I insisted on driving. I was late to school, and she had to go to work. I thought I was helping us…helping her. Instead, I killed her."

"It was an accident. She wouldn't blame you."

I'm not sure if I said it aloud, because he ignored the statement. "I had no other family, or so I thought. Mum told me my dad passed away right after I was born. Then a man turned up at her funeral, claiming to be my biological father. He'd read the obituary. Naturally, I didn't believe him, but the blood test was pretty damn conclusive. Everything changed for me. I moved to New York and became heir to a hotel empire. It fucking sounds like a Dickens novel, doesn't it? I can't even comprehend it myself. I didn't ask for any of it. I'd give it all back, every fucking nickel, if I could relive that day and call a fucking cab."

"I'm so sorry, Liam."

A warm fat tear rolled down my face. He wiped it away.

"What are you sorry for, love?" His voice inched up a level. "What happened to me or because you're leaving me?"

How did he have the ability to see through my façade?

"I can't do this."

"It's not as if you've been forthright with me."

"You lied to me, Liam. You weren't in senior management." I looked around the opulent room. "You own all this."

"Do you have an aversion to wealth? Does it somehow taint me in your eyes?"

"No."

"Then what the bloody hell is your problem?"

"Nothing."

"You're acting ridiculous."

"I'm a ridiculous girl, Liam."

I refused to look at him. Liam had become my weakness. I stared straight ahead. He grabbed my trembling hand.

"Look at me, please, because I really need you to hear what I am saying."

My head warned me not to, but my traitorous body could not resist his command.

"It may not seem like it, but I fought my feelings for you." He let out a cynical laugh. "I don't want to want you. We're complicated, aren't we? We have very different pasts and no future. But none of that matters to me. And you want me, too. We have an opportunity to spend some time together and enjoy each other. Whatever promises I can make to keep you here, I will. If you want no sex and a separate room, that's fine by me." He swallowed. "That's a bloody bald-faced lie. It's not fine by me, but I'll do it. Because as much as I crave all of you, I'll take whatever you'll give me. I told you once there is a power between us, but it is you who controls it."

I should have grabbed my bag and ran. "Liam…"

"Shhh. I'm not done. Despite all my good intentions, I want you so much it frightens me. But if you feel you cannot be with me, then I'll wish you well and let you go. I won't chase after you. That's not who I am. I have no idea who hurt you so badly you won't give anyone a chance to be in your life. I want to tear him apart for harming you. But what you're doing? This impenetrable shield you've created around yourself? You're still letting him hurt you, baby. That's killing me." He took a deep breath and stood. He put on his suit jacket and headed for the door. "I hope you'll be here when I get back."

I stood, my knees shaky. "Like I said, I'm going out, but I'll be back in a few hours. No need for separate rooms."

The muscles of his back relaxed. "See you soon, love."

Chapter 19

Mary

I shivered in the dark, cold room. My head spun from whatever drugs they had given me. They forced me onto my knees. A huge hand, stinking of tobacco, gripped my shoulder. A switch flipped. Harsh yellow lights burned onto me.

"What's happening?" I asked, or maybe I didn't, because no one responded.

I stared straight ahead at the monitor. On the screen, I saw a man, a huge looming shape whose face was in shadow. Behind him was what looked to be a statue of a gold tower and a painting that depicted a grove of tall, spindly trees, their white branches twisting into each other as if they were embracing.

"Hello, Mary. You may call me Sahib." His deep, Western voice resonated from the computer. I strained to hear. I squinted my eyes, trying to focus on him, but all I could make out was the picture behind him.

"Does she not speak English?"

"She does, Sahib," the guard said. I heard fear in his own voice when he replied. This man on a monitor far from here frightened them, too.

"Address me, girl!"

"No," I said, sure I'd formed the word this time.

"Ah, you have some fight in you. I like that. But understand this, girl. I paid for you. I own you. That means you do as I say."

"No one can own anyone. My papa will find me. You will pay."

He laughed mercilessly. "Explain it to her."

The hand on my shoulder gripped harder as another slapped me across the face. Blood gushed down my nose. Then he kicked my side.

"That's enough!" the man said.

I lay on my side, hugging my knees.

"I am a rich man. Rich enough to buy and sell you. Rich enough to own you. Out of all the girls in the world, I chose you. I will break you like I break a wild mare. You will call me Sahib. Now get up."

I didn't. My body refused. Air wafted over me before a fist connected to my rib.

"Don't hit her. She has to do it on her own."

"She won't, Sahib," the guard said. "She is insolent. We have other ways to make her do things."

"I don't want her drugged."

The world was quiet for a moment. The floor was cool. I focused on the pattern of the tiles, trying to steady my breaths.

"You have her sister, correct?" the monster asked.

"Yes, sir. She was a witness. Shall we dispose of her?"

"No!" I cried.

"That got your attention. Refer to me by name, slave. Sit up and say my name."

I winced with pain. My hands pressed into the ground. After a few tries, I managed to get on my knees. I bowed my head. "Sahib. Master. Owner."

"Good girl. I'm coming to visit you myself. It won't be long till we meet face to face. In the meantime, we're going to play a few games, you and I. You enjoy games, don't you?"

"Yes."

I tried to swallow, but it was painful. I kept Hannah in the back of my mind. By doing that, I could be what he wanted. I could play the games he set out. I could even go somewhere else in my mind.

I woke up in the back seat of the car, stuck in a midday Bombay traffic jam. The driver looked at me in the rearview mirror. "Are you alright, madam?"

"Fine, thank you."

I rubbed my face, wondering why the hell my nightmares were resurfacing. Liam was rich, but nothing like the man who tortured me. Part of me feared his wealth because money, especially his kind of money, had power to destroy. Liam was right about how I let my past hurt me. Just because I escaped, didn't mean I survived. Survival was not about existing. It was about living. For the first time in my life, I felt alive. I refused to allow the darkness of the past to infiltrate my time with him.

"How much longer?"

"Not long, madam."

It took an hour to make the ten-kilometer journey to the cemetery. Someone had tended Papa and Hannah's plots. Fresh orange marigolds covered the ground in front of their stones. I fell to my knees before them.

Bowing my head, I took out the cloth beads. I ran my fingers over them, repeating the rosary.

"Hi Papaji. It's been a long time, but I think of you and Hannah every single day. I never appreciated your lessons when you gave them, but I understand them now. I'm grateful for everything you taught me. I miss you. I love you."

I turned to Hannah's grave. I traced the two dates etched onto her gravestone. The span separating the years was much too small for the huge impression she left.

"Hi, Hannah. I'm sorry I've been away so long. I ran away from everything after you died. You see, I thought I died, too. It took me a long time to realize I hadn't." I patted my heart. "I'm so sorry, sister."

I took Liam's book from my satchel. "Remember how you wanted me to read this to you? I hope you still want to hear it, because it's long overdue."

I cleared my throat and began reading, trying to make up for my selfish actions long ago.

Chapter 20

Liam

Mary looked uncomfortable and pissed. She went to the other side of the long rack that held an assortment of clothes.

"Since I didn't know your size, she brought up three of each. I didn't pick any of it out, but I'm sure the salesgirl was competent in her selections. It turns out the boutiques in our hotels have a better selection of women's clothing than men's pajamas. I asked her to mix up western and eastern clothing since you wear both." No response. I stood in front of the long rack and bent my head. "Mary?"

She pushed back the clothes. The sound of metal hangers against the rack screeched like nails on a chalkboard. "You bought me clothes?" She looked at the bottom of the rack where an assortment of heels were lined up. "And shoes?"

"Is that an accusation or a question?"

"Why?"

"Because I want to take you out. Looking at the size of your bag, I doubt you have more than three outfits in there."

"Think I don't know how to do laundry? I was a maid, remember?"

"How can I forget when you remind me every two minutes?" I rubbed her arms. "I want to take you to nice places while we're here. The nicest places."

She blew out a frustrated breath, causing a strand of hair to flutter over her forehead. "This wasn't part of our agreement."

"I don't recall this being one of your rules."

"Well, I'm adding it."

"I'm afraid it's too late to amend our original agreement, Miss Costa."

"I don't want any of this. Why would you do this?"

"You're right. What kind of bastard am I to purchase you anything? I'm a fucking monster." Judging from her expression, my sarcasm was not appreciated.

"It's not funny."

"I promised you two things, and I'll keep those promises. You bought me gifts, and I didn't throw them back in your face. Now stop arguing with me and get ready. We have reservations."

She stomped over to me, a fire raging in her dark brown eyes. "I have my own money."

I wasn't sure if I wanted to hold her or spank her. Instead, I just smiled. "Perfect. You shall pay for dinner. Fair warning, I am not a cheap date. You better wine and dine me, girl, especially if you wish to get in my trousers tonight."

Her mouth crinkled at the corners. "Did you say 'trousers?'"

"I did. Pants…kind of an undistinguished word, don't you think?"

"What is wrong with you? I am mad at you."

"You're crazy for me?"

"Mad as in angry." The mouth curved a little more.

I pulled the first garment from the rack. "Then be mad at me in a sexy, low-cut dress."

"You realize you're holding a nightgown, right?"

I looked down at the sheer pink, gauzy fabric on the hanger. "Yeah, not this one."

She snatched it from my hand. "I think it's just the thing, Mr. Montgomery."

"Now we're talking." I looked at my watch. "We have roughly an hour."

"You misunderstand." She held it over her body. "I am planning to wear this to dinner."

I grabbed the hanger back. "Like hell you will."

"Why not, sir?" She fluttered her thick eyelashes at me, faking innocence.

"Are you trying to turn me on or piss me off?"

"Trying to please you, sir. Sexy and low-cut is what you ordered." Her hands ran down the fabric. "This fits the definition. Please excuse me."

She was teasing me or maybe challenging me, but either way, this girl never ceased to shock me. She turned to head for the bathroom.

I grabbed her elbow. "No way in bloody hell you're wearing that thing."

She jabbed her finger against my chest. "Why not?"

I took the scrap of fabric and flung it across the room. The damn thing floated lightly in the air until it landed on the bed. Not quite the dramatic gesture I was aiming for. I gripped her arms. Her mouth parted, our anger fueling the sparks of lust between us. I circled my thumb across her skin.

"I'm a jealous man when it comes to you, Miss Costa." I nodded toward the gauzy scrap of a garment. "You in that thing would bring my wrath on every man in the room. They would surely fall under your spell just as I have. In turn, I would have no choice but to use my fists to break whatever enchantments you cast on the male population of an extremely populated country. Regardless of my strength, I am certain I would sustain grave injuries. The outcome would be devastating for you. Don't you agree?"

"Any injury to you would greatly upset me."

"It's you who misunderstands now, Miss Costa. The real tragedy is that my body will be far too bruised to properly pleasure you tonight. Now, do you really want to risk it?"

Her face moved forward, diminishing the gap between us. I pulled her against me, kissing her hard and without apology. I swallowed her moans and bit her lip. She melted in my arms, or maybe I did in hers. Whatever it was, I was grateful. We parted, both of us breathing hard, our lips chapped.

"No."

A single word, but it robbed me of my sense. I had plunged headfirst from whatever tightrope we walked. "No?"

"No, I won't risk my own pleasure."

I gave her arse a playful spank. "Good. Now, put on a proper bloody dress. I'm taking my girl on the town tonight."

It wasn't exactly low-cut, but the simple black dress she chose did hug all her curves. Her long hair fell in silky waves around her. I led her to the hotel restaurant. It had a modern color scheme and had recently been rated one of the best cuisines in all of Mumbai. She emptied three glasses of wine to my one.

"Planning to get sloshed, Miss Costa?"

"Perhaps."

"Where did you go this morning? I was worried about you."

"I found a quiet spot to read."

"There is a quiet spot in Mumbai?"

"Yes." One word answers, all part and parcel of the nuanced language of furious female.

"You look beautiful."

"Happy to meet your approval." She looked around, sighed, and pushed the empty wine glass toward me for a refill. I obliged.

"How long?"

"How long what?"

"How long are you planning to stay in passive-aggressive mode? I thought we were over the clothes."

"We are."

"Then what is it?"

She leaned into the table, her voice a husky whisper. "Everyone is staring at us. They all know who I am and how we met."

"I'm sure they do. Gossip spreads faster than the speed of light in any language in any country. Don't let it bother you."

"That's easy for you to say."

"I thought you didn't care. That's what you said when you chose to stay with me when I fell ill, isn't it?"

"I could walk away from it then. We weren't on display like zoo animals. We should have ordered room service."

"That would have defeated the purpose. We've had enough meals locked away behind closed doors. I wanted to sit across from you and share a bottle of wine. To help you into your chair and make you laugh. I don't give a damn what these people think. The only person whose opinion counts is yours."

"I understand what you're saying. But honestly, dressing me up and parading me in front of everyone is not a special evening to me. I am not your pretty woman."

Mary was the proudest person I'd ever met. In fact, her pride was the thing I most admired about her at times.

This was not one of those times. "My pretty woman?"

"The movie."

"I'm not familiar with the film."

She smacked the table. "You're joking. I'm Indian and I've seen it. Both the Hindi and English versions. Next thing, you'll ask me to wear a red evening gown, present me with a diamond necklace, and take me to the opera."

"Want a diamond necklace, Mary? Would you care to go to the opera? Do they have opera here?"

"Certainly not, no, and I doubt it."

"Too bad. I think you'd enjoy it." My jaw tightened. The waiter headed for our table. I waived him away.

"Liam…"

I drummed my fingers against the table. "What is it, Lotus Girl? Are you not going to let me kiss you on the lips now? That would be a very severe punishment, considering how much I love your mouth. Even when I hate the words coming out of it."

Her fingers tightened around the stem of the glass. "You have seen the movie then."

"Everyone has seen it. Your analogy is complete rubbish. You are not my whore. Call yourself anything you want. My lover, my companion, my muse, my friend. All appropriate terms, but this…this analogy is not. You insulted me, which is bad enough. What's worse is you insulted yourself. That will not stand with me."

She was quiet, taking small sips of her wine. "You're right. I'm just not used to this." She straightened in her chair, clasping her hands. "I'm sorry, Liam. Thank you for the clothes. They are lovely."

"Welcome."

I followed her gaze around the room. Several sets of eyes focused on us before turning away. "You're right as well. Although my intentions were sincere, this was a bad choice. I never meant to put you in a humiliating position." I stood and helped her from her chair. "We can order room service."

Her hands clasped around mine. She gave me a real smile. "I'm all dressed up. You're…well, as always you're very dashing. We're both starving. We should go out. Just not here, okay?"

I grinned. "I'd like that."

We left the restaurant and the hotel. We weaved our way through humid air and crowded streets.

"We should have taken a car. We could have gone to the Taj and dined there."

"The competition?" She giggled as if I'd made a joke, the effects of three glasses of quality Bordeaux.

I shrugged. "Why not? Either way, I hope we find something fast. I'm starved, and you, my love, are very drunk."

She pouted. "Am not."

"Baby, if you sway anymore, you'll be doing a salsa. Not that I'm complaining."

She spun around to face me. Her hands settled on her hips. "Sir, I swear I am sober." Sir came out shure. Swear was shewar. Sober was shober. Hell, Mary managed a better Sean Connery than I did. She was battered and fried, this one.

"All the same, I'd like to get some food in you. Where shall we go?"

"I have no idea."

"You've lived here. Surely, you have a recommendation."

"I haven't been here in years, and I'm sure the restaurants I frequented are not the same ones you'd choose."

"Try me."

She didn't. Instead, she stopped another couple on the street. "Excuse me, can you recommend a nice restaurant in the area?"

"Chili's," the girl said. "The best food, and it's just down this gully."

Mary turned to me. "Chili's, then?"

"It does sound exotic."

Fifteen minutes later, we were being greeted by a waiter in a referee uniform, surrounded by walls covered in sports pendants. I laughed at the irony.

"What's so funny?" Mary asked.

"This is the same exact Chili's they have in New York."

She looked around the room. "Really?"

"Right down to the numerous pins the wait staff wears. I wanted to take you to a five-star establishment, not my neighborhood bar and grill."

The waiter set down the huge margarita in front of her and a beer for me. Her eyes widened as she sipped from the glass. "I'm happy with this."

"You really think a margarita is a good idea? You've had a lot for someone who only partakes during communion."

"You're right. The liquor is really loosening my inhibitions."

I leaned into the table. "Oh, yeah?"

"I want to rip off all the buttons of your shirt…with my teeth."

I held up my hand to get our waiter's attention. "What are you doing?" she asked.

"Not sure. Either asking for the check or another round."

She laughed, falling back in her chair. "I am sorry it wasn't the exotic five-star cuisine you expected."

"No worries, love. I planned a feast for later."

"I hope I'm invited."

"Darling, you are the main course."

The rose color spread across her cheeks. She took a long sip of her margarita, licking the salt off her lips. "Next time, we'll try something more ethnic. Pizza Hut, perhaps?"

I laughed so hard I sloshed my beer.

Chapter 21

Mary

We crawled through Mumbai traffic. Liam took in every sight, looking awestruck at the massive crowds and architecture.

"Where are we going?" I asked. He hadn't told me much, except that he wanted to show me something and asked me to dress conservatively. I wore a traditional cotton Salwar Kameez, which consisted of a long embroidered blue shirt and loose cotton pants.

"Just a place I want you to see. Actually, I want to see it, too."

We pulled up to a large brick building. The sign over the gate read Community Center with smaller script beneath stating *auspices of Wilshire hotel*. Although the facade was unremarkable, walking inside was like stepping into the pages of a child's coloring book. The walls were a sunny yellow, with renderings of clouds and children.

"What is this?"

"It's sort of a catchall. The center offers classes to help women learn work skills. There is tutoring and art therapy for their children. I believe this mural was done by some of the students." He touched the wall. "Pretty impressive."

"It is. What types of classes do they offer?"

"All kinds. Basic reading and writing to computer skills. There are also craft classes in sewing and embroidery. If students show an interest in a subject, the center helps them in finding work. Or we pay for raw materials and assist them in setting up online businesses to sell their creations."

We passed several classrooms where instruction was taking place.

"Mr. Montgomery, it's wonderful to finally meet you," a portly man said, practically running up to us. He shook Liam's hand vigorously. "My name is Ram. Please sir, let me take you on the tour."

"Thank you. This is Mary Costa." The man shook my hand with the same vigor.

"You have no idea what good works you are doing here. Entire generations have hope because of you."

"Not me, Ram. The Wilshire funds this project."

"Yes, with your approval." He smiled widely. "Come."

Ram took us into each room, where he made grand introductions in Hindi to announce Liam. The women and children clamored around him. He shook each of their hands and asked them questions about their work. Ram and I took turns translating. An elderly woman bent to touch his feet, a gesture of respect. Liam stopped her, looking a bit horrified. She turned toward me, speaking in rapid Hindi, moving her head from side to side.

"She wants to thank you. She says her daughter is receiving an education because of you. She says they have a proper home now."

"Tell her she created all that. We only provided a resource. That's all."

I repeated his phrase. His humbleness surprised me, but it rendered her speechless.

Many people came up to him. He took his time, listening to all of them. A woman explained to Liam how her son had cancer, and she could not afford his medicines. The center had been a saving grace to her family. As we left, Liam gestured to Ram. "See that her son gets in with a doctor. Make sure it happens."

"Yes, sir, it will be done."

"And also, I think we should have a cafeteria that provides at least one free meal per day. Some of the students spend eight hours here. I noticed very few of them leaving for the food stalls."

"The stalls are rather overpriced, sir."

"See to it, Ram."

* * * *

"I can't believe something like this exists," I said as we left many hours later.

"There are several projects up and running. We built an irrigation system in a remote African village. We have a school for girls in South America. There are a few other proposals we're looking into."

"It's really an amazing concept, Liam."

Ram and a few children waved to us as we drove away. "I wish I could take credit, but it was Stephen's idea, one of his best. He proposed we start a charity for the hotel to sponsor certain projects in the countries where we had property. It's a way of giving back to the community. Stephen runs the whole thing. I just sign off on them. I have to admit he does an admirable job."

"Why don't you get along with him?" my mouth blurted out before consulting my brain.

Liam's jawline clenched. I'd stumbled onto sensitive territory.

"I have my reasons."

I thought of Hannah and what I would give up to change a few memories. "He's your family, Liam. Your only family."

"Stephen ruined our relationship before it even formed. You see, we're close in age. He's always hated me for existing."

"I don't follow."

"Our father had an affair, Mary. I was the outcome. I was sixteen when I moved to the States. Stephen made sure I never felt welcomed in his house. He had all the advantages I never did. He turned people against me. Made up rumors about the kind of person my mother was. Who I was. We're adults now, and we have a business to run. We do it, but it's not easy. Mostly, we just divide and conquer."

"But you were both so young. Surely, you don't hold the things he did as a teenager against him? He was very concerned when he called to inquire about your health."

I couldn't reconcile the man who had sounded so relieved when I told him Liam would be all right, the one who ran this charity, with the same man Liam regarded with such disdain. Were we speaking about two different people?

"Are you sure it's concern you heard? Maybe he was disappointed I would recover."

"I'm sure."

"Let's drop this topic. It might have taken place a long time ago, but Stephen's actions are unforgivable."

"I used to hold anger inside me, too, once. I used to let it rule my decisions. It took a long time for me to realize it was another method of hurting myself. When you forgive someone else, it's not for their benefit, but your own."

"Some things cannot be forgiven."

"Maybe not all things, but most things."

He raked his hands through his hair and let out a frustrated sigh. I should have moved on. He'd asked me to. He'd respected me when I created lines he couldn't cross. But there was some deep hurt in Liam.

He carried it silently, almost as if he thought showing it would make him weak. He'd let me see that side of him, but only a few quick glimpses before he shut down.

"Mary, understand one thing. If I could cut Stephen out of my life, I would. He's toxic. I think the only reason my father left me half of the family business was because he figured Stephen would blow it. I'm sure the original plan was for his legitimate son to inherit everything. Stephen holds that against me, too. That I barged into his life, an uninvited guest. As if I even wanted to be there in the first place." Liam's laugh was heavy with cynicism. "Or maybe our father did it to punish us both. The old man wasn't exactly gracious."

Who would Liam have been if his mother hadn't died? I suspected he'd be a passionate artist. A selfish part of me, a part I hated, rejoiced he'd taken a different path. Otherwise, I'd never have met him.

"Why did your father think Stephen would fail?"

"Stephen has a talent for fucking up his life. He's been to rehab more times than I can count, not that any of them have helped. It's a miracle he functions as well as he does. His ideas are crazy, but most of them turn out profitable—not just profitable, almost visionary. We are the only hotel chain our size that recycles ninety percent of our refuse, and our energy use is lower than any of our competitors thanks to some innovative construction techniques. Did you know that?"

"No, I didn't."

"It's become a model for other hotels. Despite his ingenuity, Stephen is on a roller coaster. Eventually, it will go downhill, and one of these times he won't recover from the fall."

"Maybe he needs family, too, Liam. He had to go through a lot when he found out he had a brother."

"This is really none of your business, is it?"

I flinched against his cold stare. I'd opened up an old wound that hadn't healed properly. "I'm sorry."

The hard ridges of Liam's face softened. "I'm sorry, love. I didn't mean to snap at you." He put his arm around me. His body was so tense he might have been in pain. We were quiet for a long time, watching the high noon sun shed light on the decay and decadence that was Bombay.

Liam's voice was low. "A few months after I arrived, Stephen invited me to a bonfire with his friends. Foolishly, I thought it was some kind of peace offering. I felt like a complete outcast as it was. I drank a few beers, flirted with a couple of girls, and was having a fairly good time. The fire was already high, burning with intensity. I hadn't noticed at first, but then

I saw what he'd used for kindling. I realized it was just some revolting prank. A rage took hold of me that night. A rage that still exists."

"What did he use?"

"My mum's books."

The rage Liam spoke about had to be contagious, because I felt it, too.

"My God."

"I became possessed when I saw that. I broke his jaw. If there hadn't been people to pull me off him, I might have killed him."

"Why did he do it?"

"He said he was high. But it's more than that. There's something evil lurking inside of Stephen. That night, it got inside of me, too. Our father's solution was to send us both packing. I went to a military school to learn discipline. Stephen went to his first rehab. Military school was good for me, though. Better than that cold mansion. I learned how to use physical activity to calm myself. They had elective classes in art. I'd always enjoyed drawing, but I developed a passion for it there."

"So you didn't interact with him after that?"

"I avoided Stephen for two whole years. Then he came to my failed exhibition with our father."

"To make amends?"

"Probably to gloat. One look at him, and I knew the rehab hadn't changed him. He was still bitter. I tried, Mary. I tried to put myself in his place. At least I had a caring Mum. My stepmother is a cold woman, and our father wasn't much better. So I put my own prejudices aside, but again, I realized how fucking naïve I was."

"What happened?"

"You remember the girl? The one who lived with me in that loft?"

"Yes." I didn't want to discuss girlfriends past, but I also wanted to hear the whole story.

"Melanie and I had been together for a few months. She wanted to be an actress. I honestly thought we could have this great bohemian life together. Even though we were young, I was sure she was the one. But I was wrong about us. About her. In a really fucked-up way, Stephen made me realize that."

"How?"

"He slept with her. He told her he knew people and could get her an audition. After that, I had a hard time trusting anyone. I've never had another relationship since. It's always casual, no strings attached."

I wondered if he considered us casual. Although we were temporary, casual was the last word I'd use to describe us. It shocked me how cruel his brother was. I had seen cruelty in its purest forms. I could understand Liam's hatred. I had forgiven more than my fair share, but I was angry again. Angry at this stranger I'd never met. Angry he hurt the man I cared about.

"You're right, Liam. Some things are unforgiveable. I can't imagine how difficult it has to be to work with him."

"We both do our level best to avoid drama. I hate my brother, but we share the same goal, to make the company successful. Sometimes I think our inheritance is our father's version of a cruel prank on me...or maybe on Stephen."

"You've never talked about all the things that happened?"

"Just once. He apologized to me at our father's funeral. He said there were many regrets in his life, and three of the biggest involved me. How he treated me when I arrived. Burning my mum's books, the only thing I had left of her. And sleeping with Melanie. I told him to shut the fuck up or I'd break his jaw again."

"I'm sorry I pried."

He tucked a strand of hair behind my ear. I kissed the corner of his mouth and said a little prayer for him. We both struggled with our past. Although we came from completely different walks of life, we carried the same heavy burdens.

"I've never told that story to anyone. I don't know what it is about you, Miss Costa. You disarm me of my shield."

"Don't look to me for answers, Mr. Montgomery. I'm facing the same dilemma myself."

Chapter 22

Mary

Liam suggested we spend his first free day at Elephanta Island. I'd never been there either. I gripped the railing of the ferry as the ship jostled against the choppy waters of the Arabian Sea. It carried us away from the bustling crowded city that was Bombay. The humid day created a smoky haze, concealing the island.

"Are you seasick, love?"

"A little bit, but I don't want to miss anything."

"Why don't you sit for a while?"

All the benches lining the boat were full, but Liam narrowed his eyes at a group of men taking up an entire bench. "The lady requires a seat."

I didn't know if it was chivalry or Liam's sharp gaze, but several of them rose to offer me their seats. Liam remained standing. He took a bottle of water from his backpack and handed it to me. I made an exaggerated show of checking the cap. He shook his head, his shoulders trembling with laughter.

A herd of tour guides gathered around us once we reached the island. Rather around Liam. They sensed a rich American tourist and used all the guile of snake-oil salesmen to win his attention.

"No guides. We can see it on our own."

Their insistence grew as they warned of mischievous monkeys and the dangerous perils of going into the caves on our own. They ushered us toward the toy train, insisting we should avoid climbing the steep steps.

Liam tilted his head at me, a challenge sparking in his emerald eyes. "The decision is yours, Miss Costa."

"I think we should go for the stairs."

"Excellent choice." Liam waived away the man's insistent warnings. "I have very good sunscreen."

He stopped before we began the climb, pulling me to the side of the stone steps.

"What are you doing?"

He reached into his backpack and pulled out the bottle of sunscreen, the one I'd gotten for him. "You didn't put any on, did you?"

"I forgot."

He squeezed a generous portion on his palm. "Come here."

It was such a little act, the way he covered my exposed skin, yet it caused the heat swelling inside me to match the rays of the scorching sun. Tourists milled around us, but I barely noticed.

"Thank you."

"I'm happy you've never been here, either. We get to do this together." He took off his navy blue cap and placed it on my head, adjusting it until it was snug. "There now. I think we're set for our journey."

He allowed me to set the pace. Gone was the commanding businesslike Liam who made me squirm with heat. This boyish version, in ripped jeans and a faded v-neck T-shirt, stole my breath. We held hands climbing over a hundred stone steps, passing by the chair taxis, where four men hoisted a traveler by painted chair. By the time we reached the top, we were drenched in sweat.

Why me, I wanted to ask. Why do you want me? Why do I want you? What crazy primal desire made us find each other? Was it fate, magic, lust...or a combination of all three?

"Why here?" I asked instead.

"I wanted to see the caves. It's an artistic marvel of sorts."

I'd grown up in Bombay and heard of them, but it was one of those tourist attractions locals didn't pay much attention to. The slabs of stone reflecting the point of the right through my sandals and burned the bottom of my feet. I let out a sigh of relief when we entered the cooling shadows of the caves.

"Wow," I whispered, afraid if I said it any louder I'd disturb the moment.

"Bloody amazing," he agreed, running his hand over one of the massive stone pillars at the entrance. He turned to me, his smile full of excitement. "It reminds me of the pillars in Rome. Funny how architecture crosses borders."

"Yes." I wanted to ask him more about Rome, but he was yanking my hand, itching to get inside.

The caves were a labyrinth of chambers, where Hindu gods and goddesses were intricately etched into the hard rock. Liam squeezed my hand. "Can you believe someone made this? Carved it into hard rock centuries ago using the most rudimentary tools? I can't even imagine it."

The guidebook said they dated back to the seventh century. Unfortunately, many of the formations were ruined by the Portuguese, who used the sculptures for target practice. We stood, a moment of silence passing between us as we mourned the damaged sculptures. "Do you think they saw the figure in the rock first, or created the figure from the rock?" I asked.

"Both. Isn't that what a true artist does? Sees the image within the blank space."

We stopped at the three-headed rock-cut statue of Shiva. It was perfectly intact, unmarred by Portuguese bullets, preserved through the perils of time and natural disaster. Liam was in his element, a mixture of appreciation and awe on his face.

"Shiva," I whispered. "The destructor. I never understood why destruction was worshipped." I shivered against the image.

"I do," Liam said. "How can you create something new without destroying the old?"

"I suppose."

Liam's eyes widened at the nude of Parvati. "Who is this beautiful girl?"

"Parvati, the second wife of Shiva."

"For a Catholic, you sure know a great deal about Hinduism."

"My grandmother was Hindu. She taught me all about the deities. It always fascinated me. Parvati and Shiva had a fierce love. Her love for Shiva transcended everything because she was, for all purposes, Shiva's other half. They were incomplete without each other. She was his strength, his power, and his calm."

"Every man should be so lucky."

His expression reflected appreciation as he took in the intricate statue, all the while his fingers twitched.

I unzipped his backpack, searching for the items I'd put inside that morning.

"What are you doing?"

"Here," I said, holding them out to him.

He stared at the sketch pad and artist's pencils. "Where did these come from?"

"You said I could buy whatever I wanted at the bookstore. I figured they were a bit better than a legal pad and mechanical pencil." I held them higher, pushing them into his chest. "I know you want to draw her."

"Why did you do it?"

He held me with his gaze, and the answer tumbled out before I could analyze the words. "I like to see you happy, Liam."

A look of gratitude flickered across his face. It flashed quickly, but it spoke volumes. He cupped my cheek and pressed his lips against my forehead.

"Come on," I said, clasping his elbow. I pulled him toward a stone step opposite the statue. While the other visitors snapped pictures, Liam captured the image on paper.

"You sure you don't mind me sketching? Maybe you'd care to go shopping while I do this?"

"I'd rather sit with you. Although I am a bit jealous you've found a new subject."

He pulled me close. His lips brushed against my hair. "I appreciate her beauty, but you, Mary Costa, are my one and only muse."

I had no response. I sat, almost as still as the statue, watching him fill the blank paper. Lines turned into shapes and shapes into a figure. As he shaded, the two dimensional form turned into three.

"It's beautiful, Liam."

He kissed my forehead. "You're beautiful."

He stood, brushing off his jeans before holding a hand out to me.

After we'd had our fill of the humbling magnificence of Elephanta caves, we dashed down the stone steps.

"I should buy a souvenir for my secretary," he said, jerking his head toward the market stalls.

Under tarps of blue and gold, we walked along the vendor's stalls, each salesperson aggressively begging for Liam's attention. A white man was a rare and lucrative sight. He stopped to examine a few miniature replicas of the cave carvings.

"How much?" he asked the old woman running the stall.

She quoted a price much too high. I moved in front of him, switched into Hindi and haggled on his behalf. At first she refused to yield. I took Liam's hand, leading him away.

"What are you doing? I wanted to purchase that."

"Just wait," I said, pulling him along.

"Wait for what?"

"Come back, come back," the women said, standing from her stall. If we'd given her another minute, she would have chased after us.

"Impressive, Mary. I could use someone with your talent for negotiation."

"Liam, most prices in India are suggestions, and they are three times higher for you because you're a foreigner. You'd do well to remember that."

"I shall try my best."

We walked back to the table. As he paid her, something caught my eye. I touched the cool, smooth beads of the necklace. I held it up to see the stones against the light.

"You fancy that, Mary?"

"No."

"It's similar to a pearl, isn't it?" he asked, taking it from me.

"They are moonstones. I had one when I was little, but I lost it."

The lady clucked her tongue. "Very bad luck to lose a moonstone."

"Yes," I agreed. "Mine was similar to this, but much larger. It was flat on one side with flecks of blue and yellow in it. It had an M engraved on the flat side."

"M for Mary?" he asked.

"M for Marco. It originally belonged to my grandfather. My *dadima* gave it to me on my sixth birthday when she came to visit us in England."

"Dadima?"

"My granny."

He held up the necklace. "It's a little plain, but it will look beautiful on you. Let me buy it to make up for the one you lost."

"You buy this for her and the lady's luck go up, up, up," the woman said, her thumb pointed to the sky. "Way way up."

I took it from him and handed it back to the vendor, wishing I'd never picked it up. "I don't want it. I was only looking."

"Stop being silly."

I shook my head. "No really, I don't want you to buy it."

"I insist. Allow me to make you happy."

"Not this, okay?"

"Why not this? It's the only thing that's caught your interest since we've been here."

"We should head back. The ferry's leaving."

The woman chimed in, not missing an opportunity to make another sale. "Yes, yes, rare and expensive, but I give discount. Special stone to"—she clasped her hands together—"join as one forever."

Exactly why he shouldn't buy it. He took out a bill from his wallet. I pushed his hand away before they made the exchange. "I don't want it, Liam!" It came out hysterical and high-pitched, causing the other vendors and tourists to stop in their tracks.

I hurried toward the dock. His longer strides caught up to me quickly. The back of his hand brushed mine.

"Do you always overreact when a man wants to buy you jewelry, or is it just me?"

"No other man has ever tried to buy me jewelry."

The ferry wasn't as crowded on the way back, and we sat together on a bench. The sea was calm, the sun setting over Mumbai Harbor.

"Was it the expense? Because I promise you, it was nothing for me. Or is it your pride again?"

I didn't answer.

"Are you planning to ignore me?"

"It wasn't the expense or my pride."

"Then what was it?"

"Didn't you hear what the lady said to us?" Did he not understand we were a fortnight, not a forever? "Do you really want to tempt fate?"

His deep rumbling laugh mocked me. "Seriously, that's your reason? I don't believe in charms, or talismans, or any of that rubbish."

"I believe in them." My feelings for Liam were tangled and messy. I could barely understand them, and I had no desire to invite fate into the convoluted equation.

"It's a stone mined from the ground. It has no special powers."

"Those carvings chiseled into rock had no meanings either then?"

"That's different."

"I disagree. And I know how powerful the moonstone is."

He placed his hand under my chin and tilted my face toward his. "Convince me then. Why is it powerful?"

"Originally, the moonstone I had belonged to my dadaji. He gave it to my grandmother."

"Forgive me. I'm still confused how that explains anything."

I sighed. "There's more to the story, but it's nothing you'd be interested in."

"You've never been more wrong, Mary. I am very interested in everything when it comes to you. Tell me."

His long fingers threaded through mine. His face looked so earnest, I found myself telling him the story my grandmother had told me years ago in a chilly flat in London.

"He was on leave from the army and in Bombay for just one day. Dadaji...Marco decided to go for a walk on the beach before the night of debauchery he'd planned with his pals. He stumbled upon the saddest, most beautiful girl he'd ever seen. Her name was Savitri. You see, her parents had arranged for her to marry a man twenty years her senior, a man with a reputation for cruelty."

I stopped the story, a small surge of emotion welling up for my dadima. He tightened his arm around me.

"Anyway, the two of them strolled the beach until day turned into night, each voicing their fears of an uncertain future. Marco's mother had given him the stone when he enlisted, saying it would protect him in any battle. It was the only thing of value he owned. That night, he gave it to Savitri."

"He didn't believe in it?"

"On the contrary, he believed with all his heart. He gave it to her because he was more concerned for her safety than his own. There is a legend surrounding the moonstone they both knew of."

"What legend?"

"If a moonstone is given with a pure heart under the light of the full moon, it binds you to the other person. It's a connection that can never be severed, regardless of time or distance."

"I take it they ran off and married each other?"

I bit my cheek. "Not as easy as that. They went their separate ways. It was an impossible situation. He couldn't abandon his post and was due to leave for Kashmir the next day. She would not go against her family's wishes and be casted from her home. Dadima said fate could be beautiful and cruel. They had seen both sides of it."

"But they got together eventually? I mean, obviously they did. Him being your grandfather and all."

I was surprised how vested he was in the story, a story I'd only repeated to Hannah who never had the years with our dadima as I did. "Not for a long time."

"They kept in touch though?"

"They never exchanged any information. They married other people and lived miserably for a great number of years. She kept the moonstone, though, and made the same wish upon it every night."

"For them to be together."

"That would make sense, but her mind wouldn't even work that way. She wished for his good health and happiness wherever he was in the world. Can you imagine how unselfish it is to wish the person you love most a happiness that doesn't include you?"

"What I really can't grasp is that they fell in love in one day."

As a child, I devoured the story, hanging onto every word, begging Dadima to tell it to me again. But as an adult, I, too, had become cynical and suspicious of it. "She said it wasn't just her reaction to him, but how he made her feel about herself."

"How did they find each other again?"

"They were both scarred by their lives. Marco lost his wife in childbirth. His son died soon after. Meanwhile, Savitri's husband blamed her for not producing an heir. He punished her by splashing acid in her face, disfiguring her for life."

"Are you serious? Please tell me he got what he deserved."

"Liam, you're missing the point. This isn't a revenge story. It's a love story."

"Sounds like a tragedy to me."

"Well, if you'd let me finish, you'd see."

"Sorry. Please continue."

"After that, her family finally stepped in and helped her secure a divorce. Not an easy task. Although she was free, she couldn't come to terms with the image in the mirror. She built a shelter around herself, never leaving the house in the daytime. At night, Savitri would walk the same stretch of the Arabian coast where she'd met Marco so many years before. She clutched the moonstone in her hand during these walks. That's where he found her, ten years later, under the light of a full moon. He'd returned to the same spot himself, trying to reclaim the memories of that night. She wore a scarf across her face. He would have missed her if it wasn't for the shining stone in her hand. When he approached her, she ran from him, believing she was hideous. He didn't give up, though. He waited for her to come back to the beach. After many nights of waiting, she did. This time he wouldn't let her run. He begged her to let him see her face. When she finally lifted the veil, he took her in his arms and told her she was the most beautiful girl in the world. You see, the stone worked its magic."

"A moonstone can cure acid burns?"

"No, Liam, nothing can do that. Her face was damaged beyond repair. But Marco wasn't in love with Savitri's face. He was in love with her soul. He didn't care what packaging that soul came in. Whatever scars they'd suffered, whatever time had lapsed, whatever distance had kept them apart all disappeared. Fate had tested them in the worst ways, but their love never died."

"They got married and lived happily after?"

"Eventually, but it took a while. He courted her, appearing at her house every single day. He made friends with her father, who was not the sort of man to approve of his daughter having a second marriage, much less to a Christian. But Marco had a strong will and the kind of personality that won people over. Savitri started believing in the possibility of a future. When she married Marco, she made a decision to never cover her face after that. She saw herself the same way he saw her. When I was a child, I always thought people darted out of our way because my dadima was so tall and regal in her elegant silk saris. It wasn't until I was older I finally recognized the looks of disgust and fear in their faces. It occurred to me why I had never noticed before. It wasn't just because I was a child. She ignored those cruel people and walked with an air of dignity. To me, she was always the most beautiful woman in the world. Whatever had happened on the outside never concealed the deep beauty and strength inside her. She had this incredible wisdom that blossomed in the shadow of deep tragedy. Do you understand?"

He tucked a strand of hair behind my ear. His attention hadn't wavered since I started the story. "Completely. It's a beautiful story, Mary. Thank you for sharing it, love."

After swallowing the large lump in my throat, I managed a weak smile. "So I've made you a believer in charms and talismans and all that rubbish now?"

"I'm still skeptical about the properties of moonstones, but I understand the rest of it. The moonstone is just a symbol, though. It didn't really bring them together."

I crossed my arms. "How can you be so cynical? Especially considering where we just came from. You felt the magic in the caves as much as I did."

He was thoughtful for a while. "It was fine art. Who couldn't appreciate the hard work and effort that went into something like that?"

"Admit it. There was a spirituality in those walls."

"Okay, I agree with you. But I still think you give an inanimate object too much credit."

"When I first held the stone, I felt something like a charge go off inside of me. I knew it held magic. You won't change my mind on that."

"I'm not trying to. I don't want to change a thing about you, especially not your mind. You have a way of seeing the world that makes me believe it's a better place."

I had no response. In a way, he did the same thing for me.

"When did she give it to you?" he asked.

I closed my eyes tight, remembering that special night. "When she visited us in England. She told me the story then, too. My dadima was sad because she had owned more expensive jewels Marco had bought for her over the years, but she had sold them to fund my father's education. She said the moonstone was the only thing she had to give me. I wish I could have told her then, but I didn't have the right words."

"Told her what?"

"I wouldn't have traded it for all the jewels in the world. Dadima said it would keep me safe and sweeten all my dreams. Eventually, I was supposed to give it to my own true love so it would bind us forever. I would sit in bed at night and clutch the stone, saying a prayer for my dadaji in heaven and for my dadima. She never complained or even told us, but I knew she was sick. The visit was the last time I saw her. The moonstone was my inheritance. It's as magical to me as the lotus flower."

I cursed myself for the way my voice wavered. For taking the context of our temporary relationship and applying a deeper meaning than necessary.

I blinked in surprise. The boat wasn't crowded, but the few passengers aboard were all staring at us...at me. They had been listening to the story. Liam followed my gaze. His attention had been on me, so he hadn't realized it either. Had I been speaking too loudly? Perhaps the story just drew in people, the way it had drawn me in when I was a child. The way it drew in Hannah when I'd told it to her. Although she had never met our dadima, she'd begged me to tell the moonstone story over and over. She'd even picked up random stones on the beach and pretended they were Dadima's moonstone.

"We can talk about this later," Liam said.

"Do you still have it?" a woman in a bright red sari asked. The girl next to her, probably her daughter, wiped her eyes.

"Have it?" I asked.

"The moonstone?"

"No." Although I hadn't meant to share the private tale with Liam, let alone a ship full of strangers, I wasn't upset. My dadima would have rejoiced if her story inspired people. Papa had always said good stories had a way of connecting people. I had seen that firsthand. Unfortunately, the ending to this story was a huge disappointment.

"What happened to it?" she asked. Her daughter gripped her mother's shoulder, perhaps warning her against the blunt question, but I could see she was also curious.

Liam cleared his throat, his irritation apparent. "I really don't think that's important."

I tilted my head to take in his expression. He wanted to defend me, to bring me under the same shield he used to keep people out. I squeezed his hand. "It's okay, Liam. I don't mind." I turned to the lady. "I honestly don't know what happened to it. It wasn't in my bag when we returned to India."

She looked disappointed in me, as did the other passengers. "You lost it?" She made a tsking sound. "This is why you should not entrust children with family heirlooms."

"You're right, Auntie."

"That's not the point of the story," Liam said a little harshly.

I'd always suspected my mother might have placed it in the discarded box with my father's old records. A horrible vindictive act of revenge against Dadima for not leaving her with any expensive jewels. Or revenge against my papa for never making enough money to buy her new jewels. Or maybe even revenge against me for never wanting any of the things she wanted for me. I'd never had the courage to confront her and seek the truth. After all, no answer would have satisfied me. If she had done it, I would never forgive her. Even as a child, I understood the complexities of our relationship. I craved her love, but even more so, I needed to love her without any reservations, without the restrictions she placed on me. So I hid my suspicions and told Papa that Dadima's moonstone had disappeared in transit. He saw how upset I was, so he didn't ask for more details or make me feel guilty. I never admitted there was a chance I lost it…not even to myself. There was a hole at the bottom of my bag, after all. If it turned out to be my fault, I wouldn't have forgiven myself for being so careless. Instead of acknowledging either possibility, I pretended I wasn't ready for the moonstone's magic, so the Hindu gods my dadima worshipped took it from me for safekeeping. In this way, I maintained my own piece of mind.

Liam stood, his long shadow falling over me. He took my hand. "Come with me."

He led me to the ship's railing. Standing behind me, he wrapped his arms around my waist. We were both sweaty from the long day with its intense heat. The scant breeze coming off the water felt good. We watched the city come into view. He whispered in my ear to preserve our private moment, although no one was listening to us anymore. "I'm sorry, Mary. Your grandmother sounds like an astonishing woman." His warm accented voice sent a shiver up my spine despite the humidity.

"She was."

"Your inheritance wasn't the moonstone. It was the story."

I had never thought of it that way.

"You also inherited other things from her that are more precious than any gem. You got her strength, her grace, and her compassion. Those things live on. She lives on because her spirit exists in you. You have it in here." He put his hand over my heart. Wasn't this similar to what I'd said to him not so long ago? Except it was much deeper than what I could say. My hand gripped the railing because my knees were shaking so hard I doubted they could sustain me. They might not have if he didn't hold me so close.

"I hope so, Liam. Thank you."

"Welcome, love. But there is no need for hope. It's true." He kissed my temple. He tapped his fingers on the railing, the sound akin to a beating drum. "You have it all wrong, though. Although I'm not a true believer about moonstones as you are, you have to realize purchasing the necklace for you would not have the same effect."

"What do you mean?"

He gestured to the horizon. "The sun is just setting, and I'm pretty sure it's not a full moon tonight. It would have just been a small gesture on my part. I like seeing you happy, too. I'm trying, and most likely failing, to figure out just how to do that."

I turned to him. I caressed the angles of his face, so perfectly sharp they appeared chiseled like the statues in the cave. "I am happy. I don't need clothes or jewels. This moment right here, watching the sunset with you, makes me happy."

"Still, I wish you'd let me do more for you."

The heavy emotions anchoring me down suddenly lifted. "You're right. We should go back and get the necklace."

His mouth dropped. I laughed and smacked his chest. "I'm kidding."

* * * *

When we got back to the hotel, Liam asked where what I wanted for dinner.

"You choose, but I have to take a shower first." I winced when I caught my reflection in the ornate mirror hanging above the dresser. My hair had morphed into a frizzy, damp mess. He stood behind me, a raw hunger in his eyes as if he saw something different in the mirror than I did. Perhaps it was the visit to the island or that I'd revealed such a private story to him. But something crackled between us, an energy that needed to be released.

"Me too." His eyes locked on mine. He took my hand and led me into the bathroom.

We peeled our sticky clothes off each other. Under a spray of warm water, his powerful, large hands ran soap over my body.

"Turn around," he said.

I leaned against his solid chest while he washed my hair with almond-scented shampoo. It was his long talented fingers, not the expensive shampoo, that left my scalp tingling. The water rinsed away any doubts I harbored about my feelings for Liam. His powerful hands massaged my shoulders and back, relaxing every tense muscle.

"My turn," he said. He gripped my hips and moved us in the opposite direction. He leaned his head back. The water drenched him, running in rivulets down his hard, lean body. I lathered the soap. I pressed my palms against his chest, working my way down in slow circles. He closed his eyes and mumbled something appreciative. I went lower. His eyes snapped open.

"Mary..." He stretched the syllables of my name in a combination of whisper and growl that left my body trembling and my mind daring at the same time.

He looked down at my hand encircling his erection. What was it about him that made me so bold? I wanted to surrender to his lead and be in control at the same time.

"If you keep doing that, I'm going to fuck you against this wall. It wouldn't be a good idea since we don't have a condom in here."

"That can be remedied, sir."

He cupped my face, his thumb brushing my cheek. His kissed my forehead. The moment was a complete duality—lusty and tender at the same time.

He skimmed my nipples with his thumbs. They turned hard at his touch. Then he slid his hands further down my body. He traced my slit, back and forth. I gripped him tighter, urging him deeper, but he kept the same movement. I'd found myself at the crossroads of agony and ecstasy.

"Please."

He entered me, his green-brown eyes piecing me with the same depths as his finger.

"You are so wet, Miss Costa."

"Well, I am in the shower."

"And you're a smartass, too."

He covered my mouth with a rough kiss. Two of his fingers curved inside me, thrusting gently. I lost focus on my own task. Until he reminded me, circling his hand over mine, showing me how he preferred to be touched, all the while his fingers penetrated me. As I moaned, he quickened his speed, his mouth laying hungry kisses down my neck. He was a conductor, commanding my body to sing as it never had. His thumb pressed into my nub.

"Liam, please."

"Please what? You have to finish the sentence." He traced the shell of my ear. Then he nipped my earlobe. "Finish the fucking sentence."

"I want you inside of me."

His fingers moved faster. "I am inside of you, lover. Do you want more of me?"

I nodded, unable to articulate anything. His lips followed the trail his fingers had made until he fell to this knees. His pressed his mouth against me, his face tilted up, his eyes watching me. It was too much and not enough. I flayed my arms for something to steady me. He hooked my leg over his shoulder. His hands tightened their grip on my waist. I lost myself in Liam Montgomery. In the feel of his mouth, the touch of his hands, the lusty glint of his eyes. Whatever dream this was, I didn't want to wake. I came undone.

I would have fallen if he hadn't kept me steady. He turned off the valve. He dried me off with a soft, thick towel. Then I did the same for him. He carried me to the bed. The satin sheets cooled my over-heated skin. I shivered against the drop in temperature until he slid on top of me, pressing me into the soft bed.

He ripped the condom packet in his mouth. With one swift move, he was inside me. I lifted my hips off the bed to meet each one of his urgent thrusts. His damp hair was the color of sand, yet it had the feel of soft silk under my fingers. Just as he'd done in the shower, he adjusted my leg over his shoulder. It felt different in the horizontal. He stretched me. My body welcomed him. Each drive was deeper than the last, leaving me breathless. Liam pulled all the way out. I groaned in protest. He lunged inside me again. I screamed in pleasure. He held my wrists down, his arms flexing with each movement. Our eyes locked. We spoke in the language of lovers…grunts, moans, and growls. Yet, in that moment, we communicated with depth and precision.

"Come, Mary," he said in his slow, commanding way.

When every nerve in my body cried out with my climax, he reared his head back, releasing a deep resonating growl as he peaked.

He buried his head in my neck. I wrapped my arms around him. It would have been an embrace, except it was more than that. We clung to each other.

"So…room service tonight?" he whispered.

Chapter 23

Mary

I went to Papa and Hannah's graves every day while Liam worked. He asked me what I did during the day, but I couldn't talk about Hannah to him. The pain was still too raw, a wound that would cause me to bleed out if I opened it again. Really, he could have asked the driver since he insisted I take a car, but he never did. I appreciated the way he respected my privacy.

I was three quarters into the book when the scent of lavender perfume surrounded me. Dressed in an elegant pink sari with a white paisley border, she looked regal. The fresh bouquet of marigolds in her hand made it clear who tended my family's graves.

"Hello, Mary," she said, falling to her knees next to me. I winced, imaging the stains on her beautiful sari.

"Divya." What could I say to this girl...woman? This friend, sister, and savior whom I'd abandoned all those years ago. Her fingers threaded through mine around the cloth beads tangled in my hand. I opened my mouth, but no sound came out. She embraced me. The way she shook caused me to do the same. We cried together at the cemetery. We cried for the little girl we both loved.

"Where have you been, *yaar*?" she finally asked, once our sobs had been reduced to quiet breaths.

"In Jaipur."

She arched her brow. "Why there?"

I shrugged. "I don't know."

She nodded. "Are you here for good? Amira will be thrilled."

"I'm leaving the day after tomorrow."

"Oh," she said, her mouth tilting downward. "You weren't even going to visit me?"

A million arrows of guilt pierced me all at once. "I'm sorry, Divya. I missed you...I did. But I thought seeing you would be like...revisiting my past. I convinced myself forgetting everything, even the people I loved, would help me survive."

"Did it?"

"No. Seeing you doesn't make me sad. It makes me remember there are people who love me. I'm so sorry, sister."

"There is nothing to forgive, *didi*. Nothing at all."

I smiled brightly as my guilt disappeared. "You look beautiful." I fingered the intricate border of her sari.

"I told you I'd wear pink every day."

"And pray to Ganesha."

"Yes, I do that, too."

"When I was in Jaipur, I would go to the Hindu temple and do the same. I also closed my eyes and thought of Amira whenever I heard the bells signaling the Muslim call to prayer."

She nodded. "Amira and I put up Christmas trees. We exchange little gifts. I think the three of us imprinted on each other. Maybe we should make up our own religion. Something to teach all of the hateful people of the world that we are not so different."

"I doubt it will work."

"I missed you so much."

"You're not angry with me?"

"We are sisters, our bond stronger than blood." She cupped my chin. "I will always welcome you home."

I gestured to the graves. "Thank you for taking care of them."

She straightened. "I loved Hannah, too, Mary. So did Amira. We take turns coming here. This isn't an obligation. It's a duty for us. An honor."

"I know."

The gold of her *mangalsutra* glinted against the sun, and red sindoor powder colored the part in her hair, the sacred Hindu marks of a married woman. The fact that she led a normal life filled me with a surge of happiness for her and hope for myself. "Congratulations. Tell me about him."

Her radiant smile took my breath away. It was an expression I'd never seen on her. "I'm blessed, Mary. He's a wonderful man. You'll come to my house for dinner tonight and meet him."

"I can't."

"What rubbish? You must. I'll invite Amira. So much has happened, Mary." Divya clapped her hands. "Amira wrote a book."

"I read it."

"What did you think?"

"I'm not sure. A part of me is upset. She took our tragedy and made a profit from it."

"She changed our names. All the profits benefit a charity that helps young girls."

I felt ashamed for not knowing that. "It was a good book. She managed to make it sound hopeful despite the subject matter. I loved her description of Hannah as the girl who brought light to the darkest places."

"Yes, I thought it was very apt myself. We'll all catch up tonight." Divya's determined expression made it difficult to argue with her.

"I'm sorry, Divya. I want to see the both of you and meet your husband, but I'm here with someone. He doesn't know about my past."

"Who?"

"A man I met in Jaipur." The statement sounded simple, but thinking of the right words when it came to Liam was difficult.

"I see. Is he…is he…?"

"He is a very good man," I answered the question before she asked it.

"Bring him with you. I want to meet him."

"We're not together like that. We are temporary. He's traveling on business."

She shrugged. "Whatever he is, I'm grateful to him for bringing you here. Come, no?"

I had made her and Amira my sisters. Actually, Hannah had since that first day we spoke. We'd lived through hell together. We were stained with the Devil's mark, and we'd each worked through it in our own ways, but a deep friendship had formed between us. I couldn't leave Bombay without seeing them.

"I'll be there."

"Bring him, too. As your sister, I have to approve of any man in your life, temporary or otherwise."

Chapter 24

Liam

I hated seeing her distressed. I wasn't sure if it was me accompanying her, or the invitation itself. Mary had fidgeted the whole way to her friend's flat. We stood at a door that was decorated with a lemon and lime garland. She clutched the box of sweets we'd brought. I had suggested a bottle of wine, but Mary thought sweets were more appropriate, though she admitted she hadn't been invited to someone's house for dinner since she was a young girl.

She opted for a more traditional outfit tonight. She took my breath away in the purple and gold sari. I wanted to slowly unwrap the yards of fabric covering her. Her dark hair cascaded in rich waves down her back.

"You don't have to stay," she said.

"You don't want me here, do you?"

"No…I mean yes, I want you here."

What was I doing here anyway? Our agreement was a fortnight. It didn't include meeting friends. But I would be lying to myself if I didn't admit we'd broken through thresholds that suggested our relationship was only a tawdry affair. Still, she held back. She wanted space. I was a man peering through the slits of narrow blinds she controlled. I hated it. At the same time, I didn't want to push so hard that she pulled away from me…again.

"I'd love to meet your friends, but if you'd prefer, I'll return to the hotel and send the car back for you. If you believe they'll judge us, or you for being with me, I won't put you through it."

She shook her head. "I would not be friends with someone who'd pass judgment on me."

"Then what's your problem? Are *you* judging us?"

I saw it then. I thought she was embarrassed about us, but there was fear in her eyes. Now I had no choice but to stay. I would have left her if it alleviated her stress level, but I could not abandon her in fear.

"The only judgment I have when it comes to us is that it feels good. This...us."

"Then ring the buzzer." I gestured to the bell.

She pressed it.

The woman who answered smiled widely at Mary. Then she took a gander at me and stepped back, her mouth dropping. "Mary didn't tell me you were white."

Subtle.

"I am?" I asked, feigning a look of shock that matched hers.

She lifted an eyebrow before she broke out into a huge laugh. "Sorry, can we start over?"

"That would be great."

Mary cleared her throat. "Divya, this is my friend, Liam Montgomery."

Friend? What did I expect?

"I'm her boyfriend," I said, stepping over an invisible threshold without invitation.

I was debating asking for a redo when I caught Mary's smile.

"Boyfriend," she repeated, or rather corrected.

"Wonderful." Divya folded her hands and bowed slightly. "*Namaste*. Welcome home."

Welcome home, she'd said. Not 'welcome to our home'—a slight shift in syntax, but a huge difference in meaning.

"Namaste," I responded.

Mary took off her shoes. I followed suit, taking note of a crystal bowl on the credenza in the entryway. There was nothing extraordinary about it, except for the necklace of patterned cloth beads circling the inside of the dish. They were similar to the ones Mary used as a makeshift rosary.

"You still have them," Mary said without looking at Divya. It was as if their friendship surpassed the normal pleasantries.

"I pray with them every day. They are my mala, after all."

"My rosary," Mary said, fingering the beads.

"My subha," a third girl said, appearing in the doorway. She wore a long dress with a colorful scarf wrapped over head and draped around her neck. I remembered it was called a *hijab*.

"Hello, Amira," Mary said.

"There she is. The lost daughter returns."

The anger radiated off Amira with such intensity that we all got a smattering of embers.

Mary embraced her. "I missed you too, Amira."

"How are you, sister?" Amira asked, her voice losing its serrated edge.

"Better now, yaar. Better."

Amira turned toward me. "Who is he?"

"Mary's boyfriend," Divya said. She put her arm around Amira.

"Boy friend." She'd separated the singular word.

"Boyfriend," I corrected.

"Come inside before you let flies in," Divya said, practically dragging Mary into the living area.

Divya lived with not only her husband, Virkram, but also his younger sister, Sita, and Vikram's parents. I caught the parents' names during introductions, but didn't dare try to repeat them because I would royally screw up the pronunciation.

"You can just call them Uncle and Auntie," Vikram said, clapping me on the back. "And I'm Vik."

Mary handed them the sweets. I glanced over at their well-stocked bar and whispered, "See, told you we should have brought wine."

"You brought us wine. What kind?" Vik asked with excitement. Either I wasn't very discreet, or he had the hearing of bat.

"Actually, we weren't sure what your preferences were, mate." I gestured to the bar. "I see you're a scotch man."

He nodded. "Nothing like a good scotch. Let me pour you a tumbler."

He had the good stuff. Chivas Regal twelve-year. I decided to have a case of Chivas Royal Salute sent to him. Nothing said "thank you" like a bottle of forty-year-old scotch.

"You're British," Vik stated.

"Guilty. I've been living in the States for the past twelve years."

"Cricket or football?" he asked.

"By football, you mean soccer?"

He tilted his glass toward me. "You really are Americanized."

I laughed. "Quite right, mate. But to answer your question, rugby is my game."

We launched into a conversation about sports, which veered into politics and business. Everyone spoke English, probably for my benefit. I glanced around for Mary, who was having a serious talk with Amira and Divya. Her eyes met mine as if she knew I was staring. She smiled. Not the carefully guarded smile she usually wore. No, this smile was radiant and happy.

"You sound like Thor," Sita said. She was around sixteen. Either she had something in her eye or she was winking at me. "Look a bit similar, too, except for the darker hair color. Not that it doesn't fit you." Definitely winking.

"Thank you?"

"Who is Thor?" Divya asked.

"Oh, *bhabhi,* try Hollywood for a change."

"Why? What's wrong with Bollywood? Bollywood doesn't teach you to flirt with another woman's man." Divya pursed her lips and pinched the girl's earlobe in jest.

Usually, a baby's cry was not a pleasing sound for me, but right now, I rather appreciated how it shifted everyone's attention. "This is who I wanted you to meet the most, Mary," Divya said, coming out the bedroom with a fussy toddler on her hip. "Mary and Liam, this is our son, Manoj."

"He's beautiful," Mary said.

I agreed. As soon as Divya put him down, he tottered over to me in the drunk man's stagger that was adorable on children, but not so much on adults.

"Hi there," I said, drawing down to his eye level. He must have mistaken my face for a drum because he smacked each side of it with his chubby hands.

"Manoj!"

"Quite all right," I told Divya. "Hello mate, we're gonna be friends, right?"

He jumped up and down, clapping his hands in agreement.

"See, Manoj likes Thor," Sita said, a look of satisfaction on her face as if she had somehow proven a point.

"Thor," Manoj said, but he couldn't quite sound the *T* so it came out more like "whore." Some children are born beyond wise. I had no doubt Manoj was one of them.

Despite Divya and Vik's corrections, he called me "whore" all night, making me look bad in front of my girl. She did her best not to encourage him or giggle, but her face flushed each time the little tyke did it. It didn't matter, though. Manoj captured everyone's attention. We'd stop talking whenever he brought out a new toy or said something. When Mary played with him, all her layers fell away. They sat on the floor together, building a stack of blocks. She asked him about each of his toys, listening with rapt attention as if he were giving her the secrets to life.

"Hope you don't mind vegetarian food," Divya said, setting a silver platter in front of me. The platter had several small silver bowls lining it.

"Not at all. This is a *thali*, right?"

"That's right. You've done your homework."

"Mary's been teaching me. It looks delicious."

"Licious whore," Manoj agreed.

Manoj and his grandparents had already eaten so they retired early. I thought the little tyke was adorable, but I was relieved to have a break from his name-calling.

I looked down at my plate. I didn't consider myself a foodie, but I enjoyed a good meal as much or possibly more than the next bloke. Divya had cooked up a feast. We ate our fill of the spicy eggplant curry, and the flavorful stew of potatoes and peas. When the heat level rose a bit too high for my English sensibilities, there was a cool mint yogurt with cucumber to quench the fire.

"How did you two meet?" Amira asked, her eyes focusing on me. Innocent question or the beginning of an interrogation? I wasn't exactly sure.

"At the Wilshire hotel in Jaipur," Mary said.

Divya turned to Mary, her eyebrow arched. "You were staying at the hotel?"

"I was working there."

"In management?" Amira asked.

"As a maid," Mary said.

"What were you doing working as a maid?" Amira prodded.

I probably should have stepped in six questions ago. I missed Manoj and his timely ability to deflect tension with his interruptions.

"It doesn't matter what she was doing there," I said. "I'm just grateful she was there."

Amira wasn't impressed. "What are your intentions?"

I had no fucking idea.

"Amira!" Divya said, using the same chiding voice she used on her child.

"We should know. She's our friend."

Mary was the one who answered. "Amira, do you think I'm a dimwit?"

"Of course not."

"Then stop treating me as if I can't make my own decisions. You are my closest friends. You're my sisters. But neither of you are my mother."

Neither of them were her emergency contact either. *Why did you leave them, Mary? Do you always run away from the people who care for you?*

"What are you doing on Wednesday?" Amira asked Mary. "I want to take the two of you to lunch."

"Mary's leaving day after tomorrow," Divya said.

"What? But that hardly gives us any time."

"It gives us tonight," Mary said.

Tonight was far too inadequate. Even I knew that.

"When I saw Mary at Hannah's grave, I pinched myself. I thought I might be dreaming," Divya said, maybe to change the conversation.

Amira smiled for the first time. "Do you remember how Hannah would beg for stories? It's funny that I was the one who wrote a book, when it was Mary who had the best stories."

"I just retold the ones I'd read in books or heard from my papa," she said, not looking up from her plate.

I had no idea who Hannah was. Just one more rung in the never-ending ladder of stuff Liam didn't know about Mary.

The chatter turned to other things. But the tension returned when Vik asked Amira how her book was doing.

"You're an author?" I asked.

"Hardly. I wrote one book."

"What's it about?"

It seemed an innocent question, but the way everyone looked at each other, I might as well have stepped on a landmine.

"It's the story of four young girls who find solace in each other."

"Sounds interesting," I said, not taking my eyes off her. "Perhaps I should read it."

Amira turned to Mary. "Have you read it?"

"I did. You wrote it well." Mary adjusted her bracelet, something she often did when she was nervous, as if the thin, cheap metal shielded her from the world. "It's not the kind of book you'd be interested in, Liam."

"Perhaps one day, you'll recommend it to him," Amira muttered under her breath.

"Dessert," Divya said, standing quickly. She hit Amira's chair. "Come help me."

I saw it then. The same burned-flesh tattoo Mary had, but instead of her back, it was on Divya's arm. I was sure Amira had one, too. I realized this dinner party wasn't the best idea. They needed time together to catch up and decompress and whatever else without all the interlopers hovering around them, including me.

"Why don't the two of you come to the hotel tomorrow?" I suggested to Amira and Divya. "The hotel spa is rated the best in Mumbai. I can set something up for the three of you."

Amira smiled for a brief second before she frowned again. "Thank you, but Divya's house is over an hour from mine. The Wilshire is in the center of the city. It will take at least two hours, maybe three depending on traffic, to get there," Amira said. "It's not something I can manage on a day trip."

"Then stay the night. I can arrange a room for the three of you. It would give you a chance to properly catch up. I can send a car for you in the morning."

Amira and Divya discussed it. Mary stared at me with such gratitude I looked away. The truth was, I wanted to do this for her, but I didn't at the same time. As selfish as it sounded, giving up a whole day with Mary was a huge sacrifice for me.

* * * *

"Thank you," she said as we headed back to the hotel. "You made plans for us tomorrow, didn't you?"

"Yeah, but nothing that can't be canceled. It's really no big deal."

"It is. It's a very big…deal." She said the word slowly, as if she wasn't sure it fit. Mary turned to the window. A steady stream of rain belted against the car. "Amira can come off brash, but she's just protective."

I didn't want to discuss Amira. "I figured that out for myself."

"Did you have a good time?"

"Yes. Who is Hannah?"

"My sister. She passed away."

"That's where you've been going every morning with the book? To visit her grave?"

"She asked me once to read it to her, but I never did. It doesn't make sense, but I wanted to atone for it somehow. So I've been reading to her every day. It's silly, no?"

"Not silly at all. Why didn't you tell me?"

"This was supposed to be a fun trip."

"Mary, I care for you. Whatever you've suffered in the past is part of who you are. You don't have to hide anything from me."

She grew quiet, her hand adjusting the cheap bracelet.

"I don't think you should read Amira's book."

I sighed, dragging my hands through my hair. "Fine. I won't."

We remained quiet the whole ride back to the hotel. She was lost in tangled thoughts, and I wanted nothing more than to cut through them.

Trust me, Mary. Lean on me. Let me in.

When we arrived home, we retired to our nightly rituals. I knew her routine now. She'd wash her face with pear-scented soap. We brushed our teeth. She used my mint mouthwash. She combed through her long silky hair. She usually slept in one of my T-shirts instead of the expensive lingerie the sales girl had picked out for her. Truth be told, I preferred it as well.

"I have to work for a while. There are some calls I need to make. It's daytime in the States."

"Of course."

She sat on the bed, reading a book while I worked. I glanced over at her a few times. It didn't take a genius to figure out she wasn't reading. I could see her working through something. It was in the way she curled a strand of hair around her finger. The rigid way she sat. How she bit her lower lip.

"Ready for bed?" I asked when I'd finished my last call.

"Sure." She placed the book on the nightstand, the bookmark in the same location as when she'd started.

I switched off the lights. We lay in silent dark.

"Are you angry with me, Liam?"

"Not angry. I understand your need to hide away from the world. I wish you wouldn't hide from me, love. We both agree there is no future for us."

"Yes." The simple affirmation cut me. Maybe because I wanted her to argue. "We're from different worlds. We are just two people crossing each other's paths and finding a little happiness in the short term."

"Right. I mean, I have a life in New York. And you…well, you'll find the place where you truly belong. I have no doubt about it." I rolled over to her. Stroking her hair, I laid myself bare. "But baby, just because we don't have a future, doesn't mean I don't want all of you in the present. Maybe it's reckless of me."

"It is."

"I've let you see me…the real me. Even the not-so-attractive parts."

"There is nothing unattractive about you, Liam."

"I'm certain I was unattractive when I was puking in a bucket."

She laughed. "Not even then."

I suppose it was easier because we exist here, but not anywhere else. Maybe it would help you to talk about your secrets."

"Why is it important to you?"

"Someone hurt you once. You carry the weight of it. Perhaps it would lift some of that burden to talk about it."

She pressed a hand to my shoulder, easing me on my back. She straddled me, her hair falling over us like a canopy. I sat up, unsure if I had the strength to push her away. She kissed my neck. I turned on the light. "Am I just your fuck toy, Mary? Is that what I am?" I took her wrists and held her back. "Answer me, please."

"No, Liam."

I wanted to wipe off the look of rejection on her face, kiss it away, because the very last thing I was doing was rejecting her. I sighed. "It's neither here nor there because I made a promise to you. I intend on keeping it. So here we are Miss Costa. You ready to fuck? Isn't that your preference?"

"Are you complaining?"

"Not at all. Your appetite matches mine."

Really, this was the part where I would have returned her affection. This was how we communicated best maybe. She still straddled my lap. I could feel her pulse quickening as I held her wrists. I let go. She reached over and turned off the light. Neither of us moved, though. The sounds of our heavy breaths filled the space between us.

"I'll tell you what it's about if you'd like."

"What?"

"Amira's book."

What the hell was this? I was trying to have a real conversation with her, not a book club discussion. "I'm not interested."

"It's based on a true story."

"Did you not hear what I said?"

She pressed her forehead against mine. "I heard everything you said. You need to listen to me now. I'm really good at telling stories. And I want to tell you this one. For God's sake, Liam, please shut up and let me talk."

The rain pelted against the building, a drum sounding some kind of warning. But the time for warnings had passed, hadn't they?

"I'm listening."

Her voice broke through the steady beats of rain that mingled with late-night Mumbai traffic. "Amira's book is about four girls who end up in a place with no hope. A place that catered to wealthy men who would pay a premium for well-bred, intelligent girls. They actually had a business model. They posted random photographs of young girls walking to school or shopping. They sent them off into the world for their clients to peruse like a catalogue. 'Made to order' was their motto." She laughed, cynical and bitter. "When someone was chosen, they plucked them right from their safe lives. One of these girls was supposed to be taking her little sister to a music class. But this girl was selfish. Even though the music lessons were her sister's favorite activity, she didn't care. She skipped them, dragging her sister to the movies instead. Of course, her sister would never complain. She had this spirit about her. All she wanted to do was make people happy. Even selfish people."

I wasn't sure if Mary hugged me or I hugged her, but we stayed in each other's arms. I wanted to offer the right words to comfort her, but Mary wanted to finish the story. She'd asked me to shut up, and I did just that.

"The show got out much later than she expected. If the stupid girl had done what she was supposed to, her sister would have been at home in bed where she belonged, not walking the streets late at night. They were trying to hail a cab when a van pulled up. A man jumped out and held a rag over the girl's mouth. She woke up with a horrible headache and no recollection of how she got there. The girl prayed her sister had escaped, but she hadn't. No one even had to drug her. She came willingly because she didn't want to leave her older sister's side. There were other girls there, too, all kidnapped right off the street, drugged, and taken to a huge house far from their homes. The inside of it looked like a king's castle, but this was no fairy tale. They were stripped of their identities, treated like products. Their flesh was marked with the corporate logo. They had to act out certain scenes, requests from the customer who chose them. Sometimes, the guards were asked to act in the scene as well. Sometimes the actual customer would show up."

She blurted out each sentence, as if she'd been trying to get the story out without thinking too much about it. God, I'd asked her to tell me, but now I wanted her to stop. I had suspected, but imagining the truth and hearing it was the difference between seeing the sharpness of a blade and feeling it pierce your skin.

"How is it possible to get past something like that?"

"They helped each other. They came up with places where they could go when they didn't want to be present. The mind is pretty powerful. It lets you escape even when you can't move. They trained themselves to do that. It helped. That, and the youngest among them, the selfish girl's sister, still had joy in a place where joy shouldn't exist. It spread through all the girls."

"Stop referring to her as the selfish girl. It wasn't her fault. The blame isn't hers to bear."

"Part of it is."

I held her back. "None of it is, Mary. Not any of it."

"Amira would agree with you. She didn't call the character a selfish girl either."

"How long were they there?"

"A few months. It didn't seem like enough time to blur the past and erase the future, but that's what it did. Eventually, they realized that despite how hard their families were looking, no one was going to find them. They formed a plan. Looking back, it shouldn't have worked. But it did."

I swallowed the rage threatening to consume me. Mary didn't need my rage. She needed my comfort. Still, I couldn't avoid asking the question, so I blurted it out. "The men who did this? What happened to them?"

"They were punished with lengthy prison sentences. But during the escape, the girl killed one of them. She took a hot poker they had used to mark her back and beat him with it. She had a fury in her. It was destructive and took root inside her."

"He deserved it and a lot worse, too." *God Mary, let me take this hurt from you. Let me carry it off your shoulders.* But as much as I wanted to, I knew I couldn't. "The…the…" I couldn't use the word customer. "The men who made the requests?"

"Everything was handled with privacy, hidden behind layers of code and data. These were powerful men. They protected themselves."

I wanted them to meet another end. I wanted to be responsible for that end. Maybe she sensed that, because she ran her fingers though my hair.

"It's okay, Liam. Don't waste your time being angry with the monster you can't see."

"Tell me the rest."

"That's the end."

"It's not though, is it?"

"No. The fourth girl, the one who gave them hope at the darkest times, caught an infection in her lungs from the damp room they were kept in. She died a few months after."

"I'm so sorry, Mary." The rain thundered against the building. I held her closer.

"With therapy and help from their families, the surviving girls were able to regain their lives. Remarkably, none of them carried any diseases from the experience. Coming back to their normal lives was difficult, but they managed it. It was a miracle in a way. No matter how dark their pasts were, they were able to find a future. To rise clean and free of any of the filth that once surrounded them."

She'd buried her head in my chest. I stroked her hair, my thoughts running rampant. "Except for one. She wasn't free, was she?"

"Yes, except for one. One of the girls could never get the stain of what happened off her. She blamed herself for her sister's death. Her father blamed himself for what had happened to both his daughters. When his already broken heart finally gave out, the girl buried him next to his youngest daughter. All she wanted was to lay beside them. She had escaped, but not survived. The other girls, the ones who treated her like a sister, suspected. They found her, still breathing, in a bathtub full of blood. It was too late, though. She was dead inside."

"So she ran away to Jaipur and became a maid."

Mary nodded. "That's not in the book, but yes, it's what happened. Her heart turned black, and she kept everyone at arm's length. She wanted to be left alone with no memories, no expectations, no obligations. She worked at a hotel for years under a constant cloud of despair of her own making. She swore she'd never speak of it again. Not to anyone. She never let anyone in, not that it mattered. No one ever looks at the maid anyway." She titled her head at me. "Almost no one."

She let out a deep breath, which led to a soft cry. Then the dam broke. I held her, cursing myself for not having the right words and for asking her to return to the very place she'd done everything to avoid. She sobbed for a long time, the emotion too great to be contained.

"Maybe you lost part of yourself, but you were never dead. You are the bravest person I've ever met."

In the dim light coming through the window, I saw her flinch. "Liam, it's just a story. You asked what Amira's book was about at dinner. I told you the story. I'm really good at telling stories. They used to call me the storyteller because I could take other people's stories and retell them in my own way. It's a few chapters in a book. That's all it is."

I could see what she wanted from me. She wanted to tell me and ask me not to acknowledge it at the same time. Because if she did give it to me straight out, she'd invite the darkness back into her life. It would hover between us in every breath and kiss and conversation.

"Okay, thanks for the synopsis. May I ask one thing?"

"What?" There was an unmistakable warning in her question.

"Is the girl happy now? Is she where she wants to be?"

She exhaled a soft breath. "Yes, she is. Happier than she ever thought she could be. But like I said, this isn't a fairy tale. She's not looking for a prince to save her. You understand?"

"Yes."

"I'm really tired, Liam."

"Me, too."

She crawled off me and slid under the covers. I shifted beside her and held her tight.

"Hey, Mary," I whispered after we lay down. She hadn't fallen asleep. Pale light crept though the windows, followed by the sounds of birds with their crazy squawking.

"Yes?"

"I understand about the lotus flower now, and why they are special."

I felt her smile against my chest.

"Finally."

"Yeah, finally."

Chapter 25

Mary

I'd had the most amazing day with Divya and Amira. Liam had made sure we'd received the royal treatment. Today, as we were leaving, he'd asked me if I'd finished the book. I couldn't hide my regret…not from him. Despite my protests, he insisted we come to the cemetery before leaving for the airport. As I read the final chapters to Hannah, I was thankful for this man beside me, who had shown me such kindness and warmth. When I neared the end of the book, my voice grew thick with emotion. The words came out garbled. How many tears could one person shed?

"Take your time, Mary."

"We're going to miss our flight."

"We'll catch the next one. There are hundreds of flights from Mumbai to Goa. It's no problem. Finish it."

My hands shook, and the words blurred. "I want to, but I don't think I can." I closed the book.

"May I?" he asked.

I didn't know what he meant, but he placed his hands on the book to steady it. I relinquished it to him.

He flipped to the page I had left off. Clearing his throat, he said, "Hannah, I'm not as good at this as your sister, but I'll do my best." Liam continued where I'd stopped, his rich baritone voice perfectly matched for Dickens's prose. He kept his arm around me the whole time. When he finished, I realized I'd never grieved for Hannah or Papa. "Thank you."

"Welcome." He looked at the gravestones. "Tell me about them, love."

"We should go, no?"

He shook his head. "We have time."

I told him about Papa and his love of books. About how he made up little games for Hannah and me at the dinner table. Opening my wallet, I pointed to the one picture I had of the three of us. Hannah wore a yellow frock with tiny butterflies around the collar, Papaji was in his sweater vest, and I wore my green plaid dress, my hair in two plaits. Liam sat behind me as I told him about how much Hannah had loved her silly dress. How she wanted to wear it every single day. Then I talked about Hannah. Really talked about her.

"Hannah had Down Syndrome. My mother thought it was a curse, which reflected badly on her. When I was younger, I blamed Hannah for our mother leaving. I never said anything, but I wasn't the most patient sister. I wish to God I appreciated her when she was alive. Papa did. He said Hannah's extra chromosome came from the angels because she was too good to get what everyone else got. I never understood it at the time, but looking back, I realize she had the biggest heart in the smallest package."

"She knew you loved her, Mary. It was enough for her. Let it be enough for you."

He stood and placed a rock on each grave. I recognized them as the flat rocks that decorated the hotel entrance.

"What are you doing?"

"It's a Jewish tradition."

"You're Jewish?"

He nodded. "I'm not exactly practicing, but yeah, my mum was Jewish, so I'm Jewish. Is that a problem?"

I shook my head, smiling. "Not for me."

"Good."

"Why rocks, though?"

"I'm not sure what the real context is. Mum said it was because rocks are solid and forever, like people. The deceased never really die. Not when they loved someone. You see them in the people they left behind. I didn't know Hannah or your papa or your dadima, but I feel as though I do. Not just because you told me about them. They exist in you, Mary. You honor their memory."

Tears dripped down my face as I touched the rocks. I didn't have the right words to show how much I appreciated this beautiful man.

"Liam, that's lovely."

"Do you want more time, sweetheart? I can wait in the car if you'd like some privacy."

I squeezed his hand. "I'm ready to move on."

My answer had more than one meaning.

Chapter 26

Liam

Mumbai was spectacular buildings and bustling crowds, whereas Goa was tropical breezes and sand. The Wilshire Goa sat right on the beach, shining like a polished majestic jewel. The grounds, all fifty-five acres, were immaculate. It was hard to believe this bright blue water belonged to the same Arabian Sea that surrounded Mumbai. Everywhere I looked, there was a spectacular view. But the greatest sight by far was Mary's reaction as she took it all in.

"Is this real?" she asked, almost to herself.

"It is."

I pulled her close while the bellman retrieved our luggage from the car. We entered the sun-drenched atrium of the facility.

"It's amazing."

"Yes, gorgeous." I wasn't referring to Goa. I was talking about the girl who stood next to me.

The chime of church bells drew her attention.

"Do you know when the last service is?" she asked the bellman.

"Madam, they only have one service every Sunday. It just let out."

"Thank you."

The mention of next Sunday filled me with cold dread. I remembered what else Goa was. Goa was goodbye.

I shoved the thought away. We had another week, and a paradise to spend it in. That was enough for me. It had to be enough. I managed a wide smile as we walked into the impressive lobby, which reeked of elegance and class mixed with just the right amount of Zen.

I'd changed the booking to a private garden villa overlooking the beach. She hesitated as she walked into the room, as if the breeze coming through the veranda might turn into a powerful wind and blow her back outside. I placed my hand firmly on her lower back.

Truthfully, I really didn't have to come to Goa. In Jaipur, I needed to see if anything could be done to salvage our property. In Mumbai, I wanted to check out a new space for another hotel. Here, in Goa, our profits soared and our ratings matched. There wasn't much for me to do. I just had to see the property for myself. It impressed the hell out of me. Now, with her here, I planned to take advantage of my first real holiday.

"Is all of this for us?" she asked, her eyes widening as she took it in. It had been designed so the interior blended with the outdoors. Because we were on a hill, it resembled a luxury tree house.

"All for us, Lotus Girl."

"This pool. Do we share it?"

"No, it's called a plunge pool. It's for our use only. There are several much larger community pools, not to mention the entire Arabian Sea is our backyard, but this one…this is all ours. There's an outdoor shower, too. Because the trees surround it, no one will see us if we decide to go without our skivvies."

She laughed, a throaty, good-hearted laugh. "It's surprising how different all the properties are."

I undid my cufflinks and unbuttoned my shirt. She watched me.

"A lot of that is location." I poured out two glasses of madeira. "You build a hotel to suit the location, not the other way around. The architecture should always fit the atmosphere. That's what separates luxury from everyday accommodations. We are not a one-size-fits-all operation. Of course, there are times when you end up missing the mark, like Jaipur. Anyway, you don't really want to hear all this."

"No, it's interesting."

Maybe it was interesting, but the last thing I wanted to think about was work. "I took the week off. No conference calls or meetings or anything. Except for touring the facilities, I plan to spend this week with you."

"That's probably the best present you could have gotten me."

"What shall we do first? Go swimming? Or we could go snorkeling or sailing or take a tour of the old Portuguese churches. What's your wish, Miss Costa?"

"Those are a lot of choices."

"Wait, do you know how to swim?"

"Yes. I'll warn you I haven't been in a while, so I might not be able to keep up with you."

"Keep up with me?" I scrounged around my luggage for my trunks.

"I've seen you swim. Back in Jaipur. You swam every morning. Probably over a hundred laps at least."

I turned and stared at her. "You were watching me."

She took in a sharp breath. I let myself look at her. Look at her exposed shapely legs in the shorts she'd worn. Her rounded breasts, rising and falling, in the black tank top. The way the breeze coming through the open sliding door played with her hair. The sexy pout of her mouth as she took slow steps toward me.

"Perhaps we don't go swimming just yet...sir."

Maybe it was because she'd opened the blinds all the way for me. Maybe because we'd struggled with our emotions and feelings for each other until we reached this point of comfort. Maybe it was the lure of this location, the taste of salt in the air, the bottle of wine we'd shared on the plane. But I didn't think it was any of those things. The way our bodies reacted to each other was a different animal entirely. I was a hungry man craving a girl with a need so fierce it should have frightened me. Yet, it didn't.

I unbuckled my belt. It hit the solid wood floor loud enough to echo. "I promise I'll be gentle one of these times," I said, "but right now is not the time."

"I don't want gentle either." She unbuttoned my trousers.

Our lips crushed, hands roamed, and some clothes were shed while others were ripped. I threw her onto the bed. My teeth grazed her nipples. She left deep scratches on my back. I held her wrists down, my forehead against hers. I kissed her as tenderly as I could before my dick strained for satisfaction. Yet, I didn't let it rule me. I ran my nose down her neck to inhale her spicy vanilla scent. I took the wine glass and poured fine madeira across her breasts. She giggled, tugging on my hair. I swirled my tongue across her body until I'd gotten good and drunk on madeira and Mary Costa.

"Liam..." My name stretched, a soft humming whisper. She said it slowly and seductively, her fingers raking through my hair.

"What's wrong, love? Want some wine?"

Although she'd turned me back into a horny teenager, I had the experience of a seasoned lover. I planned to utilize all my techniques to please her. To worship her like the goddess she was. Her mouth parted. I traced the outline of her lips. She sucked on my finger.

Oh, fuck.

I shifted up. I trailed my hands down, my fingertips following the curve of her voluptuous body. She squirmed beneath my touch, begging me for more. Grasping her hips, I spun her around. She gripped the sheets with tight fists as I slowly followed the path of her spine with my tongue. The swell of her arse, the arc of her hips, and the narrowness of her waist led to a nicely defined dip on her lower back. I did everything with a shaking control on the verge of chaos. Finally, I could hold back no more. I knocked over a lamp fumbling for my wallet. Damn fucking condom.

My attempts were clumsy, but I managed to get it on.

"On your knees."

I bent over her, a possessed animal desperate for his prey. We fucked with the frenzy of rabbits and the ferocity of lions. She leaned her back into my chest. My arm was beneath her breasts. She reached her arm up and caressed my cheek. I wanted to come, but even more, I wanted to see her face when I made her come. To see the expression where she was the least guarded and she belonged to me completely. I flipped her. Then I entered her again, deeper this time.

Her warmth closed around me. Her hips bucked, meeting each of my thrusts. Mary closed her eyes and parted her mouth, her moans turning to grunts. She curled her hand around my bicep, her fingers pressing into my skin. When she let go, it was impossible not to follow. In the harsh breaths of the aftermath, I held her close, the wild beats of our hearts merging. We were tangled limbs bathed in sweat and fine Portuguese wine.

I cupped the back of her head and kissed her softy. "I have to paint. I have to paint you. I have to paint you right now."

I figured she'd tell me I was mad. Maybe I was. How could I explain my need to fill a blank canvas was similar to my need for her? How I wanted to memorialize with detailed strokes all the delicious lines and curves I'd touched and tasted. But I didn't need to rationalize it.

"Where can we buy paint?" she asked with a bright smile.

I laughed, feeling incredibly lucky this girl understood me in a way I'd never been understood. I rang the concierge, requesting an assortment of items. He delivered in less than an hour, just enough time for us to use the outside shower and go for a quick dip in the plunge pool.

I tipped him generously, grateful he'd managed to find most of them. A few fine artist's brushes of various sizes, a proper canvas, and a standard set of acrylics paints.

"Take off your robe," I said.

She looked unsure.

"This is for me only, Mary. No one else will ever see it. I promise you."

She undid the knot. I slipped the thick white robe off her shoulder. It landed in a puddle at her feet. The candles cast shadows and gave the room a soft glow.

"This might take a while, so I asked the concierge to get you something to pass the time." I handed her the paperback novel. I flipped on the light on the nightstand.

She smiled. "A highlander romance. It's perfect."

"Hope you haven't read that one."

"No."

I positioned her on her belly. She crossed one leg over the other, an incredibly feminine pose I rather liked. I brushed her long wet hair to the side so it grazed just one of her shoulders. I adjusted her arm so she was up on her elbows.

I kissed her temple. "Thank you." There were no other words for my appreciation at the reawakening of a dead desire.

"Liam, no one has ever looked at me the way you look at me. I'm afraid you see something that doesn't exist."

I tried not to be irritated that she couldn't recognize her own beauty. Stroking her hair, I said, "You have no idea how breathtaking you are. But I'm not going tell you. I'll do my best to show you. You need to be still for me. Understand?"

"Yes."

"Yes?"

"Yes, sir."

I slapped her ass playfully. "Let's begin."

Scriabin's "The Poem of Ecstasy" harmonized with the lapping surf coming through the open window. The piece sounded even more implicit…erotic tonight. There was no easel, but I covered a table with towels. I used a large piece of cardboard to palette my paints. I created a makeshift easel balancing the canvas against a vase. I doled out big blobs of rich, thick colors full of possibilities. Dipping the brush in the glass tumbler filled with water, I began.

The brush in my hand felt right, as if it had been waiting for me to reclaim it. I had no proper scraper to move and mix the paint, so I used my fingers, a business card, and a butter knife to give life to the image in my head. I flicked water on the canvas to dilute the hues when needed. The tools were rudimentary, but they worked.

I looked at the girl who had laid herself out for me. The one who made me question all the things I took for granted. Titan had his Venus. Manet had his Olympia. Dali had his Gala. And I had my Mary. I took liberties painting her with a cool blue tone surrounded by bright tangerine light.

When I had finished, the wax candles had burned down to liquid pools, barely holding up their wicks. Every classical piece on my iPhone had played twice. My fingers cramped. I was exhausted and exhilarated.

She had maintained her posture the whole time, although I could see her muscles strain, felt her need to stretch her limbs and shift her position. "I'm done, baby."

She collapsed onto the bed.

I sat on the edge of the mattress and ordered room service, holding the phone in one hand and rubbing her back with the other.

"You're stiff." She had to be in pain.

"A little. May I see the painting?"

"Let me take care of you first." My fingers kneaded into her warm, dark flesh until her knots released.

She made a noise somewhere between a sigh and a moan, a definite signal of contentment. "Better?" I asked.

"So much better."

The food arrived. We sat on the bed, feasting on oysters, crab, and lobster. We sipped vintage port. I fed her fat, juicy strawberries dipped in spiced dark chocolate.

We stacked all the empty plates back on the room service cart, and I took it down to the kitchen so she wouldn't be distracted. When I returned, Mary walked with slow steps toward the table where the canvas lay drying. She turned her head back to me, asking for my permission. I nodded, although I was nervous about her reaction.

I had planned to paint some stars around her. But my hands didn't always follow the plans of my head. The stars had become much larger and rounder, almost translucent, with flecks of deep color inside them. Instead of a starry sky, I'd painted a landscape of moonstones around her, each one emerging like bubbles from a field of lotus flowers. Her figure floated above them, her body lined in black and colored with cerulean blue number seventeen.

She gasped, her hand flying to her neck. She blinked her eyes, bending closer for inspection. *Do you see the moonstones, Mary?* If I had one right now, I'd give it to her.

"I didn't expect it to be so detailed. It's different from your sketches."

"I always enjoyed sketching, but painting is my passion."

"It's beautiful." She swallowed, her voice thick with emotion. "Do you really see me this way?"

"It's the way I see you, and it's also the way you are."

She hugged me. I picked her up and carried her back to bed. This time when we made love, it was slower.

"I don't think I ever want to leave this room, Liam," she whispered right before we drifted to sleep.

I don't think I ever want to leave you, Mary.

Chapter 27

Mary

We did eventually leave the room. We'd had a few solitary days where we explored nothing but each other's bodies. We napped on a hammock in the afternoons. I wouldn't think something made out of rope would be comfortable, but it was the best sleep I ever had.

But the sea called to us. Liam and I walked the sandy shores of Baga Beach, our feet skimming the ocean. He splashed me playfully. I jumped in his arms when I saw a crab. He tossed me into the water, drenching my sundress. He kicked up sand as he ran off. I chased after him. He let me catch up.

We fit the image of tourists well. I wore a floppy sunhat and a bright sarong with yellow and pink paisleys. He dressed in a casual white linen shirt, open at the collar, and long khaki shorts. His skin had turned a golden bronze, adding even more definition to his sinewy muscles. His hair was disheveled. The dark stubble from not shaving for two days accented his strong jawline. How did Liam make being messy so beautiful? We had made it to the marketplace before his palm brushed against my backside. He gave me a look that spoke volumes. We headed straight back to the room.

We sat at one of the beach restaurants drinking from straws pierced into fresh green coconuts. I read him passages from my highlander novel. Then he crooked his finger. I leaned closer to him, inhaling his clean, spicy, masculine scent. He whispered to me, his voice tinted with an imitation of a Scottish brogue. "You're a fine bonny lass, ye are. I aim tae have me way with yee." Heat flushed my face as desire filled my belly. We retired to the room.

In the mornings, he'd swim in the plunge pool. I treaded water in more ways than one. I dressed in a bikini for him in the privacy of the veranda. We didn't make it to the room. We had sex right in the pool.

Today though, there was no turning back. We were in the middle of the sea on a private chartered boat.

"You ready, Mary?" he asked, checking the snaps on my life vest for the third time.

"Are we really going to ride a motorbike across the Arabian Sea?"

His excited laugh startled the birds resting on the ship's ledge. "It's called a jet ski."

"The word 'jet' doesn't make me feel any better."

He placed his hands on my shoulder, his gaze turning serious. "I'll keep you safe."

I believed him.

Liam jumped on the vehicle like a cowboy mounting a horse. I was less graceful and required his assistance.

"I wish I could take you for a ride on my bike," he said as we were floating on the water.

"You have a bicycle? Is it built for two people?"

He let out another laugh, but it held no humor. "It's a motorcycle. A Ducati, actually."

"I don't know what that means."

"Doesn't matter." The jet ski throttled to life as he turned the ignition. "Anyway, we got this thing, yeah?"

"Yes, we have this." *We have today, Liam. Stop thinking about tomorrow and make today last as long as possible.*

"Trust me?" he asked, his grin mischievous.

"I would still be on the ship if I didn't trust you."

I'd still be on land.

I'd still be in Mumbai.

I'd still be in Jaipur.

"Good." He pressed the handlebars, the engine roaring much too loudly for such a small machine. "Just the same, hold on tight."

I almost fell back when he took off. Tightening my grip, I adjusted. My eyes shut tightly as the wind whipped my hair in all directions. I'm not exactly sure when my body stopped clenching and I started to enjoy the flips my stomach made as he took a turn. A mixture of exhilaration and adrenaline coursed through me. Water splashed our feet and sprayed our faces. I pressed close to him, the scent of sun and sea and Liam drifting everywhere. He rode fast, the machine either cutting through or jumping the waves. I tightened my hold around him as we flew in the air, my voice hoarse from excited screams. He slowed down and eventually came to a full stop. The boat was a distant dot in the horizon.

"Why did you stop?"

"Let's trade places."

"You're joking."

"Why not?"

"I can't drive this thing. I can't even drive a car."

"I have no doubt you can do anything you want to, Miss Costa. Don't worry. This is simpler than a car, and there isn't anyone out here."

His praise gave me a boost of confidence. "Okay," my mouth said without checking in with my brain.

"On three, we'll stand. Me to the left. You to the right. And we switch. Count with me."

We counted. I thought for sure I'd fall into the water, where a shark would be sharpening his teeth, ready to make a meal out of me. But I didn't. Liam instructed me how to maneuver the boat and adjust speed.

"Ready?" he asked.

"Yes." I replied with more confidence than I felt.

Liam's large hands rested on my thighs, his fingers spreading. I pried his wrists off me.

"I'm nervous enough without your naughty distractions, sir."

"Well, I have to hold onto something." He gripped my hips, shooting a flurry of butterflies into my tummy.

"Not there either."

He wrapped his arms over my breasts. I could feel the tension even through the padding of the life vest. "Liam!"

"Okay, keep your hair on, lass." He moved them over my waist. It still made my insides quiver, especially combined with the tender kiss on my neck, but it would do.

I swallowed back any hesitation. I went much slower than Liam did. But I had to admit, it felt amazing to drive this strange vessel.

"I'm doing it."

"You are."

"Liam, I'm driving a jet boat!"

"Jet ski, baby. Can you drive it bit faster, though? A school of sea turtles just passed us."

I laughed, revving the motor higher. I didn't go fast enough to jump any waves, but the speed was definitely challenging.

"Stop."

I slowed us down to a crawl and then stopped. "Did I do something wrong?"

"No sweetheart, you were doing well. I wanted you to see this. Look over there." I turned in the direction he pointed to. Several gray fins rose out of the water.

"Are those…"

"Dolphins."

Thank God, I thought they were sharks. "Wow."

We watched them for a while. They leapt out of the water in a graceful dance. Liam leaned his chin on my shoulder. He traced the line where the swimsuit met my thigh. Then he slipped his fingers underneath the material.

"What are you doing?"

"Relax, no one can see what I'm doing…except maybe the dolphins. They have very good eyesight, you know."

I opened my mouth to protest, but only a moan escaped as his fingers slipped inside me.

"You like that, baby? You're always so fucking wet for me. I love it."

I closed my eyes and ground my hips into his thrusts.

"Dolphins have no official mating season. They fuck all year long." His voice turned husky. I parted my mouth and licked my lips. He nibbled on my ear, his erection pressing into my back. "They are very sexual creatures."

"Just like you," I said in a strained tone.

"And like you, too, my little nymph. Or should I say nympho?" He kissed along my jawline with soft, wet presses of his lips.

My legs shook. The waves rocked us while his fingers rocked me. Small pulses of pleasure built higher and higher until a tidal wave exploded.

"Ready to trade places again?" he asked. "I think it's your turn to pleasure me now."

"Liam, you have the libido of a dolphin."

"And the sharp bite of a shark," he hissed before he nipped my neck.

* * * *

That night, Liam and I dined on the boat, gorging on fresh Kingfish ceviche and prawn ravioli cooked in curry leaves. Before I met him, all seafood was disgusting to me, but he made trying new things exciting. The chilled wine, flavored with apple and dark grape, tasted as smooth as Sidr honey.

When the ship reached port, we decided to laze about on the beach and watch the sun go down. We laid on towels. Liam rested his back on a boulder, his arms around me.

"I've never seen anything like it," he said, gesturing to the other beachgoers nearby.

"What? People enjoying a sunset on the beach?" I asked.

"Cows enjoying a sunset on the beach."

I peered closer at the direction where he pointed. He was right. Two large cows casually roamed the sandy shores as if they were out for a romantic walk. They mooed to each other. We laughed.

"He's telling her he wants some tail," Liam said.

"She's telling him to behave since they're out in public."

As the sun set, Liam's smile waned. He laid his head in my lap. I combed my fingers through his thick hair. Usually, this was the kind of thing that would have one of us suggesting we return to the room.

"Is something wrong?"

"We only have two more days."

I stopped touching him. "I know exactly how much time we have, Liam. I keep track, too."

"Today I was thinking about this particular property."

"You're not working this week, remember?"

"Still, I couldn't help notice the hotel lacks something."

"It has every amenity anyone could want."

"It doesn't have a bookstore."

"It's a good idea."

"I'm glad you feel that way. I need someone competent to run it. Someone who has a passion for books. The position would come with nice accommodations. Of course, I'd have to come and check on the progress personally."

"Stop it."

"Just hear me out, Mary. We can make it work."

"We agreed. When this is over, it's over. It's not as if I live in a different village than you. I'm across the world."

"Don't you feel the same way I do?"

"That doesn't matter."

His mouth tightened into a grim line. "It's the only thing that matters."

"Don't you understand? I don't want to spend my days wondering when you'll call, when you'll visit, or who you're with when you're not with me."

"I wouldn't be with anyone else."

"That's not the point, Liam."

"Well then, come up with another fucking solution."

"There isn't one. You're being irrational."

He sat up, narrowing his eyes. "I'm irrational? Tell me you don't feel what I do. Fucking tell me."

"Let's head back."

"You're avoiding the question."

I stood, brushing the sand from my skirt. "Don't spoil the next two days with this." The warning edged somewhere between frustration and fear.

He didn't respond. We walked in silence, each lost to our own thoughts.

"At least tell me where you'll be."

"I'm not sure yet."

"When you are there, you still won't tell me, will you?"

I spun around toward him. "What difference would it make?"

"How will I know if you're all right?"

"You won't, Liam. That's the point. We'll go on with our lives without the constant worry." I didn't add the other elements—the jealousy, the loneliness, the resentment.

"What if you need me?"

"What if you need me, Liam? I can't exactly get to you. Don't you see? It's better not to spend our days filled with thoughts of each other." I wanted to sooth the hurt in his face. Didn't he understand? I wasn't doing this to hurt him. Nor to hurt myself. I pressed my hands against his chest. "I will cherish every moment with you, but I'm going to let you go because it is the best thing for both of us. In this way, I can look back on these memories with fondness. I can pray for your happiness…even when it doesn't include me. Do you understand?"

"No, I don't fucking understand. Why are you doing this to us? What is it? Some stupid sense of pride? Or are you just this stubborn?"

It wasn't stubbornness. It was self-preservation. Having him in and out of my life would be like mourning him over and over. I had prepared myself for our end, but I lacked the strength and discipline to do it repeatedly.

"I'm following our agreement."

"Your fucking agreement. Your bloody rules."

"You agreed to them." I inhaled a deep breath. "Let's not fight." I kissed the exposed area of his chest, tasting his salty skin as I unbuttoned his shirt.

"What the hell are you doing?"

"I think you know…sir." My hand cupped him.

The raw anger in his eyes both attracted and frightened me. I had become a moth drawn to an intense fire. He gripped my arms and pulled me against him. "I'm trying to have a conversation."

"We can't have one when you're not listening to anything I say. Right now, there are better things you could be doing with your mouth than arguing with me."

He pushed me against a wall, his harsh kiss claiming me. "Is that what you want? You want me to fuck you?"

"Yes, Liam. Fuck me. Fuck me hard."

His eyes blazed with fury and lust. He gripped my hair and pulled it back, exposing my neck. The hard muscles of his chest collided against me. His teeth grazed me, nipped me, bit me. He wanted to mark me, punish me. I wanted to be punished. He threw me on the bed and stripped off my clothes. He crawled toward me on his knees. He slid a silk tie across the detailed metal scrollwork of the headboard. Grasping my wrist, he secured it with the tie. He kissed the scar on my other wrist with such tenderness I almost cried. Then he secured that one, too.

"Tell me you want this," he said.

"I want it, sir."

"If I go too far, you'll ask me to stop." It was a statement, a command, and a question all in one.

"Yes."

"Don't speak again unless you want this to end." He covered my eyes with the widest part of another tie. The soft silk cooled my heated skin.

His fingers slid down my body. They taunted me with soft touches. They startled me with hard grips. I arched my hips, begging him to stop teasing. He'd made my punishment some special brand of torture where I wasn't allowed to touch him. Not allowed to voice my need for him. Not allowed to reciprocate his affection.

The mattress lifted as he stood.

Music leaked into the room, its harsh beat raw, primal, and sexual.

"Nine Inch Nails," Liam said, answering the question I wasn't allowed to ask.

The room grew darker. He must have switched off the lights. I thought he would leave me like that. Alone and tied up with a million rampant thoughts. But he didn't. My heart beat faster with each of his footsteps. Hard liquor and sweet limes mingled with his own masculine scent. Time had no measure. It was his moist breath on my ear. It was his long fingers trailing down my flesh. It was the sticky, sweet honey he dripped onto my skin. His tongue warm, wet, and hungry lapping it up. Mmmm…soft bristles of a paintbrush, circling my nipples, causing them to harden like little pebbles. Every nerve ending rose up in silent protest. Warm wax from a melted candle against my tummy. My entire body became over-sensitized with each new sensation.

I parted my legs, begging him for more.

He stopped touching me.

"You don't get to make any decisions right now, my love. You're abiding by my rules. You'd do well to remember that."

Liam bit into the soft flesh of my thighs. He gave me a tongue lashing, which I never wanted to end. I surrendered to the language of lust, one spoken with no words. He swirled his tongue, tasting me…savoring me. But he pulled back right before I climaxed. I cried out in protest.

"Shhh."

Slowly, his fingers spider-crawled up my legs. He slid them inside me. He thrusted gently, his thumb circling my tense bundle of nerves. His movements became faster and deeper, drawing me in. I climbed to the peak, unable to control the moans escaping me. He withdrew.

"No!"

"What's wrong? You want me to stop."

Through clenched teeth, I made my stance. "I want you not to stop."

His laugh was cynical and sad. "That's not how it works, baby."

He pressed the head of his cock against my opening, sliding it up and down. I bucked my hips. But he never entered me.

So this was my punishment. He'd take me to the precipice without releasing me. It was cruel and excruciating. I hated it. Another part of me, which only existed with him, also loved it.

He played with me for a long time, a tiger toying with his prey. My body riled in response. A hot tear slid down my face.

"Please…" I begged. "I can't."

"Can't what? Submit to me? Listen to me? Let me love you?"

I never had a chance to answer. The faint sound of ripping foil gave some great relief.

Time had become Liam inside of me. Liam grunting with each thrust. Liam's harsh kisses. Liam's strong hands cupping my bottom, his long fingers pressing into my flesh.

Time had become my enemy.

Chapter 28

Liam

We laid in the hammock for an afternoon siesta. She had fallen asleep. Her silky hair tickled my skin. I couldn't sleep. The minutes ticked by, their speed almost exponential. I hated it. I also didn't want to miss a second. I had the sketch pad, but I didn't want to sketch her. Not today.

"What are you drawing?" she asked, rubbing her eyes.

I looked at the blankness of the page. "Nothing. Did you have a good nap?" I asked, kissing her head.

"Yes. Your chest is my favorite pillow." She sat up, stretching her arms. "Will you paint when you're back in New York?"

She'd asked me that once before. "Didn't we have this conversation, lass?"

"You said maybe. I wondered if you had a more definitive answer now."

"I doubt I will."

"You should."

I started sketching, well, more like doodling. The chaos in my head wouldn't translate to anything real.

"That's the beach, isn't it?" she asked.

"Yeah, I suppose it is. Or at least my interpretation of it." I handed her the pencil. "You draw something."

"I can't draw."

"Sure you can. Everyone can. Let's collaborate."

She took the pencil from me, her hesitation apparent.

"Dogs?" I asked her when she'd finished.

She elbowed me. "Cows. The cows on the beach."

"Oh, yeah, I see it."

"Told you I couldn't draw."

I took her hand and kissed the pad of her fingers. "I beg to differ, lass."

"What's your life like in New York?"

I shaded the black spots on the cows. "Why do you ask?"

"I just want to imagine you as accurately as possible."

I handed her the pencil. She drew a bottle of wine.

"It's nothing exciting."

"New York isn't exciting?"

"Oh no, New York is definitely exciting. I'm not."

She didn't reply. She wanted a real answer.

"I get up a six and go for a run."

"Even in the winter?" she asked, drawing a huge sun.

"Every day. I need it. Then I go to work."

"Then?"

"When I reach home, I have a late supper. I have an indoor pool so I go for a swim sometimes or read a book."

"Your building has a pool?"

"My flat has a pool."

"Like the plunge pool?"

"No, Mary, like an Olympic-sized pool."

"How can you fit a whole pool inside a flat?"

She had no idea how rich I was. "It's four levels."

"I see." She chewed on the bottom of her lip. "What kind of books do you read?"

"Usually texts on economics. Occasionally, a classic here or there."

I took the pencil from her and sketched a few books. They were open, flying through the air like the huge hulking birds of Jaipur.

She listened to all of it as if she was trying to imagine it herself.

"Told you it wasn't exciting."

"I hope you paint, Liam. It makes you happy, and you're very good."

"You're a little biased, don't you think?"

"Maybe biased, but I'm not blind. You have talent."

She handed the pencil back to me. I drew the boat we sailed on the other day. She drew something that made me laugh.

"Is that your favorite body part of mine? I'm concerned about the proportions."

She looked at the paper and back at me, her mouth gaping. "It's a banana and two mangos. It represents our breakfast."

"Oh, thank God, I thought for minute I had Elephantitis."

She laughed. I tickled her. The hammock swung violently.

"Stop, you're going to make us fall."

I kissed her forehead. "Okay," I said, laying on my back again. "Draw something else."

She drew what I imagined was a plate of ceviche. Back and forth we went until it was apparent we drew our time in Goa. Then I sketched the caves in Mumbai and jars of honey. She drew the fountain in Jaipur. I added the lotus flower blossoming in the middle of it. Soon, we had filled up the entire page.

"What shall we call our masterpiece?" I joked.

She didn't smile when she looked at me. "How about we call it *The Best Time of Mary's Life?*"

I threw down the sketch pad and took her in my arms. "Or *The Best Time of Liam's Life*. It's also a fitting title."

"Liam…"

"Yes, love."

Tell me you changed your mind, Mary. Tell me you'll try.

She gave me a soft, sad smile, the kind of smile that had goodbye written all over it. "My world is better because you were in it."

I resigned myself to this fate. "Mine, too."

Chapter 29

Mary

I combed through his hair, still messy from this morning's tryst.

"You stay at the hotel as long as you need to. Order anything you'd like."

I nodded. I had already made up my mind to leave shortly after him, but I didn't want to waste our time with those conversations. The room would feel too big, too empty without him.

He kissed me the last kiss. It was a quick peck. I wanted to pull him back to me, but it wouldn't matter. Liam had become an infinity symbol for me. The more of him I had, the more I wanted. I looked away, my gaze falling to the nightstand.

I went over and picked up the envelope. "You forgot something."

He adjusted his tie, almost fidgeted with it nervously. A strange gesture for Liam. "Actually, that's for you. Open it after I go."

I held up the envelope with his drawing of a lotus flower. Judging from the expression on his face, he hadn't expected me to find it until he left. "What's in here?"

"It's a check. It's not much…not to me. I just want to make sure you have enough to keep you safe."

I opened the envelope. I had to recount the zeros twice. "I don't want this." I handed it to him, but he folded my fingers around it.

"I'm not trying to offend you."

"Why would I be offended when a man conveniently leaves me an envelope full of money on the nightstand after we engaged in passionate sex? What's offensive about that?"

He titled his head. Once I broke a smile, he laughed. "Okay, you got me. It was in bad taste, but I swear, my intentions were honest."

I shoved it toward him. "Thank you, but I'll be fine."

"Don't take it for you. Do it for me. It'll relieve some of my anxiety."

"All right."

"Really?" he asked, suspicion casting over his face.

"Yes, really. Thank you. You should go. You're already running late."

"Good-bye, Mary." He picked up his laptop case, swung it over his shoulder, and turned.

"Liam," I called before he walked toward the door. I ran up to him and swung my arms around his shoulders. *"Main tumse pyar karti hoon."*

"What does that mean?"

"It means have a safe journey."

"You too, Mary. Godspeed."

Chapter 30

Liam

I sat on the plane, my thoughts consumed with her. I had tried and failed to convince myself it was the allure of traveling that incited these feelings. No, what I felt for Mary was pure and real. It wasn't just how I felt about her, but how she made me feel about myself.

I loved her.

It hit me hard...the simple statement. I thought I'd been in love once before with Melanie, but it wasn't love. We were compatible and comfortable. Mary, although compatible, wasn't exactly comfortable. She challenged me in ways I'd never been challenged. We'd known each other for less than a month in total. How could I love someone in such a short time? I dismissed the question. I had no answer, except that I did.

But she didn't reciprocate those feelings. Even if she did, it's not like I could take her to New York with me, right?

Bloody hell, why couldn't she come to New York with me? She had to feel it, too. But would she uproot herself and continue our crazy journey? There were a lot of logistics, but logistics I could conquer.

Main tumse pyar karti hoon.

Safe journey, my arse. We'd watched a Bollywood flick one night with the same phrase. How had I not made that connection?

"Drink, sir?" the stewardess asked.

"I need to get off this plane."

"We've already boarded."

I stood and made myself clear. "I need to get off this plane right now."

Word to the wise, it was not a good idea to stand up and dramatically announce the need to get off your international flight. It worked well in the movies, but in real life, they took you to a room and asked you a bunch of uncomfortable questions. Then they asked you to strip and subjected you to certain searches. They could have at least bought me a drink first.

It took me two hours to get back to the hotel. It figured—my phone had up and died. I almost jumped out of the cab and started running. By the time I bolted through the front doors, I was an out of breath, bloody mess.

"Sir? Are you all right? Did you miss your flight?" the front desk attendant asked.

"Is Miss Costa in the room?"

"I'm afraid she's left, sir."

Something inside me snapped. "Did she say where she was going?"

His face brightened, giving me a ridiculous sense of hope. "No." *Goodbye hope, it was nice knowing you.* "But she did ask me to post this to you."

I didn't have to open the envelope to know my check was inside. Stubborn, proud Lotus Girl, the love of my life, the thorn in my side, the girl who killed me, the one who saved me. I stuffed the envelope into my pocket.

Bloody hell.

"Shall I have your bags taken back to the room? The maid is cleaning it now."

"Yeah. Thank you."

How would I find her? This was a huge country. One that was easy to get lost in. I made a mental list of the places to search—the rail and bus stations for starters.

I walked outside in the warm Goa sunshine. "Can you get me a car?" I asked the valet.

"Right away, sir."

I heard them in the distance. Chimes. Really, the soft sound should not have carried or been strong enough to pierce my wayward thoughts.

"Are those church bells?"

"Oh, yes sir. Service is just getting out."

Mary had asked about church service, hadn't she?

He said some other things, but I was already bolting across the street.

People were exiting the building when I got there. I prayed I hadn't missed her, if she was even here to begin with.

I watched them, a procession of parishioners, all shaking hands with the priest.

She wasn't there.

I stood, holding my breath, until the very last person exited the church. The priest walked back inside and closed the ornate doors.

Yet, I could not leave. I climbed the steps. Nothing could stop me from entering, although I wasn't sure if I was breaking some cardinal rule. After all, I didn't exactly have a membership card.

I adjusted to the dim light filtering through the bright colors of the stained glass windows. The strong scent of incense lingered in the air. Finally, I let out a long deep exhale.

Welcome back, hope, I've missed you.

She sat in the second pew, her head bent in prayer.

"Mary…" I knelt in the aisle next to her. Her dark brown eyes were tinged with red. The tracks of dried tears and wet tears made a roadmap out of her beautiful face.

"What are you doing here, Liam? You'll miss your flight."

"I already missed it, love. I got off the plane."

"Why?"

"I forgot something."

She stood, her shadow falling on me. She fell to her knees. We stared at each other in the middle of the church aisle. She placed her hands on my shoulders, shaking me, or trying to. "What could you have possibly forgotten that was so important you missed your flight?"

I clasped her wrist and kissed the back of it. "You."

She blinked. "I don't understand."

"Come with me to New York."

Her silence killed me. But I let her process the statement.

"Another holiday?" She shook her head. "I think we've extended this one as long as possible, don't you?"

I held her face and leaned my forehead against hers. "I'm not interested in a holiday. I want to make a life together." A stretch of silence passed until I finally cleared my throat. "*Mai tumse Pyar karta hoon. Tora Dost Daram. Mai Taunu Pyar Karda.*"

She put her hand over my mouth. "You don't have to say it in seven languages."

"I memorized ten."

She laughed and cupped my face. "Ten…very impressive."

"You said it to me first. Why did you lie about what it meant?"

"I wanted to say it aloud. It's something I'd kept bottled up to a point where it erupted. I didn't want you to know. It seemed almost selfish to express it, since we couldn't do anything about it."

"We can do something about it. Say it to me in English, please. I need to hear it."

"I love you, Liam."

I couldn't hold back anymore and kissed her. A long, deep kiss. When we finally broke apart, she shook her head. "Liam, it's not as simple as that, is it?"

"Why isn't it?"

"It's difficult to get a visa here, especially for the States."

I smiled huge, the kind of smile that comes from great relief. "You let me worry about that, love. I can make it happen." She chewed her lip, the tension in her body tangible. "What else?"

"I'm afraid of leaving everything I know. I had forgotten what happiness meant until I met you. I'm afraid of tempting fate. Of not being strong enough. I'm afraid of being surrounded by darkness. I won't survive it again."

Now, I was the tense one. "You're the strongest person I know. This journey we're on? I feel it's right in my soul. I think fate is what brought us together in the first place. But I understand I'm asking a great deal of you." I tucked the loose tendril of hair behind her ear and made a vow I wasn't sure I could keep. "Anytime you want to come back, I promise I'll let you go. I won't make it difficult for you. Mary, you have to fight for your own happiness in this world. This is me fighting for mine. If..." I wasn't even sure how to complete the thought.

"Okay."

"What?"

"I'll fight, too. Yes, I'll go with you. But the promise you made to me? The same goes for you, Liam. If it's too hard to make us work, you let me go, too. I will not make it difficult for you."

That was never going to happen, but she kissed me so deeply I chose not to ruin the moment with more words.

Chapter 31

Mary

My excitement was a contained pot, ready to boil over or explode at any minute. I did my best to control it. I never thought a visa would be approved, so I didn't allow myself the same excitement as Liam. I had no idea how much the right amount of money and contacts could accomplish. Liam spent vast amounts of cash, buttering up important people. It helped I already had a passport, although expired. We updated it first. Within a week, I had an official tourist's visa granted by the U.S. embassy. Something people spent years trying to obtain.

But I still didn't let myself believe it, not even during our layover at the Mumbai airport for the flight that would take us directly to New York. I feared someone would tell me this was all a cruel joke. I'd suddenly wake up back at the fountain in Jaipur wearing a scratchy sari.

I read the two dates they stamped on my passport once more.

"What happens when it expires?" I asked.

"I need to talk to you about that. There wasn't a lot of time. We settled for the only visa we could get."

"Talk to me now."

"When it expires, you either have to go back or we get married. I have dual citizenship so as my spouse, you'd be granted a green card."

I would have dropped the papers if he hadn't held his hands over mine.

"Are you asking me to marry you?"

"Not yet. I want to, though. I wouldn't have come back for you and stormed into that church if I wasn't sure I wanted to spend the rest of my life with you. But you have to be sure too, Mary. I will ask you to marry me once you tell me it's okay."

"So I have to tell you when?" There were so many niggling thoughts in my head. What if I didn't fit into his world? Truthfully, I didn't even fit in my own world. In a way, it was a relief to set a time period for straightening out all my tangled thoughts.

"I'm not going to pressure you."

I wanted to tell him this fierce love I felt for him would never waver, but I couldn't make that promise. He was right. Liam had become my power, my strength, my calm. But I couldn't make assurances to him until I knew I could support him as he supported me.

They started boarding calls for first class passengers.

"One more thing," he said. "Because we booked the flight on short notice, I wasn't able to secure two seats together. I could only obtain one first class ticket. I know flying makes you nervous, and this is going to be the longest flight ever. I'm sorry."

"I'll manage."

"You should get going, sweetheart."

I was puzzled for a moment, until he handed me my ticket. Liam, the consummate gentleman, had given me the first class seat.

"I'll see you in New York, love."

I opened my mouth to argue, but he pointed me toward the gate. "Go on."

Little butterflies fluttered in my belly as I found my seat. I was going to America with this man. Everything was changing so fast. I was sure my heart was pumping fast enough to fly the plane.

The stewardess approached me, welcoming me by name. She explained how my large, comfortable seat folded into a flat bed. I closed my eyes, clutching the arm rest as the plane took off, watching as the bright lights of Bombay disappeared. The seat offered enough legroom for three of me. I thought of Liam's tall, broad frame squashed into an economy seat for over 20 hours.

As soon as they turned off the seatbelt sign, I grabbed the stylish carry-on bag Liam had purchased for me and headed back toward the economy section. Luckily, Liam was tall, and I spotted his head over the rows of seats. Stuck between a chatty lady and a portly man, he had his nose in a book. The person in front of him had leaned their seat all the way back, giving him even less room.

"Liam."

"What are you doing?" he asked.

"This is stupid." I gestured to him. "Look at you. Take the first-class seat."

"I'm fine, love. I plan to sleep the whole way, just as soon as I finish this chapter."

I handed him the ticket. "Then sleep in first class. You'll be more comfortable."

He sighed, shaking his head. "No. Now you should head back." He arched an eyebrow. "Unless, you want to join a special club with me?"

"What kind of club?"

He shook his head. "Never mind, I've already had my fair share of troubles with this airline." His grin sparked with mischief. "We'll save that for another time"

"I don't care where I'm sitting. But I'll feel horrible imagining you all cramped back here. You're so much bigger than me."

"No kidding. But I'm going to insist on this. You think I'd rest easy knowing I took the better seat? Now go back up there, lass. I'm serious."

The woman next to Liam piped up. "I wish someone would offer me a first-class ticket. You wouldn't hear me arguing about it."

I looked at her and back at Liam. He shrugged his shoulders, picking up on my silent suggestion.

"Please, Auntie, take my seat."

"*Arey*, are you being serious?" she asked, but she was already standing up, her hand on the ticket.

I nodded. "What I want more than anything is to sit next to him."

The woman turned to Liam, probably for confirmation. "Yes, please take it with our gratitude."

She clamped her hand on the ticket and pinched my cheek. "*Achha*, thank you, beta." She shook her head. "Young people, so sweet and silly." Liam helped her with her bag before getting back into his seat.

I sat next to him. He put his arm around me and kissed my temple.

"You're crazy," he whispered.

"So are you."

Liam, the seasoned traveler, fell asleep right away, his arm stretched across me. Although I felt better sitting next to him, I couldn't sleep. The plane filled with the snores of other passengers.

I shifted to my side. A little girl with huge blue eyes and curly black hair smiled back at me.

"Hi," she said, giggling as if she knew a secret.

I returned her smile. "Hello."

"Sarah, shhh. Don't bother her," her mother said. She was a young, pretty woman who had the same smile as her daughter.

"I don't mind. I can't sleep, anyway. She's adorable. How old is she?"

"Thank you. She's two." She wrapped her arms around the little girl. "She's a bit overexcited about her first big trip." She combed her fingers through the baby's curls.

"I don't blame her. My name is Mary."

"Shyla," she said. "This is Sarah, as you know." She jabbed her thumb into the air, indicating the seat behind her. "That guy, sound asleep back there, is my husband Nick and our other daughter, Nalini."

I glanced at the seat where a man was sprawled with an identical little girl slumbering on his lap. She sucked her thumb. I imagined he probably had blue eyes like his daughters.

"Twins?"

"Yes."

"One has a Hindu name and one Christian?"

"We named them after the two women who raised me."

We spoke in quiet hushed tones about her interesting life, while I made funny faces at Sarah, who laughed with glee.

"I saw what happened," Shyla said. "It was very sweet of you to give up your seat."

I stared down at Liam's hand across my waist. "I just wanted to be next to him."

"My husband is like that, too. He's pretty upset we couldn't get four seats together."

"Do you live in New York?"

"Nick is from there originally. We met there, but we live just outside of Mumbai. We're going to New York to visit friends, and I'm giving a few lectures."

I wondered what had made him shift across whole oceans and continents.

The answer was clear when the man woke and his expression changed to one of bliss when he looked at his wife.

I imagined it was the same way I looked at Liam.

Chapter 32

Mary

"This is Anderson," Liam said, introducing me to the driver. "Anderson, meet Mary Costa."

"Nice to meet you, miss." We shook hands. "Welcome to the new world."

Indeed it was a new world. The sky was a shade of gray I'd never seen. No matter how hard I searched, I could not find a trace of the sun. "Thank you."

"How are you doing, mate?" Liam asked, helping the older man put the luggage in the boot.

"Can't complain, Mr. Montgomery. How was your trip?"

Liam looked in my direction, a wide smile on his face. "Excellent."

A gust of wind sliced through me. Tiny snowflakes swirled in the air, landing in odd places. I wrapped my arms around myself.

"Did you bring it?" Liam asked Anderson.

"Oh, yes, sir." Anderson pulled out a long black coat.

Liam held it out for me. It was definitely the protection I needed. Liam didn't wear a coat.

"Snow," I said in awe. I held out my palm to catch a flake.

"It's starting early this year." He buttoned my coat. "First impressions?"

"It's lovely."

"The truth, Mary."

"It's cold. Is it always this cold?"

He laughed. "No."

"Good."

"Just for the next four or five months."

"You could have kept that to yourself."

He kissed my cheek and gestured me into the huge limo waiting for us. I rubbed my hands together. He took gloves out of the pocket of my coat and slid them over my hands.

"I can't believe I'm in New York."

"Actually, lass, this is Newark."

"That's what I said, New York."

"Newaark." He spoke it slowly, expanding each syllable for me. "We're in New Jersey right now."

I concentrated, repeating the word slowly as he had, but it didn't sound the same coming from my mouth. The roads were smooth, too smooth. I kept waiting for bumps or pits or cracks, but none came. The roads in Bombay were insane, but the traffic kept everyone moving at a snail's pace. I thought that somehow made it safer than this ridiculous speed we traveled over slick surfaces. When we reached the tunnel, all I saw were bright red lights and cars. No one even honked.

"Is this a traffic jam?"

"It is," Liam said.

Anderson regaled us with a story about the storm of 1983, when the ice had built up so much, they closed the tunnel and people abandoned their cars right on the road.

When we emerged into the city, night had fallen. It didn't matter, because every building was lit up. There was so much to see, I wasn't sure where to look first. Then the honking started, and I was grateful because it reminded me of home.

"Welcome to New York," Liam said, his fingers folding over mine.

When we reached his building, I craned my neck to take in its massive height. Then he introduced me to Clawson, the doorman.

"Welcome back, Mr. Montgomery."

"Thank you."

Liam pushed the top button on the lift. As the doors closed, I caught my reflection in the shiny brass doors. I winced at the mess of tangles in my hair.

Liam unlocked the door of his flat. I went to step in, but he reached for my arm.

"Wait, let's do it proper." He swooped me off my feet.

I laughed, wrapping my arms around him.

"Isn't this supposed to happen after marriage?"

He kissed me. "We're not very traditional people, are we?"

"Definitely not."

He carried me inside. "Would you care for a tour?"

"I'd love one, but perhaps you should put me down first?"

He let me down. Slowly, I turned around, taking it all in. Liam lived all by himself in a palace on top of the world. He took my hand and led me from room to room. Then from floor to floor. Each floor had an entire wall of windows that reached the ceiling, giving a panoramic view of the city below. The dark wood floors gave way to muted gray walls. I stared at the two paintings in his living room, knowing Liam didn't paint them. I doubted he even picked them. They weren't really his style. Or at least I didn't think they were.

He opened the double doors to the master bedroom. Against the ornate king-size bed, the wall was covered with intricate paper. I traced the design. Everything was symmetrical and balanced with smooth lines and dramatic angles.

"Liam, it's amazing."

"Thanks," he said, taking off his shirt, "but I can't take credit. The place was staged, and I purchased it with all the furnishings."

"Would you have chosen the design?" I asked.

He shrugged. "Probably not. I just wanted a nice place to sleep."

I was relieved, because this flat didn't feel like Liam. He liked brighter colors and Moroccan architecture. A niggling worry worked its way forward...maybe I didn't know Liam as well as I thought.

"Hungry?" he asked.

I nodded and yawned at the same time. My inability to sleep during the flight had caught up to me.

"I'll order us a pizza. Then we'll take nice bath and off to bed."

I stared out the window, a surge of fear rising through me. He put his arms around me, dissipating some of the fear the same way the snowflakes dissolved when they hit my skin. I leaned against his chest.

"Mary, I want you to be comfortable here. You tell me what you need. If you want to change anything, you let me know. This is your home, too."

His phone rang before I could respond.

"I'll be right back."

I sat on the edge of the bed to remove my shoes. Pressing my hands into the thick mattress, I noticed a small circular stain on the wallpaper. Disguised well by the intricate design, it was barely discernible. I focused on it, realizing I had found the one thing that wasn't perfect in Liam's home.

Well...maybe there were two things now.

Chapter 33

Mary

I slept for a few minutes before Liam woke me up.

What a meanie he was.

"Morning, love."

I rubbed my eyes. Surely, he was joking. "It's morning? We just fell asleep."

He chuckled. "Yeah, about twelve hours ago."

"Why didn't you wake me?"

"You needed sleep. It's common to be overtired after you cross over time zones and oceans. You rest. I only woke you to tell you I have to go into the office."

I sat up. "Already?"

"I have a lot of catching up to do. Miss Jenkins can see to you, though. She can fix you whatever you'd like."

"Miss Jenkins?"

"My housekeeper. She comes every day."

"Oh." He had on a dark grey suit with green striped tie that I wanted to strip him of. "Let me get up. I'll have coffee with you."

He stroked my hair. "You rest. I'll be back around six."

He stared at me with such intensity, I shivered. "Why are you looking at me like that?" I smoothed back my hair, hoping it didn't resemble a hastily built bird's nest.

"I love seeing you in my bed, Miss Costa. My bed." He kissed my forehead. "Our bed."

"Me too, Liam."

* * * *

Liam's shower required a degree in engineering to operate. It had a million settings and just about as many heads. Cold water shot into my side. Then Mozart played, mocking me as I screeched. I pressed a few more digits. One changed the temperature to scalding hot water and another to music. I never managed to get it to the right setting, but I settled on a lukewarm spray accompanied by the same opera Liam was playing the first night we spent together. I let my mind drift back to that night. The taste of Sidr honey and Liam's mouth. By the time I emerged, my fingers were wrinkled from the water.

Last night, one of Liam's staff had laundered and hung all my clothes in the massive closet, which was larger than the suite in Bombay. I put on a cream-colored cotton blouse and a pair of jeans. The material felt thin and vulnerable. Looking through Liam's side, I found several thick wool sweaters. I wrapped up in one of them, inhaling the clean fresh scent.

Miss Jenkins was an older lady with a permanently sour expression, as if she'd just swallowed a whole lemon.

"Hello, I'm Mary."

"What will you be having for breakfast, Mary?"

"Chai and toast, please."

"We only have coffee. Mr. Montgomery drinks coffee." I had known that already. The one British man who didn't drink tea. "I'll add it to the list," she continued." I only go shopping on Thursdays, so you'll have to wait. That is, if your still here by then."

Ignoring her jab, I smiled brighter. "Thank you. What does Mr. Montgomery usually have for breakfast?"

"Cold cereal. He's not much of a breakfast person. I'll get you a bowl."

I didn't want cold cereal, especially not when it was freezing outside. "It's okay, Miss Jenkins. I can fix myself something."

She shrugged and went back to dusting the chandeliers.

I opened the cabinets, but Liam didn't have many choices.

Miss Jenkins voice traveled to me. "He usually eats out or tells me what he wants. I wasn't sure when he'd be back. His trip kept getting delayed."

"Yes, he fell ill."

"What a shame. I had a bad feeling when he left. I told him to get all his shots."

I settled on a box of oatmeal. "He did have all his shots. That's not why he got sick."

"Yes, I know. He told me all about it this morning. You can't trust anyone these days, especially not in a foreign country. No one."

I searched for pans. She didn't offer their whereabouts, and I didn't really want to ask. "Just so we're on the same page, miss, he prefers me to cook for his overnight guests."

She emphasized the word "guest." She wanted me to know there were others, and I was in the same league with them. "No worries, Miss Jenkins. I am perfectly capable of fixing my own breakfast."

I located a pan and turned on the stove. I threw in a few cups of water. The steam rose faster than I expected. I threw in a packet of oatmeal and found a stirring spoon. I searched the cabinet again for something to flavor it up. I smiled, thinking about the jar of Sidr honey. Of course, we'd used all that up. I couldn't find anything….no raisins or coconut shavings. Not even any spices. Which was odd since Liam enjoyed spicy food. Or maybe he didn't.

"Mr. Montgomery doesn't care for people rummaging through his house." Her tone was rife with judgment.

I could feel her eyes on me, scrutinizing me. The sensation swallowed me up. I ignored her because there was something mean about her. She wanted my response. She wanted to prick at my doubts until they flooded me. I refused to give into her. My thoughts ran so rampant I didn't notice the smoke thickening around me.

"What are you doing?" she said, running into the kitchen.

The oatmeal had turned into a burnt brown mess.

"I'm sorry. I didn't realize how quickly it heated up."

She switched off the stove and pointed to the pan. "What is this mess?" She wasn't looking at the pot. She was looking at me.

I stared at what remained of the stirring spoon. I set it on the stove where it melted. "I'm s-s-sorry," I stammered.

The look of revulsion she shot my way made me cower. She threw the ruined spoon into the sink where it clanged loudly. "I'll make you the oatmeal. After I clean this up, that is."

I mumbled about not being hungry and going out. Suddenly, the large expanse between the walls was closing in on me. A desperation to flee pitted into my stomach.

Grabbing my purse and the coat Liam had gotten me, I headed out. I passed Clawson on the way.

"Going out, Miss? I'll call Anderson for you." He had a deep, gruff voice that seemed at odds with his small frame.

"Thank you. I'd rather walk, Mr… I'm sorry, I don't know your surname."

He was a short man with tufts of silver hair peeking out beneath his cap. He smiled warmly. "Clawson is my last name. First name's Bill." He put his legs together and saluted me. "Bill Clawson at your service."

"Mr. Clawson, call me Mary, please."

"Only if you call me Bill."

"Bill, can you help me with something?"

"Help a gorgeous woman? That's my sole purpose in life, ma'am."

I might have been uncomfortable if his flirting wasn't so good-natured. "Is there a place I can get a cup of chai? It's Indian tea."

He chuckled with heartiness. "It's very popular here, too." He opened the door for me and walked into the street. I could physically see my own breath. It roared out of me as if I was a dragon. "Straight down this lane and on the left."

"Thank you, Bill."

"You sure you'll be all right?"

"I will be great." Entire clouds came out of my mouth. I wanted to swallow them back.

The crowds jostled past me. I picked up my pace, but I wasn't keeping up. Someone bumped me and then gave me a dirty look as if I was to blame for the incident. I forged straight ahead, pretending none of these things penetrated me. I tried to be as strong as the concrete and brick surrounding me.

I wasn't sure if I saw the sign or smelled the hot caffeine first, but I found the shop with no trouble. I crossed the street, following the cues of the crowd as they rushed forth when the signal changed. It was such a small feat, but I looked at it as an accomplishment of sorts. The café was crowded. If a few more people came in, the line would spill out to the street. I was so busy staring at all the brilliant displays with the foiled packages we weaved around, I missed the growing gap between me and the front of the line.

"Heelllooo," an impatient man grumbled.

I hurried forward. "Chai, please."

"Size?" The clerk asked without looking up.

"The largest one."

He told me the price. I raised an eyebrow, wondering if I'd heard him correctly. I could eat, and eat well, for an entire week on the price he quoted.

He repeated it louder, making it clear I'd heard correctly. I fumbled through my purse, cursing myself. I only had rupees. Why had I not exchanged my money? The clerk drummed his fingers against the counter. I heard the disapproving sighs rise from the line behind me. My fingers wrapped around the thin piece of plastic. I pulled it out with a false sense of triumph.

"Will you take this? Credit?"

He didn't answer, except to give me a frustrated stare. He pointed to a machine instead. When I looked back at him in confusion, he pointed again. "Swipe it."

"Swipe?"

He snatched the card from me and ran it through the tiny gap in the machine. Something chimed.

"Declined," he announced, almost gleefully. A chorus of synchronized groans followed.

"Are you sure?" It was attached to my bank in India. I had over three-hundred thousand rupees, which equated to a few thousand dollars. Liam wanted to take care of me, but I was happy I had some money. My bank was international. I hadn't thought there would be any problem. I'd used the card once in India, and it worked. A sinking fear gripped me. What if my money had been stolen? I hadn't changed my address. What if they shut off my account when my mail was returned unopened? I was in a country with no money. What little shreds of independence I had slipped away.

"Look lady, if you don't have another way to pay, I need you to move along."

"You don't have to be so rude," a man said, stepping forward. "Put this on my bill. I'll also take a café renversé and a beignet."

I tilted my head at the man who had stepped forward. He was tall with dark hair and tanned skin. He wore a plaid scarf and smelled expensive.

"Thank you, but I can't accept."

"Too late," he said, gliding his card along the gap.

He gestured me forward to the area where machines sputtered and cups clinked. "I believe this is yours." He put a circular piece of cardboard around my tall decorative paper cup.

"I'll pay you back."

He laughed. "You're new here."

"It's that obvious?"

"Oh yeah, you might as well have a sign flashing H1-B."

"H1-B?"

"Your visa status."

"I'm here on a visitor visa actually."

"I see. Don't worry. Many of us were new here once. You're Indian?"

"Yes." I held out my hand. "Mary Costa."

"Chetan Singh. Everyone calls me Chet."

I took in his brown skin and dark hair. "You're Indian, too."

His smile flashed brightly, a row of blindingly brilliant white teeth. "From Toronto actually, but I am of Indian descent. So my *nani* keeps reminding me."

"Canada, right?"

"Right." He looked down at his watch and back at me. "I have a few minutes. Let's sit."

I looked out at the cold street, involuntarily shivering at the prospect of walking outside again. "Okay."

We found a booth by the window. I gripped my coffee with both hands, thankful for its warmth against my trembling fingers. I looked at his plate with the sugar-covered rectangle. He slid it forward and handed me a fork.

"Oh no, I couldn't."

He stood and fetched another fork for himself. "I shouldn't have the whole thing, anyway. Do me a favor and share it with me."

My stomach rumbled, and it smelled divine. I cut into a corner. The sweetened fried dough melted inside my mouth. "Does this magic have a name?"

He grinned. "I know, right? It's called a beignet."

He must have sensed his answer puzzled me. "A fancy French doughnut."

"Oh."

"You don't know what a doughnut is, do you?"

"Afraid not."

"Think *gulab jamon* with powdered sugar."

Now *that* I knew.

"I see the resemblance, but it's more like a distant cousin, no?"

"I suppose." His face turned wistful. "What I wouldn't give for fresh gulab jamon soaked in sweet syrup."

"You don't get that here? I thought you could get anything in New York."

"The Indian restaurants serve it, but it's from a can. My *nani* makes it from scratch. Once you've had it like that, anything pales in comparison."

"Yeah, I would agree."

"So Miss Visitor Visa, you here with your family?"

"No." He waited for me to add to the sentence. "I met a man," I blurted out.

"I met a man," he repeated, his grin widening. "Are there four more dangerous words in all the English language?"

"I don't think so." The disappearance of my money and independence shrank as I talked about Liam.

"This man let you leave without any money today?"

"No, that's my own fault. I hadn't planned to go out. He definitely would not approve. I'll be fine as soon as I figure out what's going on with my bank account."

"Tell me about this man."

My mouth curved into a smile. "He's an artist. Well, he's really a businessman, but an artist, too. We are as opposite as two people could be, or at least it seems so on the surface. In fact, we're very similar. I recognized a part of me in him. I think he did the same."

"And you came here to tell him this?"

"Oh no, he asked me to come here. We met while he was doing business in India. He's leaving the choice to me."

"Choice?"

"To figure out if I can find my place here. I have ninety days…well, a little less than that now."

"So you're kind of a ticking bomb? You're giving yourself ninety days to figure out if you belong together."

"Actually, Liam is giving me time to decide if I want to have this life with him here. The U.S. government is giving us ninety days." Truthfully, we'd had many expiration dates. We'd surpassed them all. I promised myself we would pass this one as well. "I love him. You would think that's enough, right?" I wasn't sure if I was asking myself or Chet. Or why I was even having such a deep conversation with a stranger. I guess once you started letting people into your life, all the walls chipped and cracked, making the entire façade easier to expose. That and Chet was easy to talk to. And I was really desperate for someone to talk to.

"Honey, I'd sure love to say yes. Things are never so easy though, are they?"

"No." I had been tense since we arrived yesterday. My muscles relaxed slowly, grateful for someone else who understood.

"That's a very long exhale for such a diminutive girl."

"I've been holding it in for a while now. I'm not exactly worldly, but I know I have to work on some things for myself. I've kind of been hiding away for a while. I'm not even sure who I am. Before I can make him any promises about our future, I want to make sure I can live in the present. He makes me happy, but I have to make sure I can make myself happy, too. Does that make sense?" I didn't want to think of Liam as the man who saved me. I wanted to think of him as the man who cherished me.

"Absolutely." He lifted his coffee toward me in a mock toast. "What an interesting dilemma for you."

"Indeed."

I looked down at our empty plate. I rifled thought my purse. "Chet, can you do me a favor?"

"Loaded question but shoot anyway."

I pulled out my card. "Can you help me find this bank? I believe they have a branch here."

"Yeah, they do." His expression turned disapproving. "Mary, don't hold out your plastic for anyone to snatch. I'm gonna teach you a few things, and that's your first lesson. Now, as for the bank, it's a bit of a walk but we can take the subway. It's not far from my office."

I tried to match Chet's confident strides as we left the café. We walked down a staircase and emerged inside a tunnel. Chet bought me tokens.

"What is this?"

"There's no such thing as a free ride, darling."

I held the odd coin in my hand and deposited it into the receptacle. He used a card he explained was a metro card. We walked into the open doors of the long underground train. I looked around at the signs, shocked to be traveling below the ground.

He took a silver case from his jacket. He wrote on the small square inside before handing me the card and a crisp twenty-dollar bill. "This is my business card. I've listed my personal number on the back. Call me if you need anything. Even if it's just to chat or vent." He instructed me about a few more things, like holding my purse over my shoulder and across my body. Also, to stand up before my stop so I could get out.

"Thank you for your kindness. I'll be sure to pay you back once I get my situation straightened out."

"Don't bother, honey. I'm serious. Just consider yourself one friend richer today."

"I am lucky." I heard the call of many conversations, some heavily accented and others in foreign languages. "Are there any native New Yorkers?"

He laughed. "You bet there are. When you meet one, they'll be sure to broadcast it." The car started slowing down. "This is where I leave you, Mary Costa. Will you be okay?"

"I'll be just fine."

"I have no doubt you will."

He held his hand out to me. I shook it, almost wanting to hug him. Then he gave me a quick peck on the check before standing up and heading toward the exit.

"Chet?"

"Yes, dear?"

"You never told me why you moved here from Toronto. What brought you to New York?"

He tightened his scarf and did a flourishing bow. "I met a man."

I sat like a loon, smiling widely as the doors closed behind him.

What a crazy wonderful world.

Chapter 34

Mary

The queue at the bank was long. But unlike the café, I prepared myself and had my documents ready when it was my turn at the window. I discovered my account was intact but frozen since I never bothered to tell them I was leaving the country. The lady switched it back on and issued me a new card. All good news.

Bad news. I was lost. I searched for the subway tunnel, but I couldn't find the mysterious staircase. I had cash now, but no idea where I lived. No doubt, this would earn me an award for the worst immigrant ever. To make matters worse, I didn't know Liam's phone number, nor did I have a phone in which to contact him. I considered taking a cab to Chet's office, but that seemed silly. How had I managed to get lost on my first day here?

Finally, I located a payphone. In the large phonebook, I searched for Liam's number, but there was no listing. I managed to find the corporate headquarters for the Wilshire Corporation, though. I entered a ridiculous amount of change and dialed the number.

"Liam Montgomery, please," I said to the girl who answered. She transferred me several times. I held so long, I memorized the pattern of music playing on the other line. At one point, the mechanical voice of the phone demanded more money. I prayed someone would answer before I ran out of change.

A woman finally came on the line. "He's in meetings. I can take a message."

I didn't want to leave him a message. After all, what sense did that make since he couldn't contact me back?

"It's all right." I hung up. I looked down at the address. It said 58th Street, and I was on 52nd, so it wasn't that far. I hailed my first cab in the new world. I gave the man the address with a fake bravado as if I did this all the time.

When I reached my destination, I leaned my head back to take in the tall skyscraper of a building. The lobby with its huge ceiling and marble floors made me feel like a miniature version of myself. People passed in and out of the revolving doors. I was tentative, almost being swept through rather than pushing. Pointed heels clicked on the fancy floors, while my shoes created a dull shuffle, followed by an embarrassing squeak or two.

"Liam Montgomery, please," I said to the security guard.

He looked at me suspiciously. "Do you have an appointment?"

"No."

"Who are you?"

"Mary Costa."

"Wait there," he instructed, pointing to a sofa. I took a seat. There were magazines. I leafed through their glossy pages and skimmed a few articles.

An hour later, a woman with shiny blond hair done in a tight knot approached me. "I understand you're here to see Mr. Montgomery."

"Yes."

"I'm sorry to keep you waiting. I just received the message. I'm one of his assistants. I'm afraid he doesn't see people without an appointment. He's a very important man. If you tell me what this is about, I can try to schedule something and get back to you."

"I'm his girlfriend, actually."

She crossed her arms as her heel tapped against the marble. "You are?"

"I am."

"Why didn't you say so?"

Yes, why didn't I?

"I am saying so. Can you tell him I'm here?"

"I'm afraid he left about twenty minutes ago. I'm sure you'll catch him at home."

I dropped the magazine. I didn't want to admit I had no idea where home was. I looked at the huge ornate clock behind her. "It's only three. He said he'd be here until six."

"Perhaps he had a date."

I didn't entertain the poisoned dart of doubt she threw in my direction, although it hurt just the same. Not because I believed her, but because I couldn't understand why she was being so cruel. "Can you call him and tell him I'm here waiting?"

She narrowed her eyes at me. "Why can't you call him? Surely, his girlfriend has his phone number." She thought I was a fraud…an imposter.

"Will you just ring him, please?"

She gave me a cold smile. "No, I won't. However, if you don't leave, I might just call the police."

I'd simmered all day until this boiling point. I stood. She was taller than me, but I met her eyes. "All you have to do is call him for confirmation of who I am. Do you really want to risk embarrassment with simple assumption on your part? Please understand when I'm speaking about embarrassment, I'm speaking of yours, not mine. Now, please call him."

She took a moment to consider it. "Wait here."

It felt as if all I'd done today was wait. This time, though, it only took two minutes until she hurried back to me, a huge smile on her face. "Miss Costa, I apologize for the misunderstanding. One can't be too careful these days." Before I could respond, she helped me up. "Let me take your coat." She took it without my response. "He requested I bring you upstairs. Mr. Montgomery is rushing back to the office at this very moment." Even as she made the statement, I could hear the inflection in her own voice like it surprised her. "Can I get you something? Coffee, tea, perhaps some wine?"

"No, thank you." We walked past the guard's station and slipped into one of the six lifts.

She pushed the button for the top floor. "I hope you understand where I was coming from earlier."

Yes, from the land of bitchdom. "Of course."

The lift opened into a plush room of creams and beige. She gestured toward a sofa. "His office is down the hall if you'd rather wait there."

"I'll be fine here."

She nodded and took the seat opposite me. She began chatting about the weather and upcoming holidays. This I didn't need. "I'd prefer to wait alone."

"Of course."

After she left, I stood and stretched. It was warm, so I took off Liam's sweater. I walked along the corridor. I told myself it was just to stretch. I was curious, though, and I went deeper until I reached another a set of ornate desks outside of two doors. Neither of them was marked, but one was ajar. I pushed it open. It didn't make any sound. The carpet was so thick my feet sank. I wanted to take off my shoes and run across it in my bare feet. There was a bank of windows here, too. All the lights and chaos of the city bounced inside, conflicting with the calm space. I sank into the large leather chair, its surface as smooth and soft as butter. Leaning my head back, I swiveled a few times until I got dizzy. All the photos on Liam's desk were promotional shots of the hotels he owned.

I picked them up, one by one, and studied them. The picture in the last frame was off-center. There was another snapshot behind it, peeking out. Really, I shouldn't have opened it. This was trespass on my part, but I found myself prying the clips on the back. Under the picture of the hotel was a photo of a gorgeous woman with hair the color of ripe strawberries. She was in a sundress on the beach and smiling at whomever took the photo. The kind of smile you reserved for a lover.

Was this Melanie?

"Well, well, you sure don't look like Goldilocks, so what are you doing sitting in my chair?"

I spun around, dropping the frame and picture. It hit the edge of the table where the glass cracked.

"Sorry," I said. "Who are you?"

He had broad shoulders, blond hair, blue eyes, and a smug expression.

"That's my question, sweetheart. I asked the agency to send a redhead. Looks like they messed up again. Don't get me wrong, you're nice to look at, but I have my preferences. I'm pretty set on it."

"Excuse me?"

"I don't negotiate." He came around the desk and looked at the shattered glass on the floor. "Jesus, what did you do?"

"I'm sorry." I shifted to the floor and began picking up the pieces of glass.

He picked up the picture and ran his hand over it, almost reverently. Tiny bits of glass fell on the carpet. "What the hell is wrong with you?"

"I thought this was Liam's office."

"It's not. Are you illiterate? Did you not read the sign outside the door that said Stephen Wilshire in big bold letters?"

"There is no sign."

He scratched his head. "There's not?"

"No."

He walked out the door and came back in. "Well, whatdaya know? I guess we'll have to fix that." I felt his eyes on me as I continued to gather the shards of glass, many of them embedded into the thick carpet. His polished black shoes were right next to my face. "Who the hell are you?"

"Mary Costa."

He got on the floor, but he didn't help me. Instead, he grabbed my wrist. "Mary Costa...the nurse? Wait, no...you're the maid. Prabhat told me you'd left with Liam, but what the hell are you doing here? If he's looking for a new maid, surely he didn't have to outsource."

"Liam…" I said, unsure how to finish that sentence under the cold glare of his blazing eyes.

He laughed. "Seriously, you are talented. How does a maid in a third-world country nab a billionaire? What is your secret? You could make a killing marketing your program."

I pried my wrist away, but he held on. His eyes narrowed in on my scar. In my haste to leave the flat, I had forgotten my bracelet.

No. No. No.

He stared at my scar, his hand curling around my wrist. "Get him to feel sorry for you, did you?"

"Shut up. You don't know anything about us."

He pulled my wrist down, almost painfully. His eyes searched my face as if he could find the answers to his questions there.

"Who the fuck are you?"

"Your brother's girlfriend. Let go of me."

He did. I scrambled to stand and backed away from him.

"What the hell is going on?" Liam's voice boomed from the doorway.

Stephen stood. He smirked at me, then turned to Liam, his smile widening. "Just getting acquainted with your girl. Why didn't you tell me about her, bro?"

Liam crossed the room in two seconds. He grabbed Stephen's shirt. "Because it's none of your business."

"Were you embarrassed?"

"Yes," he seethed. "Of you."

"Liam," I whispered. He ignored me. The chiseled lines of his face all hardened. "Liam, please." I placed my hands around the crook of his arm and tugged. "It's okay. Let's go."

Liam pulled Stephen closer. I thought I misheard at first, but Stephen's laugh was unmistakable. "Just like old times, eh?"

Liam slammed Stephen against the desk with each of his statement. "You don't look at her. You don't talk to her. You don't even think about her. Understand me?"

"I didn't invite Goldilocks into the bear cave. She came in here all on her own."

"I swear to God, Stephen, I will not stop at your jaw this time."

"Please, Liam." My voice sounded small and distant. I repeated it, hoping it would anchor Liam before the waves of rage took over.

Liam let go. I reached for his hand. He pulled me through the door, and then into the second office. It was identical to Stephen's.

He slammed the door and turned to me, rage still on his face. Except this time, it was plainly aimed at me. "Where the bloody hell have you been all day?"

"I was…out."

The vein in his neck pulsed. "Out?" he asked as if he'd never heard of the concept.

"Liam, are you all right?"

"No, I'm not fucking all right. I've been calling the house all day. Miss Jenkins said you went out. Then Clawson said you left to get tea and never returned. I've been going mad with worry. Clawson went to the fucking café to look for you. Anderson was out searching for you as well. Finally, I couldn't take anymore so I canceled my afternoon meetings and joined the search. It never occurred to me you might come here. Why the fuck didn't you call?"

Guilt pricked at me for wasting everyone's time. "I did, but they said you were in meetings."

He dragged his fingers through his hair. "Where did you go?"

"It's a long story. I'd love to tell you, but not when you're yelling at me. I'm sorry I worried you. I've never had to answer to anyone before."

"Jesus, Mary, I'm not your boss. You don't answer to me. You tell me where you are so I don't worry. That's all. It's what being in a relationship is about."

He took off his jacket and flung it to the couch by the door before slumping in his office chair. I saw his real emotion when the mask of his anger fell away. It was fear. I padded over to him. "I'm so sorry, Liam."

"I'll have Anderson take you home. I'm behind schedule now. We'll talk later."

Behind him on the credenza was a picture of me standing in front of the massive pillar at Elephanta Cave wearing his navy blue cap. He must have had it printed today. Doubts had crept through me all day, aided by Miss Jenkins, Liam's assistant, and most of all Stephen. I feared he might be embarrassed of us…of me. But there I was, front and center in his life. When I turned back to him, I knew, although unintentionally, I'd hurt him.

I bent to caress his cheek. "Look at me, Liam. Please."

He pulled me onto his lap and held me tight. His heartbeat had the rhythm of a war drum.

"I can't explain myself rationally," he whispered against my hair.

"You don't have to."

He grasped my waist and sat me on his massive desk. In one swift move of his arm, all the contents spilled to the floor. His body pressed against mine, his mouth hungry as it devoured me in passionate kisses. The flush of heat wrapped around my body. He pushed my shirt up. His teeth slid across the cup of my bra, biting the fabric, tugging it lower. His tongue swirled around my breast. Tangling my hands in his hair, I moaned. He went lower, punctuating each increment with hard presses and nips and bites. Somewhere I heard the familiar rip of a condom. He gripped my hips so hard I was sure his fingers would leave marks. The first thrust was swift and deep.

"Tell me you're mine." Although he said it in a low voice, the command was urgent.

"I'm yours, Liam. Only yours."

His eyes blazed with a raw energy that captured me. He lowered his head to watch himself entering me. I did the same. Each thrust was more urgent than the last. Every muscle in my body vibrated with his movements. I bit my lower lip to keep from screaming out my ecstasy. He tugged it free with his own mouth. He swallowed my moans as I released. Heat filled between my legs. When we regained our breath, he kissed me. Not the rough kiss of claim or the passionate kiss of lust. This was a soft kiss against my lips...pure and sincere.

He went into another room of his office, which I assumed was a bathroom. He brought a damp washcloth and cleaned me. Then he leaned back on the desk. We stared at the ceiling for a while.

"I was going out of mind." He reached for my hand. "Don't ever do that again. I know you can take care of yourself, but you're in a new city. A new country. A million things passed through my mind today. None of them good. You have no idea all the horrible things I imagined these last few hours."

"I promise I won't worry you again."

He stroked my hair. "I'm sorry too, Mary. I should have made sure you had a cell phone. I was going to have Anderson get one for you today. I didn't think you'd be going out. I shouldn't have gone all starkers on you. I saw you in there with him...and something snapped."

I turned on my side to face him. "Liam, you don't have to keep asking me. You asked once if I trusted you, and I do. But you need to trust me, too. I love you."

He twisted a strand of my hair around his finger. "Next time have Anderson drive you."

"I didn't plan it this way. It just happened."

He kissed my head. "Tell me about your day, sweetheart. What did you do?"

It seemed a bit silly to have this conversation lying naked on his desk. But yet, it was completely normal, too. I told him everything—from the beignets at the bank to my first friend, Chetan.

"Should I be jealous?"

I laughed. "You're probably more his type than me."

"I would have helped you with the bank thing. You know you don't have to spend your money. I'd rather you spend mine."

"Liam, you're paying for everything. I can at least purchase for my own coffee." Even as I said it, I did the mental calculations and realized I couldn't pay for my own coffee for long.

"Have it your way."

"Thank you."

"You rode the subway?"

"Yeah, it was fun."

He kissed my forehead before standing. "Shall we go?"

"Don't you have work to do?"

"I can finish up at home. Besides, I want to take my girl to dinner. I can hear your stomach rumbling."

On cue, it complained again. The beignet, as sweet as it was, had become a distant memory, and I was starving.

We walked to the lift. A gorgeous, tall woman with red hair walked out. She smiled at Liam. He didn't react, but I squeezed his hand as she headed toward Stephen's office. "Is she from…the agency?"

"Stephen has always preferred company he can pay for. Let's not waste any more time talking about him."

I wondered how I had missed Liam exiting the lobby. As it turned out, he didn't go through the lobby but an underground parking garage. The lights of a flashy red car turned on as we approached. He opened the door for me.

"This is your car?"

"One of them. Get in and buckle up."

The inside gleamed. He drove it through the city, shifting gears, weaving us in and out of traffic in an almost graceful way.

He took me to a small Italian restaurant. I discovered lasagna… possibly the most addictive dish in the world. The layers of cheese melted in my mouth. So many kinds of cheese living in harmony in one dish. Surely, this was a delicious metaphor for the world.

"How did you get along with Miss Jenkins?" Liam asked, cutting into his steak.

I thought about my reply. If I told him I didn't care for her, he might fire her. Everyone was entitled to a bad day. Besides, if I really wanted to maintain my own independence, I'd have to learn to fight my own battles. "Fine."

After we ate, he took me across the street to a brightly lit store.

"What are we doing here?"

"Getting you a cell phone." He took out his wallet. "This is a credit card for your use. Don't argue with me. You'll need to purchase some warmer clothes. I love the way it looks on you, but you're practically swimming in my sweater."

I didn't argue.

Chapter 35

Mary

I couldn't move. His body had to be heavy, to be crushing me, but I didn't feel anything. I was there, but I wasn't. The shadow on the monitor was real. He had come for me, but I was the shadow now. I moved my mouth, but no words came out. He grunted as he sat up.

The colors in the room faded together in a blur, as if they bled into each other. Every time I blinked, the shapes and colors shifted like the picture in Hannah's kaleidoscope. I heard the sound of harsh slaps over and over. I didn't feel it, yet, but I knew it was my flesh. Just as I knew the faint warmth between my legs was blood.

"She is useless to me. You gave her too much."

"She fights, Sahib."

"I wanted her to fight. I enjoy the fight." A ringing sound invaded my head. "Shut up," he said.

"Hello, dear. Yes, I arrived safely."

I tried to make a sound, but it only came out a muffled choke. A hand pressed against my mouth.

"It's street noise. Darling, I have to go. It's the last leg of my trip." He sighed. "What's your problem? I always go to Jaipur every few years. This is business. What do you mean, he found it? Just calm him down." His voice rose with each sentence. I struggled to scream, but he pressed down harder. Then I struggled to breathe. He was going to kill me while having a phone conversation.

I tried to focus on him, but I couldn't shift my head. It lay to the side, my cheek pressed into the pillow. There were two gold birds on the nightstand. They started moving, running to the edge of the table. They flew around my head. Concentrate, I told myself. It's not real. But his hand felt real. Why weren't the birds real? They liquefied and shimmered as they circled me. Their wings made a hard metallic thrashing sound as they flapped. I thought they might rescue me by carrying me away from this place. But they only flapped around my head, mocking me. They were vultures coming to pick at my dead flesh. I would be the carrion that sustained them.

"It's not what it looks like. You explain that to Bobby. You know how his mind works. No, wait. I'll call him myself. The lines are bad here. I'll call tonight when I arrive at the Wilshire. I have to go. Love you."

This monster was capable of love?

His hand moved. I gasped and choked a lungful of painful air.

The darkness came. I fought it.

"Get the other girl."

"Sahib?" The guard said, his voice hesitant. "Which girl?"

"You know which one."

"But sir..."

"You heard me."

No. No. No. No.

Not her. Take me. Please, please, please.

"I already had you, bitch." A glob of wet slime drooled down my face. He had spit on me. But it didn't matter. I could speak. He'd heard me. My voice worked.

Hannah's screams marred me deeper than any cut. They marked my soul, turning it black.

"Hannah, think about moonstones with shades of blue and yellow in them. Think about ice creams, sticky and sweet, dripping on your fingers. Think about the red balloons the toy-wallah sells. How you always let one go, and we would watch it fly into the air and disappear into the clouds. Think about all the stories I told you. God, Hannah, go somewhere else in your head." I wasn't sure if I said it aloud. I prayed she heard me. Because no matter how hard I tried, I couldn't move. This was the only protection I could give her.

Her screams stopped. I prayed it was because he was done and not because the gold birds had taken my hands and lifted me. They were carrying me far away.

The darkness came.

I surrendered to it.

I woke up with a start.

"Are you all right, love?" he asked. "You were having a nightmare."

"Fine."

He rubbed my lower back.

"Where did you go?" I asked, tugging at his sweatshirt.

"For a run. Do you want to talk about it?"

I shook my head. "It was just a weird dream." I hadn't had the dream in so long. Truthfully, I wasn't even sure if it had really happened, or if I'd just sewn faded bits and pieces of my fears together.

Liam held me tightly until the sun rose, filtering light into the room. "Are you sure you're all right?" He kissed my cheek.

"Yes, I'm sure."

"You up for taking a shower with me?"

"Definitely."

"I'll meet you in there. I have to make an overseas call real quick."

I ran into the bathroom and started the water. He opened the glass door, completely naked. I pulled him inside with me.

"Why is it so bloody hot?" He moved to the far corner where I stood.

I ran my hands down his front. "Because you're in here? Also, it might have to do with the fact I have no idea how to operate this technology you call a shower."

He laughed, cupping my face. "Lola, I was under the impression you were a tech wiz."

I feigned the silly southern accent he claimed turned him on. "No sir, it's the one area I don't excel in."

He showed me how each of the functions worked, all the while kissing my shoulders and neck.

"I want you right now," he whispered in my ear.

"It's mutual."

"Did you bring a condom in here with you?"

"No."

"Speaking of, will you go on birth control, love? It'll make things more convenient and less risky for us." He massaged my shoulders.

"Yes, I can do that."

"Good." He swept up my hair and kissed the back of my neck. I didn't even flinch when he lowered his lips and kissed the burned part of my flesh. Then his fingers worked down my spine. *Dear God, I cannot escape my nightmare, but please don't let me wake up from this dream.*

Chapter 36

Mary

I braved the conversation with Miss Jenkins. I handed her the revised grocery list. "I've made a few changes."

She looked at it as if I'd written it in a foreign script. "I don't know how to use these ingredients."

"No worries, I'll be cooking dinner for Mr. Montgomery."

She shook her head. "He doesn't care for heavy spices."

"I'm afraid you're wrong on that account. He enjoys them very much. I think we both made a bad first impression the other day. Miss Jenkins, I understand you've been working for him for a while. I respect that you do a wonderful job here. But I need you to respect who I am. I'm an important part of Liam's life. I'm not a guest. I suggest you recognize that sooner than later."

Her mouth gaped for a moment. I waited for her response.

"Yes, ma'am."

Things between us would never be friendly, but I settled for cordial. Cordial was just fine by me. Anderson took me to a special market that carried ethnic foods, and then to the retail stores. I almost thought the saleslady would pull a *Pretty Woman* and tell me they didn't cater to my kind, but she was very helpful. I stocked the cabinets with masala chai and the closets with warm clothes. I wanted to use my own money, but the prices were so outrageous, it would deplete me. Besides, Liam would be upset, so I swiped the credit card he gave me.

I learned how to use the kitchen. I hadn't cooked since I made meals for Hannah and *Papaji*. I missed the smells of frying and baking and sautéing.

Thoughts about Stephen kept intruding at the oddest times. I hated him for what he'd done to Liam. At the same time, he reminded me of the story about the proud lion who had a pin stuck in his paw. He chose to live his life in pain rather than ask for help. I saw pain in Stephen, recognized it beneath the layers of his well-tailored suit and arrogance. As soon as I had them, I whisked the thoughts away like I did the eggs for our omelets on Sunday we ate before I left for church.

Liam bought me an e-reader. He handed it to me with an air of nonchalance, as if it wasn't the greatest gift in the world. One I would never refuse.

We laid on the sofa in the media room, his arm around me. "You mean I can download any book. Any book at all? Then I can read it right away?"

"Yes, Mary, for the third time, you are correct."

I stared at the device with suspicion. "Don't deceive me with promises of grandeur, sir."

"Oh, my sweet girl, you think I'd make false promises when they would get me locked up in the doghouse?" He took the device from me. He typed *highlander romances* in the subject line. The screen filled up in an instant. "Look here. Which one do you want to read first, lass?"

I shrieked with joy. I didn't even realize there were that many highlander romances in all the world. "All of them."

"So it shall be." He highlighted each one and downloaded them for me.

I'd seen people with these devices at the hotel, but I never realized the lure until now. It was instant gratification at its best. He might as well have handed me drugs. "Liam, this is so dangerous. You may never see me again."

He nibbled my ear. "Really, never again?" His hand traveled down my body. "Would you choose fiction over…friction?"

"Keep convincing me, sir."

"Let's find something naughty to read instead, shall we?"

He cleared his throat, and his clipped British accent filtered into the Scottish brogue he did so well. It wasn't a very sexual scene, but I didn't even make it to the end of the page before I told him to bookmark it.

And he did.

When I got bored, I went downstairs and chatted with Bill. He told me about his daughter in the military and his son in college. He asked me about India, his fascination evident with each conversation. Sometimes I'd cook him lunch. He raved about my saffron rice. Other times, he brought an extra sandwich for me. I was partial to egg salad.

On a particularly chilly Tuesday, I went to the lobby for my daily chat, but Bill was busy.

"Who is this handsome fellow?" I asked, pointing to the four-legged creature with hair whiter than the drifting snow outside.

"Figures, all the girls are crazy for him. This is Charlie. He belongs to the Seville Sisters in 14-E. Their dog-walker couldn't come today due to the weather, so I offered to fill in."

I looked outside the revolving doors. The snow rained down in heavy sheets.

"You're going out in that?"

"Already did. Now I'm waiting for Miss Danvers to arrive with her trunk full of shopping bags. I'm not really sure how I'm going to manage this one. Charlie barks when he's tied up."

"I can take him back for you."

"You sure?"

"Positive."

I grabbed hold of the leash. The dog jumped in my arms.

"Some mutts have all the luck," Bill said, petting him good-bye.

I punched the button on the lift. "You're a pretty boy, aren't you?" He licked my face in agreement. He had a glittering pink collar and fur softer than silk.

An elderly lady answered the door, her gorgeous silver hair resembling a halo. Her ears dripped with glittering diamonds. She wore a pink-checked suit. Although she was very different, she had the same air of grace that Dadima had. "Well, hello. I was expecting Bill."

"I was doing him a favor. I live in the building, too." Charlie jumped out of my arms and into hers.

"Hello, Charlie boy. Have a good walk?" She kissed him.

"Goodbye," I said. "Have a good day."

"Wait, dear." I wondered if she was going to tip me. Instead, she opened the door wider. "It's time for high tea. Sister and I can use a bit of youth to freshen up the old place. Won't you join us?"

"I'd love to."

"I'm Dorothy Seville, and this is Lucille."

Lucille pushed a walker. She was older than Dorothy, but held a lively and mischievous smile, making her seem younger. I liked them both immediately.

"Mary Costa."

Their apartment was plush sofas with soft floral patterns and tons of antiques. A small table was set up with linen napkins and floral dishes holding small white sandwiches without crusts. A shiny silver tea setting sat in the middle.

"I haven't seen you before. Are you new to the building, dear?" Lucille asked me.

"Fairly new. I recently moved into the penthouse."

"I thought the young British man owned the penthouse."

"He does. I'm his girlfriend."

"Ah, I see," Dorothy said, her eyes sparkling as much as her ears did. "My, he's a handsome one, although he is a bit of a loner. I offered to set him up with my granddaughter, you know. He graciously refused. I'd almost thought he was more interested in the rougher sex."

I almost choked on my tea. "Rougher sex?"

"Jesus, Dorothy, just say what you mean. She thought he was a fruit."

"A fruit?"

"A homosexual, dear," Dorothy said.

"Oh, I see. He's not."

"Well, hot damn." Lucille slapped my knee. "Well done, child. He has manners. He not only holds the elevator open, but he assists me inside. Plus, he's a hottie, as the kids say. Bedroom eyes, yank-able hair, and that butt is like a work of art."

I laughed at her analogy.

"Yes, he has all those things. I'm a lucky girl."

Dorothy rolled her eyes. "Excuse my sister. She forgets her manners and her age."

Lucille huffed. "Everyone should be so lucky to forget their age. I swear, if I were ten years younger..."

"Then you'd be young enough to be his grandmother," Dorothy replied, a warning in her voice.

I expected Lucille to combat her with another quip, but she simply crossed her arms. "True."

"I was married to a British man once," Dorothy said as she poured me a cup of tea. She opened a decorative tin containing tiny square lumps of sugar.

"How many, dear?"

"One, please."

She twirled a silver spoon in my cup. It was all very sophisticated. I took a sip of my tea. I held up the cup, pinkie out. "What type of tea is this?"

"Sorry, we should have told you it's laced with brandy. Perhaps I can make you a fresh cup?"

"This is delicious."

"Oh, good."

"What happened? To the British man you were married to?"

"He asked me to make him Bubble and Squeak."

"What is that?"

"It's a god-awful British dish. Anyway, I prided myself on being a decent homemaker. Our mother taught us well. We were trained in the art of wifery at a young age. Always wear a strand of pearls and make pushing out babies look painless and all that. I excelled on those accounts. So I made him Bubble and Squeak. In return, he bubbled and squeaked all night."

Lucille huffed. "That was the end of husband number three. You think you've found James Bond, but in reality it's just Mr. Bean in disguise."

"You divorced over that?" I asked, my tone full of disbelief.

Her ruby-colored lips curled into a sad smile. "Not quite, dear. There were many other issues. Some men confuse women with property. We are not continents to be conquered, but gardens to be nurtured. Always remember that."

"I will."

During the course of our tea, the sisters delighted me with stories of their past adventures. Within the tapestry of our conversation, I worked out the ladies had many marriages between them. They were like old romantic figures from an Austen novel, the ones who always had great advice and antidotes. I soaked it all up, enjoying each and every story while savoring cucumber mint sandwiches and tea laced with brandy.

"You have a lovely accent. Where are you from, dear?"

"India."

Dorothy clapped her heavily jeweled hands. "How wonderful. When you come for tea tomorrow, you must regale us with your own adventures in the far east."

I attended tea most days.

Chapter 37

Mary

Liam didn't like his job, but he was dedicated to it. He worked long hours, often apologizing for being late. I never let him feel guilty. We snuggled on the sofa under a warm blanket. He introduced me to action films, which I loved. He laughed when I requested we watch Thor. It turned out Sita was right about his voice. We watched Bollywood movies, too. Although there were subtitles, I often whispered the more romantic dialogue in his ear.

Liam showed me how to use a computer. He set up an email and Facebook account for me. Divya, Amira, and I chatted daily. I was so grateful to have them back in my life. Although I wasn't eligible to work due to my visa status, I did enroll in a few cooking classes at a nearby restaurant.

Anderson drove me to Dr. Chivel's office after my first month in the States. Liam had heard she was the best in Manhattan. He insisted I see her even though she was booked for weeks. I sat in a paper gown waiting for her to examine me. She started our session with questions. Tons of questions about my sexual history and health. I answered them with a complete honesty that shocked me.

"I've only had one committed relationship. The one I'm in now. I've had other sexual partners. I've had unprotected sex twice but was tested afterward."

Dr. Chivel removed her glasses. "You know how dangerous that is, dear?"

"Yes. Those times weren't by choice, doctor."

She tilted her head, digesting my statement. She gave me a sympathetic smile. "I see. Have you ever had therapy?"

"Yes."

"I'd recommend you go again. Especially if this is your first committed relationship. It will benefit you. Also, I'd like to run another blood test before I prescribe anything."

I had no qualms about another test. I loved Liam. I wanted to protect him, and I would never jeopardize his health. She gave me the card of a therapist and took a blood sample. A week later, I presented my results to Liam. "I thought you should see it."

"Thank you," he said, folding it up and handing it back to me.

"Liam, I've been thinking about this. I hope you're not offended, but I'd like you to have a test, too."

"Why would I be offended?" He gripped my hips, lifting me to the countertop in the kitchen. "I love you, Mary. That means I won't let anyone harm you, especially not me. I'm already on the same page, though."

"What do you mean?"

He pulled out a paper from his jacket. "Here."

"What's this?"

"When you told me you were having a test, I scheduled an appointment for myself. We're both clean."

Liam made no distinctions between us. Of course he'd want to protect me, too.

I cupped his face and kissed him. "You nurture my garden, Liam Montgomery."

"Is that suppose to turn me on? 'Cause it just sounds really weird."

"I guess it does. I only mean that I love you very much."

"I love you, too, Mary." He shuffled his feet. "So…are we safe?"

"Yes."

His smile turned sinful. "Then why are your clothes still on, lover?"

"I'm waiting for you to take them off, sir."

He growled before he carried me into the bedroom. I'm not sure who took off whose clothes, but we both ended up naked on the bed. He slipped an eye mask over me. I couldn't see anything, not even with the lights on.

"Lay on your front, love."

I turned around. He adjusted my face so my cheek was lying on the pillow. "Remember Goa? I want the only sense to be my voice and my body. I have fucked you and made love to you, but tonight…tonight I'm going to ravish you. Do you want that, Mary?"

"Yes, sir."

"If you don't like anything I'm doing, then I want you to say the word...'honey.' I will stop immediately. Can you do that?"

"Yes."

"Say it now."

"Honey."

The mattress sunk with his weight. He secured my hands behind my back with soft rope. Liam kissed my shoulder. Then he bit it. He pulled me up by the rope.

"Kneel for me."

"Yes, sir."

In this position, I expected something rough from him. Something I wasn't sure I wanted at all. Except, he wasn't rough. His hands slid down my body. He suckled my earlobes. Soft leather skimmed my spine. He moved it across my face. My breaths quickened. He rolled my nipples between his fingers.

His fingers entered me. I leaned against his back, spreading my legs. I was restrained and free at the same time. "Help me please you, Mary."

He untied me, rubbing each of my wrists. "Show me how you please yourself." I didn't know what he meant until he took my hand and lowered it. I touched myself, owning my own seduction. He shifted away from me. I cried out for him. Then I felt his tongue inside me. "Keep going, lass. I'm watching you." He moved to the same rhythm I set.

"You taste so fucking good." His husky voice sent a shiver right though me. "Fuck, I can't hold off."

"Then don't."

I heard his breaths, felt the closeness of our bond, and smelled the masculine scent of his skin. I reached my hand out. He grasped it and pulled me against his lap. He groaned as he entered me. I threw my arms around him, my breasts bumping against his chest. He pulled my hair back. He slammed me into the bed.

"You were made for me."

"Yes. I was made for you." He was made for me, too, some grand design beyond my understanding.

Liam wasn't gentle now. Rolling his hips, each thrust had a new urgency. I wanted to beg him to take off the mask, but I was incapable of voicing my needs. He must have understood, or else he wanted to look at my face just as badly, because he tore it off.

"Tell me you're mine. All mine."

"I'm yours, Liam. All yours."

With his lips against me, I shuddered with pleasure. He reared his head back, his face looking so beautiful with his release. Warmth flooded inside of me. We were both out of breath. He managed to recover first. Pressing his forehead against mine, he told me exactly what I needed to hear. "I'm yours, too. Master, servant, lover, friend. Just as you are mine."

I almost feared my own joy. Anything this good was surely dangerous and precious. "You are, Liam. You are all those things to me."

He went to the bathroom. When he came back, he had a warm washcloth. He cleaned me. I looked at the bed. I picked up the item he must have brushed against my skin. It was a handle with several soft leather braids on the end. There were metal clips and handcuffs and long beads as well.

"Where did you get all of this?" I asked, gesturing to the rope and mask.

"I bought a Dom-in-the-box kit from Amazon."

I sat up. "Really?"

He winked at me, his smile turning mischievous. "No, not really. Although I did order it."

"What's this?" I asked, pulling out a long object sheathed in a silk pouch.

"It's for you, love."

"Oh, my God, is this…this is…"

"Yes, it's a dildo. I have to go to Mexico for a few days. Unfortunately, you can't come due to your visa status."

"I'll be fine."

"I have no doubt you will. However, your appetite is as voracious as mine. I brought this for you so you could pleasure yourself while I'm gone. But just so we're clear, I never want you to use it in front of me. And I will never use it on you."

I doubted I would ever try it either. I couldn't even operate the shower, and this was one area I didn't want to accidently scald or worse…electrocute.

"What will you be doing to entertain yourself in Mexico?"

He looked wounded by my question. He cupped my face. "I promise I will never cheat on you. To me, it's the worst form of betrayal. I'd never intentionally hurt you, especially in that way."

"Oh Liam, that's not what I meant. I trust you completely. I was asking if you have any devices to relieve your…cravings. That's all."

He chuckled. "No, sweetheart, it's not really my thing." He held up his right hand and wiggled his fingers. "I'll manage in my own old-fashioned way." He kissed me, opening my mouth and tangling our tongues. "I'll be thinking about you pleasuring yourself in front of me the whole time. You're my muse in every way, love. Every. Fucking. Way."

"I'll be thinking of you, too." I held up the device. "But this…this I'm not sure about." I flipped the switch. It buzzed so loudly I dropped it. We watched as the device spun around on the bed as if possessed.

We laughed. He smiled the wide smile that made the indented line on his cheek appear. I traced it with my finger.

"It's kind of small, don't you think?" I asked.

"I was looking for something to tie you over. Not a replacement."

"Unless it's going to hold me and tell me I'm pretty afterwards, it won't be much of a replacement."

He roared with laughter. "No, it definitely won't do those things, but I will. I'll call you every night, yeah?"

I sat up on my knees and kissed him back with the same wild passion he'd used on me. "You better. But out of curiosity, why won't you use this on me?"

Liam stared at the device, still buzzing in the middle of the bed. He turned it off and threw it in the nightstand drawer. He arched his brow, his smile turning a shade coy…an odd expression for Liam. "I'd rather not say."

I gripped his face. "Tell me."

He kissed my nose. "I'm such a jealous man when it comes to you, Miss Costa. I cannot stand the idea of another dick being inside of you. Even a fake one."

"I understand, sir."

Chapter 38

Mary

I'd been meaning to pay Chet a visit for weeks. When I kissed Liam good-bye the day he left for Mexico, he reminded me. Anderson drove me to Chet's office, but his receptionist told me he was off-site for the day.

"Do you want to leave that for him?" she asked, gesturing to the glass dish in my hand. I considered it, except this was a dish best served hot, and I wanted to deliver it myself.

"It's okay. I'll try another time."

"If you'd like, he's at the shelter today. I can give you the address."

"Yes, I'd appreciate it."

She jotted it down for me. Anderson seemed skeptical when I repeated it to him, but he took me anyway, cautioning we had to leave before dark. This was a part of New York I hadn't seen. The stores had bars across the windows. There was very little greenery. We pulled up next to a large brick building, its façade marked with spray paint.

I found Chet right away. He wore a dark suit jacket with blue jeans.

"Mary Costa, how are you?" he asked, as if he'd expected me.

"I'm well. I'm sorry to drop in on you like this, but I made something for you. I didn't think it would keep long." I handed him the glass container and a twenty-dollar bill. "I wanted to thank you for your kindness."

"You didn't have to pay me back."

"I sorted out my bank situation. I wanted to."

He lifted the lid, his eyes lighting up as he sniffed. "Gulab jamun. No cans, right?"

I lifted my hand. "Swear."

"Watch out. I might just fall in love with you."

"If I only knew you were that easy," a man said, walking up beside him. He had blond hair spiked with lime green tips, and tattoos on his hands and neck.

"Tony, meet Mary. She's the one I told you about."

"Ah yes, the ticking-clock girl."

"The very one. Mary, this is Tony, my paramour."

"I don't think I've ever heard the term 'paramour' used in normal conversation," I said.

"Yeah, well, Chet's kind of a crazy romantic," Tony said. He eyed the glass dish and turned back to Chet. "You planning on sharing?"

"Can't say I was."

Tony seemed to be Chet's polar opposite, but one look made it clear they were very much in love.

"Tony's an artist, too," Chet said. "His medium is ink and skin."

"I don't follow."

"Tattoos. I'm a tattoo artist."

"Did you do all those?" I asked.

"I designed them, but someone else did them. I don't work on my own body. I consider it a conflict of interest."

"Is that a rose?" I asked, gesturing to his hand. He held it out for me, palm up, so I could see the red rose with its twisting thorny vine going down his arm.

"It is."

"It's beautiful...so detailed. Does it mean something?"

"When I was going through a tough time, I forgot to see the flower inside the thorns. I only saw the thorns. It reminds me to always remember they lead to a bloom."

"Did it hurt?"

He stuck out his tongue, revealing a silver ball. "Not as much as this."

Sympathy pain shot through my own tongue. "You pierced your tongue?"

"Pierced a lot of things."

"Why?"

"I'll tell you when there aren't children around."

"I'll hold you to it." I looked around the large room. Groups of women and children sat at cafeteria-style tables. "What is this place?"

Chet held up the dish. "I'll let Tony explain. He's an actual employee. I just volunteer. Mary, you mind if I share?"

I took in all the faces. "Not at all. I wish I had made more."

"I think there will be just enough."

"Want a tour?" Tony asked.

"I'd love one, if you have time."

"Time I got. Follow me, kid. We call it 'the shelter.' We house about ten families. It's temporary housing for folks who are down on their luck. The idea is to help families in times of crisis. Unfortunately, there are always more crisis than room and board. We do our best."

"What made you want to do this?"

"I had a few times of crisis myself. I was homeless for a while. People helped me. I always wanted to return those favors."

Although the outside needed a fresh coat of paint, the inside of the building was modern with bright colors. Tony showed me the kitchen and cafeteria. He pointed down a corridor where the bedrooms were.

Tony was not only a tattoo artist, he was also a social worker. He'd met Chet at a conference. A year later, Chet moved to New York.

I listened to Tony, but my attention kept drifting to a little boy in the corner, a large box of crayons almost obscuring his face. "That's Marcus," Tony said. "He's pretty introverted. Can't blame him. His family has had a rougher patch than most. His older brother got involved with gangs. Marcus was there when a car drove by and shot his brother."

"Oh, my God."

"He and his mother are staying with us. But she's out looking for a job right now. We're trying to help her."

All the other kids were taking turns playing video games, but Marcus sat by himself. He had the face of a cherub and almond-shaped eyes. I saw Hannah in him.

"How old is he?"

"Physically, he's twelve. Mentally, he's about eight. He has autism. What he saw really set him back emotionally."

"May I talk to him?"

"He's not much of a talker, but you're welcome to try."

I approached him slowly. "Hi, Marcus. I'm Mary."

He didn't answer. I took the seat next to him and watched him color in the picture of a turkey.

"I can't get in the lines," he said after a while. He broke his crayon in frustration. "There is no brown. Turkeys are brown."

"Who said you need lines? Or that turkeys have to be brown?" I ripped the paper and turned it over.

He blinked his eyes. "Are you allowed to do that?"

"Sure," I said, not sure at all. "Draw whatever you want. Any color."

He drew on the backside. "My turkey is gonna be purple."

"I like purple." I pointed to the backpack on the table, which had purple stars scattered across it. "You must like it, too."

"It's a girl's backpack. The only one left. The big kids got to choose theirs."

"What would you pick if you could choose?"

He shrugged. "Not sure."

He drew a box with a triangle over it. It had no resemblance to a turkey at all.

"Is that a house, Marcus?"

"Not my house. Someone's house."

"It's a very nice house."

He held out his arms. "This is my house."

"I used to live in a place like this, too."

"A shelter?"

"Sort of." The orphanage wasn't exactly a homeless shelter, but it was where I went when I had no home. I took one of the plates Tony had laid out with the gulab jamun on it. "Try this," I said, passing it to Marcus. "I made it."

He looked at it suspiciously. "What is it?"

"It's like...like a beignet."

He rubbed his hair. "What's that?"

"A doughnut, Marcus," Chet said, taking the seat beside me.

"More like a doughnut hole," Tony offered, taking the other seat.

He took a bite, followed by another. Pretty soon he had an empty plate. "It's not the doughnut or the hole," he announced. We all agreed. I wiped his mouth. He started coloring again. "It tasted good."

"Thank you. May I come back tomorrow and color with you?"

"Will you bring more of those?"

"I can."

He gave the smallest nod. Then he smiled. It was a brilliant smile that lit up his face. Even though his innocence had been cruelly stolen, this little boy's spirit couldn't be broken. Like Hannah, he had a pureness and joy in his heart.

"You're good with him," Tony said, walking me out.

"My sister had Down Syndrome."

"He doesn't usually open up like that."

"I don't think he opened up. He said less than a paragraph to me."

"It's a paragraph more than we usually get. We can always use volunteers, Mary."

I became excited thinking about it. I had been searching for something to fulfill me. This felt right. "I'd enjoy that, Tony."

Anderson pulled up and Tony arched his brow, which was also pierced. "Maybe you don't bring a limousine to a homeless shelter tomorrow, though."

Chapter 39

Mary

I had just pulled out the last batch of oatmeal cookies, Marcus's favorite, when the buzzer sounded. Miss Jenkins was shopping. I answered the door and almost shut it again. Stephen stood there, shuffling his feet.

"What do you want?"

"I'm well and yourself? I know you're not from around here, but that's how we traditionally greet people."

"I have no interest in greeting you, Stephen. Liam's still in Mexico."

"I'm here to pay you a visit, Mary. I believe it's long overdue."

I backed away.

"And also to bring this." He held out a brightly colored package. "It's a Christmas present for Liam."

"Christmas isn't for another month."

"I meant Hanukkah. I believe it arrives earlier."

I took it and set it on the table. "What do you want?"

"Can we go for coffee?"

"Why would I go for coffee with you?"

"We can do this here if you'd prefer."

"Do what?"

"What are your intentions with my brother?"

I blinked, wondering if I'd heard correctly. "I care for him." The statement didn't reflect my depth of my feelings, but I wasn't about to share them with this strange man.

"Really? Because where I stand, it doesn't make a whole lot of sense."

"It doesn't have to make sense to you, does it? Why don't you ask him?"

"I would, but every time I say your name, he makes a fist. You know when people say the bark is worse than the bite? Well, that's bullshit, especially when it comes to Liam. His fist hurts like a mother." He worked his jaw as if he were in pain. "I have no interest in drinking meals from a straw for the next six months. So I'm asking you. Are you a gold digger? Or do you have some other agenda?"

"How dare you?" I marched toward him. "The man who pays for services to fulfill his loneliness is actually questioning our loving, committed relationship."

"You've got some balls, lady, talking to me like that."

"Now will you leave?"

"No. I see a change in him. He's different. He smiles more. He whistles sometimes. It's fucking annoying."

"Are you here to do what you did with Melanie? Because I'm not her. I'm not attracted to you or scared of you."

"She came onto me."

"It's no excuse."

"I know that." He pinched the bridge of his nose, breathing out a long sigh. "Look, can you just have a cup of coffee with me?"

Everything told me I should push him out the door and slam it in his face.

If he hadn't sounded so concerned when he called about his brother's health in Jaipur, I might have.

If he hadn't started several charitable projects benefitting people around the world, I might have.

If I hadn't been so curious about what he wanted, I might have.

If I didn't have demons of my own, I might have.

Instead, I grabbed my coat and followed him out.

The snow swirled around us. We walked in silence. He held the door for me.

"Why did you burn his books?" I asked as soon he set down the cups. "What kind of person does that?"

"Someone who's on very serious hallucinogens. I can't blame him for not forgiving me. I don't forgive me, either. For any of it. For all of it. I have no excuse except I was pretty fucked up back then."

I circled the rim of my cup. How did he know to get me chai? "And now?"

"Not as fucked up."

"Liam said you still take drugs."

Stephen rested his elbows on the table, his fingers clasped. "Prescription drugs, mostly. Once in a while, when I need to take the edge off, I snort a little coke. See how honest I'm being right now? I hope you'll return the favor."

His honesty did surprise me.

"You should stop."

"Well, thanks for the PSA. I'll take it under advisement." He gestured toward my chai. "Drink up while it's hot. Think I poisoned it?"

"I was debating."

He laughed. "Mary, villains aren't always evil. Everyone needs a day off."

"Who said you're the villain?"

"Liam does. If he is the hero, then surely I am the villain."

"Nothing is ever black and white. Except that I love Liam." I took a sip of my chai, maybe to prove something. The cup shook when I set it back down. "I believe you love him, too. That's why you're asking about my intentions. You're worried about him."

"Look, the damage between Liam and me cannot be repaired. I'm not asking you to do that. But if you think I'm going to let you Yoko your way into our company, you've got another thing coming."

Okay, so I was wrong. Maybe this did all come down to checks and balances. In Stephen's mind, I threw everything out of whack. "I don't want his money."

"What do you want?"

I straightened in my chair and met his eyes. "His happiness. Our happiness. If you think you can scare me off, you'll find out I've got some villain in me, too."

He took a long sip of his coffee, his icy blue eyes staring at me over the rim of the cup. "I believe you care about him. I had to hear it for myself, you understand."

"Just like that?"

"Not just like that. You've been volunteering at a homeless shelter. I know your best pal is Liam's doorman. You walk a dog every day and pick up his shit without blinking." He eyed my sweater with a harsh glance. "And frankly, you could dress a whole lot better. I know Liam's given you a credit card, but you hardly use it. Either you are not a gold digger, or you are just really lousy at it. I think it's the former."

That's how he knew I would like chai. "You've been following me?"

He let out a cynical sound, not quite a laugh. "I'm a busy man. I don't have time to follow you."

I tried to focus on something else besides the rise of blood in my ears. "Then how did you know?"

"I hired people to follow you," he said, as if that made it better.

I laughed because Stephen, in a very strange way, was attempting humor. Or maybe I was the strange one, because I graped the joke. "You're crazy."

"Takes one to know one. But hey, you're all right in my book. Maybe we can be friends." I replayed his request in my head, detecting no notes of sarcasm. I waited for him to laugh again, but his expression was sincere.

"Are you serious?"

"Yes."

"Why would I be friends with you?"

He held up his hand, undoing his gold watch. It landed on the table with a thud.

"Is that some kind of payoff?"

"No, sweetheart, we're way past the part where I offer you a check. Unless, of course, you want the watch. Take it, friend. It is a Rolex, after all. Although I think it would look odd on you, it would be an improvement on your current choices. Seriously, do you shop at the granny store?"

"I don't want your watch or anything else. Not that my style of dress is any of your business, but let me explain something. First, it's freezing outside. If it would be socially acceptable, I'd tie a flock of lambs around me. Second, you're horrible at this friend thing. You should quit trying."

"Yeah, so I've been told." He held out his hand, splaying his fingers wide. It was almost imperceptible, but I noticed the tremble. "To answer your original question, we can be friends because we're part of the same club, you and I."

The scar was faint and no doubt old, but its purpose clear.

"Getting me to feel sorry for you?" I asked, echoing his words the day we met.

"No."

Too bad. It was working.

I played with the thick brown packets of sugar on the table. "When did you do it?"

"I was nineteen. I take it Liam didn't tell you?"

"No."

"After it happened, he visited me in the hospital. Visited me every day, as a matter of fact. The only visitor I had. We didn't talk much. Really didn't talk at all. He brought over a game console. We played *Call of Duty* for hours. He didn't even like video games. He just knew I needed someone to care. And there was no one else. Even though I burned his books and slept with his girlfriend, he still came. Yeah, he'll never forgive me, but he's all I got." Stephen shook his head, his laugh too sad to be cynical. "The only person who cares about me also hates me. Pretty pathetic, huh?"

"What about your mother?"

"If you met my mother, you wouldn't ask the question."

"Why?"

"Because she's a cold bitch who cares more about her social standing than the welfare of her son."

"I mean, why did you do it?"

"Things happened. It messed me up. I see the same messed-up shit in you. Some strange part of me believes if I help you, I can get past some of my own stuff. I understand your suspicion, but maybe we just meet for coffee and talk once in a while." He gestured to my outfit. "Maybe I can give you a couple of tips."

"You need a therapist, not a friend."

"I have one. I see him once a week, lately twice. Do you see one, Mary?"

"No, but I'm going to start."

"That's good. I attend this group, too. I haven't gone in a while, but if you'd like, I could take you."

"What kind of group?"

"People who know all about the dark matter in the universe, and I'm not talking about space."

"I don't need your help."

"Maybe I need yours. This isn't anything creepy. Well, I guess it is. But not sexual creepy. I told you—"

I held up my hand. "I know, you prefer redheads and you hate the way I dress."

"Sweet of you to remember."

"No worries there. My heart belongs to Liam. He owns it outright."

"Good, so there is no issue then."

"There's a very big issue. Liam wouldn't approve of our friendship. He would see it as an act of disloyalty. I see it that way, too."

Stephen smirked. "You do everything he tells you to?"

"Not everything, but I wouldn't do anything to intentionally hurt him or jeopardize our relationship. If you really cared for him, you wouldn't, either."

"Ouch."

I stood, my chair scraping against the wooden floor. "Good-bye,

Stephen. Stop following me. I can't be your friend, but I promise if you do anything else to hurt Liam, you will make an enemy out of me."

"See you around, Mary," he called out as I walked away.

Chapter 40

Liam

I dropped my suitcase on the floor. I was exhausted. "Mary?"

She rushed out of the kitchen straight into my arms. I picked her up and swung her around. What a welcome home this girl could give. Suddenly, I wasn't so tired. We'd talked on the phone every night, but there was no replacement for this.

"I missed you so much." She punctuated each word with a kiss.

"Me too, love."

"Are you hungry? I made dinner."

"Starving, but not for food."

She laughed, her head falling back, her silky hair falling on my arms. "Then take me to the bedroom, sir."

We collapsed on the bed.

She straddled me, undoing the knot in my tie. "I have so much to tell you."

"Me first, love."

"Okay."

I pulled out the box from my pocket. "I had this made for you in Mexico."

Please don't reject this, Mary. Please let me give you a fucking nice gift for once.

She gasped as soon as she opened the case. "It's beautiful." She undid the bracelet from the velvet box. It was a solid silver band with tiny lotus flowers etched on it.

"I'm glad you think so. There's an inscription."

She turned it over. "To my Lotus Girl, with love, always yours, Liam." She looked at me with a big smile, completely at odds with the tear rolling down her face.

"Hey, what's this?" I asked, kissing it away.

"Liam, I love it. I will always wear it."

"Good. What did you want to tell me now?"

She bit her lower lip and turned her face away.

"What is it?"

Mary pointed to the nightstand, where a gift-wrapped package sat.

"You got me something, too?" I picked it up.

"It's from Stephen, actually. He came here to drop it off. We went for coffee."

I wanted to punch the wall. The gift shook in my hand. "You went for coffee with my brother?"

She twisted a strand of hair. "Yes. I'm telling you about it because it would feel underhanded if I didn't, but nothing underhanded happened. We only talked."

"I'm still trying to figure out why you'd go with him." I saw my past collide with my present. Was she trying to hurt me?

She took the package from me. Then she took my hand in both of hers. "I'm not sure. He asked about my intentions. I know it's strange. I think it came from a place of concern...concern for you. Then he asked me to be his friend. That was even stranger, but it sounded sincere. I told him 'no.'"

I exhaled a long, ragged breath. "Stephen only cares about Stephen. I'll make it clear to him he's not welcome in my home." Maybe I could even hold the conversation without beating my fists into his head.

"He's your brother. Your only family. I don't want you to have regrets like I do with Hannah."

"Not the same thing."

"He told me about how you visited him in the hospital."

I sighed, dragging a hand through my hair. This was the last thing I wanted to discuss. "Only because no one else did. Don't you see what he's doing? He's manipulating you. He's trying to fuck up my life."

"Are you going to at least open his gift?"

"It's the latest *Call of Duty* game. What he gets me every year. Just like all the other ones, I will donate it."

"That's the game you played when he was in the hospital. Don't you think it's his way of reaching out to you? Trying to make peace?"

"It's complete bollocks."

She flinched. "How do you manage to run a successful company with someone you hate?"

"We all do what we have to, Mary. One thing you don't have to do, that you shouldn't have done, is go to fucking coffee with my brother."

She turned away from me, staring at the wallpaper. I stood, groaning in frustration.

"Where are you going?"

"To take a shower. Good night."

I leaned against the shower wall under the hot spray for a long time. Long enough to realize I'd reacted from the fears of the past. Mary was not Melanie. She would not hurt me in a way I could not forgive. That much I knew. I came back to bed and slid beside her. "Still awake?"

"Yes," she said.

"I think you see the good in everyone, even a sod like Stephen. I trust you. But you trust everyone. He's not a good guy."

She rolled over and laid her head on my chest. "Liam, do you not remember who I was when you first met me? I trusted no one. I spoke to no one. Give me some credit. I don't see the good in everyone. What I have seen is evil. I've seen it firsthand. Because I have, I can recognize it. Stephen is insulting and brash. He's done evil things to you, perhaps even unforgiveable things, but he is not evil. He's like us."

"How's that?"

She pinched her fingers together. "A tad tortured."

I grabbed her waist and rolled us over, so I was on top of her. "I appreciate your being honest with me. You're not a naïve, gullible girl. I'm sorry if I made it out that you were. I'm in awe of your strength and bravery and compassion. I understand you're trying to help me, but baby, you can't un-sink a ship. All I thought about in Mexico was this moment when I got to hold you and kiss you and worship you."

She kissed the corner of my mouth. "Let's get started on that right away…sir."

That's my girl.

Chapter 41

Liam

We didn't talk about Stephen, but it was still a sore subject. Instead, she told me about the boy over breakfast. Her face lit up with excitement. Then she told me about her plans.

"Absolutely not," I said, slamming down my coffee cup.

"Excuse me?"

"You heard me, Mary. You're not working there."

"Volunteering, not working. I can't work because of my visa status."

"Well, you're not volunteering, either."

She paced the room. All the excitement in her face had disappeared. She chewed on her lower lip, throwing me steely glances. I had a moment of regret, but when I thought about what she was asking, it didn't last long.

She stopped in front me, hands on her hips. "I think you're mistaken. I wasn't asking you for permission."

"You don't have to ask. I'm telling you."

"What is your problem?"

"It's not a good area. Don't you dare fucking say you can take care of yourself, either."

She put her hand on my shoulder. "Liam, I love you, but I can't sit here and wait for you to come home every day. Is that what you wanted? Someone to wait for you every day?"

"Of course not."

"Then why are you being so stubborn? You told me to find my place, and that's what I'm attempting to do."

"I'm stubborn? Because I don't want the woman I love to go to a place where random shootings are a daily occurrence?"

"You're exaggerating."

"If you want to volunteer somewhere, I can give you a list of acceptable opportunities."

"I want this."

"I understand you think you can make a difference in this boy's life."

She stamped her foot. "You don't understand at all." She clenched her teeth. "He makes a difference in *my* life. Not the other way around."

"No, Mary. It's not going to happen."

"You can't command me."

"You love it when I'm commanding."

She shook her head, her shoulders slumped. "Not like this."

I broke her some. Whatever strides we'd made, I'd managed to set us back. Did she not realize how much I worried about her? I wanted to protect her. Why wouldn't she let me?

"I have to go to work. Are we done here?"

"No need to dismiss me, sir. I have nothing further to say."

I slammed the door on the way out.

What was happening to us?

* * * *

I headed to Stephen's office first thing.

"Morning, Liam," he said without looking up.

"Stay away from my girl."

"I looked into her past."

I clenched my fists and counted to ten, trying to control the fury inside me. "What gave you the right?"

"Do you know about her? About her past?"

"I know everything."

He nodded. There was no smartass remark or smirk. Instead, he stood from his desk and looked me in the eye. "Don't hurt her, Liam. She's been hurt enough." It was the last thing I expected him to say. It caught me so off-guard, I had no response.

I worked for a few hours, but my mind kept reeling back to our fight. I stared at the photo on my desk. It was a candid shot I took of her on the beach, the waves lapping at her feet and a breathtaking smile on her face. It wasn't in the picture, but she was watching some children building sandcastles.

What had she said about the lotus blossom?

It's strong but delicate. You can't change the habitat without destroying it.

Mary was strong but delicate. Was I destroying her?

Moneypenny came in with contracts for me to sign. "Can I get you anything else, Liam?"

"Will you sit?"

She raised her eyebrow. "You need me to take notes?"

"Not exactly."

"What's wrong?"

"Did I tell you I fell in love in India?"

She slid into the chair. "You didn't have to. I saw the picture. That and the new perma-smile you're sporting."

"I love her so much it frightens me."

"It should frighten you. That's how you know it's real. You're putting your hopes and faith in someone else. You don't have control over it. It's one of the greatest risks, but it's also the best reward in the world."

"Right you are, as always. You're brilliant, Moneypenny."

"So brilliant I deserve a bonus?"

"And cunning... I forgot cunning."

"I'm kidding, Liam."

"I'll take it under advisement anyway, but for now, I need you to cancel my afternoon."

She cupped her hand over her ear as if she didn't hear me. "Everything?"

"Clear the schedule, Moneypenny. I'm playing hooky today."

Chapter 42

Liam

When I walked into the bedroom, Mary whirled around. She had her back against the wall, as if she was hiding something.

"What are you doing, love?" I asked.

"Why are you home?" she countered.

"We didn't finish our discussion."

"I don't want to argue anymore."

Her arms were behind her.

"Are you hiding something?"

She sighed and stepped aside. I couldn't see anything, so I moved closer. She pointed to the tiny tear in the wallpaper about the size of a dime.

"I was trying to clean it. I scrubbed it so hard, I tore a hole instead. I'm sorry."

I laughed and took her in my arms. "It's fine, lass. It's kind of ugly anyway."

"It's ruined because of me. I tried to get rid of the stain, but I made it worse."

I'd never noticed any stain in the wallpaper, but I realized that's where her eyes always went when she entered our bedroom.

I peeled the edge of the hole and then ripped it some more, making her dime-sized hole into a tennis ball. "No big deal. Feel better?"

"No." Her mouth gaped. "I can't believe you did that."

"Come here," I said, leading her to the bed. "Let's talk."

"You changed your mind?"

"No, Mary. It's not safe."

"Then there is nothing to talk about." She turned toward the spot.

I tilted her chin, turning her face to meet mine. "Stop worrying about the bloody wallpaper."

"Do you think we can fix it?"

"Fix what?" *Our relationship?* It wasn't broken, at least not to me.

"The wallpaper."

Suddenly, I knew what we had to do. It might not have made sense to anyone else, but I knew my girl. I knew how she thought. What she needed.

"Not fix it, sweetheart. We can make something new, though." I held out my hand. "Let's go out."

"Where?"

"We'll need supplies."

* * * *

We'd chosen a color between sea and sky. Actually, we each picked a swatch. I went for sea and she went for sky. We found something in the middle. When I went to pay, she tapped at the bill tucked into my wallet. The rupee note she'd given me as payment the first night I sketched her.

"You still have it?" she asked.

Why was she surprised? This note, this symbolic gesture, meant a great deal to me. I put my arm around her and kissed her head. "Best money I ever earned."

Bill came up to help me move the bed. It wasn't easy removing that God-awful wallpaper.

The work was good, both distracting and cleansing in a way. Maybe because we were busy doing something, it was easier to talk. I'd promised myself I wouldn't broach the subject of her impending decision, but I saw her struggling with this new life. "Are you having a hard time here, love?"

Paint spattered her T-shirt as she rolled. "It's an adjustment. Things are different."

"What things exactly?"

I figured she'd say 'me" or 'us,' or something along those lines.

"Units of measure. I keep converting things in my head. Distances take a lot longer than I plan on."

I covered a spot she missed, wondering if I heard her right. "Units of measure?"

"It's a small thing, but there are a lot of little things like that. They add up. It's hard being an immigrant."

"You're having a tough time with units of measure?" I was relieved. Because this...this I could help her with.

"Don't tease me."

"I'm not, Mary. I get it. If anyone gets it, I do. Why didn't you talk to me about it? I was an immigrant myself, remember?"

She smiled. "I forgot. What was the hardest thing for you when you came here from London?"

"The date. It still is. Sometimes I still write the day first."

"I haven't done it much, but I got it wrong when I signed the bank papers."

"It'll take a while. Don't even get me started on 'Celsius' and 'Fahrenheit.'"

She laughed. "Oh, my God, so true. Every day when I hear the weather, I get so excited thinking it's going to be thirty degrees. Then I remember that means slickers and coats and gloves here."

"Exactly. Once in a great while it happens to me, too. You'll get used to it. What else are you having trouble with, Mary?"

"The prices. I do the exchange rate in my head. I calculate it twice, usually. I can't believe how much things cost."

I wanted to tell her not to worry, but the words would be meaningless. "I understand."

"Don't get me wrong, Liam, I'm adjusting. There are things I love, too. I love Central Park and the subway and how the stores are decorated for Christmas."

"I think you're the first person to ever utter affection for the subway."

"I haven't had the courage to attempt it on my own yet. I'm not really sure how to navigate it."

"There's an app. I'll download it on your phone. You just type in where you want to go and it sets the route for you, station to station. Although, I can't comprehend why you'd choose the subway when you have a car and driver at your disposal."

"I don't either, but sometimes I want to."

"We need to talk about stuff like this more."

"I agree."

We weren't exactly professional. We had a few drips. I used a fine paintbrush to cut the corners. When it was done, we sat on the floor against the door and admired our handiwork, a bottle of chilled white wine between us. We didn't even bother with glasses.

"Why did you want to paint the room?" she asked, passing me the bottle.

I took a long swig. "Because that hole would continue to cause you anxiety. I don't want anything in our bedroom to bother you. This is the room where we sleep and dream and make love. It's our sanctuary, yeah?"

"Yes. It's a really nice color, don't you think? It reminds me of Goa."

"Me, too."

"You haven't painted since we got here, Liam."

"Were you not here? I just painted a whole bloody room."

She laughed. "You know what I mean."

"I do." My fingers twitched thinking about it. "Are you upset with me about the shelter still?"

Mary crawled onto my lap. I put my arms around her, inhaling her spicy vanilla scent mixed with the tang of fresh paint.

"Liam, I love you, but you can't be my entire life."

"Doesn't mean I don't want to be."

She hugged me. "I even love you for saying that. But I have to have something of my own here. You told me to find my place. That's what I'm trying to do."

I kissed her head. "Don't stay any later than six."

She tilted her head. "What are you doing?"

"Compromising."

She smiled, the excitement back in her face. "Okay. No later than six. I promise."

"Have Anderson take you every day."

She shook her head. "I can't take a limousine to a homeless shelter, Liam."

"Baby, don't you care about Anderson? He has a family to support. You're going to make his position redundant."

"I talk to Anderson, Liam. I happen to know he usually drives you because you like to make calls and reply to emails during your commute. So in a sense, me utilizing Anderson and you driving yourself is a waste of resources."

Damn, this girl was a sharp negotiator.

"Fine. But you'll take a cab. Don't take the subway there. Every night, I'll pick you up."

"I agree to those terms."

I held up the bottle of wine. "Here's to a successful negotiation."

Chapter 43

Mary

I had bargained for his surprise. I also prepared for his dismissal. Instead, he grinned in that boyish way of his. He walked around the easel and supplies I'd set up. I'd covered the floor with the drop cloths we'd used when painting the bedroom. I hesitated on the purchase, worried the artist inside him had gone back into hibernation. He touched every tube of paint, his eyes glinting brighter as he handled each one.

"I found this small art supply store. I don't know if I purchased the right materials."

He threw off his suit jacket. "I'll make it work." He undid his cufflinks. "Thank you."

"You're welcome. What are you going to paint?"

"My favorite subject." He loosened his tie and unbuttoned his crisp white shirt. He stripped down to his boxers.

"Why are you stripping?"

He stared at me, a hunger in his eyes that robbed me of all senses. "I'm not going to risk getting paint on anything. I can be very messy, Mary."

He lifted my blouse and then reached behind me to unclasp my bra. My skirt followed.

"Leave your knickers on."

He moved a chair to the middle of the room, his excitement growing. "Sit here, lass."

"Like this?" I asked, sitting very straight.

He undid the clip in my hair. "Bring your feet up. I've seen you sit that way before. It's comfortable for you, yeah?"

I nodded and did as he asked.

"You look beautiful, Mary." His lips grazed mine.

He went to the easel. I remained as still as possible for as long as possible. I snuck glances at him in my peripheral. He was definitely in his element, the passion evident on his face. I wasn't tracking the time, but the dim sky had turned dark, and I couldn't maintain my position any longer. "I need a break, Liam."

"Right."

He came over to me. He massaged my legs and stretched them. "You're very tense. I should have noticed. Sometimes I get carried away."

"I'm fine."

He steadied me as I stretched. "Want to see it?"

"Yes."

He'd done me in a black background with shimmering gold light around me. I marveled at the way he captured little details, like the white half-moon tips of my fingernails. He put his arm around my waist. He had paint splatters all over his chest. "I love it."

"Thank you."

"You *are* messy."

He took the brush, dipped it in a dollop of bottled green, and painted on my stomach. I looked down at the smiley face he drew. "Now we match."

"Not quite." I took the brush from him and tried to make a heart on his arm, but it looked more like a weird circle.

"Oh, you'll pay for that, Miss Costa." He tickled me so hard I fell to the ground. He moved on top of me. We rolled around, knocking into the table. The paint tray fell on us. Paint dripped down his back and across my side. He traced the line of my hip with citrus orange. I painted his back in an earthy red. Paint was everywhere. In our hair, on our bodies, and flowing onto the hardwood floor like lava. It would take forever to clean up, but for once, I wasn't paying attention to the mess. I was so deliriously happy, I wanted to splash color on everything.

"Liam?"

"Yes, my love."

I swirled all the colors with my fingertip. Then I took his left hand and drew a solid circle around the base of his ring finger.

"What are you doing?"

"I'm telling you it's okay."

"Okay?"

"You can ask me to marry you."

He smiled a huge smile. I traced the crease on the side of his face with dark purple. He kissed my forehead. He held me close, our bodies slick with paint. "Thank you, love. I know how much you miss home."

"You're my home, Liam."

Chapter 44

Liam

I wanted to fly out to California for the long weekend and propose at the Wilshire Pacific, but Mary was intrigued with the idea of Thanksgiving. She asked if we could have people over.

I had to admit, she'd managed to make closer friendships in two months than I had in all my years in the States. She had been animated when she talked about menus and guest lists and table centerpieces. And a bunch of other stuff my masculine tendencies precluded me from understanding. Regardless, I couldn't deny her. Then she'd asked in a tentative whisper if we could invite Stephen. I didn't know who was more shocked when I had agreed.

"What can I do?" I asked, putting my arms around her as she stirred a pot.

"Not distract me."

I kissed her neck. "That might be difficult."

She closed the lid and went to the opposite counter to peel potatoes. "Will you cut the onions? They always make me cry."

"I can do that."

I heard something roll onto the floor. I bent to pick it up. She turned around, her hands clapped against her mouth.

"Yes, Liam!"

"Yes what?" I realized the position I was in and what she thought. Shit. "You dropped this," I said, handing her the potato.

Disappointment coursed through her face.

I arched my brow, trying and failing to hide my smile. "Thought I was proposing, did you?"

"Maybe," she said, turning back around.

I spun her toward me. "I plan something much more romantic than kneeling on the kitchen floor while you're peeling potatoes."

"You don't have to be romantic."

"Yes, I do, Mary. You deserve it."

We finished preparing the meal and getting ready just as our first guests arrived.

The Seville sisters were interesting. They brought Bubble and Squeak, which I never really enjoyed. For whatever reason, this made Mary giggle like a school girl.

"He is British, and it was the only British thing I could make," one of them said.

Then the older one winked at me and commented what lovely cheeks I had. Cheeks she wouldn't mind pinching. I had a feeling she wasn't talking about my face.

Clawson, whose daughters weren't coming home this year, came next, bringing some kind of pork stuffing.

"Hello, mate," I said, taking the casserole dish from him.

"Mr. Montgomery, thanks for the invite."

"It's Liam. Call me Liam."

"Okay, as long as you call me Clawson."

I stopped in my tracks. "That is what I call you."

"So it won't be an issue then."

Stephen came next, carrying a bottle of wine and a weary expression. "You sure about this, Liam?"

"No, but what the hell? You're here." I held up the bottle. "And you brought good wine." I lowered my voice so Mary couldn't hear me, but the warning was unmistakable. "Behave yourself. This is a big deal to Mary. She's been working all day."

"Behaving is not a problem, bro. But let me ask you something."

"What?"

"What the hell kind of cheap bastard are you? You didn't cater? Everyone this side of the Hudson caters."

I cracked up, because I did sound like a cheap bastard. "I suggested it. Mary insisted on doing it all herself. Just so you know, she's never made a turkey."

"You think she'll botch it up?"

"I have no idea, but no matter what, you're going to eat everything on your plate and tell her it's the best damn bird you've ever had, yeah?"

"Got it."

Stephen strolled over to the painting in the living room. I had done it last week, and it was the only one that was appropriate for public display of any kind. There was no way anyone was going to see the nudes except for me. In this one, she wore my blue oxford shirt and a pair of fuzzy white socks.

"You're painting again?"

"I am."

"I'm glad, Liam. You have a talent."

I would have treated a compliment from Stephen with suspicion if not for the sincerity of his delivery.

Mary wore an emerald green dress with a deep v-line. Her long hair cascaded in soft waves. The bracelet gleamed against her wrist. God, she was gorgeous. I debated kicking everyone out, sliding all the dishes off the dining room table, and having my way with her.

"Hello, Stephen," she said, holding out her hand.

Stephen kissed her cheek instead. I strained not to break my wine glass. "Looking good, Costa. You went shopping."

"Yes, I did."

"Find any lamb coats?"

She laughed. "Not yet."

"Well, I hope you bought an evening dress, too. There's a pretty big party next week."

Shite.

I let out an aggravated sigh directed at my brother. "I told you, Stephen, I have no interest in going."

"I don't want to go, either," he said.

"Then why are we discussing it?"

"Potential investors will be there, and we're taking the company public, so it's an important event for us. Besides, it's for charity."

"What charity?" Mary asked.

I sighed. "My stepmother throws an annual charity ball to support protecting endangered species. We don't have to go."

She looked worried. I wanted to hit Stephen in the back of the head for bringing it up when she was already stressed.

"Is it important for you to attend?" she asked.

"It's a matter of opinion," I said.

"No one wants to go. I think we've all established that," Stephen said. "But we need to go. Our biggest clients and future investors will be in attendance. My mother's friends aren't exactly worthwhile people, but they are influential, and we need their backing."

"Then we'll go," she said, offering me a hesitant smile.

I nodded at Stephen. He was right. "Okay, we'll go." I clapped my hands. "Let's get this dinner party going. Are Chet and Tony coming?"

"Not until later. They'll be here for dessert."

"Then let's eat."

Thank goodness for the Seville sisters, because they could definitely entertain.

"My Charlie is constantly licking my face. I have to tell him no," Dorothy said.

"I don't mind it," Lucille countered. "If only I could get him to stop biting."

"You encourage him. Just as you let him into your bed every night. He belongs on the floor."

Stephen looked at me questioningly. I shrugged.

"Who's Charlie?" I asked, afraid of the answer.

"Whoever he is, he's sure getting a lot of action," Stephen muttered.

"Their dog," Mary said. Bill burst out laughing.

Oh, thank God.

Mary tapped her glass with a spoon. "I heard about this tradition where we all go around and say something we're thankful for. Shall we try it?"

I nodded. "Sure, sweetheart."

She turned to Stephen to start. He cleared his throat. "I'm thankful the strip clubs are open tonight."

"Stephen!" I barked, although I sort of wanted to chuckle.

Mary tensed, and everyone looked uncomfortable. He sighed and started again. "I'm thankful to have people to spend Thanksgiving with."

Bill was thankful for his daughters and said a special prayer for the one in the service, which we all said with him.

"It's your turn, Miss Lucille," Mary said.

"I'm thankful the strip club gave me the night off," she said.

We were all silent for a second.

"So is everyone at the strip club," Dorothy muttered.

Everyone at the table, including Lucille Seville, broke into laughter.

"In all seriousness," Dorothy continued. "I'm thankful that no matter how large the gap exists between the old and young, we can still laugh together."

"I'll drink to that," Stephen said, lifting his glass. We all toasted.

Mary went next. "I'm thankful, grateful rather, for friends who mean so much they become family, and family who can get past their struggles and become friends."

I smiled at her, mouthing the words, "I love you."

Mary inspired me in all ways. She was the catalyst for my passions. But even more, she made me want to be a better man.

When we finally quieted down, I cleared my throat. "I'm thankful for the girl at the other end of this table. The one who challenges and supports me." I stood. "Mary, there's something important I need to ask you."

She gasped, a blush creeping into her cheeks. "Yes, Liam?"

"What's burning?"

Her jaw dropped. "Shit." She ran into the kitchen. I followed her.

She took out a blackened dish. I had no idea what it was except, judging from the smell, the onions I had chopped were definitely in there somewhere.

"I forgot about it," she said.

"We've got plenty of food."

"I thought you were going to ask me to marry you. Pretty mean, Liam."

"I'm sorry for teasing you. But you've made me wait so long, you can wait just a bit, can't you? A proposal is a thing of grand gestures. I want to make it perfect for you."

Her lips twitched, fighting the smile. I tickled her until she gave in. "Okay, I forgive you."

"Are you guys coming out here?" Stephen called. "The strip clubs are opening soon."

Chapter 45

Mary

The sisters Seville shook their heads every time I modeled a new outfit. "Well, this is the last one," I said, walking out in an understated knee-length black dress with slits on the side.

"Dear, that's a lovely gown, but it belongs on a lady of mature years," Dorothy said, pouring me some tea. "Someone our age."

Lucille huffed. "Speak for yourself. I wouldn't wear it."

"I couldn't find anything. I went to at least ten stores. I even used a personal shopper. But whatever fit in the waist, didn't look right in the bust. I don't have time for alternations."

Dorothy handed me a cucumber sandwich on a tiny plate. "Well, you are well endowed. That's a blessing and a curse."

"It's hopeless," I said.

Dorothy's teacup rattled when she set it down. She clapped her hands, animation coloring her gray eyes. "Sister, do you know what I'm thinking?"

"I can barely figure out what I'm thinking these days."

"The Givenchy beaded gown."

"What is that?" I asked.

"My second, and by far wealthiest husband, Hubert Rourke, bought it for me at a Sotheby's auction. It was originally designed for Audrey Hepburn. Luckily, Miss Hepburn and I shared the same svelte figure, so tailoring wasn't necessary. I bet you'd fill it out well."

"I couldn't."

"You must," Dorothy said, standing. "I'll go fetch it. I've kept it in immaculate condition all these years. It'll be wonderful to see someone wear it again."

The dress was nothing short of spectacular. It hugged my curves, with a plunging neckline and open back. Tiny crystal beads were sewn into the fabric and outlined the hem. It was a work of art.

"Wow," I said, staring at myself in Dorothy's full-length mirror.

Dorothy adjusted the straps. "This is a true vintage couture piece. I knew you would do it justice."

The reflection in the mirror was of a sexy, confident girl, who, until recently, had been a stranger to me.

"You'll have to wear your hair up," Dorothy said.

I gathered it in a low bun.

"No, dear, all the way up with a few scandalous wisps in just the right places. This is backless dress, and you have just the back for it. Hiding that would be akin to draping an oil cloth on the shoulder of Apollo. Show it off."

I thought of the scar on my back and how it would look. It wasn't just marred flesh. I'd let it define me and make choices for me. I wasn't going to do that anymore. I wasn't going to hide. In this room with the Seville sisters, I felt my dadima's presence looking down at me and nodding with approval.

"You're right," I said.

Chapter 46

Mary

Liam and I were in a hotel once again. His stepmother's home was a few hours' drive from the city, so we stayed at the Wilshire Montauk. He jerked his head toward the bed, his eyes smoldering. I was tempted, but he looked too perfect in his tux. Meanwhile, I still wore the hotel robe.

"Later, sir. We're running late."

"I hate how right you are. Let me check your ink, at least."

He brushed the hair away from my neck. Liam had held my hand the whole time Tony worked on recreating the lotus flower from Liam's rendering. I'd been thinking of a tattoo ever since I met Tony. What better symbol to show I had emerged clean, regardless of the darkness in my past? Liam had rubbed the ointment on it every night.

He ran his fingers over it. His touch made my body shiver with need. "It's healed."

He referred to the tattoo, but I felt healed in all ways.

"I hope these match your dress," he said, holding out a velvet box to me.

"Liam!"

"It's not a ring." My body slumped. I'd been so hesitant before, but now all I wanted was to marry him. He kissed my shoulder. "Don't be disappointed. We're going on a trip tomorrow."

"A trip?"

"As soon as we leave here, we'll head straight for the airport. Then we're off to Hawaii for a few days."

"But..."

"I called Tony. He switched your schedule around. I packed you a suitcase, although you might need to buy a few things. I even remembered your passport."

"Why do I need my passport for Hawaii?" I wondered if I'd gotten my geography mixed up again.

"You'll need photo ID. It's the only one you have."

I turned around. "I want to, Liam, but I promised to help Marcus's mother with her job interviews. Besides, can you take another holiday with the IPO coming up?"

"First, she has a job and an apartment now."

"What do you mean?"

"I took care of it. They'll have a home and be moved in before Christmas. When we get back from Hawaii, I told her we'd help them paint. We're both pretty handy at that."

Both Liam and Stephen had written large checks to the shelter. So large they could accommodate additional families and start new outreach programs. But this...this warmed my heart so much, I could have melted into a puddle. "Liam, you sweet, sweet man. I love you."

He pressed his lips against my forehead. "Second, things are going very smoothly. Stephen can handle it for a while." He settled his hands on my hips. "C'mon, lover, walk on the beach with me again."

"I can't wait."

"Open your gift." He tapped the box I was holding. "This is just a little something I picked up. Consider it an appetizer."

I lifted the lid, blinking against the shine of emerald earrings done in a paisley design. "These are gorgeous. They'll look beautiful with the dress."

"You would be beautiful in anything, Mary." He smacked my bum. "Or nothing at all. In fact, I think I want to paint you in nothing but these earrings."

"Seriously, Liam, you and your dolphin-sized libido need to leave me alone."

He laughed. "Baby, you're about to make the great white shark in me come out."

* * * *

My mouth dropped as I took in the dazzling ballroom with its sparking chandeliers and massive Christmas tree. I walked with nervous steps, hoping the heels didn't buckle on me. A firm hand pressed against my lower back, giving me the boost of confidence I needed.

"This is some dress. I'm not going to be able to keep my hands off you," Liam said, his whisper heavy and husky.

"Then don't."

"No worries there. Come and meet some people."

He introduced me to so many people, I forgot all the names. We sipped pale champagne and chatted casually. Stephen joined us. He and Liam even exchanged a few jokes.

"Mary, meet Janet Waters. She designed the interiors of several of our hotels." I shook her hand. Stephen stiffened beside me.

"I love your dress. It's stunning," she said. She had hair the color of strawberries. There was something familiar about her.

"Thank you."

The air stilled when she glanced at Stephen.

"Hi, Jan," he said. "Didn't know you were coming."

"Liam invited me."

"I see," he said, sounding disinterested, although his fingers tightened around his wineglass.

Liam led me to the dance floor. I noticed Stephen, standing in the corner, talking with Janet.

"Who is she?" I asked Liam.

"She went to college with Stephen. I believe they dated for a bit. He suggested her for this job. I have no idea why he was acting so cold to her. Then again, I rarely get what's going on inside his head."

I got it. It dawned on me why she looked familiar. She was the picture behind the picture in Stephen's office.

Liam looked down at his watch. "I'm counting down the minutes until we can leave. I hate this house."

"I'm sorry."

We danced through two songs before they announced dinner. Liam and I sat apart during the meal. Stephen was seated next to me. He downed one drink after another, keeping his eyes on Janet's back the whole time. Once she turned in his direction, he looked away.

"How are things, Mary?" he asked.

"Wonderful. What about you?"

"Can't complain. I'm going to get some air."

"May I come?"

"I wouldn't mind the company."

He helped me from my chair. We went outside to a heated patio. I worried it would be cold, but the heat lamps made it feel like a warm summer night. Everyone else was still inside. The naked trees stood close together, their branches twining as if they were embracing. A shiver ran up my spine. Stephen leaned against a railing and lit a cigarette.

"I didn't know you smoked."

"I have to keep some vices." He smiled at me. "How's therapy?"

"It's good. Liam is going to start coming with me, too. How's your therapy?"

"Not bad. I've been clean for over a month."

I bumped his shoulder. "You have? That's great."

"I got a keychain and everything." He bumped me back. "I never really thought about myself as an addict since I always managed to function in my life. I figured as long as I maintained a balance, I was fine. I just needed something to take the edge off once in a while."

"And now?"

"I figured out I need edges in my life. If you make the pain disappear, how would you ever recognize the pleasure?"

"True."

He stubbed his cigarette on the railing. "I hate this house," he muttered.

"Liam does, too."

"One thing we have in common."

I gestured inside. "You love her, don't you?"

"Who?"

"Janet, the girl with the red hair."

"I love all redheads." He wiggled his eyebrows. "They're freaks in bed."

"Don't lie to me. That's why you always ask the agency to send one. Do you pretend they are her?"

"You're a brazen one. Yeah, you got my number. What of it?"

"Why don't you tell her how you feel?"

"Some ships sail too far and deep to anchor. Understand?"

"Ummm, no, I have no idea what that means."

"I couldn't give her what she wanted then, and I'm certainly not capable of it now."

"What did she want?"

"The usual—marriage and kids. Security. Anyway, I let her go. That's what you do for someone you love. You let them go so their dreams don't die."

"Rubbish."

"What?"

"Rubbish. If you loved her and she loved you, then you fight. You fight for the person you love. You work hard to make each other's dreams happen or create new dreams."

"Look at you, Miss Freud."

"Sorry, yaar, I spoke out of turn."

"What does that mean? Yaar?"

"It's Hindi. It means…friend."

He smiled, a real smile, not a trace of condescension in it. "C'mon, yaar, let's go inside."

They were clearing dinner. Liam's hand pressed into my back, his spicy masculine scent intoxicating me. "There you are. I've been looking for you."

"You found me."

"It was easy. I just followed the gazes of all the men in the room. I think I liked you better when you wore my huge sweaters."

My laugh was cut off by the woman approaching us. "Hello, Liam. I suppose your mother never taught you, but it's rude not to greet your host."

Liam's jaw tightened, but he maintained the smile. "She did teach me that if I didn't have anything nice to say, I should shut my mouth." He turned to me. "Mary, this is Lorna Wilshire, Stephen's mother."

The woman embodied elegance in her floor-length gown, her hair the color of spun gold. "Also Liam's stepmother." There was judgment in her stare. I wanted to take a step back, but Liam's arm kept me grounded.

"It's nice to meet you."

"Yes," she replied, her eyes scanning me like a package containing something foul. She turned to Liam. "Did Bobby tell you I'm selling the house?"

Who was Bobby?

"No, he didn't."

"I'm permanently relocating to the city." She smiled as people passed us, making it appear we were having a friendly chat. "You have some things in the attic. I was going to donate them to the poor, but then I remembered you were pretty poor yourself, so I doubt they have any value to anyone. Shall I throw them out?"

Liam nodded, his arm tightening around me. "Do whatever you wish."

She patted her golden hair. "I see you're wearing them. They were his favorite. Of course, I thought he'd leave them to his legitimate son. Then again, you managed to inherit a great deal from your father." I followed her gaze to Liam's sleeve. He wore gold cuff links in the shape of birds.

Liam smiled brighter. "I'd be happy to return them."

She waved her hand in a gesture of dismissal. "Don't bother. That's not the point, is it?"

"I completely understand your point, Lorna. I've understood since I was a teenager. But back then, I actually cared. I won't make the same mistake again."

Her mouth gaped for a second. She quickly recovered, fixing us with an icy stare. "In any case, they look good on you. They are definitely appropriate for the evening, since the bald eagle is on the endangered list. Speaking of, I'm starting the presentation soon. I hope my son isn't too inebriated to join us." She walked away, leaving a heavy trail of expensive perfume behind her.

"Who is Bobby?" I asked, feeling uneasy.

"It's Stephen's first name…Robert. He's Robert Wilshire the Second. He decided to go by his middle name a few years ago. Lorna does not approve." Liam laughed. "She constantly lectured him about how lucky he was to carry the family name and legacy. I didn't live here that long, but there were loads of fireworks in this house, I tell you."

"I can imagine." My voice sounded distant to me.

"Are you alright, sweetheart?"

"Can you get me another glass of wine?"

"Maybe you should have water." He touched my forehead. "You feel warm." He took my hand and led me to a seat. I slumped into it, swallowing down the bile. *Stop it, you're acting ridiculous.*

I forced a smile, ignoring the irregular way my heart beat. "Wine, please."

"Okay, love, I'll be right back."

He brought me a glass, but it was weak. I drank it anyway. The lights dimmed as Lorna Wilshire took the stage.

"Thank you all for coming. This was an important charity for my husband. As you know, he dedicated his life to preserving endangered species, not just in this country, but all over the world. He was a humanitarian, a successful businessman, a philanthropist, and a wonderful husband and father."

I almost laughed at the last accolade.

"Friends, my words are hollow. He said it so much better than I can. He may be gone, but he is still in our hearts. So listen to him, and while you're at it, take out those checkbooks and jot down a lot of zeros." A few people snickered. "Or plastic if you prefer."

Then the screen behind her lit up. A distinguished-looking man sat at a desk. There was a gold tower behind him and a painting of trees twisting into each other.

"Hello, friends," his deep voice resonated.

I covered my ears. I didn't want to hear anymore. It was the same voice that haunted me.

Liam knelt in front of me, his face full of concern. He took my wrists and pried them off my ears. "Mary?"

I recognized the lines and curves of the picture. They were made by the same hands that held me every night. "You painted that. It's the trees in the back of this house."

"Yeah," he replied. "It was the portrait he bought at my exhibition. I still can't believe he hung it up in his office or that my stepmother never took it down."

Everything blurred, one color bleeding into the next, as if I was looking inside a kaleidoscope.

"Mary, sweetheart, look at me. What's the matter?"

I looked down at his cufflinks, waiting for the birds to carry me away.

"I was wrong."

"Wrong about what, love?"

"I thought they were birds of prey." They were supposed to eat my flesh and peck away at my soul until there was nothing left of me.

"Birds of prey?"

Vultures, I wanted to say. But I slipped into the darkness. It grounded me. It protected me.

Chapter 47

Mary

I was on a couch in a dim room. Liam sat beside me, holding my hand. His face lit up with relief when I opened my eyes. "Hey, there you are. You just fainted. Thank God, there was a doctor in attendance. He thinks you're dehydrated, so you're cut off for the night." Liam held a bottle of water under my lips. He offered me a half-hearted smile that couldn't conceal his worry. "I checked it personally. It's safe." I took slow sips.

He caressed my cheek. For the first time, I backed away from his touch. Hurt flickered across his face.

"Can we speak outside, Mr. Montgomery?" asked the man who must have been the doctor.

"Later," Liam answered, irritated.

"Go, Liam, I'll stay with her," Stephen said. Stephen...Bobby...the Monster's other son.

The door closed. I sat up, a dull ache in my head. The ache sharpened as I took in the room. The painting, the desk, the gold tower were all there. I used to dream of killing him in this room. Of taking the tower and smashing it over his head.

"Lay down, Mary," Stephen said. "You shouldn't be up."

Stephen...the man who'd asked me to be his friend. The man who thought he could help himself by helping me. It all clicked.

Stupid, stupid, girl.

"You knew." It was an accusation.

"Knew what?"

"You knew who I was. How?"

He took a step back. "You don't understand."

I stood and pushed him. Then I slapped him hard across the face. "What did you do, you sick bastard?"

He winced. "Calm down."

I kept going, spitting out the sick, twisted thoughts as they entered my mind. "Did you watch the videos? Did you and your father watch them together?"

I held my hand up to slap him again, but stopped in midair. He looked wounded and lost. Almost as if he wanted me to slap him.

"Listen to me," he pleaded. "I found a video on my father's computer. I had no idea what it was at first. Then I realized and wished to God I had never found it. I saw you in it. I recognized you that day in the office. I thought you had come to get revenge on us. Oh, God, Mary, I'm sorry. I confronted my dad about it, but I was just a kid. I was weak. My mother told me it would ruin us if I said anything, and no one would believe me anyway. She destroyed all the evidence. But I never forgot your face. It was burned into my memory. I have a lot to atone for since you weren't the only victim. Just the only one I met. After I saw you, I did some research into your background to confirm what I already knew."

I had fallen in love with the son of the man who had destroyed my life. The knowledge hit me so hard, I had to lean on a side board to keep from collapsing.

"Why didn't you tell me?"

"How could I? I was suspicious of you. Like I said, I thought you were looking for revenge, and that's why you were with Liam. Isn't that why you were a maid in Jaipur? The daughter of an educated man. Isn't that what you were doing? You honestly didn't know who Liam was? Who we were?"

"I didn't know your father by name. I only knew his voice, his smell, his shadow. Those things were seared into my soul. I'd heard him say he'd be back at the Wilshire in Jaipur in a few years. I decided when he returned, I would be waiting for him. I wanted to kill him."

"He's already dead."

"Then dig him up for me." *I'd dance on his bones and spit on his grave.*

"Mary, you have to calm down. I understand what you've been through. I've been where you've been."

"You don't fucking understand, Robert Wilshire the Second."

Stephen cringed. "Don't call me that."

"It's your name, isn't it?" I jabbed my finger into his chest. "Do you know what it's like to be tortured? To be raped? To feel as if you're nothing but a speck of dirt, upswept and sullied? To watch as your little sister had her innocence ripped away? To be relieved when she got ill and prayed she would die because she'd never find joy again? Do you fucking know what it's like to watch your papa blame himself?"

He dragged a shaky hand through his hair. "Stop...please."

"Don't tell me you understand me. That you've been where I've been because you feel guilty you saw something on a video once."

"No...I haven't been there, but I understand more than you think. He liked boys, too, at least young boys. He's behind every sharp edge and dark night of my life." He choked out a bitter sound. "When I realized I wasn't his only victim, some fucked-up part of me decided..." He sucked in a breath as a tear slid down his face. "Better them than me. Better you than me. God forgive me."

"Maybe God will forgive you, but I won't."

Stephen's body slumped in resignation. "We have the same monster, Mary. I'm begging you to let me atone for my sins. What can I do?"

The room closed in on me again. My head ached and a nauseous heat grew inside my belly. "Get me out of here."

Chapter 48

Mary

I waited for Stephen in his car. I watched as the lights turned on in every room of the massive house.

He opened the door. "I found your suitcase and your coat. Liam is going crazy."

"Did you talk to him?"

"Are you kidding? He probably thinks I kidnapped you. I snuck past him. This is ridiculous. You need to go back into the house."

"I'm never going to step foot in there again."

"Then I'll tell him to come out here."

"No."

He sighed. "Fine. Want me to take you back home?"

"Yes," I said, grateful he gave me the answer I searched for.

"Okay, we'll go back to the city. Then we'll call Liam."

I shook my head. "Take me to the airport."

"That's not going to happen." He opened his mouth to argue some more, but I slapped my hand over it.

"You owe me this. I want to go home. This is your chance to atone, Stephen. So shut up and drive."

I let out a breath when the car started moving. We were silent. Stephen's phone buzzed constantly, like some silly song on repeat.

"Liam's called eight times, Mary. I have to tell him something."

The next time it rang, I picked it up. "Liam."

"Mary, thank God. Where the hell are you?"

"I can't do this. I can't marry you."

"What? Have you gone mad?"

"Stephen's written me a huge check, large enough so I don't have to marry you. That's all I really wanted."

"You're lying." The hurt in his voice would have caused another tear in my heart if it weren't already completely broken.

"I'm not. I'm sorry."

"You just fainted. Obviously, you're not thinking straight."

"I am. I see everything for once."

"Sweetheart, tell me where you are. I'll come to you."

"Liam, if you really love me, you'll let me go. You need to understand my happiness means not having you in my life. You made a vow to me in a church that you'd let me go if it didn't feel right anymore. I need you to honor that vow now. Good-bye, Liam." I disconnected.

Stephen banged his hand against the steering wheel. "He's never going to believe that."

"It's better than the truth. I'm not going to tell him what kind of monster his father was. I'd rather have his hate than his pity. He's strong. He'll recover."

"He won't, Mary. You can work through this. It's not Liam's fault."

I closed my eyes, trying to summon strength I didn't feel. "It's not about fault. It's circumstance." Every time I looked at Liam now, I would hear Hannah's screams. I would go back into the darkness and never find my way out. I thought I'd emerged clean like the lotus blossom. But I was wrong. I remained rooted in the mud and muck.

The phone buzzed in my hand. I threw it against the dashboard. It bounced back on my lap. It buzzed again. I picked it up and threw it in the backseat. It buzzed some more. I craned back to find it. I opened the window and chucked it.

"I could have just turned it off," Stephen said.

I laughed hysterically. I had been outside of myself, exceptionally calm. But I felt everything inside me break at once. I buried my face in my hands and cried. He slowed the car down.

"Mary…" He touched my shoulder.

I recoiled. "Don't touch me. Keep driving."

We reached the airport in record time. The next direct flight was in eighteen hours. But there was one to London Heathrow leaving in two hours. I could make the connection there, so I booked it. I wanted out of this country as fast as possible. Thank God, Liam had packed my passport. I didn't have anything to declare. I didn't even have a bag to check, since I could carry the small suitcase with me. This was final. Once I left and my visa expired, I wouldn't be allowed to come back for years. The need to escape was so strong, I had no doubts about my decision.

"Do you need money?" Stephen asked.

I shook my head.

He clasped my arm. Then his eyes widened at my reaction. "I'm sorry." He let me go. "Don't do this. Don't let that man ruin your life. He's already destroyed so many."

"Good-bye, Stephen. Thank you for the ride."

I turned toward the security area. I looked back once. I saw him bury his face in his hands, his broad shoulders shaking.

It's not what it looks like. You explain that to Bobby. You know how his mind works.

I'd remembered that bit. Replayed it in my head over the years. Staring at him now, it was clear the choices of the past haunted him. He needed something from me. Although my stomach churned and my head reeled, I wanted to give him this. The peace of mind he'd always sought.

I ran back to him. He pulled me into a needy embrace. "I'm so sorry, Mary. I am."

"You're not to blame. You were a child."

"I threw up when I watched the video. I fucking puked all over his desk. I still taste it in my mouth every fucking day of my life. I taste that day over and over. You're wrong. It was my fault...some of it. A lot of it. I could have stopped it. I could have made him pay. I chose to be a coward instead."

I cupped his face and gave him the thing he most wanted from me. The thing he'd been asking from me since we'd met. "I forgive you."

"Thank you, yaar."

Chapter 49

Liam

I couldn't breathe. Tiny knives pierced my flesh. I jumped off the couch, ready to choke him. He threw a fucking bucket of cold water on me.

"What the fuck, Stephen!"

"Look at you. You're a mess."

"Yeah, you're one to talk."

"When's the last time you ate?"

"I'm on a liquid diet these days," I said, grabbing the bottle of rum.

He threw the bucket. Then he swiped the coffee table of all the wrappers and garbage. "Happy New Year, buddy. It's time to pull yourself together."

"What's your issue? I come to the important meetings. I still do my job. I'm functioning fine."

"This isn't about work."

"Don't pretend you care."

He shook his head. "I do care."

"Get the fuck out of my life."

He grabbed my shoulder and hoisted me up. I swung my fist but it missed. Hell, I was still half-drunk. He dragged me down the hall and threw me into the bathroom. "Take a shower. And while you're at it, shave off the beard. You look like a fucking British mountain man."

"Get the hell out of my house, Stephen."

"Listen, man, you may not like it, but you need me right now. I'm not very good at this, but I am all you have, so get in the fucking shower."

Somehow, that made sense. I got in the shower.

When I came out, he'd cleaned up the living room. Two cardboard boxes sat on the coffee table. "What's that?"

"Something to take your mind off it." He took out the video game console and hooked it up to the television. "You remember how to play?" he asked when the green and black graphics came up.

"I'm not doing this."

"Fine. I'll play by myself," he said with the haughty flourish of a spoiled teenager.

He sat on the floor, his back to the couch.

"We're not kids."

"Definitely not."

I joined him on the floor, drank my rum, and sulked. "Is she all right?"

"You ask me that every day. The answer is still the same. I have no idea. I haven't spoken to her."

"Tell me where she is."

"I told you, I don't know that either."

The doorbell rang. He paused the game to answer. My stomach grumbled as the aroma of hot, fresh pizza filled the room.

He pushed the box toward me. "Eat some pizza. I'm going to make coffee. We'll play a few games."

"I'm only going to ask you this one time. Did you do anything to her?" The ice in my voice was enough to make him shiver.

His jaw stiffened. "You think I hurt her?"

"The thought crossed my mind. You drove her to the airport, and she didn't sound like herself. So I repeat, did you fucking do anything to her?"

"I took her to the airport. That's all."

I let out a breath I'd been holding for a while. I didn't think he had, but I needed to ask the question just the same. I still couldn't come to terms with the fact she'd left me. It was so sudden and didn't make sense. No matter how much I questioned Stephen, he never gave me any concrete answers. Mary and I were happy together, weren't we?

"Why did she leave me?"

"Ask me a question I can answer, bro."

"What's in the other box?"

"Mom sold the house. It's your stuff that was still in the attic. She was going to throw it out, but I stopped her. I figured you'd want it. Nothing can make up for what I did to your books, but it's something."

"You should have let her throw it out. It's junk."

Stephen shrugged. "It's some old jewelry. It must have meant something to you if you lugged it here all the way from England."

"There wasn't time to pack. I just threw a bunch of stuff in suitcases. I probably threw in some of my mum's things by accident."

"Well, I tried." He held a controller out to me. "Want to play now? I have two controllers."

I stared at the screen with its brilliant details. "They've made a lot of improvements."

I snatched the controller from him. We played. We stopped talking. What use was it?

* * * *

He came over every night for a week. We played *Call of Duty*, ate pizza, and drank a few beers. I suppose it was some fucked-up version of male bonding.

"Why did she leave me?" I asked as I did every night, more to myself than him now.

Stephen turned off the game.

"I was winning."

"You won, Liam. I'm going to tell you. She asked me not to, but I can't keep doing this. I've held on to evil secrets for many years. They've ripped me apart from the inside out. I think they exploded inside me, and I became evil myself. But this one...this one I can't hold anymore. I'll warn you, once you know, you'll wish you didn't."

I wanted to break his jaw again. He'd been keeping things from me. I calmed myself with deep breaths. After all, if I broke his jaw, how could he speak? "Say it."

"You think I hated you because you took my inheritance."

"What other reason did you have?" I wanted to ask him why we were talking about us and not Mary, but I held it in. Stephen had paled a few shades since we began the conversation. He kept swallowing, so whatever this was, it wasn't easy for him.

"You didn't pay your dues. Our father was a sick man. You were too old when you came to our house to pique his interests."

"What are you saying?"

"I'm saying I was his favorite boy. He did things to me."

"Our dad molested you?"

He didn't answer. He didn't have to.

"I'm sorry, Stephen. I had no idea."

"He did stuff to you, too, Liam. You just don't know it."

"What stuff? Just say it, man."

"Your exhibition? You were set up to fail. Dad had a lot of contacts. He made that happen because he wanted you in the family business. He'd lost faith in me and needed a backup."

I laughed, because what the fuck else was there to do? "I sort of suspected. But the whole idea was so Machiavellian, I thought it was too dramatic to be real."

"You were right to suspect. You're a good artist, Liam."

"What does this have to do with Mary?"

"I'm getting to it. Just give me some slack." He chugged his beer, maybe to give him a break from the revelations. "Did you ever wonder why your mom never told you who your father was?"

"I asked him once. He said something about her being selfish and wanting to keep me to herself. I found it difficult to believe."

"A few years ago, I started researching into anything and everything to do with Robert Wilshire Senior. Your mother filed an accusation of rape."

"He raped my mother?" I was a product of rape?

"Nothing ever came of it. He had it covered up, Liam."

I always knew something was wrong, very wrong about my life, but I had never imagined this. Of course, I'd never imagined it. My mum had never shown any hatred or animosity toward me. Only love. My God… my poor mum. And Mary.

Mary!

I felt sick.

"Mary…"

The beer can crushed in my hand.

"Calm down, Liam."

"Don't fucking tell me to calm down. Say it. Say it right now."

"Our father was a pedophile. He did things, things that were easier to do abroad, like buy children for his disgusting personal amusement."

"Jesus Christ. He raped her? Why did you keep this from me? Why didn't she tell me?"

"She didn't have his name and never his saw his face. She only knew him by his voice and manners. And that he'd be in Jaipur every few years. That's why she was there. She wanted revenge." He told me some other things about how he'd come across the knowledge, but blood rushed into my ears, drowning out the rest.

I replayed everything. All the pieces made sense. All I wanted to do was destroy the puzzle. "So did he…rape her?"

"Not just her." He gripped the sofa. "Her sister, too."

Oh, God.

I threw the controller across the room. Something snapped inside me. I thought I'd felt rage once before in my life, but it was nothing like this. I didn't remember destroying the room. When it was over, I stood amidst a rubble of broken furniture, a ripped painting, and a cracked big screen. There were cuts in my hands, a gash on my foot, and I was gasping for breath. It wasn't enough. My father had destroyed everything she loved. His blood ran though my veins.

Mary, I'm so sorry.

"Feel better?" Stephen asked.

I leapt to the bathroom. I vomited a week's worth of pizza.

He handed me a wash cloth. I sat on the floor and closed my eyes. Repulsive images kept replaying themselves like a silent movie. Was this what Mary saw when she closed her eyes?

"I need you to leave, Stephen. I have to process this."

"But…"

"Please leave."

He did.

Chapter 50

Liam

Stephen peeked into my office. "Hey."

"What can I do for you?" I asked, not looking up from my computer.

He strolled inside and took a seat. "Just wanted to check in. You doing okay?"

"Fine. Busy gearing up for the IPO. Did you review the new contracts?"

He sat down. "Liam, you know what I mean. I've left you alone for a month now. We need to talk about this."

I leaned back in my chair. "I'm really sorry for what happened to you, Stephen. I understand some things better now. You've had a hard life."

"I'm not here to discuss me, Liam."

"I'm fine."

"You're not fine."

"Is there anything else? Because we really need to get those contracts out. We're ringing the Wall Street bell in less than a month after all."

"I hired a private detective to find her. I wanted to make sure she was all right."

"And?"

"He couldn't find her. He did confirm she arrived safely, but I guess it's easy to get lost in a crowded country where cash is the primary method of payment."

"You didn't have to do that, Stephen."

"I'm not trying to overstep, but I had to make sure she was all right. The way she left. I couldn't talk her out of it."

"That's not what I mean. You didn't have to do it because I already know where she is."

He sat up. "She called you?"

"I haven't heard from her at all." It stung me to even say it. "But I had to know, too. I called her friends. They confirmed she'd been in touch but wouldn't give me any more information. I checked a few other things, too. I almost gave up. Then about a week after our little chat, Dorothy Seville asked me to tea. They had gotten a package from Mary. Mary posted a dress back to them. Although she asked them not to tell me, Dorothy said she couldn't stand the idea of it. The package was from Goa. I did some more checking. She's working in a restaurant there."

"That's great."

"Yeah, she always enjoyed cooking. I'm sure she'll do well."

"What the fuck, Liam? You're not going after her?"

"She doesn't want me. She made that clear. I can't blame her."

"Then change her mind. You were so good together. What happened was a tragedy, but this…this just makes it worse."

"She made her decision. I'm going to respect it. I'm letting her go." I vowed to her that I would, and in a church no less. *How could I break my word?*

He leaned forward, pounded his fist into the desk, his face animated. "Bullshit. If you love someone, you fight for them. You know where I heard that?"

"Dr. Phil?"

"I heard it from Mary. Go fight for her."

Didn't he realize I wanted to make her mine again more than anything else in the world? I'd give up everything for her. But I had promised her I would make her happy. Maybe the only way I could was to leave her alone. So I would. In this way, I could pray for her happiness, even when it didn't include me.

"Read the contract, Stephen. We have a board meeting in twenty minutes. I have to get back to work."

Chapter 51

Liam

I hadn't slept in our bedroom since she'd left. I hated being in there even to change my clothes. There was a huge party tonight at the Wilshire Times Square to celebrate our successful public offering. It was the first social event I'd attend since that God-awful night she left me.

Instead of reaching for my suit, I grabbed Mary's wool scarf. I could picture her wrapping it over her neck and smiling at me before we went out for brunch. I bunched it up in my hands and held it to my face. Her scent no longer lingered. Still, it made me feel closer to her to hold it.

God, I missed her every single day. I still painted, but the images were poor imitations of the vivid colors I once knew. *Do you miss me, Lotus Girl?* Maybe we were never meant for each other, but she had given me a peace and strength and serenity I'd never imagined.

I tossed the scarf back on the shelf. Then I decided it should be folded the way I'd found it. So I reached for it again. It hitched onto something. When I tugged, a box fell at my feet, the content spilling out. The box Stephen had brought of my mum's things. I had shoved it in the closet and forgotten about it.

Kneeling on the floor, I gathered up strands of broken necklaces, random beads, and wire, throwing them back inside. Something sharp pricked me.

Shite.

I dislodged the pin.

I blinked, realizing it was the lotus flower pin I'd helped my mum make all those years ago. All the silver wires were shaped into petals, and a milky stone sat in the center. There was something about that stone. I held it up to the light. It had flecks of green and yellow in it.

Fuck.

It was a moonstone.

My mind spun back to that rainy afternoon in our Luton flat when Mum had told me how she found it at a thrift store.

Impossible.

I rifled through a drawer until I found a flat-head screwdriver. I pried the stone loose. It popped out, bouncing under a bureau. I almost slid on the floor chasing after it. My hand wouldn't reach. Shoving the bureau aside, I found the smooth flat stone with the veins of subtle color. I gripped it and rushed to the window.

Holding it up to the light, I saw the faint M etched onto the flat side.

M for Marco.

M for Mary.

M for mine.

I smiled for the first time in months.

Chapter 52

Mary

Dev rushed into the kitchen, his round face scrunched with worry. "There is a Westerner outside who demands to see the cook. He says the *parathas* are too spicy."

I wiped my forehead with the back of my hand. "Doesn't he know he's in India? Everything is spicy."

"I've already spoken to him, but he doesn't want the manager. He insists on speaking with the cook."

I stared at all my boiling pots. I had much to do. "I'll take care of your orders," Dev said. "He's outside on the veranda. You probably need a break anyway."

Talking to an irritated customer wasn't my idea of a break, but I was sweating like a pig, so any opportunity for air was welcome. I hurried to the veranda. Then I stopped short, feeling as if I'd run into a brick wall.

Liam.

My knees almost buckled. He wore a crisp white shirt and faded jeans. His sandy hair forked over his forehead just above the dark sunglasses covering his eyes. He stood and removed the sunglasses. His eyes focused on my face with such intensity I couldn't rip my gaze from him. Then he went lower, and his face hardened as he took in my swollen belly. I put my hands over it as if I could mask the obvious. I grappled between running full force into his arms and rushing the opposite way. I did neither. I stood, still as a statue, my heart pumping fast enough to fuel a train.

Liam crossed over to me. He stopped, keeping a sliver of a gap between us.

"Why are you here?" I asked.

"You're pregnant," he said at the same time.

Unable to answer, I simply nodded.

The breeze blew his spicy, clean, masculine scent toward me.

He took my hand and led me to the table. "I'm not supposed to sit out here."

"Sit," he growled.

I sat.

"Why are you here?" I repeated.

"You're here."

"Go home, Liam."

"You are my home, love."

He slid his water bottle toward me. "Drink. You look parched."

I took a long sip. The sun shone against the silver of the bracelet on my wrist.

"You still wear it," he said, his expression softening.

I hadn't taken it off since I arrived. All I'd done was mourn Liam and curse the way the past always ripped through any chances for a future.

He sighed. "Were you going to tell me about the baby?"

"I needed time."

"Jesus, Mary, how long were you going to keep my baby from me?" He raised his voice, not too loud, but Liam's voice was deep enough that other diners turned in our direction anyway.

"I'm working right now. I can't have this conversation with you."

"You've been sacked, and you're coming with me, even if I have to drag you."

I crossed my arms. "You're not my boss."

"You think I'm going to let the mother of my child work in these conditions?"

I stood and took his plate. "I don't think you have a choice."

I returned the kitchen, my hands shaking so hard I nearly dropped the plate. I should have known better than to think I could simply walk away from him.

"Sir, you can't come back here," Dev said.

He pushed past Dev and rounded the corner.

"Answer one question. Do you still love me? Can you still love me?"

"That's two questions."

"Answer me."

Every day I'd replayed the series of events that had brought us together and eventually torn us apart. I'd been living in darkness for the past few months. Seeing him was like having a veil lifted and bright light flooding in. I squinted against the sight, still grappling with my own fears. As if the baby disagreed with me, she gave me a swift kick.

He didn't wait for my answer. He crushed his lips against mine. My bum hit the counter. The kiss, aggressive and passionate, stirred me awake. He slid his tongue inside my mouth. He tasted of sweet mint. I kissed him back. His long fingers threaded through my hair while his other arm wrapped around me. I felt all the warm, hard muscles of his chest.

We were both breathing heavily when he let me go. He smiled. "I thought so."

"It's not enough."

"It's a nice start. I'll be outside."

Before I could respond, Liam walked away, nodding toward Dev, whose mouth was almost as wide as his face.

Dev told me to leave straight away. I had no doubts Liam had arranged that. When I walked into the busy street, Liam leaned against a green Mercedes, waiting for me as promised. I didn't see a driver.

"You're driving...in India. Are you mad?"

He laughed and opened the passenger door. "I've figured out the cows have the right of way. Once you know that and how to properly use your horn, it's not so bad."

He grabbed the seatbelt and belted me in. Despite my anger and confusion, I almost leaned forward to kiss him. "You had me sacked."

"I got you the afternoon off."

"How long have you been here?"

"About a week. I had a few things to set up. I would have come sooner if I'd known..." His voice trailed off, but I could finish the sentence. If he'd known I carried his child.

He handed me a wrapped package after he got into the driver's seat.

"What's this?"

"A little gift. Open it."

I unwrapped the paper, revealing a beautiful hardcover of Jane Austen's *Persuasion*.

"Fitting title since I aim to persuade you."

"Why are you doing this?"

He shrugged, starting up the car. "Me? I'm fighting for the woman I love. What the hell are you doing?"

"Trying to survive."

His jaw hardened for a second. "Open it. I know you want to."

I told myself not to, but I still flipped open the book. A note card with a rendering of a lotus flower fell out. I read his scrawled script. "My world is better because you are in it. Yours in every way, Liam."

Although my fingers shook, I placed the card back inside the book and snapped it shut. "I said that to you once."

"Words don't die, Mary. You throw them into the universe, and sometimes they come back to you."

I had said that too, hadn't I? A long time ago when he was just a beautiful stranger to me. I swallowed back the surge of emotion. "Take me home, okay? I'm really tired." My voice quivered. "We can talk tomorrow."

He nodded, although he looked disappointed. "As you wish, love. I can be patient."

He didn't ask where I lived. Clearly, he already knew, but he did grimace when we pulled up to the building.

I fiddled with my seatbelt. He put his hand over mine.

"I lied. I can't be patient. You're not going in there. We don't have to talk, but you're coming home with me."

I opened my mouth to protest, but he sped off back in the direction of the beach. I stayed quiet because I didn't have the strength or courage to argue with him. Most of all, I didn't want to cause him any more pain.

We pulled up to a pretty blue cottage with Moroccan shutters. Palm trees and sweetly scented honeysuckle lined the path.

"You're not staying at the Wilshire?"

"No."

He ran around to open my door. The house was done up in earthy colors. A wall of windows framed the beach. He led me to the sofa. We sat in silence for a while, each lost in our own thoughts.

I rubbed my belly. "I don't know how it happened, Liam. I swear I was careful."

"I'm happy we're going to have a child, but I have to know why you kept it from me." His eyes darkened, a deep sorrow on his face. "Do you think I'm like my father? Is that why you didn't tell me?"

I'd wounded him with my hasty selfish actions. "I didn't think that at all. Not for one second. You are nothing like him."

He looked relieved. "Good."

"I needed time to sort it all out. I don't expect anything from you."

He narrowed his eyes, the vein in his neck throbbing. "Expect anything? This is my child, Mary. If you think I'm not going to be a major part of his or her life, then you're very mistaken. Maybe you don't want me, but I promise you my child will know me."

"I never said I didn't want you to be a part of our child's life."

"But not your life?"

"I had so much rage in me for a long time. All I wanted was to make your father—"

"Don't call him my father."

"Make Robert Wilshire suffer. I blamed him for every tragedy in my life. Even the things that had happened before, like my mother leaving. When I figured it out that night, all that rage came back inside me. I wasn't afraid of you hurting me, Liam. I was afraid of hurting you. It was all too much."

"We could have talked about it." There was defeat in his statement.

"After I had some time to digest it all. The real fear was that you might leave me."

"Why would you ever think that?"

"Everyone leaves me."

He kissed my forehead. "I will never leave you. You are everything to me. Besides, the fates brought us together. It's impossible to fight fate."

"What?" The baby kicked me as if to tell me to shut up. I pressed my palm to my stomach.

"Are you all right, my love?"

I missed his nicknames for me. Missed the way he said them slower than the rest of the sentence. "I'm fine. She likes to kick."

His lips curled into a beaming smile. "It's a girl?"

"Just a guess. I didn't want to call him or her an 'it,' so I settled for 'her.'"

"May I?" he asked, gesturing to my tummy. He looked nervous, as if I might reject him.

I nodded. He lowered his head, pressing his palms flat against my waist. My pulse raced with his touch.

"I don't feel anything."

Taking his wrist, I moved his hand lower and to the side. "Wait for it."

Maybe she felt her papa's hand, because she kicked three times in a row. Liam's face lit up. "That's our baby, Mary." His voice turned thick. A tear rolled down his cheek. "Our baby."

I caressed his cheek. "She's feisty."

"Like her mother."

My stomach growled.

"What was that? Are you okay?" Panic laced his questions.

I laughed. "Just hungry."

"I'll go start dinner. Would you like to take a bath?"

I wanted to ask him when he'd learned to cook, but the idea of a bath was too enticing, so I nodded. He showed me the bathroom and ran the water in the large claw foot tub. I took a long soak and scrubbed myself with lemon soap.

I pulled on the soft silk robe hanging on the door. I piled my wet hair on top of my head and secured it with a band. Liam was still in the kitchen when I walked into the living room. The house was right on the beach. The curtains danced as the sea air hit them through the open veranda doors. There was an entire wall of blank, white canvases except for the painting in the middle. My feet were sore, but I had to get a closer look. I gasped, taking in the artwork. It was the picture we'd drawn together the last time we were in Goa. Liam had taken the sketch and painted it, leaving everything exactly as we'd drawn it, even my wonky dog-cows. On the top in black letters it read *The Best Time of Liam's Life.* On the bottom in red letters, it read *The Best Time of Mary's Life.*

"You're still painting."

He came out of the kitchen, a dishtowel on his shoulder. "I was able to finish two works since you left. That one and another."

"It's beautiful. Why are all the other canvases blank?"

"They represent the best times yet to come. We'll fill them all up, won't we?"

Yes...we will.

"Why don't you sit, sweetheart?" he asked, leading me to the couch.

"Where is your other painting?"

"It's here. It was your Christmas present originally."

"May I see it?"

He gestured to the far side of the room where an easel was set up. A linen cloth was draped over it. I walked toward it with slow steps. A steady, firm hand pressed into my lower back. Then he removed the cloth. My knees did buckle this time. But he didn't let me fall. He picked me up to carry me back to the couch.

"Please, I want to look at it," I begged.

"Okay, but I'm not putting you down." He turned back toward it. I had no idea what the right word was for this feeling...this feeling of warmth and hope and love. He'd painted Hannah and Papaji and me.

"I did it from the photo in your wallet. I made a copy of it when you were sleeping."

"I don't know what to say. This...this is the most amazing gift in the whole world."

"I'm glad you think so. We're just getting started."

I didn't think I could take any more. He said he'd come to fight for me. Didn't he know I had surrendered the moment I saw him? I was wrong. There was nothing sick or evil about us. I had nothing but love and joy in my heart for this man. He was my best friend, my lover, my muse...my home.

"Liam—"

"I'm going to feed my girl now. She's hungry and so is my baby. We'll talk some more after you eat, yeah?"

I nodded, resting my head against his chest as he led me back to the sofa. He came out a few minutes later with a plate filled with cheese, fruit, and hummus with pita chips. "I have some things in the oven, too."

I started nibbling. He unrolled some papers. "Someone else made you a few paintings, too. Apparently, you're not just my muse." He set down a few simple paintings of houses. The paper curled on the ends. I held one side straight while Liam held the other.

"Marcus did these."

"Yes."

"I can see him in them. Just like I see you in your work." I ran my hands down the shapes. "He's moved on from crayons to paint."

"I've been going to see him and showing him a few things. He misses you, Mary."

"I miss him, too."

He rolled up the pictures and put them back in their case. He sat down and picked up my feet. "Your feet are swollen, aren't they?"

"A little."

He began massaging my feet. It felt so good I moaned.

"Why do you think we're fated, Liam?"

"I have it on good authority, but I'll keep that nugget for later. Right now, you need to finish eating, love."

I polished off my plate. He took it from me and went back to the kitchen. "Ready for a feast?"

"I thought that was the feast."

"No, love, that was just something to whet your appetite."

When he came out, he was rolling a cart full of covered dishes.

"When did you make all of this?"

His smile turned mischievous. "I'll admit, I had it catered, but I did plan the menu." He removed each cloth with a flair. "It's all part of our journey."

None of the dishes went together, but I recognized them because they all held a memory. Spiced lamb stew with hot buttered naan to remind me of Jaipur. Buffalo wings similar to what we ate at the Chili's in Mumbai. A ceviche from Goa. Pizza reminiscent of New York. My mouth watered as I took them all in.

Then he set down the thing I could not resist or get enough of—a large glass jar of Sidr honey. Okay, counting Liam, there were two things that fit that description.

He sat on the couch and handed me a fork. "Dig in."

"What are you trying to do?"

"Romance you. Make you remember every delicious moment we shared. Remind you that you are mine and I am yours."

Something inside me broke. I threw my arms around him. He held me tight. My mouth found his. I let out some wild sound between a joyous cry and relieved laugh.

"I missed you, Liam."

"Me too, lass. Me too."

"I'm sorry."

"Shhh, we're not going to apologize to each other. We can't undo the past. We can only plot the future. That's all I want to do with you."

"I love you so much, Liam. I promise I will never leave you again."

I lifted my head and attacked him, crushing my lips into his, threading my fingers through his hair, tasting his delicious, naughty mouth.

"Baby, if that's how you kiss me, I can't wait to see how you fuck me."

I laughed. "Let me show you. Take me to the bedroom, sir."

He picked me up and carried me outside.

"Where we going? Isn't the bedroom inside…sir?"

"Lotus Girl, believe me, I have an erection the length of the equator. There is nothing more I want than to have my way with you. But first, there is something I need to give you. Something that belongs to you."

He set me down in the courtyard. We stood in the middle of three fountains. Each one was lit up and bursting with gleaming white lotus flowers.

"Oh, my God. Did you do this?"

"Yeah, the plan was for us to have a dance right here, but I don't think it's wise since your feet hurt."

The flower on the far fountain was the largest. I sat on the stone ridge of the structure staring at the blossom. It had a soft pink tinge on each petal. I knew it to be mine.

"Liam, I swear this is my lotus flower from Jaipur."

"It is, lass. The new owners hadn't started construction yet. I convinced them to let me have it. I had it flown here."

"You did all that?" I pointed to my chest. "For me?" *My God...was he real?*

"I wanted to prove a point to you."

"What point?"

He sat next to me. "The blossom maybe delicate, but it is strong, too. It can always find a new home."

I leaned my head against his chest. "Don't let go of me."

"Never, but this isn't what I wanted to show you."

"I can't handle anymore."

"Sorry, lover, this one, this one we can't skip. It's a full moon, and I've timed it just right." He scooped me up in his strong arms and carried me to the beach. He set me down on the sand so we were facing each other. The foamy sea lapped against our bare feet. "I'm so relieved you didn't make me wait ten years, but I would have. I would have come down to this beach every night, waiting for you and praying for your happiness at the same time."

He took my hands and fell to his knees.

"Liam," I gasped. "Yes, I'll marry you!"

He shook his head, stood, and brushed the sand off his knees. "Shit, this isn't a ring either."

"Oh," I said, not hiding my disappointment. "How about you stop getting on your knees in front of me?"

"Yeah, in hindsight, it wasn't the most fitting gesture."

He took a rock out of his pocket, an actual rock, and handed it to me. I stared at it, wondering if he was doing some sort of symbolic Penguin gesture. Then I saw what it was. "It can't be."

"It is."

"How did you...?"

"My mum bought it. I helped her fashion some wire into a lotus flower pin. We pasted this in the center. I didn't even know I had it until Stephen dropped off this box of my old stuff. I've had it all along, but it really belongs to you. I'm giving it to you under the full moon."

I held it up against the moonlight. I said a prayer for our happiness. Then I handed it to him and closed his hands around it. "Dadima told me to give it to my true love. So I'm giving it back to you. I am bound to you in every way."

"I was hoping you'd do that." He hugged me and whispered in my ear, "I love your soul, Mary Costa."

"I love your soul, too."

I shivered against the breeze. He picked me up again, and this time he did carry me to the bedroom. We fed each other strawberries dipped in Sidr honey. He made love to me. I finally let the darkness go.

I finally survived it.

* * * *

When I woke in the morning, he was staring down at me.

"Morning, *janu*," I said.

"What does that mean?" he asked, twirling a piece of my hair in his fingers.

"It means 'love.'"

"I like it," he said, stroking my hair.

"How long can we stay here?" I didn't want to break the spell of this magical place, but I knew we had other, more practical things to talk about, like where we were going to live. Not that it mattered as long as we were together.

He smiled. "You like the cottage, lass?"

"I love it."

"How does forever suit you?"

"What are you saying?"

"I bought it. It's ours."

I sat up. "Don't you have to work, Liam?"

"When the IPO happened, I sold my stock. I gifted a few shares to Stephen, giving him controlling interest."

"You sold your stake in the company?"

"I never wanted it, Mary. I just thought I did. I gave the lion's share to charity, but I kept enough so we'd be comfortable while I pursue a new career choice."

"You're going to paint?" I asked with excitement.

He grinned. "No, baby, I'm going to be a professional arm wrestler. What do you think?"

I elbowed him. "Liam!"

He tickled me. "Yes, I'm going to paint. But only if my muse promises never to leave me again."

"I promise, janu."

His kiss was tender and fierce at the same time. He tasted like Sidr honey.

His expression turned serious. "And you, Mary. What would you like to do?"

"First, I'd like to visit Marcus and say a proper good-bye. Then I want a nice wedding with all our friends who have become family and all our family who have become friends."

"Brilliant idea."

"Then maybe while you're pursuing your passion, I'll go to school and learn some culinary techniques?"

"A woman who can feed me. I'm such a lucky man."

"But before any of that, you have to propose to me."

"I have plans for that," he said, kissing my neck. He worked his way down to my breast. His tongue flicked across my tender nipple.

I yanked his hair, pulling his face up. "After last night, I don't need anything else. You literally swept me off my feet. I think if you do one more grand gesture, my heart might just burst right out of my chest. I don't even need a ring. Just ask me."

"Oh, I got a ring. You sure about this? Because I have a plan that's already set in motion."

"Positive."

He opened a side drawer and pulled out a box. He kissed my stomach before placing a light blue box on it.

"Mary, me—"

"Yes," I screamed.

"I wasn't finished."

"Oh."

"Mary..." This time he paused, smirking. "Me and you have been through so much."

I sighed. "Liam, please stop teasing me."

I expected the amused smile. Instead, he inhaled. "I'm sorry. I'm kind of nervous."

"Don't be. We already belong to each other."

His smile was full of relief. "Yes, we do. Mary, *mai tumse pyar karta hoon.* I love you. I promise to be a good husband and the best father I can be. I will always safeguard your happiness. Marry me and make me the happiest man in the world." He opened the box. Inside was a stunning platinum band with diamonds shaped into a lotus flower.

I cupped my hand over my mouth, afraid to touch it. It was so lovely. He slipped it onto my finger and kissed the underside of my wrist.

"You're suppose to respond. That's the tradition."

"*Mai tumse pyar karti hoon.* Yes. Yes. Yes."

Epilogue

Mary

Liam was a grand gesture *Raj*. He'd already put so much work into the proposal, he insisted on carrying out his original plans. A fortnight later, he took the ring back from me and told me to go out to the beach. I stood there alone, a cool breeze flowing in the air, ripe with the scents of coconut and honeysuckle and spices, wondering what was going on.

Then the music started. Musicians, dancers, and singers dressed in colorful outfits descended around me. They did a mash-up of Bollywood, Dusty Springfield, and even a little opera. Somehow, it all blended into the most harmonious song I'd ever heard. Then Liam made all my highlander fantasies come true by galloping down the beach on a white horse. Yes, a real white horse, and in a kilt no less. I don't think I've ever laughed so hard in my life. It was a huge epic spectacle of over-the-top corny, but I loved every minute of it.

We married in New York in a beautiful outdoor ceremony in Central Park. Spring in New York made me appreciate the city a hundred times over. All our friends were there. Liam surprised me by flying out Divya, Amira, and their families. Stephen was Liam's best man. He brought a very lovely woman with hair the color of strawberries as his date. Next month, we were flying back to New York for Jan and Stephen's wedding.

All of those huge memories would always hold a special place in my heart. But this...this right now was the kind of moment I couldn't get enough of.

Lying on the hammock of our veranda and watching my husband and son stroll the beach. I was wrong about our child being a girl. We had a beautiful, healthy baby boy. Marco had rich, dark curly hair and the same green-brown eyes as his daddy. He giggled as he ran down the shoreline, turning back to his dad. Liam ran after Marco, grabbing the boy around the waist and swinging him onto his broad shoulders. Then my janu turned to me, a goofy grin on his face. I returned his smile, my heart expanded to a level I didn't think was possible. Wasn't that the magic of love? Just when you thought you reached a level of fullness, the boundary lines stretched once more.

I had lived through hell. Then made my own purgatory. Now…now I finally had emerged from the dark waters to find a love and happiness I would always fight for.

Meet the Author

M.K. Schiller is a hopeless romantic in a hopelessly pragmatic world. In the dark of night, she sits by the warm glow of her computer monitor, reading or writing, usually with some tasty Italian ... the food, that is! She started imagining stories at a very young age. In fact, she got so good at it that friends asked her to create plots featuring them as the heroine and the object of their affection as the hero. She hopes you enjoy her stories and find The Happily Ever After in every endeavor. M. K. Schiller loves hearing from readers. Find her on Facebook, follow her on Twitter @MKSchiller, and visit her website at www.mkschillerauthor.com.

mk@mkschillerauthor.com

MK Schiller's first cross-cultural romance, Unwanted Girl, has received a starred review from Publishers Weekly and an Amazon editor pick. A heartfelt tale not to be missed.
On sale now!

Unwanted Girl

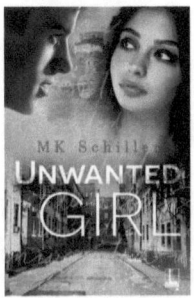

When a man loves a woman

Recovering addict Nick Dorsey finds solace in his regimented life. That is until he meets Shyla Metha. Something about the shy Indian beauty who delivers take-out to his Greenwich Village loft inspires the reclusive writer. And when Shyla reveals her desire to write a book of her own, he agrees to help her. The tale of a young Indian girl growing up against a landscape of brutal choices isn't Nick's usual territory, but something about the story, and the beautiful storyteller, draws him in deep.

Shyla is drawn to Nick, but she never imagines falling for him. Like Nick, Shyla hails from a village, too…a rural village in India. They have nothing in common, yet he makes her feel alive for the first time in her life. She is not ready for their journey to end, but the plans she's made cannot be broken…not even by him. Can they find a way to rewrite the next chapter?

Chapter 1

Nick Dorsey ran every morning, although he no longer ventured to guess whether he was chasing dreams or fleeing demons. As he exited the brick building on Bleecker to a grim, grayish sky, the promise of another sunless day revealed itself.

His feet pounded the pavement in a stride that ranged from sprint to run to jog, matching the same footpaths as TS Eliot, Faulkner, and Poe. He'd insisted on the Village because it was a literary mecca. Although, these days, it could be argued the high rents favored capitalists over the creatives.

He'd hunted for months with a petite blond realtor until she found a place in his price range. The realtor was intelligent and assertive—during negotiations and sex—two traits Nick valued. In the end, it got him a nice place in the West Village with a working elevator, architectural charm, and original hardwood floors. It got her a fat commission check and about the same number of orgasms. Too bad the only thing he turned on these days was his computer...and that relationship was near terminal.

He rounded Thompson Avenue, passing the bookstore where his latest novel occupied the window. He allowed the smallest flicker of pride before picking up speed. How far he'd come from the poor kid whose life was hand-me-down clothes and secondhand books.

He reached Washington Square Park ready to do a complete loop. Nick's runs used to consist of random thoughts about his characters and plot points. The beauty of being a writer was you could work anywhere anytime. One of the best scenes he'd ever written was during a tax audit. Now, his mind lacked the spark required to conjure creativity. He emerged from the park, slowing his pace until he reached the glass door of The Ole Time Floral shop with its annoying wreath of greenery and bells that signaled his arrival.

"A white rose, please," he said to the florist, who was already reaching into the barrel to retrieve the item.

"You know, dear, its romantic how you buy her a rose every day, but I'm sure she'd be more impressed with a whole bouquet at once."

Nick frowned. "I don't want to impress her. I just want her to know I'm there."

The lady arched a bushy brow, waiting for further explanation, but Nick did not intend to satisfy her unsolicited curiosity. He shoved the money at her and clutched the thorny bud in his hand. She no longer asked if he wanted it wrapped with a sprig of greenery.

He ran an additional mile until he reached the tranquil snow-covered grounds behind an ornate metal gate on Sullivan Street. It looked like a park with its lush landscape of willow trees and benches, but the stone angels, marble pillars, and simple markers jutting from the ground gave away its identity.

He fell to his knees, the crunch of fresh snow against hard earth disturbing the serenity. Nick gulped in the cold desolate air, reading her gravestone for the thousandth time, even though every curl of the fancy lettering chiseled on the surface was already etched into his brain. He'd become a creature of habit, and the repetition of every act provided a strange comfort. He bowed his head, joined his hands together, and begged in silence for forgiveness that would never come.

An hour later, showered and freshly dressed, he walked through the heavy wooden doors of the old church on Grand, the location of his second daily errand. Nick originally chose the ten a.m. timeframe to avoid crowds. It was flawed logic, bordering on reckless naiveté since the term "avoid crowds" was a fool's ambition in this city. Although there weren't any stockbrokers or executives, plenty of actors, singers, and housewives packed the large room. They all chatted amicably while drinking percolated coffee, which Nick, a coffee connoisseur, admitted was the best he'd ever had.

He sat in the uncomfortable metal chair, waiting for the meeting to come to order. When the time came, Nick spoke clearly and honestly.

"I'm Nick Dorsey, and I am a meth addict. It's been eighteen months, two weeks, and three days since my last fix." He talked about his addiction until his three minutes of indulgent introspection were up and his Styrofoam cup runneth empty.

He arrived back at the Bleecker Street loft with all his errands accomplished, but no sense of accomplishment for it. Gaping at his keyboard, a fresh cup of caffeine in his hand and a stifling lack of imagination, he sat down.

Wanting to alleviate the harsh glare of the blank page, he clicked on the keyboard in quick snapping strokes. *The rain fell in thick sheets as if the sky weighed in on Max's decision.*

Shit.

Did he actually start the fucking book with a weather report? The greats—George Orwell, Charles Dickens, or Dr. Seuss were capable of such openings, but Nick Dorsey was not. He hit the backspace, erasing every individual character with a scorning strike. He wondered what other words could describe rain. He walked over to the large bookshelf that spanned an entire wall. As it turned out, Webster's had thirty-two words for precipitation from the descriptive *drencher* to the very simple *wet stuff*.

He slammed the book shut, tired of his pathetic attempts at procrastination.

He didn't mind the timid knock at nine p.m., though. That was a welcome break from the unrelenting flutter of the cursor.

Sandwich girl was here and right on time.

He opened the door, and there she stood as she had almost every night for the past year since he'd discovered the corner deli delivered. The tall, thin girl with raven hair offered a nervous smile. He often speculated on the length of her hair. She always wore it in a tightly coiled bun except for the few loose strands that framed her face.

When her smile widened just right, it would create the slightest dimple on her left cheek. As much as he enjoyed the appearance of the dimple, what struck him the most was her accent. He'd heard all kinds of Asian accents, but never one as lyrical as hers with each simple word drawn out softly, a seductive hum as it left her lips. Her loose trench coat, too mild for this weather, slipped off one shoulder as she inched her knapsack higher on the other.

"Hello," she said cheerfully, handing him the brown paper bag that contained his turkey and Swiss on whole wheat.

"Hiya, Sandwich Girl." It was their usual greeting. No names—the time for civilized introductions had passed long ago.

He fished a twenty from his wallet. She shoved her hand in her pocket searching for change.

"Keep it," he said.

"Thank you. That's very generous."

Why they went through the same motions, he didn't know, except she was polite and unassuming, and he found a certain comfort in the repetition. "Don't mention it."

Her head began shifting downward, but she paused and lifted her gaze to meet his. In the beginning, the shy girl would never look him in the face, throwing the bag at him and taking off before he yelled after her that he had yet to pay. Then she'd slowly shuffle back, her head down, holding out her trembling hand. Now, they held actual conversation between them, and although it lacked any depth, those few minutes became the most enjoyable part of his scheduled day.

"It's getting nicer outside. I think spring will arrive early this year," she said.

"Is that so?" Maybe she believed Nick never went out, and her weather reports were a necessary service to give him insight into the subtle climactic shifts of his own environment. Or maybe she was just making small talk.

"Yes, but it might rain." She dropped her voice as if conveying a secret. "I think it *will* rain actually."

"Will it be a soaker, a mist, or a monsoon?" he asked, happy to apply the seldom-used words to his vernacular. The thesaurus hadn't been a waste of time.

She clutched her jacket around her. "Definitely a drencher. I don't think we have to worry about monsoons on this side of the world."

"Your forecasts have never been accurate…not once."

She bit her lower lip, her expression thoughtful. "Really?"

"Nope. But in case you're right, do you have an umbrella?"

"I don't have far to go."

"Wait here." He set the bag on a console table and grabbed an umbrella from the hall closet. "Take this."

"Oh no, I couldn't."

"You can return it tomorrow." He held it out to her until she gripped her fingers around it.

"Thank you."

"Be safe."

She'd rewarded him with a brilliant, dimple-inducing smile the first time he'd said that, and it became his customary farewell to her in the days that followed. The smile never disappointed.

"Good-night."

"Night," he said, leaning against the doorjamb until the elevator arrived.

A minute later, he strolled to the window and watched her exit onto the street, headed north on Bleecker, her coat flapping around her. He reassured himself it was the comfort of routine along with the quality deli meat he craved. It had nothing to do with the delivery girl. Never mind he opted for Chinese or pizza on Wednesdays and Sundays—her days off. Sure, she was a pretty girl, but definitely not his type. He preferred the kind of women he wrote about...buxom blondes and rambunctious redheads with confident personas and hungry appetites.

This girl was shy, awkward...and for some reason, intriguing. He had no idea why he looked forward to their silly chats, except they made him a little happier. Any ounce of happiness was such a rare occurrence in Nick's life, he seized it gratefully.

Nick started the process of shutting down the computer. He'd eat, work out for a few hours, take a shower, read, and go to bed. The same as he did every night. He hesitated at the customary question of *Do you want to save changes?* There were no changes to save.

He cracked his knuckles and stretched his back. His fingers landed on the keys like a mocking friend, both beckoning and humiliating him in that order. Except now, the words coursed through his hands with great speed and little consideration as the page filled.

Sandwich girl, you are a mystery. A sweet, sad smile that never reaches your big brown eyes. Silky hair tucked and clipped away as if forgotten, save for the few rebellious strands struggling for freedom. Would you welcome my advance or retreat into the shadows? I can see your inexperience, an odd fit, wrapping around you like another coat. But there's something else there, too. A profound strength that exists as if you're a lone soldier, battling your way through a battered life.

Nick highlighted the section and hovered a finger above the delete key. Instead, he labeled the document *Sandwich Girl* and saved it to his hard drive. It wasn't his best work and nothing he could use in a novel, but it meant something to him. It represented the first paragraph he'd managed in almost two years.

* * * *

Shyla Metha watched his window from a darkened corner some distance away. On warmer days, she'd stand in this area for twenty minutes until sufficiently shamed by her lurking. Still, she was drawn to him.

It wasn't just his looks, although she couldn't deny the pull of his broad shoulders, sandy hair that fell somewhere between brown and blond, and dark ocean-colored eyes. The beard was interesting, too, creating an air of mystery around him. Funny, she'd never expected to be attracted to physical characteristics so different from her own, yet she'd developed a dimwitted crush on this boy...man.

He'd been aloof in the beginning, and she was timid, a combination that never mixed, but one day she'd added a comment about the weather, and he had grinned, the rigid stiffness of his posture easing for a few seconds. Although they came from different worlds, they had something in common. Nick Dorsey was lonely and sad...perhaps even broken.

She clutched the black umbrella in her hand. Her time was growing short. She'd be returning home when her student visa expired at the end of the semester. Now was the time for risks! Or rather tomorrow when he ordered another sandwich.